THE CHINOOK MUST DIE

THE CHINOOK MUST DIE

MICHAEL O'REILLY

JANUS PUBLISHING COMPANY
London, England

First Published in Great Britain 2002 by
Janus Publishing Company Ltd,
76 Great Titchfield Street,
London W1P 7AF

www.januspublishing.co.uk

British Library Cataloguing-in-Publication Data
A catalogue record for this book
is available from the British Library

ISBN 1 85756 547 9

Typeset in 10pt Times New Roman
By Chris Cowlin

Cover Design Hamish Cooper

Printed and bound in Great Britain

Prologue

Thursday 2nd June 1994

There have been five major inquiries into the circumstances and events surrounding the helicopter flight from Aldergrove Airport, Belfast, on the evening of Thursday, 2nd June 1994. Two of them were open to the public. The other three were conducted in great secrecy at the very highest level of British Intelligence, making use of the most skilled and experienced investigators. None of the inquiries was able to come up with the answers that were desperately needed. They were able to describe in elaborate detail what had happened. But this failed to tell them why it had happened. From the evidence and testimony gathered, it is possible to reconstruct the sequence of events.

At 5.30 p.m., RAF Flight Lieutenant Jonathan Tapper sat in the cockpit of the helicopter, running through the final check-list with his co-pilot, Flight Lieutenant Richard Cook. Tapper was reckoning on a relatively short and routine round-trip. The giant HC Mark II Chinook helicopter ZD 576 had recently been serviced by the makers, Boeing, and had arrived in Aldergrove Airport, Belfast, just two days ago. It was the first Mark II to go into service with the British security forces in Northern Ireland.

Tapper and Cook were more used to the slower Mark I but they had completed the two-week conversion course for the Mark II, had taken the new helicopter up a number of times and were already familiar with its different components and procedures. Tapper, aged 28, was an experienced and highly professional pilot, known to be particularly safety-conscious. He would have been relaxed about the trip, which he had made many times. It was certainly a lot easier than the many occasions he had flown under battle conditions or on search and rescue missions in stormy weather.

The destination was Fort George, located on an isolated peninsula eight miles from Inverness in Scotland. It was headquarters for the 600 officers and men of the Royal Scots but it was also used from time to time by British government agencies for top-level security meetings. Surrounded on three sides by water and with only a single road providing access, Fort George was probably one of the easiest places in Europe to guard against attack. Normal security

1

measures had been stepped up for this conference, with a special SAS unit sur-rounding the area. Tapper and Cook, as well as the two loadmaster sergeants, Graham Forbes and Kevin Hardie, who made up the four-man crew, were also on SAS secondment. But there would be little time for the usual camaraderie at Fort George. Tapper thought it a bleak and cheerless place and would be happy enough to get back to the relaxed atmosphere of the officers' mess in Belfast.

If the flight itself from Aldergrove to Fort George was a routine one for the crew on this fine summer's evening, the passenger list was highly unusual. Twenty-five of Britain's top intelligence chiefs on a most secret mission.

The sergeant in charge of flight arrangements sighed inwardly when he saw Flight Lieutenant Jonathan Tapper was the pilot. Tapper was highly respected as a professional but he did have this tendency to be over-cautious, worrying away at problems that didn't exist.

"I'll do a complete re-check," the sergeant promised without being asked. He mentioned his own problem. "By the way, I still haven't been given any pas-senger details and it would be helpful to know in case there are any special arrangements. There's been a lot of flapping upstairs today so I gather they're an important bunch. What's the story?"

Tapper shrugged. He handed the sergeant a sheet of paper that had a hand-written name and address. "Here you are. Phone the Major at noon tomorrow and he'll give you all the details you need. They're mostly RUC as far as I know."

In fact Tapper knew precisely the passengers he would be carrying. He had been briefed earlier that he would be transporting Britain's most senior intelli-gence officers operating in Northern Ireland, the top men-and one woman-in MI5, MI6, Royal Ulster Constabulary Intelligence and the SAS, together with agents who had been undercover for years. "These are the best there is and they're getting ready to kill all the IRA without an anaesthetic," he'd been told. He knew some of them, like Special Branch chief Brian Fitzsimons, Senior MI5 officer Matt Maltby and Intelligence chief Major Gary Sparks who had been flown by Tapper to various locations in the past. Some of the others he knew by reputation.

Now, Tapper saw them briefly as they left the helicopter lounge, awkwardly adjusting their cumbersome immersion suits and lifejackets, as they formed into lines to board the Chinook. A loadmaster stood between the two lines as they boarded through the rear, checking that their survival gear was worn properly and handing out ear-defenders. Inside, they were strapped into two

2

facing rows.

As soon as the passengers were aboard, the rear door was closed and within minutes the twin rotor blades began spinning. At 5.43 p.m., the Chinook lifted off and headed east. Three minutes later, as he passed the airport boundary, Tapper laconically advised the duty controller:

"Approach F40 at zone boundary, VFR operational, good day."

The message confirmed that he was now clear of the controlled airspace zone and was flying low using visual flight rules rather than instrumentation. Effectively, the flight was now totally under Tapper's control and he was not scheduled to make voice contact again until he was approaching Fort George.

To people in the village of Carnlough, beyond the airport, the huge helicopter appeared to skim the housetops as it thundered overhead. Military helicopters in Northern Ireland almost always flew very low or very high as an operational necessity to avoid giving the IRA a ready target. The Chinook soon had the land behind it and was flying across the short strip of the Irish Sea that separated Northern Ireland and Scotland. Over the water, Tapper gradually increased his altitude to 500 feet, then higher.

As the Scottish coastline appeared, Tapper noted that the weather forecast he had been given was accurate. The sky was overcast over the Mull of Kintyre, with low clouds and large patches of Scottish mist. As he neared the coast, visibility was deteriorating. The lighthouse, a familiar navigational landmark, was half hidden in fog. He made no attempt to climb above the fog. His orders specified low level altitude for the flight and, in all probability, he wanted to use the flight as a low altitude training exercise on the Mark II which was now fitted with all the latest technology available.

He switched on the navigational equipment. The Mark II had two recently installed state-of-the art independent positioning systems. The Racal RNS 252 Super TANS, positioned in a console between pilot and co-pilot, processed information from the Global Positioning Systems (GPS) network of twenty-four satellites circling the earth. The Doppler Velocity Sensor provided velocities of the aircraft in relation to the earth's surface by transmitting signals from the aircraft to the ground and measuring returns.

As he headed into the swirling grey fog, with the beautiful rugged countryside barely visible below, he carefully scanned his instruments. They all showed that the Chinook was on course and at the normal correct altitude to clear the misty mountain comfortably, just as both pilots had done as a matter of routine many times in the past.

Cycling slowly along a pathway that meandered across Beinn na Lice

Mountain, 1,405 feet high, a local farmer, Angus Macdonald, had heard the steadily growing sound of an aircraft. He stopped cycling abruptly as the roar increased in volume and felt the ground and air around him begin to vibrate. The aircraft sounded frighteningly low to the ground and very close and it seemed almost to be somewhere directly in front of him.

Suddenly, it came charging out of the fog barely a hundred yards away like some enormous bellowing primeval creature. His heart lurched painfully as he realised that it was heading straight as an arrow into the mountain. Instinctively, he shouted a warning, though the noise was deafening. As though hearing him, the helicopter jinked, then far, far too late, it began to turn and, with engines screaming, its nose rose slightly in a futile attempt to claw its way upward.

The Chinook slammed into a rocky outcrop above and to the left of Macdonald with tremendous force. (Later, it would be calculated that its speed was over 140 knots when it hit.) A figure hurtled through the front windscreen to be dashed on the rocks. The helicopter bounced back into the air, turning over completely. For several moments, it was flying in the air upside down. Transfixed, Macdonald thought he glimpsed spinning limbs and a white bloodied face through the round portholes. Then everything seemed to happen together. The body of the Chinook split, then disintegrated in a huge shower of pieces of fuselage, metal shards, bits of equipment and human bodies. With a *whooosh* the spewing fuel burst into flames. There was an enormous explosion that hurled both flaming engines and a thousand pieces of debris into the air. The remains of the helicopter, broken in two, hit the ground like a pair of fiery comets. And then all was silent, apart from the crackle of flames.

Angus Macdonald emerged slowly from his mental and physical paralysis and turned away. He heard a voice repeating over and over, "ah no, ah no" in a monotonous chant. He realised it was himself and he stopped. He was lying on the ground but couldn't remember falling. His groin felt wet and sticky and he looked down, expecting blood. He was more embarrassed than relieved to discover that he had involuntarily urinated. He forced himself to look again at the blazing inferno above him. He knew there were no survivors. He quickly picked up his bicycle where it had fallen, turned it round and began to pedal furiously in the direction of the nearest telephone, several miles away. Long before he got there, senior security officers in Fort George were being informed that the Chinook had failed to establish radio contact on schedule and it was not responding to calls. They were already beginning to start thinking the impossible-that British intelligence had just suffered the greatest disaster in its history.

4

Prologue

* * *

THE CHINOOK CRASH----STILL A MAJOR INTERNATIONAL MYSTERY

"BRITISH RESIST INQUIRY IN WAKE OF 'NEW EVIDENCE' ON HELICOPTER CRASH" (Irish Times, 25 November 1997) "The British Government is resisting pressure to re-open inquiries into the cause of the Chinook helicopter crash on the Mull of Kintyre in 1994 which killed all 29 people on board. Labour Party ministers recently announced support for the RAF board of inquiry that the accident was due to gross negligence by the pilots. Last night the Ministry of Defence stated 'pilot error' was to blame."

"SUPPORT FOR FINDING OF HELICOPTER PILOT ERROR" (Irish Times, 26 Nov. 1997) "The British Armed Forces Minister Dr. John Reid said he and the Defence Secretary Mr. George Robertson had examined the findings of the civilian and military investigators and; 'We have satisfied ourselves that the verdict of pilot error was fully justified'."

"MPs FIND DOUBTS ON CHINOOK SAFETY" (Irish Times and News Agencies) 30 Nov. 2000; An influential committee of MPs has concluded that there were 'real reasons' to doubt the safety of the Chinook Mk2 helicopter when it crashed and has insisted that the verdict of gross negligence against the pilots should be set aside. The committee of Public Accounts at Westminster charges the Ministry of Defence with 'gross arrogance' in defending the 'unsatisfactory' findings of gross negligence against the pilots."

"THE BRITISH GOVERNMENT AND MOD REJECT FINDINGS OF IT'S COMMITTEE OF PUBLIC ACCOUNTS AND TELLS MPs THAT THE CRASH WAS DUE TO PILOT ERROR" (Sky News and News Agencies later on Thursday 30 November 2000)

2001 May 1; "NEW CHINOOK INQUIRY" (The Times London.) "PEERS BACK NEW CHINOOK CRASH INQUIRY" (The Independant, London.) "LORDS SEEK NEW INQUIRY INTO CHINOOK CRASH" (The Daily Telegraph.)

2002 February 6; "MOD REFUSES TO CLEAR CHINOOK PILOTS" (The Times) "LORDS INQUIRY CLEARS CHINOOK CRASH PILOTS" (The Daily Telegraph) "LORDS SCORN RAF ACCIDENT FINDINGS-BLAIR UNDER NEW PRESSURE TO OVERTURN VERDICT BLAMING CHINOOK PILOTS. IN A DAMNING REPORT, A CROSS-PARTY HOUSE OF LORDS COMMITTEE UNANIMOUSLY CONCLUDED THAT THE TWO PILOTS SHOULD NOT HAVE BEEN BLAMED" (The Gaurdian).

TEN YEARS EARLIER

Grand Hotel Brighton

Friday 12 October 1984

The actress spent the last hour of her life contemplating, as she often did in recent months, her incredible good fortune. It was after midnight and she was back in her hotel suite, still flushed with the success of yet another great performance. This evening, the audience had been made up wholly of adoring fans who watched in rapture her every move and hung on her every word. So many important people, she thought, the cream of British society, the movers and shakers, the familiar faces from television and newspaper photographs. And all eager to congratulate her, shake her hand, engage in a few brief words of conversation with her.

She crossed to the bar in the corner of the room and poured herself a neat Stolichnaya. Her preferred brand of vodka would have raised quite a few eyebrows among her public, she thought with a smile. She settled herself in a comfortable armchair. She still wore the make-up and the designer costume of what she called her one-woman show. She had been performing the role for two years now to sustained critical acclaim from those whose opinions she really valued. Two years, and she had been assured that the show would run for another ten, perhaps longer.

She truly believed this night that she was one of the luckiest of people. Oh, she worked damn hard at her job, more than most of the people she had known over the years in her profession. But then she had always been a hard worker and where had it got her? Nowhere, until that extraordinary night almost three years ago.

She had been alone in a small dressing room in a small theatre in Guildford, feeling sorry for herself. It was only the second night of what had been scheduled for a fortnight's run of *The Importance of Being Earnest* and audience numbers were already well below expectations. Advance bookings were meagre and there were rumours among the cast that the show would close at the end of the week and the planned tour of the South of England might now be curtailed or even cancelled.

Sitting in the dingy dressing room, out of costume and heavy make-up, she looked in the mirror at a tired woman in her early fifties and wondered what was going to happen to her. She always tried to avoid indulging in self-pity but, my God, it was so easy. Her family dead, no close friends, a short, painful marriage begun and ended many years ago, and now an uncertain future. Damn Charles Bonnington! How did that ridiculous albino dwarf ever get to direct a play. She was proud of her Lady Bracknell. She believed that she had successfully avoided the usual clichés of the part and had created an interpretation that was subtle and different and would have been certain to attract favourable press comment. But bloody Charlie, for reasons that defied theatrical or any logic, had his own ideas about how *The Importance of Being Earnest* should be staged, including switching the period to the 1920s, and introducing, for Heaven's sakes, a Charleston dance sequence.

It was all too bad, a bitterly disappointing end to what had looked like a real opportunity to get back on the boards after yet another long period of resting. She had entertained such high hopes when her manager had called out of the blue and told her that she had the part of Lady Bracknell in a two-month run. "Maybe three, more," he said. "And listen, if it does as well as everyone expects, and Charlie's such an outstanding talented guy, this one could finish up in the West End. Plus the money is good."

Yes, the money was important. The bank manager's politeness was dropping perceptibly with each successive reminder about the size of her overdraft. But it wasn't just the money, it was the potential. The passing of the years had not really dimmed her belief that the big break was just around the corner. How often it had hovered teasingly before her just to vanish the moment she almost had it in her grasp. Yet always she believed that it would all come right the next time. Now, she was losing faith.

And then there was a knock on the door and Stan Laurel and Oliver Hardy came strolling into the dressing room and changed the course of her life.

"Miss Simpson," said Mr Hardy. "Forgive the intrusion, please, but I have to say that it is the greatest honour to meet you."

Almost immediately she saw that her first impression was wrong and that her two visitors did not really look like Laurel and Hardy. Yes, one was a big man, in a dark three-piece suit. He was wide of girth and beneath his small moustache he was beaming happily. His companion was smaller, dressed in a grey suit and his smile was more tentative as though unsure of his welcome. But the big man on closer inspection was more muscle than fat and the thin man was lean and wiry. She could imagine that, in certain circumstances, both could be hard, dangerous men. But right now they managed to give the impression that they were slightly overawed at meeting her.

The big man had been carrying a large cellophane-wrapped bunch of flowers and he now presented it to her with a flourish.

"We so enjoyed your performance tonight, dear lady," he said. His voice was deep and pleasantly modulated. "But, please let me introduce ourselves. I am George Gooding and my colleague here is Robert Grayford. I do hope you can spare us a moment."

"Absolutely," murmured Grayford politely.

"How really kind of you," she said, surprised and flattered. Few men had called on her backstage in recent years and it was wholly unexpected. Earlier, she had watched a number of young men and women congregate outside the dressing room door of the young blonde actress from the TV soap who was playing the part of Cecily. But Lady Bracknell did not usually draw the fans. She invited them to sit down, uncomfortably aware of the shabbiness of the room and the cheap cane chairs.

With another wide smile of pleasure, Gooding dropped into one of the chairs, which creaked at his bulk. Grayford looked doubtfully at the other none too clean chair, then perched himself carefully on the edge of a large wicker basket.

"I must confess," said Gooding, "that I have long been one of your great admirers, ever since I saw you in *Last Testament*. And then, of course, there was that marvellous film, *The Hollow Man*. You were magnificent." He raised his hands in an expression of admiration.

She was utterly taken aback. *Last Testament* was more than twenty years old and was the only movie in which she had featured in a starring role, as the young governess of a crippled boy whose devotion to duty eventually wins the love of the rich and handsome widower. At the time, she was convinced that the role would be her passport to Hollywood. But the movie had been a critical and box office flop and, like the public, she had long forgotten it. *The Hollow Man* was another failure, a TV series based on the locked-room murder novels of John Dickson Carr that didn't survive the pilot programme. And, here, astonishingly, was someone who not only remembered them, but was actually rhapsodising about her performance in them.

She was momentarily at a loss for words but Gooding was in full flow.

"But in my opinion, Miss Simpson, Lady Bracknell is one of your finest roles to date. So many great actresses have put their stamp on the part that one has come to expect merely inferior echoes of them. You, on the other hand, have recreated the part in a most fascinating way. It never occurred to me until

11

I saw you this evening that Lady Bracknell is none other than one of our leading political figures." And he chortled.

"Please call me Emma," she said. "So, you recognised my Lady Bracknell. I wondered if people would notice."

"How could they not?" he boomed. "I have to say candidly that I was not at all persuaded that this production fits comfortably into the years of *l'entre deux guerres*. Happily, you completely transcend this curiosity and, indeed, give us something altogether new and exciting."

She could never remember being the recipient of so much lavish praise in all her life.

"You are a perceptive man, Mr Gooding," she said. "Are you perhaps in the theatre yourself?"

It was Grayford who unexpectedly replied. She had almost forgotten him in Gooding's larger than life presence. He had been sitting quietly on the wicker basket, nodding contentedly at the conversation. Now he stood up and said, as though glad to get to the point:

"Yes, we are very much in the theatre business, Miss Simpson-

"Emma, please," she broke in.

"Yes, of course, eh, Emma. The fact is that we are putting together a fairly major production and both George and I are hoping that you might consider the leading part."

Gooding spoke up quickly. "Tut, Robert, let's not rush into business. And this is not perhaps the ideal place to discuss it." He waved a hand dismissively at the dressing room. "Emma, would you by any chance have the time for a spot of supper with us? We have the car just outside the door."

Trying to hide her eagerness, she agreed to join them below in a few minutes.

"Excellent, excellent," said Gooding, giving his companion a hearty clap on the back as though they had achieved some great coup. They departed the dressing room in a flurry of good humour. As she carefully applied her make-up, Emma Simpson forced herself not to think about what their offer might be. Her spirits were soaring, a combination of the flattery and the possibility of solid work. Somehow, Gooding and Grayford did not strike her as men who would be associated with failure and, if their praise meant anything, they were surely talking about a substantial role.

She could vividly recall her mounting excitement of that night. Their car was a black Bentley and there was a chauffeur, a polite, athletic young man who also had the look of someone who could take care of himself. It was a two-minute drive to the Jarvis hotel on the cobblestoned High Street. Dinner was in a private room. At Gooding's insistence, they started with champagne, then smoked salmon, followed by beef wellington and fresh strawberries. Gooding took charge of the wines, ordering the most expensive Sancerre available and a full bodied Spanish red, Scola Dei Tinto.

It had been a very long time since she had been dined so lavishly and in such congenial company. The talk was mainly theatre gossip, of which not only Gooding but, surprisingly, Grayford knew a great deal. Gooding was, of course, the life of the party, laughing uproariously at every anecdote, including his own. Grayford seemed also to loosen up and showed a tendency to giggle. Emma found herself studying the two men and was intrigued to notice the subtle indications of a more personal relationship between them than she had first realised.

It was only when the meal had ended and they sat contentedly sipping brandies that Gooding brought up the business of the evening.

"As Robert mentioned to you, we are in the final stages of putting together a show. It will be really big, our financial backers are extremely generous and we are satisfied that it will run for a long time. And we so much want you, dear Emma, to take the leading role."

It was all sounding too good to be true. "Do continue," she said trying for a non-committal interest and hoping that her face did not betray her.

Gooding nodded happily, as though pleased with her response.

"We realise, of course, that we will be asking you to commit a great deal of your time and that you will have to turn down many other offers. That is why we will be offering fair remuneration." He named a sum and Emma almost dropped her glass. It was at least four times her earnings in her best ever year.

Gooding frowned deprecatingly. "The figure is net of tax, incidentally. There will also be an apartment in Carlton House Terrace, which I think you would like, reasonably good expenses, a paid holiday."

"Even perhaps a pension scheme," added Grayford, who had been watching her closely.

Mellowed by the alcohol, Emma realised that this was all way over the top. She got a sudden sinking feeling.

"Who else will be in this play" she asked as lightly as she could.

"Just you," said Gooding with a grin of delight.

There was a long pause. Finally, trying to blunt the edge of a sharp disappointment, she said in her Lady Bracknell voice: "Gentlemen, I must admit that I am somewhat bewildered by what you have just told me."

Gooding let out a whoop of delight at the quotation from the play but she continued: "I begin to fear that your proposal involves something either immoral or illegal or possibly both."

"Bless my dear mother's soul, far from it," exclaimed Gooding in apparent genuine surprise. "Let me assure you that among our backers are at least three members of the Cabinet, two Law Lords and the Commissioner of Scotland Yard himself. In fact, some of these gentlemen are quite looking forward to meeting with you very soon. Please allow me to explain."

He did and she immediately accepted. It was not just the astonishing possibility of a life free forever of financial worry. It was not that she knew instinctively that she would be able to play the part to perfection. It was something else that decided her there and then to give this role everything she was capable of. She was no fool. She knew that Gooding and Grayford (though she had learned that these were not their names) might so easily have taken a totally different approach. They might have said: "Miss Simpson, your career has not brought you fame or fortune. Your name is not up in lights and, sadly, never will be. You are no longer a young woman. Your bank overdraft is over your limit. You have no family, few friends. Your prospects are hardly bright and you have little choice but to take our offer." She would have been forced to agree. But instead of humiliation, they had treated her like a great actress, still at her peak. They had respected her pride and her dignity. And for that, she would be profoundly grateful to them and to their "backers" and she silently promised herself that she would never let them down.

Nor had she, reflected Emma Simpson, as she poured herself a second Stolichnaya in the lavishly appointed sitting-room in the Grand Hotel, Brighton. She had more than met everyone's expectations. And, in turn, it had been the most wonderful two years of her life. The role had largely taken over her life so that, even when alone, she often slipped into the character in her actions and even her thoughts. She would never, she believed, take for granted the applause, the cheering crowds, the adulatory looks.

She glanced at her watch and quickly finished her drink. It was almost 2.30 a.m., time for the changeover. They would be calling for her soon.

* * *

Outside the hotel, hidden in the darkness of a doorway, the watcher was cursing the sharp cold of the October night that seemed to freeze face and hands and penetrate the dark heavy overcoat. A few minutes earlier, almost every floor of the hotel was a blaze of lighted windows, giving it the appearance of a great ocean liner at sea. RMS Titanic, thought the watcher sardonically. Shortly after 2 a.m., the bar closed and one by one the lights were going out. But, looking through the latest US army nightscope binoculars, the watcher saw with satisfaction that the lights were still on in that suite on the first floor. They had figured it exactly right. She would be up late, working on her speech for the following day. Despite the time, there was a lot of activity at the front of the hotel. The security remained alert. But they couldn't stop things now. This operation had been twelve months in the planning and had taken everything into account.

The watcher waited out the last few minutes, shivering with the cold and also with an element of nervousness. It was not fear of what was about to happen or getting caught or anything like that but an anxiety that, through accident or stupidity, there would be a failure to do the specific job that had been assigned. It was the watcher's first time on active service, after two years as a sleeper in London.

"Keep a low profile, Sam," they had said. "Do your job, keep your social life to a minimum, never talk politics or religion, be one of the crowd. We'll call when we need you." The call had come at very short notice for such a well-planned operation. The person originally assigned had suddenly fallen ill. Maybe. Or maybe it was a test. It was known within the organisation that Sam did not agree with this type of operation.

Sam, the watcher, looked again at the time and thought, here we go. It was 2.50 a.m.

* * *

Emma Simpson was in the bathroom, hastily removing her make-up, annoyed with herself for spending too much time daydreaming. They would be calling for her any minute now and she didn't want to keep them waiting. She had the bathroom door open to hear their knock. They wouldn't say anything or even give the appearance of impatience if she wasn't ready. But she liked to be ready to leave immediately. It was more professional that way. Nearly ready, she thought, glancing around the room to make sure that everything was in order for the next occupant. At the beginning of her new career, she had spent a lot of time with her. Since then, they had never met, though Emma carefully watched tapes of her every public appearance, always checking her voice, how she pronounced new words, any new personality

15

quirk. Emma had no wish to meet with her face to face again and she suspected that the other would also wish to avoid such a meeting. In different ways, it would be unsettling for both.

She went back to the sitting room, took the black wig out of its box and returned to the bathroom. As she caught her image in the bathroom mirror, she noticed, with a slowly dawning surprise, that she seemed to be floating several inches above the ground and that her hair was spreading outwards in an extraordinary way, as though caught in a sudden draft. A crack ran swiftly across the mirror and it began to buckle inwards. There was a great roaring noise in her ears, increasing in volume, as though some huge audience was rising in ovation. She was still staring with incomprehension at the mirror when the room exploded around her and everything went black.

* * *

From the vantage point, Sam saw the explosion moments before hearing the thunderous noise of the blast. The whole frontage of the hotel collapsed slowly, with tons of rubble cascading down through the floors of the hotel. The noise was deafening. It was followed by a long eerie silence. Then Sam heard the screaming and shouting. People began to pour out of the hotel, first in twos and threes and then in a milling, panicked crowd. They were mostly in night attire and many were barefooted. The few uniformed police and security people were quick and efficient, gesturing people to move away from the hotel, afraid possibly of another bomb. Sam recognised several members of the cabinet, some with wives and family members, standing dazedly and unprotected in the crowd at the waterfront and reflected that, had an active service unit been in place or a second bomb strategically planted, the second devastation would have been even more lethal. But tonight there was really only one target and Sam was the watcher whose job it was to confirm the kill.

There was the distant wail of an ambulance siren and the blaring horn of a fire truck and then the night was echoing with oncoming emergency vehicles. Within minutes, the area in front of the hotel was filling with the flashing multicoloured lights of police cars, fire engines and ambulances. Dozens of emergency workers and volunteers were scrambling in the mountain of rubble, lifting piles of masonry in search of survivors. Sam finally removed the heavy black overcoat, stepped out of cover, and walked quickly across to the hotel, just one of many figures in a white coat.

It was easy to mingle with the rescue services in the devastation and confusion. Sam scrambled over the wreckage of the hotel, pausing twice to assist a group haul bricks and slabs of concrete away and gently lift people onto waiting stretchers. One, a young man, was naked and dead, his eyes and mouth open in surprise. An older woman, with a gaping hole in her cheek and the bone of her arm sticking through the skin, looked fixedly at her rescuers and said calmly: "I told Gerard that we should have taken the train. Now, you see, we can't go home."

Sam moved steadily in the direction of what had been the Prime Minister's suite, feeling no emotion. Like it or not, this was war, and a soldier couldn't get emotionally involved without cracking up which would be no use to friend or foe. Finally, Sam stood on the periphery of a large group of emergency workers who had just stopped their frantic scrambling. A body had been taken out, dirt-covered and misshapen, a policeman was bending over it. Sam instantly knew who it was. A man in the group, wearing a suit but no shirt said to no-one in particular: "Oh God, the bastards have killed Mrs Thatcher."

Sam moved away. It was well over time to get out of this place and make the phone call announcing a successful mission. But it took longer than expected to clear the site. Almost immediately, a fire chief was calling for volunteers to help get at some trapped people. Sam was in the fire chief's line of sight and had no choice but to help. It took almost half an hour of digging before two injured men were brought out. Sam finally slipped back to the edge of the crowd. A woman stopped by with a tray full of cups of tea and Sam took one and was grateful for the strong, scalding brew. Nobody paid any attention as the figure in the now filthy white coat walked off. Ten minutes later, Sam was behind the wheel of a Rover driving out of Brighton, listening to the news on the radio.

They were still scrambling to get the story. The announcer spoke of a massive bomb that had ripped apart the Grand Hotel, Brighton where the Conservative Party conference was being held. One person was so far confirmed dead and many people were believed seriously injured. No organisation had yet admitted responsibility for what was clearly a terrorist outrage. "Don't be impatient," muttered Sam. "You'll have our announcement soon enough." What an incredible coup if it turned out that Mrs Thatcher was the only person killed. Precision like that would unnerve British security. But Sam knew that this was an early news report. Later, the number of deaths would be higher.

The first phone box, about two miles outside the town, was vandalised. So was the next. Sam swore and drove on, watching out for the next phone box and only half listening to the radio. Suddenly, Sam braked the car to a stop and listened to the radio intently. A flash announcement. It had just been confirmed that the Prime Minister was safe and was uninjured.

"What the bloody hell?" shouted Sam aloud. Thatcher was dead. That mangled body couldn't possibly have been alive. It certainly wasn't uninjured. There could be no mistake. If it looked like Thatcher and dressed like Thatcher it had to be. And suddenly Sam knew.

"Our leading customer had a double and the double accepted delivery in full." Sam was in a phone box, this one in working order. The person at the other end, in a house in the suburbs of north London, swore angrily, then became philosophical.

"We can't think of everything, Sam. But we've sure scared the shit out of her. I feel sorry for her, you know, with all her clean underwear blown sky high. Think we should let the world know that she hides behind a double?"

"I suggest that we don't," said Sam slowly. "Never let them know what we know about them. That way, they won't know all their weaknesses."

"Maybe so," said the man non-committally, "We'll think about that. Thanks Sam, you did well to find out about it." The phone clicked off.

Sam replaced the receiver. It had been sheer good luck not getting to a phone earlier and announcing that Mrs Thatcher had been killed. Now they would be thinking: Sam is sound, didn't rush things, checked carefully before calling, saved us the embarrassment of a premature announcement.

It was important to Sam that the job of watcher had gone right and that the organisation believed they had an intelligent, careful operative. There would be bigger things ahead, more responsibility, an opportunity to influence decisions and move the organisation away from spectacular but ultimately pointless bombings and into new directions that would bring about the results they all wanted.

The IRA put the best face on it. A few hours later, they formally announced responsibility for the bombing. Their statement included a message to Mrs Thatcher: "Today we were unlucky, but remember we only have to be lucky once. You have to be lucky all the time." There was no mention of Mrs Thatcher's double.

LONDON
Thursdays 24 & 31 January 1991

Milton Keynes, near London

Thursday 24 January 1991

Douglas King stopped his new BMW 501 outside the gates of his factory at 7.30 a.m. and instantly the half dozen minor business problems that had been preoccupying him vanished when he saw the two men who were waiting for him. He knew immediately who they were. He had hoped that he would never hear from them again. He had done his best to lose them, moving several times before settling down in Rickmansworth and Milton Keynes, changing his name, taking his number out of the phone book. He had almost believed that his past was behind him. Now it was in front of him.

They were standing beside a mud-spattered white Ford transit van. One was in his early 30s, tall, dark-haired, intelligent-looking, and was impeccably dressed. He was wearing an expensive black overcoat and silk scarf, with a well-tailored suit and what looked like Church shoes. The other was about the same age, with a mop of blond curly hair, skinny but tough-looking and dressed in a donkey jacket and denims.

The well-dressed man came forward, his hand outstretched. King shook hands without thinking about it. "Douglas King, I believe," said the man with a pleasant smile. His accent was a kind of neutral English middle class with an underlay of the posher suburbs of Dublin. "My name is Kieran Delaney. We haven't met but I think you'll remember Terry, here. He was just a teenage hoodlum when you last met him. Now, as you can see, he's a fully grown hoodlum."

Terry grinned. He stayed where he was and waved amiably at King then put his hands back in the pockets of his jacket. "How's it going, Colum, or should I say Douglas? You've put on a bit of weight since the last time. I'm wondering if you'd be able to make it over the wall again under your own steam?"

King said nothing. Delaney stamped his feet. "It's a bloody cold morning, Douglas, and I'm sure we'd all prefer not to be seen together hanging about the Queen's highway. I think you'd better invite us in. We won't be taking up too much of your time."

"Right you are, " said King heavily, his mind numb. He took out his keys, opened the gate and swung it back. He went back to his car and drove into his usual parking spot. Delaney got into the van and drove in after him. Terry walked into the yard and stood admiring King's BMW. "Nice wheels," he said. King nodded as he unlocked the main door of the factory and disconnected the alarm. For a brief moment, he thought of rushing into the building, slamming the door in the faces of the two men, relocking the building and-then what? His shoulders slumped. They followed him down the corridor and into his office. King had spent a lot of money on his office and knew that it impressed visitors with its large size, custom-made Swedish furniture, back-lit drinks cabinet, rich blue carpet. Now, he wished it was small and cramped, over-flowing with papers and files.

King and Delaney sat in two of the leather lounge chairs that surrounded the marble coffee table. Terry, after looking round him with an appreciative whistle, stood in a corner of the room, hands still in pockets.

"Your old friends send their best wishes," said Delaney, lighting a cigarette. "Kinda lost touch with you for a while. But, they are delighted to see you doing so well for yourself. Makes them happy that they sprang you out of jail, how long ago was it, nearly twelve years? Even with good behaviour, you'd still be inside today if they hadn't got you out."

He glanced around the room. "You've built yourself a nice business, Douglas King. And no-one's saying that you don't deserve it. You gave a lot to the movement in the old days. That's not been forgotten."

King sighed and shook his head as if to clear his mind. He looked levelly at Delaney. "I was good then," he said. "But I'm not that man anymore. Three years in that hellhole of a place took too much out of me. I didn't have the mentality to be cooped up and I thought I was going to be there forever." He shuddered at the recollection. "When they set up the escape, I knew that the moment I got outside the walls, I was going to run from them as much as from anyone else. I'd be no good to them anymore, thinking all the time of being caught again and sent back in. I had to start all over."

He thought of what he had achieved. He was the boss of a small but highly sophisticated light engineering and electronics factory close to Milton Keynes's town centre. This location gave his trucks fast access over five miles of dual carriageway to the M1, the heart of the British motorway system. He was proud of the work of his 25-strong labour force, many taken from the dole queue to train himself. They were loyal, worked hard, and didn't join a trade union because, like the American plant nearby, he looked after them well with productivity bonuses, an extra week's holiday, presents for their children at

Christmas and a few other perks unknown to the taxman.

His products were selling well nationally, and he was exporting to Germany and Holland, with plans for Japan and the US market. The business was a good earner. He had the Georgian house in Rickmansworth, a beautiful wife, two young children, he was a respected member of the local Chamber, was on the committee of the golf club, he had a four-week time-share villa in the south of France and;

Delaney broke in on his thoughts. "We thought you might do us a small favour, for old time's sake," he said.

King was silent for a long time. Then he said: "I don't suppose I've much of a choice about it."

Delaney frowned and looked like he was going to snap out an angry retort. Instead, he leaned over and patted King's arm. His voice was quiet. "You've got it wrong, Douglas King. There's no pressure. We'd like your help and it won't be a big thing. But if you decide you don't want to help, we'll understand. Say the word and we'll walk right out of here and right out of your life." He paused. "If that's how you really feel about things now."

"Oh, sweet and holy Jesus," said King, wondering if he could believe him. The involuntary ejaculation brought back an unexpected recollection. He was back in the prison cell again, at the end of another day of tedium and petty harassment from the prison guards. He could hear Bill Turley, the fat fool, snoring and farting in the overhead bunk. He prayed: "Sweet and holy Jesus, get me out of this place and then give me the strength to break the necks of the fucking Brits who put me in here." A blasphemous prayer, of course, but he thought that Jesus would understand him, even if He couldn't help him.

He realised that Delaney was looking at him with concern. King smiled weakly. "Just recalling happy days. OK. What do you want me to do?"

"Thank you," said Delaney. "Like I said, it's not an onerous thing we want. The Ford outside. We'd like to leave it where it is for a few days. Make certain nobody goes near it until we come back to pick it up. We'll need a spare key to the gate." He stood up and lowered his voice. "Glad we can count on you, Colum."

There were no more words needed. King shook hands with his visitors and they departed.

Next day, Saturday, King drove down to the factory. It was closed for business at the weekend and King, who usually went in for a few hours in the morning, knew the van was safe enough where it was but was determined to see what was inside. He locked the gates carefully behind him and approached the van. Since the meeting with Delaney and Terry he had been surprised to find that he could be almost his normal self in work and at home. He had managed somehow to blank the van out of his mind. But, since he had woken up, the tension had been growing. He knew he should do absolutely nothing until the van was collected. But he had to confirm his suspicions.

He walked around the van. Four years old, in reasonably good condition, London licence plate. All the doors were locked; he had expected that. He peered through the side window at the driver's compartment. Everything neat and clean. 55,000 miles on the clock. He slipped into the factory and came back with a bunch of keys, a file, and gloves. As he worked on the back door lock, he saw that his hands were shaking. He knew it was madness but he couldn't walk away. A frighteningly clear image flashed into his mind of a bomb inside and an anti-personnel trigger waiting for him to open the door. He didn't stop and gently probed the lock with the keys until, after a little filing here and there, it snapped back.

Gingerly he opening the doors. His whole body was shaking now, and he felt perspiration on his back and in his armpits. "Sweet and holy Jesus," he thought.

The mortar bombs looked innocent enough but nearly twenty years ago his two best friends had been blown to pieces without even getting the missiles off the ground. These were an improved version, but he knew just how unreliable home-made mortars were no matter how carefully they were handled. They could go off anywhere, anytime or not at all.

Part of the van roof had been removed and the opening covered with some material. The mortars would be set off by an electrical timer which, if fired from the van, should give the driver time to escape before the explosion. Maybe. The steel casing was made from pipes and was about 4ft long, probably 6inch in diameter and weighed about 10 stone, he reckoned. The detonator was in the nose and fins had been welded to the tail to give more accuracy than the ones he remembered. He had no idea what explosives were being used. The mortars he remembered carried about 50lb of a home-made explosive. A dangerous mixture of sugar and sodium chlorate obtained from farm fertiliser had provided the explosive propellant charge. Maybe they were using Semtex now.

"Hello, Douglas," someone called and his heart lurched. He quickly closed the doors and when he came round the van and saw the police car outside the gate, he all but collapsed. He took several deep breaths and walked quickly towards the car. It was empty. Then two policemen came into view. He recognised Sergeant Parrott from the golf club. "Someone reported a possible break-in here but we guessed it was you," he said, looking slowly around the yard. "Still, no harm checking." He glanced at the van without interest.

"Good of you to do so," said King. "Few things I had to sort out, auditors coming Monday." Couldn't they see his shakes, hear his heart banging painfully against his chest?

"Aye, fiddling the books again," laughed the sergeant as he got back into the car. "You can buy me a large one at the clubhouse on Wednesday on the taxman."

"You blind git, you could have had me if you hadn't called out just then. Promotion for you and twenty years for me," thought King gratefully, leaning against the gate and watching the car disappear down the road. "You could have had me and a bloody IRA car bomb except that you called out just then." He wished he had a large one in his hand right then.

He took a roundabout way home to give himself a chance to calm down. He let his mind wander. Why were they still using such unreliable weapons? With what he knew now, he could make-he closed off the thought abruptly. That evening he surprised his wife and children by suggesting they go to Mass, something they had not done together for a long time. It worried his wife more than if he had arrived home dead drunk. But she asked no questions. On Wednesday morning, when King arrived at the factory, the van was gone.

Number 10 Downing Street, London

Thursday 31 January 1991

The Prime Minister, John Major, called the Cabinet meeting to order at precisely 10 a.m. There were 15 Government ministers and senior officials in the room. Others were held up in traffic by the snow and frost that morning. The Cabinet was on a war footing due to the Gulf war with Iraq and they got down to business quickly.

Major was sitting in his usual chair facing the windows of the Cabinet room. To his right was Sir Robin Butler, Cabinet Secretary, Sir Percy Cradock, his foreign affairs adviser, Andrew Turnbull, his private secretary and Len Appleyard, the minute-taker. On Major's left was his senior private secretary Charles Powell and press secretary Gus O'Donnell. With their backs to the big windows and facing them across the table were: Sir Patrick Mayhew, the Attorney-General, Chancellor Norman Lamont, Energy Secretary John Wakeham, Industry Secretary Peter Lilley, Foreign Secretary Douglas Hurd, Defence Secretary Tom King, and the Chief of the Defence Staff, Sir David Craig.

Treasury Secretary David Mellor was speaking, giving a summary of his money-raising mission for the war. It was going well, he reported. It had already been known that Saudi Arabia and the Gulf States would pick up much of the tab. But other countries, notably Japan, who were not making a military input, were going to kick in some hefty financial contributions. Major was about to interject a question, when suddenly the room shook and there was a loud bang.

Outside, people heading to work in the snow were amazed to see three mortar shells soaring across the rooftops of Whitehall towards the Prime Minister's residence. The first missile landed and exploded in the back garden of No 10, a few feet away from the windows of the ground-floor Cabinet room. Since the Brighton Grand Hotel bombing, the security at Downing Street had been extensively overhauled. At the touch of a button, reinforced armoured plates would rise up from the road itself to prevent a frontal attack by the IRA. Additional security posts for police sharpshooters had been set up on the rooftops overlooking the maze of offices in 10, 11 and 12 Downing Street. All window-panes had been replaced by toughened security glass and there were heavy fine steel imitation net curtains held down with lead weights. These precautions almost certainly saved those in the Cabinet room from serious injury from flying glass. As it was, the men in the room were unscathed and if they were shaken they did not show it.

Within minutes, the Cabinet meeting was resumed in an underground bunker in 10 Downing Street. Major calmly asked David Mellor to resume his briefing. The Home Secretary, Kenneth Baker, arrived, was immediately given responsibility for working with deeply embarrassed security officials, and began to draw up a preliminary report for the Cabinet before the meeting broke up.

* * *

In a suburban house in Belfast, three people were watching the news on television, switching occasionally from Sky News to the BBC and ITN. They watched a news reporter standing behind a police barrier, cold but excited:

"Witnesses report seeing three cylinders, several feet long flying over the roof of Downing Street. We are told that one landed in the rear garden of No 10 and exploded, blowing out windows at the back. The other two landed on Foreign Office Green and burst into flames but did not explode. If they had fallen a few feet shorter, they would also have hit No 10. Our information is that the bombs were launched at 10.08 a.m. from a white Ford Transit van that had parked at the corner of Horse Guards Avenue and Whitehall, some 200 Yards from No 10, just two minutes earlier. A man jumped from the van onto the back of a companion's motorbike and had just disappeared when the rockets were fired and the van exploded in flames."

"A close one," said the Chief of Staff, running a hand through his thinning white hair. He was wearing a casual woollen pullover, pants that had seen better days and slippers. He sounded tired.

"But no cigar," said the Belfast Brigade Commander. Like the chief, he was in his sixties. But he was leaner and fitter and was smartly dressed in a dark blue sports jacket and sharply creased pants. "At least the boys didn't do themselves an injury. And it's going to give us a lot of very positive publicity. What do you say, Sam?"

The IRA's Director of Intelligence, the youngest person in the room, nodded agreement. "We've probably come out ahead by not blowing up Major and his merry men. British security is going to come out of this all arse and elbows. I expect that Major will issue a statement about keeping a stiff upper lip and not giving way to terrorism. But the net effect will be to bring him round to taking negotiations seriously."

The Brigade Commander poured himself a cup of tea and stared across at the Director of Intelligence. Still a youngster, really. But the best DOI to date. Very clever, with a complex mind that never lost track of where it was going. "You surprise me, Sam. You were very much against this operation, so you were. Something changed your mind, eh?"

"No, I'm still of the same mind," replied Sam carefully. "I just think we're trying for the wrong targets, making life difficult for ourselves. John Major is the least trustworthy politician I know. But his steel is soft and he's going to bend. If we'd had taken him out this morning, the next guy could have been worse. And with a slaughtered Cabinet around his neck, he'd be slow to think of coming to the table."

The Chief turned from the television and said: "Truth of it is, I don't know if you're right or wrong, Sam. You've made a good case for switching targets and what you're proposing may be the answer. A lot of people on the Council are leaning your way, even though they're not economists. And you're giving them time to work things out for themselves. That's good. But what we're watching on the telly here is going to bring in a goodly number of recruits and a lot of extra US dollars. And more people in Britain are going to be asking questions about what their government is doing in Ireland."

"Hitler bombed London for years and where did it get him?" asked Sam.

"Don't worry," said the Chief. "John Major is no Churchill. Deep down, he wants to wave a bit of paper and declare peace in our time. We'll bring him to the table because the man doesn't really give a tinker's curse about Ireland one way or the other. A few more doses of today's medicine and he'll be ready to do the business."

Sam knew better than to pursue the argument. As the Chief said, the Council was slowly coming round. It was just a matter of patience. And Sam was good at that.

**The City of London
Friday 10 April 1992**

The City of London

Friday 10 April 1992

More than 200,000 people work in the famous financial centre known as the City of London which, together with New York and Tokyo, controls most of the world's wealth in one way or another. The man and woman in the white Toyota Transit van had expected the City to be quiet at this time. It was 8 p.m. and the banks and other financial institutions had long closed for the day. But this evening, they were driving through fairly heavy traffic and the pavements were busy with pedestrians. Pubs and wine bars were overflowing with staff from the nearby banks and financial institutions, noisily and happily celebrating the unexpected Tory victory in the General Election.

The man and woman were worried but they knew they had to go through with it. A lot of planning had gone into this operation. Everything was in place, and the warnings would be given in good time for the police and the anti-terrorist Branch to clear the streets before the bomb would go off at 9.20 p.m. The man drove, saying little. The woman beside him was frowning over a London A-Z map spread on her lap. They had gone over the route several times but she still found it confusing. She looked nervously over her shoulder at the 100lb Semtex bomb in the back of the van. She knew that the Army Council did not want any civilian casualties. That was all very well, she thought, but who could predict what would happen when a bomb this size went off. She could only hope that the police would move quickly once they got the warnings and clear the area in time. If it weren't for the bloody election celebrations everybody would have gone home by now.

She was looking for Leadenhall Street and suddenly they were on it. The Commercial Union, one of the tallest buildings in London, and the old Baltic Exchange loomed over them, probably the bomb blast might reach the half mile to the Bank of England itself or even Lloyd's of London. They drove down a little side street, St Mary Axe, parked the van and set the timer. Arm in arm, the couple made their way leisurely to the nearby Underground. The man glanced up at a public clock and confirmed the time by his watch. "Eight forty-five," he said. "They'll be phoning in the warnings just about now." He sounded only mildly interested. The woman envied him his coolness. Her nerves were taut and she half expected at any moment to hear footsteps running towards them, shouts to stop. She began to relax as they descended the steps to the trains.

Two other members of the IRA's Active Service Unit No 5 were already on their way in a white Bedford van towards Staples Corner, one of the main traffic junctions in the capital, where the A5 passes underneath the North Circular Road and the M1. By the time the bomb went off just after 1 a.m. on Saturday morning, wrecking the motorway system, they were back with the others in a safe house in Camden Town watching the television reports.

* * *

"Three deaths," said one of the women. "The Army Council won't be happy. I expect we're going to get our arses kicked over that."

"I expect we won't," retorted one of the men. "Car bombs are not precision instruments. We went for as much destruction as possible and when you let off a bomb that size, the chances are that someone will get killed. We knew that. We did what we could, gave them plenty of time to clear the area. But we knew what could happen and so did the Council. All things considered, with pubs and streets full of well-oiled yuppies, it was a clean job and I don't expect to hear any whining from Belfast."

He turned back to the television to hear the top of the hour news summary.

"Three dead as London counts the cost of IRA bombs. The blast was heard five miles away. More than 50 important financial institutions have been comprehensively damaged. Among the worst affected companies in the City are Commercial Union, Baltic Exchange, James Capel, Hong Kong and Shanghai Bank, National Westminster Bank, lawyers Norton Rose, Exchange of Shipping, as well as numerous small brokers and underwriters whose computers and records may have been destroyed. The blast cut through hundreds of phone lines, many providing vital links with money and share markets. British Telecom reports that as many as 175,000 telephone lines had been put out of action. The Edgware Road flyover, target of a second blast, is expected to take a year to rebuild."

He was about to switch off and go to bed when a follow-up story caught his attention. A news reporter was saying that Commander George Churchill-Coleman, the leader of C13, the Anti-Terrorist Branch, was again likely to face criticism from the media and already there were calls to give MI5 overall responsibility for the fight against the IRA.

He snorted. The media didn't have enough of an inside track to give an informed opinion on who should be in charge of fighting the IRA. Obviously, MI5 was being quick off the mark in taking advantage of the bombings to feed some friendly journalists a line that would undermine the Anti-Terrorist Branch. If MI5 was lobbying the media, they were almost certainly pushing all the buttons where they had influence. He made a mental note to talk to Belfast about it. But it wouldn't be his problem for a while. Active Service Unit 5 of the Irish Republican Army in London, while always involved in observation, identifying targets, checking security, and working in their normal jobs, would not be called up again for a military operation for at least six months. But this time, the two senior officers, Kieran Delaney and Tara Barry, were very wrong.

New York
11 November 1993

New York

11 November 1993

Martin Carter strolled into the shop in the Waldorf Astoria to pick up his morning newspaper and saw the pickpocket taking the credit card from the girl's handbag. The girl was obviously an out-of-town tourist because she carried it on a strap over her shoulder in a way that was an open invitation to a petty thief. She was checking the price of postcards with the assistant behind the counter and the man stood beside her, apparently pre-occupied with selecting a pack of chewing gum, while his hand slipped the credit card out of the bag.

Carter walked over to him and said amiably: "Hello, pal. I'm with hotel security and I'd be obliged if you'll walk down to my office for a chat."

The man turned quickly. He was a big, red-faced, beefy white man in a tweed suit that didn't fit him well. He looked like an off-duty cop.

"Who the hell are you?" he demanded, then suddenly he moved past Carter and ran for the door. Carter kicked his ankle as he passed. The man shouted in pain and began hopping towards the door. Carter was reaching out to grab his jacket when another man entered the shop, carrying a shopping bag in each hand. The pickpocket reached out for the man's tie, swung him around and into Carter. They both went down.

Carter tried to get up but the man was holding onto him protectively. "What is it?" he shouted. "What's going on here?" With an effort, Carter shrugged him off and ran down the corridor into the hotel foyer. No sign of the pickpocket. He went out onto Lexington Avenue and immediately saw the man two blocks up, limping heavily. The man turned and saw him and went into a side street.

When Carter got to the corner, the man had made less than fifty yards. He saw Carter coming and stopped, his hands on his hips, breathing heavily. As soon as Carter got within range, the man went into a boxing stance and threw out a punch. He looked strong but he was clumsy. Carter moved inside the punch and snapped three of his own into the man's nose and felt the crunch as it broke. The man reeled back, blood cascading from his nose and sat down heavily on the sidewalk. Two men with briefcases hurried by, ignoring the fight.

The man pulled a dirty handkerchief from his pocket and tried to staunch the blood. He looked up aggrieved at Carter. "Bastard," he mumbled. "You've broken my nose."

"Go call your lawyer," said Carter. "But first give me the credit card."

"Fuck you'self," said the man.

Carter hit him again on the nose and the man screamed. "Give me the goddam credit card," said Carter, angry with himself for hitting the man who was now past defending himself.

The man glared at him, put his free hand in his pocket, took out the credit card and threw it on the ground. Carter picked it up and saw that it was a Bank of Ireland gold Visa. He pocketed it.

"Get a doctor to fix up your nose and don't come within a mile of the hotel again," he said to the man. He left him sitting on the ground, moaning into his handkerchief and returned to the hotel.

The girl and the man were both waiting for him in the shop, looking anxious. Carter handed her the card. "I want to apologise on behalf of the hotel. We try to make sure this doesn't happen to our guests."

"What happened to the man?" asked the girl. Carter looked at her closely for the first time. She was a beauty, tall and slim, with long dark red hair and green eyes. She had a strong Irish accent. "Oh God, you're bleeding," she exclaimed.

Carter looked at the bloodstains on his sleeve. "Not mine," he said briefly. "The guy got away but he threw down the credit card."

The man said: "Listen, I'm sorry I got in the way but I didn't know what was going down." He was a few years older than the girl and his hair was a lighter shade of red and close cropped.

"Sister and brother?" Carter asked.

The man laughed. "We just can't hide the fact. I'm Sean Quinn and this is Eileen. As you can probably guess we're over here on holiday from Ireland." They shook hands, Eileen letting the handclasp linger.

"Hey," said Sean impulsively. "We'd really like to thank you properly for getting the Visa back. How about we get together for a drink this evening?"

"I'd like that," said Eileen.

"I'll take you up on that," said Carter. "I'll be off duty from five. How about meeting up at six?"

It was agreed.

Carter walked back to his office, poured a cup of coffee from the percolator and put his feet up on the desk. Now, just what was that all about, he wondered. It was a set-up, and not a particularly good one. The beefy man was no pickpocket. Sean's appearance in the shop doorway, the ease with which he had let himself be pushed around, his clumsy attempts to hold onto Carter had been amateurish. The plan had obviously been to let the man escape. He had seen the panic when they saw the blood on his jacket. Obviously, Sean and Eileen wanted to build a quick relationship with him and he was curious enough to follow their play.

They met in Eamon Doran's bar on 2nd Avenue their choice. It was crowded but they found themselves a table. Carter let the talk flow as he sized them both up. He didn't see Sean as a clothing salesman. He was small, well muscled and had the air of a man who was used to taking charge. He had an inner tension and it took him an effort to relax. Eileen, he suspected, was the brains of the duo. Laughing and joking came easier to her. She was openly flirting with Carter, but she couldn't hide the calculation in her eyes.

Over pints of Guinness, they told him their story. Sean and Eileen owned a small clothing manufacturing company just outside Belfast, inherited from their late father. The business was doing well and they had both come to New York to check out the possibility of getting export orders. They were combining a little business with a lot of sightseeing. No, they were not staying at the Waldorf. They had cousins in Queens who were putting them up for the visit. "Everyone in Ireland has a relative in New York," said Eileen.

"How about you?" she asked Carter. "Chances are you've got a bit of Irish somewhere in your background."

He shook his head. "Scottish, I think."

"There you are,"said Sean. "You're a Celt and that makes you one of us."

"I knew an Irish guy once, came from a place called Wicklow. We were in the same outfit in Vietnam. Everyone called him Padder and I thought it was because of how he would pad silently through the jungle at night. But it turned out his name was Peader, which was the Gaelic version of Peter."

"That's right," said Eileen.

"He told me once that the basic Irish skills were farmin', fishin' and fornicatin'. Was he right?"

Carter had said it to see their response. For a moment, Sean's dark eyes flashed a wild look of anger and Eileen threw him a warning glance. Then the wild look was gone and Sean answered easily. "That's true enough but there is a fourth, fighting. We tend to be bloody good at that when we have to."

Eileen quickly changed the subject and the rest of the evening passed pleasantly if a little dull for Carter. At the end of the night, they invited him to come back to the house in Queens. He was going to refuse but Eileen quietly put her hand in his and he accepted.

The big house on Howard Beach seemed to be empty when they arrived. They sat around the kitchen for a while with a bottle of Bushmills. Then Carter said he was tired and was shown to a spare bedroom. He lay awake in the dark, trying to figure their game. He tensed when he heard the bedroom door open quietly and a figure moved swiftly across to his bed. He almost hit her before he realised it was Eileen and she was nude. She stood in front of him for a full minute, slowly stroking her body. Then, without a word, she got into bed beside him.

* * *

When he woke up the next morning, he was alone. He washed and dressed quickly and went downstairs. In the kitchen both Sean and Eileen were cooking rashers, sausages, eggs, black and white pudding, some dreadful mixture from the Old Country. "What you need is a good Irish breakfast," said Eileen. What he really wanted was fresh orange juice and a pot of black coffee.

He joined them at the table. Eileen was friendly and happy. But she gave none of the signs a secret smile, a private eye contact-of the lover. Sean was intent on demolishing his breakfast.

"Hey, Martin," he said suddenly as if a thought had just occurred to him. "How would you like to come with us to Florida and places onwards? We've decided to get out of New York, see something else of America. We're going to fly down to Miami early tomorrow morning. Then maybe after a couple of days we'll move on to Las Vegas. We'd love you to come along as our guest."

"It would be great fun having you along," said Eileen enthusiastically. "Please say yes."

The proposal was bizarre. For a moment, thinking about the possibilities with Eileen, he was almost tempted. But his mind rebelled at the idea of trailing around assorted tourist spots in America while he waited for the pair of them to get around to letting him know what was on their minds.

He gave a shrug of regret. "Sounds pretty fantastic, but it's no go for a working stiff like me, I'm afraid."

Sean persisted. "Surely you can take the time off, Martin. And, like I said, don't worry about the money. We've got a lot of dollars to spend."

"I wish I could, but I'm going to have to take a pass," said Carter firmly.

For a while, Sean ate in thoughtful silence. Then he asked: "When are you due back at the hotel?"

"Not until six this evening," replied Carter. "I've got late duty tonight."

Sean brightened. "Then, tell you what. My cousin is due back in about an hour from now. Let's wait for him and we'll all go into Manhattan and see some of the sights."

Carter agreed. Sean went out of the kitchen. A minute later, Carter heard his voice low on the phone. Eileen came up behind him and put a hand on his shoulder. "I was really hoping you'd be able to come with us to Miami," she said. But her heart didn't seem to be in it.

Sean came back and the three of them made small talk. Sean got out a map of New York and asked Carter to recommend places they could visit that afternoon.

An hour later, a white Range Rover pulled up outside the house and three men got out. They reminded Carter of professional wrestlers who hadn't been in the ring lately, big brawny men with beer bellies. Sean introduced them.

"This is my cousin, Mack McCarthy, this is Liam O'Donnell and this is his cousin Bull Owney. I'd like you to meet Martin Carter who saved us from being robbed in broad daylight." They shook hands and chatted for a couple of minutes. All three looked interchangeable characters to Carter, except for the one called Bull, who was taller than the others and had a scraggly beard. He also carried a black leather suitcase that he handed to Sean who placed it on the floor.

Mack McCarthy, who apparently owned the house, took a six-pack of Coors out of the fridge. The three of them headed back to the Range Rover, Mack explaining that there was a problem with the heater that they wanted to take a minute to sort out.

Sean sat back at the kitchen table beside Eileen and placed the suitcase on it. "Come over here, Martin, " he said. "Something I'd like to show you."

Carter sat down facing them, his back to the wall. Outside, he could see the three men talking and sipping their beer in the car. They didn't seem interested in fixing the heater.

Sean flipped open the suitcase and stared at Carter. "This is yours," he said. The suitcase was half filled with neat bundles of dollar bills, $50s and $100s.

Carter ran his hand along the side of the suitcase. "I like it," he said. "Good quality, real leather."

Sean looked confused for a moment, then found his place in his script again. "There's $100,000 here. That's a lot of money in any language. We're prepared to pay you this Martin in return for something you can do for us." He stopped.

After a pause, Carter said, "Haven't you more to tell me, Sean. Like, for example, what you want me to do."

It was Eileen who answered. "You just have to do what you do best, Martin."

Carter began to get irritated. "Why don't you both stop the cryptic comments and say exactly what's on your mind?"

Again, the wild look was in Sean's eyes and just as quickly faded. He nodded. "Fair comment. I'm going to level with you Martin. Our meeting yesterday was no accident."

Carter feigned mild surprise.

Sean continued: "We have invested a lot of time and money to find you, Martin. To find someone like you. And I'll tell you honestly that we've had you checked out very thoroughly. We know a lot about you and you come highly recommended. Former Green Beret, former Special Forces, Vietnam hero, one-time CIA agent and now freelance hitman. One of the best in the business, a mechanic I believe they call you."

"Only in the movies," said Carter politely.

"Whatever." Sean waved it away. "The fact is that we are in the market for your talents and we're prepared to pay well for them."

"And who is the target?" enquired Carter, genuinely curious.

Sean shook his head. "You don't need to know that yet. I can tell you that the hit will be in New York and the timing is maybe a few months away. We want you to be on stand-by. When the time comes, you'll get a calendar from Ireland in the post. A date will be circled. From the date, the target will be obvious."

Carter looked at him astonished. "You work this out yourself? Look, Sean, you've got IRA written all over you and your friends sitting outside. I know a little bit about the IRA. They're one of the most successful terrorist organisations or liberation armies or whatever you want. They're good because they're professional.

"But you're not in Ireland now, you're in the United States. You're on my turf and you're talking my profession. That means you plan by my rules, which doesn't involve mysterious calendars and guess the target games. So, we stop playing games and get down to it. Who do you want me to kill?"

"Margaret Thatcher," said Eileen quietly. "We have learned that she is coming over to New York in the very near future for the start of a US tour of very well-paid speaking engagements. There will be tight security, we presume, but not too tight since she is a private citizen now. Someone with your background should have no problem in penetrating American security arrangements."

Carter thought about it. "I'm prepared to take the assignment. But the fee is $400,000, plus $50,000 for expenses. All paid up front before I even begin to think about it."

"You are fucking out of your mind," snapped Sean. "Just who do you think you are? Hey, let me tell you something about yourself, Martin. You're in a dead-end job as a junior hotel dick. You're overdrawn with your bank. You earn $25,000 a year and a big slice of that goes in alimony and support to an ex-wife and two children in Hartford, Connecticut. Don't try to play games with us. $100,000 is big, big money to you right now."

"Maybe you've got me dead to rights, Sean. Then again, maybe what you've managed to get with all your checking is my cover. Maybe I have an ex-wife and, what, two children in Hartford, Connecticut. Maybe I haven't. But don't let's waste too much time over it. My price is still $400,000."

"Don't be foolish, Martin," said Eileen. "This is your one big chance to be very rich or maybe very dead."

Carter turned to her and in doing so he knocked a spoon off the table. He bent down, picked it up and replaced it. He said nothing.

Sean said slowly: "I think maybe we've picked the wrong man."

Carter began to get irritated with the dramatics again. He said: "Eileen, look under the table please and tell Sean what you see."

Eileen frowned but leaned her head down. She said calmly. "He's got a gun in his hand."

"Yes," said Carter. "And it's pointed at your nuts, Sean. I never go out with strangers without an ankle gun. You know, my best move now would be to get you to call in your three boyos from out of the car and drop them as soon as they walk into the room. Then I kill both of you and walk out with the money."

"You wouldn't live to spend a cent of it," said Sean, not moving.

"Maybe, maybe not. But that's not it. I can think of a better reason for not doing it. Five kills work out at only $20,000 each and I don't like cut-price jobs. So let's stop talking about killing each other and decide if we're doing to do business. I've given you my price."

Sean shook his head. "We don't have that kind of money."

"Crap," said Carter. "Where did this lot come from?" He nodded at the suitcase. "My guess is that you've been tapping into some wealthy Irish-

Americans, guys who like to see a big bang for their bucks. Tell them what the money is for and they'll ante up. That's up to you. As far as I'm concerned, I'm going to give you a bank account number in the Cayman Islands. When I hear that $450,000 has been deposited there, I'll start planning. You won't hear from me or contact me. You'll just read about it in the papers."

Sean grinned. "Maybe we've got the right man after all. OK, Martin, we'll do it your way right down the line. And you're right, I think we'll get your money."

"Two more things and we're done," said Carter. "First, I want a contact, one of your men here in New York. He doesn't contact me, I contact him only in an emergency."

Sean looked out at the car. "Mack is your man."

"Fine. The second item is an abort code. If for any reason you decide to call it off, Mack or whoever gives me the message 'Teddy Roosevelt is Dead.' You got that?"

"We've got it," said Eileen. "But I guarantee that you'll never get it. There will be no abort."

Carter stood up. "Can you get one of the boys outside to drive me into Manhattan?"

"No problem," said Sean. He looked at the suitcase. "What about this? Don't you want it as a deposit?"

"I don't do cash," Carter said.

1994
February * March * April

Jurys Hotel, Dublin

Saturday 5th February

For the past five years, the Annual General Meeting of O'Sullivan Precision Steel (Subcontract Services) Limited was held in Dublin in early February on the Saturday of a home international at Jurys Hotel in Ballsbridge, adjacent to the Lansdowne Road rugby grounds. Each year, the supporters of England, Scotland, Wales or France whichever happened to be playing away in Dublin on that Saturday poured into the capital by air, sea and car in their thousands. This year, the Welsh colours were everywhere as most of their supporters made a week of it, while some even missed the game.

Jurys Hotel was one of the most popular meeting places for rugby fans, and from early morning, the hotel was thronged. Many firms used the occasions of the International Rugby matches to entertain important clients. Many more made sure to have meetings scheduled for Dublin that weekend, to give them an excuse to be in town for the game and for the fun afterwards. Nobody paid any attention to the seven people who arrived at 10 a.m. and made their way to the small private room that had been set aside for a company meeting and reception.

It was usual on those occasions for a company to have two assistants as PR girls outside the door to greet those arriving, to keep out those not invited, and organise the coffee and refreshments when required. It was unusual that these attractive cheerful young ladies had arrived an hour earlier to sweep the room for listening devices or other forms of surveillance. Even more unusual, each had a compact Uzi submachine gun in her expensive black leather briefcase under the table but always close at hand. In the hotel foyer, a group of four young men, similarly armed, were quietly drinking coffee.

As soon as the last of the seven people in the room, the Chief of Staff took his seat at the head of the small boardroom table and the others joined him, three on each side. Two of them who had not seen the Chief for several weeks noticed that he was visibly ageing. His mind was alert as ever but physically he looked tired and ill.

Placed neatly in front of them was the draft annual report and accounts for

O'Sullivan Precision Steel (Subcontract Services) Limited. The documents were ignored, as was the side table display of the company's products, small components for the automotive industry. O'Sullivan Precision Steel was a legitimate company that supplied customers in France and Italy. Occasionally, its raw material imports included items that had nothing to do with car parts. The owner-manager of the company was in Dublin that day for the rugby match but he made a point of staying away from Jurys. He was happy to provide cover for the meeting.

The Deputy Chief of Staff distributed the real Agenda for the meeting and they got down to business. The document was marked "Confidential" and on another side table, the latest Sharp shredder was already plugged in, waiting to make tiny confetti out of the papers and any notes made at the meeting. Later, the shredded paper would then be burned carefully in the metal waste paper bins. Nothing was to leave the room.

The Deputy Chief took a document out of his briefcase, put on his spectacles, glanced at the first page, then put it aside. He was a small, neat little man, who owed his position entirely to his long friendship with the Chief, an association that went back to their schooldays. They had joined the IRA together and each had been best man at the other's wedding. He was essentially an administrator, inclined sometimes to be fussy and pernickety, but was well liked by members of the Council. Two of his sons had died in recent years, one by an SAS bullet, the other in a Loyalist pub bomb.

"Let me give you the gist of the introductory report," he said conversationally. "It's available for anyone who wants to read it before we leave today, but it really just summarises what we here are all familiar with.

"At our last Special Meeting in Belfast which, as you will remember was long and at times heated, we made a crucial decision. After what diplomats might describe as a full and very frank exchange of views, the Army Council agreed by 4 votes to 2 with one abstention that a cease-fire would take place within the next nine months, subject to a number of conditions being met. I can now tell this meeting that all the elements we want are in place and we are on target to declare a cease-fire on 31 August this year."

He paused and looked quickly around the table as though expecting an interruption. There was only an attentive silence.

"The reason for our cease-fire will be an invitation to the Republican movement to participate with others in discussions on the future of Northern Ireland without preconditions. The pressure on the British to come to the negotiating table is gathering heavy momentum and it is revolving around three people who will be calling the shots."

"Or calling off the shots, as the case may be," said the Chief.

"Exactly," said the Deputy, missing the joke. "First, we have Albert Reynolds in the Republic. Since he became Taoiseach, he has had one over-riding ambition: to ditch his coalition partners, call a general election and return to government with an absolute majority. To do that, he needs to pull off a political spectacular that will swing the voters behind him and he knows that if he can take credit for bringing about a cease-fire, he'll be the most popular man in the Republic. We are also absolutely convinced that Albert Reynolds has a second big ambition. He believes that if he is seen as the leading light in a cease-fire, and gets himself a key role in the negotiations, he will bring about a united Ireland within ten years, with himself as President. He can already see himself in Stockholm, accepting the Nobel Peace prize."

There was some laughter and the Deputy frowned. "Don't underestimate Reynolds. He has the mentality and attitude of a small-time businessman who has beaten all the odds. And I mean that as a compliment. Reynolds has made himself a millionaire by selling his dogfood to English supermarkets. He's built up the business by following his own gut instincts, ignoring professional advisors, playing it tough when he had to, and gambling heavily when he thought it was worthwhile. He's exactly the same in politics and in govern-ment. The civil servants are telling him to play it cautious on Northern Ireland. He pays them no heed. He has his own agenda and goes straight at it. Most important, he is putting a lot of pressure on John Major to start open negotia-tions. And Major is finding it extremely difficult to say no.

"Next important person is President Bill Clinton. He is the first President in the history of the United States who sees a political advantage in actively sup-porting Irish freedom. Partly, it's those 40 million plus Irish-American votes. Partly, he needs the support of Ted Kennedy and other big hitters in the US Congress who are on our side. Mostly, though, Bill Clinton is the first US President since Franklin Roosevelt who isn't hung up on the Anglo-American special relationship. In particular, he doesn't like John Major on a personal level. He has a good memory for the fact that Major sent some British politi-cal gurus to advise George Bush in the presidential campaign. Reynolds has been working on the Irish-American lobby and, as soon as the time is right, we believe that Clinton will put the US four square behind the call for negoti-ations.

"The third person in the frame is, of course, John Major. For a while we couldn't get a handle on Major. We had hoped that he would show a bit of the pragmatism and realism about Ireland that was sadly lacking in Margaret Thatcher. So far, he has been pursuing the same old line. A couple of things we need to take on board about John Major. For a start, he has very little ideological baggage. In fact, his political views are a bit blurry. We know that he really doesn't give a damn about Northern Ireland and he'd be a happy man if the whole island of Ireland sank under the Irish Sea. What really worries him is that, if he starts the ball rolling in the direction of what might turn out to be a United Ireland, then Scotland will look for its independence, Wales will follow and he'll be left with Little England, a fifth-rate world power. That's why he is resisting the pressures to call for negotiations. And that's why he continues to listen to the security chiefs who tell him that they can wipe out the IRA. As of now, he still believes them."

There was laughter around the table. Again, the Deputy didn't join in. "We're going to have to give John Major a sharp dose of reality in the very near future. His Achilles Heel is this: he is utterly convinced that he can win the next general election in Britain. He is undoubtedly the only person in the Tory party who believes that. But he believes he can pull it off. To do that, he needs an economy that is booming, with lots of new jobs and inward investment. And this is where we will hit his weak spot and force him to the table.

"The car bomb in the City of London was our single most effective action ever against the British. We knew that it caused huge damage. We're only now finding out just how badly we hit them. We have seen a highly confidential report prepared for the British cabinet that puts the direct and indirect cost to the British economy of that one bomb at over £2.4 billion. Their biggest nightmare is that we will do something like that again. If we do, it could put the British economy into a tailspin that would take years to recover from. And Major could kiss goodbye to his political future."

The Deputy sat back. "That's the background. I'm now going to hand you over to our Director of Operations who has combined his report with one from Intelligence."

He was the second youngest at the table, dark, intense, controlled. He spoke without preamble in a strong Derry City accent that at times at least two of those present had difficulty in understanding.

"We have identified 20 major economic targets that will cripple the British economy world-wide if we hit them now and have completed files on each one. They include The Stock Exchange and Lloyd's of London, the Bank of England and International Financial Futures. They are all vulnerable. There are lesser but important targets where we literally have only to press a button.

Over the past twelve months, a special team has placed our new, small but very powerful computer-detonated electronic Semtex devices in twelve buildings in London, Manchester, Leeds and Birmingham. These devices are very reliable and we can leave them where they are for years without danger of either discovery or premature explosion. Alternatively, we can activate them all in one night. They are state of the art technology from NASA and the CIA.

"Our policy is to avoid civilian casualties and we have taken this into account in our planning. But, as you know, we have hard evidence that, on more than one occasion, Special Branch and M15 have deliberately delayed having buildings and streets cleared in order to ensure that there are injuries and even deaths for propaganda purposes. It is incredible that, despite our best efforts, not one serious British newspaper is prepared to check out this story.

"These are our primary targets. I am satisfied that, should the need arise, we can hit any or all of them, at once or over a period. Now, let me mention two other high-profile targets. While London is a very exciting city, there are more interesting things under the ground there than above it. You might have read that the tower that houses Big Ben is in danger of becoming like the leaning tower of Pisa. They have already placed electronic monitors around it after discovering it has shifted on its east face and there is the risk of subsidence from tunnelling on the Jubilee line Tube extension.

"We have learned that the foundations supporting the 96-metre-high clock tower are 13 metres wide but only 3 metres deep, with Thames gravel mixing with London clay. Toppling Big Ben would be a nice publicity stunt but there's more to it than that. The Jubilee line, which is to connect Canary Wharf and the Docklands to the West End will pass through Waterloo station underneath Westminster to Green Park. In the Big Ben Parliament area, there are also the District and Circle lines, a mass of electricity supply cables, water and gas pipes, and something even more interesting secret Ministry of Defence tunnels which connect Whitehall and the Parliament buildings, about 10 metres underground. Just two carefully placed bombs would devastate the area, causing damage of upward of £500 million. We have, as you can guess, put a lot of planning into this already.

"The second special target is the new 50-mile-long Thames Water Ring main that supplies more than six million Londoners through a very sophisticated system, as we know from the plans we have stored in our computer in Spain. It cost £250 million and it is highly vulnerable.

"These are the main targets of opportunity. Which of them are we planning to hit?" The Operations Director paused, took a sip of water from the glass in front of him and continued. "Most likely none. And I'm going to let the Director of Intelligence explain why."

The Chief of Staff spoke. "I think this is a good time for a coffee break." The Director of Intelligence pressed a button on a nearby mobile phone and almost immediately one of the two girls entered the room.

"Time for the coffee and biscuits please, Mary," the Chief asked politely as he shifted in the uncomfortable office chair. His body ached. The years in prison had caught up with him now and he had no regrets about the announcement that he would make later. He sipped his coffee, only half listening to his Deputy telling him about some complex plans to shift money into new bank accounts in the Republic. The two members from Belfast and the one from Derry were chatting together over the coffee while the member from Crossmaglen was trying to chat up Mary, a stunning 21-year-old brunette who had just entered the room with a plate of biscuits. The members from London and Dublin were discussing the match and they could hear outside the hum of the early crowds arriving for the big game.

After fifteen minutes, the Chief brought everyone back to business and called on the Director of Intelligence to report. The Director was young for the position but had already proved more than capable. A person worth watching, was the general view.

"Seamus has listed our priority targets," the voice was cool, decisive, confident. "The security forces are guarding those targets in the City of London around the clock. They are expecting us to hit them. Their intelligence is very good because it has come from us. I believe that we will never have to hit any of these targets because the very possibility that we can destroy them, and the cornerstones of the British economy, will be sufficient to persuade John Major to start waving the white flag. Through a special agent in Paris, we have leaked information to select international financiers that we are about to launch another City of London bombing campaign. The financiers are very worried and are leaning on their governments who, in turn, are going to be leaning on the British. And that's how John Major is going to be dragged kicking and bleating to the negotiation table."

The member from Derry broke in. "I'm sorry to interrupt, Sam, but do I understanding you aright? Are you saying that all we have to do now is threaten the British government, and that we don't need to bomb a single target?" He sounded politely sceptical.

"No," said the Director of Intelligence. "It would make our lives easier if it were as simple as that, but it isn't. We have a specific operation planned, a

London target that British security is not expecting us to hit because they don't know that we are even aware of it."

The Director opened a brown manilla folder, took out a press cutting and placed it on the table. There were sharp intakes of breath when they saw the headline: "£10 billion Channel Tunnel Nears Completion."

"God almighty," said the member from Derry softly. "We're going to blow up the Channel Tunnel."

"Not quite," replied the Director of Intelligence, placing the news cutting back in the folder. "We have over a long period, at close range, devoted an entire special unit to the Channel Tunnel. Security has been quite incredibly lax. It's a strange thing that the British seem to have forgotten that the Irish are the world's acknowledged experts in major tunnelling works, especially men from Donegal who have the skill in their blood for many generations. We've had qualified engineers reporting to us on the Channel Tunnel for the past year. They have confirmed an important piece of information about what is down there. Britain's answer to the possibility of a major IRA attack on the City of London.

"Almost immediately after the last bomb, the British Cabinet put together a combined security and technology team, with the highest classification, to develop a response to any further bombs in the City. They have built, at great speed and enormous expense, a state-of-the-art communications centre that will, in effect, duplicate the City's own communications infrastructure. We understand that the budgeted cost was £1 billion and that it has overrun considerably. It will provide a complete back-up to power and telecom lines. It will be linked to several thousand computer servers and terminals in offices throughout the City, and will automatically download and store all data transmissions on a continuous basis. If the City is bombed again, the centre will come into operation immediately. They estimate that 90% of telecommunications utilities and 75% of vital data can be restored within 24 hours.

"This communications centre, which is known as CITON, has been located in a spur off the main Channel Tunnel line. We found out about it by sheer good luck. The operation is so complex and sophisticated that the British needed to buy in some international telecoms software expertise. One of the people they approached happened to be our man in Spain. They produced a vague and deliberately misleading RFI, that's a request for procurement information and they didn't select him in the end. But he got enough information to be able to work things out. Two months later, we got a confirmation from a member of one of our active units in Britain whose day job is with an industrial trade magazine."

The Director tapped the manilla folder lightly. "CITON is currently undergoing its shakedown tests and is due to be fully on-line early next month. As soon as it is fully operational, we intend to blow it up. If we succeed, I think it's reasonable to assume that the tremors and shockwaves from the blast will be felt all the way to 10 Downing Street. Apart from a massive financial investment vanishing in a puff of smoke, the British government will know that the City is vulnerable and that we know it too. They will realise the focus of our attack and I don't think they will be able to risk the consequences."

When the Director finished speaking, there was a long, thoughtful silence. Then spontaneously the members around the table gave a round of applause.

After that, it was difficult for members of the Council to concentrate on the rest of the proceedings but the Chief of Staff went methodically through the agenda. There were important points that needed discussion and agreement. The Chief emphasised that, when the cease-fire came, there would be no letting down the guard. Even though negotiations would be conducted in the full glare of publicity, no-one at the table trusted the British government. There was a long discussion on the best way to prepare the rank-and-file for a cease-fire. It was crucial to avoid discontent that could result in a splinter group of hard-liners refusing to accept the end of the fighting. It was agreed that the IRA political prisoners, in British and Irish jails, would be the toughest to persuade. A cease-fire would almost certainly be followed by an early release programme, and this could be a factor in swaying the views of the prisoners.

Finally, the Chief of Staff looked at his watch and was surprised to see that it was almost 1 p.m. "I'd like to move on to Any Other Business," he said. "I have just one item to raise. I have decided to retire as your Chief of Staff with immediate effect."

No-one spoke. His decision was not unexpected. They looked at him and saw the tiredness and the pallor of his face. He saw their expressions.

"Yes," he said. "My health is not very good and it's not going to get any better. If I remain in office any longer, I'll become a burden to you all. So it's right and proper that I should resign now. Now, you all know me pretty well and you know that I have no great liking for flowery speeches and lengthy goodbyes. You'll do me all a favour by accepting my decision without comment. For my part, I'd just like to say how terribly, terribly proud I have been to serve as your chief of staff and how much I have appreciated your support in times that were-" His voice cracked and he broke off. With an effort, he continued: "Anyways, I'd like to thank you all. From the bottom of my heart. As Hamlet said, the rest is silence."

Then he laughed, as though already relieved that he had made his decision. "Actually, the rest is not silence, after all. I have one more thing to say. As I have discovered lately, the job of Chief of Staff calls for someone with the stamina of youth and the wisdom of experience. It is a rare thing to find this combination in one person and, when we do find it, we must make best use of it. I therefore have pleasure in proposing to this Council that the Director of Intelligence be elected as Chief of Staff."

All hands were raised in assent as the IRA Army Council formally elected its youngest ever Chief of Staff. The new Chief sat relaxed as though nothing of major significance had occurred and spoke quietly. "Thank you for your trust. I'm going to respect Joe's wishes that his resignation is accepted without comment. Therefore, I won't embarrass him by saying that he has taught me everything I know, that he has been father and brother to us all, that without him we would not have won this war and would not now be ready to win the peace."

"Please don't say any more of what you're not going to say," interjected the former Chief with a chuckle, and general laughter eased the tension. But when the new Chief continued, there was no humour in Sam's voice.

"This has been one of the most productive and positive special meetings of the Council. I'm sorry that I have to end it on an unhappy note. A serious problem has developed in Belfast. A small group of volunteers has been acting without the authority of the Council. To date, there have been two bank robberies and one abduction and assassination. The man killed was a known child molester and he's no loss to the community. But no approval was sought for the operation."

"Who are we talking about?" asked the member from Dublin bluntly.

Down the table, the member from Belfast answered: "Sean and Eileen Quinn."

"Jaysus," said the man from Dublin. "Two of our best."

The Chief nodded: "That's the real pity of it. But what I've told you is only the tip of the iceberg. We have now learned that this group has come to the conclusion that this Council has gone soft. They have been doing their own fundraising in the United States, and have been seeking to purchase their own stock of weapons and explosives. They have been quietly recruiting in Armagh, Dublin and New York. And I can tell you that they have drawn up their own plans for high-profile assassinations of British and Northern Ireland

Unionist political figures. I am taking care of this matter. Are there any questions before the meeting concludes?"

There were none. He had forgotten to mention John Hume who was also putting on the pressure for peace talks, but that was the problem with his memory these days.

* * *

Although unofficially retired for years, now the job was done! The chief was feeling his seventy-five years as he settled into his favourite armchair beside the coal fire. It had been an eventful life, one that should have ended several times earlier if God or luck had not been on his side. In moments like this, he often remembered those days in the dark, damp, dreary prison cell waiting for his execution. It was more than fifty years ago that he, together with five IRA comrades, had been sentenced to death for the killing of the police constable Murphy on Easter Sunday 1942. They were all young men then determined to get the British out of Ireland and a tear came to his eye as he thought of the month spent with Tom Williams, G Coy, IRA, who was only nineteen when he was hanged right there in Belfast Prison, the last IRA man to be executed in the Six Counties. The Chief himself was also awaiting death but was granted a last-minute reprieve. There had been many escapes since then but Joe Cahill, chief of staff of the IRA, had decided in the early 1970s that it was time to hand over to younger men like Gerry Adams in Belfast and Martin McGuinness in Derry. He was pleased that they also, when their turn came, had stepped back for the next generation and had decided to take the British on politically by building up Sinn Fein. He remained as fully committed to a 32-county Irish Republic as he had been when a young man, but took little active part now, except, like Tom Clarke the old Fenian in 1916, when the young men asked for his advice. Adams and McGuinness were doing a great job on the political front but he was still able to make a worthwhile contribution when needed. He was, as often happened, falling asleep now, the house was quiet, the place secure, with only his memories and his dreams.

Intercontinental Hotel, Geneva

Saturday 5th March

The penthouse suite of the Intercontinental Hotel in Geneva was, as might be expected, luxurious and the view over the lake from the picture windows was breathtaking. But the ten men who sat around the oval table had other things on their minds. Between them, they represented and spoke for the greater part of the world's industrial and financial power. The meeting was being held under the auspices of G7 and had been called at relatively short notice. Elaborate steps had been taken to ensure complete secrecy and those in attendance expected as a matter of course that nothing said in the room would ever appear in the media. There were no leaks in this rarefied world of high finance.

All seven countries who made up G7, the richest nations in the world, were represented at the table. Five from the United States, Germany, Britain, France and Japan were senior Treasury officials. Italy and Canada had sent lower-echelon civil servants who would be essentially interested observers. The other three represented the governments of Saudi Arabia, the Gulf States and the Sultanate of Brunei.

The US representative, an Assistant Secretary of the Treasury Department, chaired the meeting. "Well, we all know the particular problem that has brought us here today. It's not the first time that terrorism has gotten to the top of our priorities but it's highly unusual that a comparatively small group that has tended to operate, in its own lights, within defined parameters and in a confined geographical area is causing us all concern. I'm going to hand straight over to one of our guests here today, the Deputy Foreign Minister of Saudi Arabia."

The Saudi official was a thin, hawkish man, with gold-rimmed spectacles, who looked uncomfortable in his expensive Western suit. He nodded politely to those around the table, all of whom he knew reasonably well from previous international financial meetings. He let his eyes rest on the British delegate as he spoke.

"We have a serious situation. We are all very familiar with the background, but let me summarise. In early 1992, a terrorist car bomb was exploded by the organisation known as the Irish Republican Army, which caused extensive destruction to financial institutions in the City of London. We have all of us experienced terrorist attacks of one kind or another and have responded with appropriate security measures. Her Majesty's government took the appropriate measures. Then the Baltic Exchange and the adjoining area of the City experienced a further serious explosion. The effects, as we know, were devastating and more than 50 companies lost their offices."

He took a cigarette from a gold holder, lit it and continued. "A large number of these were international businesses based in London. They included banks, investment houses, insurance companies and international financial consultants among others. Some came close to going out of business as a result of losing records and invaluable data. My own country lost a considerable sum of money due to the disruption of business. Following these events, we did some candid talking together. We were forced to advise Her Majesty's government that certain assurances were required. Global finance is built on confidence. We stated that, however regrettable the reasons, the City of London was becoming an unsafe place and that, if the highest level of security was not guaranteed, it was inevitable that we would have to review the scale of our financial interests in London. We are now concerned that this security is not sufficient to prevent a disaster in the immediate future."

The British representative sounded puzzled. "My government fully appreciates your concern. We have taken the most comprehensive precautions to safeguard the City and there have been no further outrages. Nor will there be any. I shall be circulating to you copies of a combined security report that will show you that we have been highly successful in reducing the effectiveness of the IRA. We have thoroughly infiltrated the organisation, we have put the worst of the terrorists behind bars where they will remain for a long time, we have cut off their supplies of explosives, we have solid evidence that they do not any longer have the resources to undertake major bombing campaigns in Britain. Their activities are confined to Northern Ireland, where our security forces, including the Special Air Services, have completely demoralised them. That is the reality of the present situation."

It was far from the reality, he knew, but the security report had done an excellent job of magnifying every small success of the past year, while ignoring the failures.

The unassuming-looking Malay who represented the Brunei Investment Authority, with its £25 billion funds, spoke up.

"We do not doubt that you are winning your war against the terrorists." His tone suggested that he had the deepest possible doubts. "But the fact is that we are receiving intelligence from some of our most trusted sources that suggest something else entirely. We are told that your IRA are getting ready to launch an all-out attack on London's financial institutions and that they have the manpower to strike within the next two months and that they intend to create a wasteland of the City."

"That is absolute balderdash," said the British representative, with icy politeness. "There is no possible way that a campaign of this sort could be planned without our hearing it and may I respectfully suggest to you that your 'informed sources' have been taken in by a black propaganda exercise."

The Head of the German Economics Ministry intervened. "My dear Sir George, we are all friends here and we must speak to each other with the utmost candour. I'm afraid that we, too, are receiving the same information of a large-scale and imminent terrorist attack that will be directed at leading financial institutions in London. We are inclined to believe the information. I was in Frankfurt earlier this week and two of our leading bankers asked me if there was any truth in the story."

"I have the same story," said the Frenchman, a respected financial advisor to the President. "We have, in fact, something more specific. Last week, the security team of a French bank in the City of London discovered a small but extremely powerful explosive device, of considerable technical sophistication embedded in the wall of an office that is directly adjacent to their computer room. I understand that this bomb was disarmed and removed by your army bomb disposal unit at night, in conditions of the utmost secrecy. I further understand that teams of Special Branch officers are now discreetly visiting other offices in the City with special detection equipment."

"I have no knowledge about this," replied the British representative uncomfortably. "Certainly, I shall check into it without delay and give you the full story. I am sure that this is something that has been completely exaggerated."

The Saudi smiled. "One of the curiosities of the English language is that when people say they are sure of something, they mean that they are not sure. But let us get to the point of this meeting. We have the greatest respect for Britain in her fight against terrorism. We hope the success you mentioned continues. But if it does not, if these stories about another attack on the City of London turn out to be correct, then many of us will be forced, with the greatest of reluctance, to place considerable less reliance on Britain as a centre for transacting business. It is something we sincerely do not want to happen. But

I do not believe that we will have a choice."

The British representative looked round the table. It was clear that the Saudi was speaking for the Gulf States and Brunei. It was also clear that Britain seemed to have few friends in the room.

He spoke formally: "I shall convey your views to my government but I assure you again that your fears are unfounded." It sounded weak but there was nothing else he could say.

* * *

Two hours later, the British representative was in his hotel suite, drafting the report he would present to the Prime Minister early next morning. He was not looking forward to the meeting. The implications were disastrous. The Square Mile of the City of London employed some 200,000 people and generated up to £15 billion a year. It probably accounted for a fifth of Britain's whole GNP.

He knew that the Arabs, who kept the City in business, were not bluffing. If they moved out of the City, the rest of the world would begin to follow suit. Over a period of five years, perhaps a lot less, the British economy could be totally wrecked.

Arab gold, he knew, was the foundation of the Bank of England reserves but, to add to the problem, almost half the banks, insurance companies and other financial institutions in Britain were depending on foreign investment, pension funds, Government loans and money from overseas. Many were already foreign owned. SG Warburg was owned by the Swiss Bank Corporation, Kleinwort Benson was strongly rumoured to be looking for an overseas partner. The other smaller merchant banks saw their future in the same way. The money market was increasingly global and partnership with a foreign financial institution was becoming a strategic necessity.

There was a knock on the door. His bodyguard entered, ushered in the Assistant Secretary of the US Treasury and closed the door behind him. Without a word, the British representative walked over to the drinks cabinet and poured two sizeable Macallan whiskies.

"Your good health, Sir George," said the American. "Well, that was one mother of a meeting."

"I have spent happier afternoons in Geneva," responded the Britisher mildly. "Cheers, Barry. Now tell me what our options are."

The two men sat down. "They mean what they say. The Arabs, the Sultan of Brunei and the Japanese are ready to haul out of London if the IRA manage to pull off another big one. Kurt sees an opportunity for Frankfurt and Pierre reckons that Paris could be the big winner. They're both dropping hints about the kind of incentives that their financiers would offer if the big money moved their way from London. But you'd expect that."

"Naturally," murmured Sir George.

"Fact is," said the American,. "neither the Arabs nor anyone else really wants to shift out of London. They'll only do it out of self-preservation. But if they do, they'll start a stampede. And you know what that will mean. They can't come right out and tell the British government how to run its own business. But what they'd like to say is this: either eliminate the IRA pronto or start negotiating with them. You know and I know that the IRA is a helluva lot stronger than you suggested at the meeting. If there's the slightest chance that they can hit the City again, you're in the shithouse without a toilet roll."

Sir George smiled. "A frightening prospect, indeed. But the fact is, Barry, that my masters are not yet ready to admit defeat. They are getting all sorts of advice from the security wallahs that the IRA can be smashed. Certainly, I grant you that I painted a rather rosy picture of the IRA being torn limb from limb at the hands of our trusty security forces. But, in fact, we believe that we're close to breaking the power of the IRA as a force that can operate outside Ulster. All we need is time."

"Well, Sir George," said the American. "You've just put your finger on the one thing you don't have. Time is running out. You can take it that if you haven't disposed of the IRA definitively within the next six months, you'd better start talking seriously to them. Otherwise, to be blunt, the money is going to start pouring out of London at a terrific rate."

"I believe you may be right," said Sir George gloomily as he got up to refill their glasses.

Belfast

Tuesday 8th March

Eileen Quinn had spent the past hour pleasantly window shopping in the city centre. She had delivered a rush order of dresses to a customer in Chichester Street and had wandered into the nearby Victoria shopping centre. It was early afternoon, a warm day for March, and she was in no rush to get back to the factory. Sean should have made the trip but he hadn't returned home the previous night. She wasn't concerned. He often stayed overnight at a friend's house in order to avoid having a routine.

She was in a small bistro, waiting to be served, when a cultured voice interrupted her thoughts

"Excuse me, ma'am, but can I get you something?"

"A glass of white wine, please," she answered and then realised that he was not a barman.

He waved for the waiter and ordered two glasses of white wine. He was in his mid-thirties, tall, over six feet, some four inches taller than she was. He was dressed expensively in a three-piece dark pinstriped suit. He was also, she noticed, a very handsome man.

"I'm so sorry," she said, unexpectedly flustered. "So stupid of me. I thought you were the owner."

The drinks arrived almost immediately.

"Here's to pleasure," he said.

A pick-up, she realised, amused. She studied him closely and liked what she saw. Well, why the hell not, Eileen, she thought, you've earned a bit of fun. "Cheers," she said. "What kind of pleasure had you in mind?"

His name was David Creary and he owned an art gallery and antique shop nearby. Eileen felt warmth in her thighs. She decided she didn't want to waste time on small talk. Creary was quick to get the message. "I've got some better wine than this plonk at my place. It's only five minutes away."

They walked arm in arm along Chichester Street and then turned into a little cul-de-sac. His mews house was large and was a miniature house of paintings and pieces of sculpture, most of it contemporary and expensive. Inside it was a treasure, like a palace in miniature.

David slipped off his jacket and waistcoat. "My late wife, that's what I call my Ex, collected everything during our twenty years together and it cost me quite a bit to hold on to it when she took off with a journalist, on the bloody *Sun* of all things. That added insult to injury, I can tell you."

He went over to a drinks cabinet and returned with two Waterford Crystal filled with wine. "I think you'll like this," he said.

"I envy your lifestyle," said Eileen, sinking into a cushioned sofa and sipping the wine. She was no wine connoisseur but was disappointed with the slightly bitter taste. But she took another sip and said: "Thank you for the unexpected pleasure."

"The pleasure has still to come, Eileen, my dear," he replied, sitting down close to her. "Do you know you've got the most incredibly lovely emerald eyes I have ever seen in my life? But maybe we should get that dreadful money question out of the way."

"What do you mean?"

"Don't tell me it is my lucky day and you are giving it away free," he said with a laugh, putting his hand on her bare knee.

Eileen shot up into the air, overturning his Waterford glass. The remains of the wine spilled slowly into the thick Persian carpet.

"I ought to beat the shit out of you?" she snapped, enraged and disappointed. He remained seated, smiling at her. And then she began to feel weak. He's put something in the bloody wine. She sat back heavily on the sofa. She recalled now the casual way he had locked the door as they came in and had slipped the key in his pocket. How could she, Eileen Quinn, have been so stupid.

"I don't believe any of this," she said but her voice was slurred. He pushed her onto the floor, saying something she could not hear. He bent down and put his hands under her short spring skirt and she brought both her knees up between his legs in one last effort. They hit the target and he hit the floor rolling in pain, his hands grasping his testicles. She crawled along the floor to his jacket, took the keys, and with what she felt was a superhuman effort, reached the door.

She saw that he was struggling to his feet so let fly with the heavy crystal glass. It struck him on the forehead and he fell down behind the sofa. She reached the door, opened it and staggered out into the mews. Looking around, she saw a black taxi parked just two doors down. With a grateful sob, she forced herself over to it.

Too late, she recognised the driver and the two men in the back. One of them opened the door and pulled her in.

"Now what have you been up to, Eileen, you naughty girl. We've been after you all morning. The Army Council just want to ask you a few questions."

Out of the frying pan, she thought, and then she passed out.

Heathrow Airport, near London

Wednesday 9th March

One of the four men in the red Nissan Micra that drove around the perimeter fences of the world's busiest airport was grousing about their orders. "Kill no-one, injure no-one and most important go easy on the property damage," said Trevor, repeating their instructions for the umpteenth time. "It's a damn sight easier said than done. You know how many people work in Heathrow?"

"Surprisingly enough, we do," replied Richie, the group's leader. "In a normal day, more than 20,000 people work here and almost one million passengers pass through the terminals every week. It was in our briefing papers and we all read them."

"Sorry," muttered Trevor. "I'm always a bit jittery before we go in. I'll be OK."

"Never doubted it," said Richie easily. "Piece of cake, old chap. Easiest caper in the world. We'll just give 'em a fireworks show and then home for tea."

The others smiled but none of them said anything. They assumed he was doing an imitation of a World War II RAF pilot straight out of a 1950s British movie. On the other hand, you never could be sure that Richie didn't take the whole heroic thing seriously.

"Here we are," said the driver as they drove into the car park of the airport's Excelsior Hotel. They drove to the predetermined spot, out of sight of everyone and not likely to be disturbed. They had been assured at the final briefing that several warnings would be given. All they had to do was fire the mortar bombs at 6 p.m., making certain that they were well away from the car before the rockets landed. The escape car was in the car park and their departure would be monitored to ensure that nothing went wrong. Nothing did. It was, as Richie had forecast, a piece of cake. Just over an hour later, they were being debriefed in a shabby office in the old Gower Street building near Euston station.

Belfast

Thursday 10th March

The new Chief of Staff of the IRA flicked through the pile of newspapers on the table and read aloud:

"IRA bombs on runway as jets land....IRA Mortar Blitz on Heathrow....Police given less than one-hour warning, unable to completely clear airport.....Crude home-made bombs failed to explode...The force of the launch, from five six-feet-long tubes caused about ten vehicles in the car park to catch fire...Heathrow airport is known to be regarded by terrorists as a prestige target and is one of the most heavily defended in the world. Terminal One was closed and passengers were ordered off aircraft, etc, etc."

The Chief swept the newspapers onto the floor and looked round the table at the other members of the Army Council. The voice was cold with rage. "Riddle me this: Why are we learning about this from the bloody newspapers?" There was a long silence. The Chief made a conscious effort to speak calmly. It was important to treat the Council members with respect.

"We've all agreed, after much debate, on our campaign strategy. And we've all agreed, and it took little debate, that freelance, cowboy operations were a thing of the past. The word has gone down the line, loud and clear. So who the hell decided to indulge themselves in this pointless bombing?"

The new Director of Intelligence spoke up. "Chief, I'll swear it wasn't one of ours. I've spent all night going around the city to find safe phones and make discreet enquiries."

There were nods around the table. British security would right now be falling over themselves, with MI5, MI6, Special Branch, RUC, Army Intelligence and GCHQ in Cheltenham all monitoring every move, every phone call.

The Director of Intelligence continued. "We've touched base with all the Active Service Units. All of them. And I'm pretty well convinced it wasn't any of our people. The other republican groups in Britain we can forget about. They don't have the resources to mount something like this."

"So what do you think?" asked the Derry Brigade Commander.

"I don't know," admitted the Director of Intelligence. "There's something very odd about this. Last night's attack had the stamp of one of our jobs. It's how we would have planned it. And the mortars were very similar to those we used in Downing Street. But what we used in 1992 was pretty crude to what we're using now. It's as though"

"A copycat bombing," said the Chief suddenly.

"How do you mean?" someone asked.

The Chief took one of the newspapers from the floor and opened it to an inside page. "What's the other important news story in today's papers?"

The Chief began reading: "Home Secretary Michael Howard told MPs of the attack shortly before they voted by a majority of 86 to renew the Prevention of Terrorism Act. Angry Tory MPs urged Major to get tough with Sinn Fein's Gerry Adams..."

The Director of Intelligence slammed a fist on the table. "It was a set-up. Heathrow is an MI5 job to make sure they got that bloody Act for another year. Once you think about it, it's clear as day. And it's not even an original ploy. MI5 and MI6 did exactly the same thing with the bombs in Dublin in the '70s that brought the Irish government into line. The damn thing is that no-one believed us then and no-one will believe us now. Although we did get their key man Captain Nairac to pay the penalty later."

There were angry voices around the table, calling for action. They died down when they noticed that the Chief of Staff was sitting back in the chair looking relaxed. "I think I know how we should respond to this," the Chief said and smiled for the first time that day.

* * *

"Again?" The young commander of the IRA's Active Service Unit No 3 in London was stunned to get the order to attack Heathrow. He had been puzzled when he heard about the previous attack because it seemed to go directly against the approach of the new Chief of Staff a person he had never met and never expected to meet. The new Chief had reorganised the IRA in London into five Active Service Units with weapons, explosives, vans and cars always ready for action. He assumed that one of the other ASUs had bombed Heathrow. The airport complex was one of the twenty specially selected targets in London that had been fully surveyed over the past three years, security weaknesses identified, and attack plans drawn up. There had been one plan, long discarded, for the entire airport to be taken over on the day thousands of Irish fans would be arriving for the rugby international against England at Twickenham.

This mission was simple in concept. His unit was to replicate as far as possible the previous Wednesday's attack. Fire a few mortars onto the runway, get out, and avoid casualties at all costs. The last bit worried him. Personally, he was against the idea of killing or maiming innocent civilians-though he would do it if ordered. No, he was concerned that he might not be as lucky as the last lot. Heathrow, after all, was the busiest airport in the world and never closed. Security would have been stepped up but he felt that the sheer audacity of a second strike within such a short time would give them the advantage of complete surprise.

They parked the car outside the Heathrow Hilton, the Semtex rockets, as he liked to call them, ready to go. The evidence of additional security was everywhere since Wednesday's attack especially when Queen Elizabeth herself had just been at the airport. With a range of little over half a mile, they would have to be careful not to hit a plane.

It only took a few hours to mount this second attack near Terminal Four but then the members of the ASU decided to go one better. The airport would be closed, in chaos, half of London disrupted so why not yet again do what would be least expected? The other car, which was holding a parking place, was quickly driven away by the young girl volunteer and another one fully loaded put in its place.

The next day's newspapers led with the third IRA airport attack. Both Heathrow and Gatwick airports were closed. There had been no casualities.

Glasgow, Scotland

Wednesday 20th April

"It's today," said the voice on the phone and hung up. Kevin jumped out of bed, put on his underpants, jeans, a multi-coloured sports shirt and leather jacket. He washed his face quickly, using the cold tap, wet his hair and patted it down with his hands. He went out and knocked at the next door in the somewhat dingy bed and breakfast house on a Glasgow side street. "Shite, go away whoever you are," shouted a muffled voice. Kevin knocked harder. There was a shuffling noise and Thomas opened the door, looking the worse for wear. "What is it?" he demanded. The three weeks' wait had been far too long. It had started to play on his nerves and he had taken to drinking too much.

"Keep your voice down," whispered Kevin. "We've finally got the word. We do it now." The change in Thomas was gratifying. The blear, sleepy look dropped off him and his eyes came alight. "Give me two minutes," he said, forgetting to whisper.

It was, in fact, 15 minutes when they got into the VW Golf and made their way out of the city. For a while, they drove without talking. Kevin drove at a steady speed, careful to observe traffic signs. He didn't mind the silence as he mentally went over again what they had to do. Thomas never was much company until he had finished his first cigarette and lit another.

"It's the drive back I'm thinking about," he finally muttered. "I just hope they don't get a copter up. They'll be sure to spot us."

Kevin didn't answer. They had talked about that many times during the long evenings in Glasgow. He picked up speed as he drove faster along the winding roads to the Scottish loch. He had driven a number of routes several times Belmore, Garelochead, Shandon before deciding on the best way.

"What time did he say?" asked Thomas, relaxed after two cigarettes and taking his third out of the pack.

"He didn't. Just said it was today and hung up. Big eejit, thinks he's James Bond." He swerved to avoid a tractor that seemed to come out of nowhere.

"Can't be too careful, though," said Thomas, who might have been referring to the tractor or the caller. "You'll have to pull up soon. I want to piss."

"We don't have time," said Kevin, exasperated. "Use your pocket or something." But a minute later, he stopped at a quiet stretch of road.

Five miles behind them, the man sitting beside the driver in a black Mercedes, who was carefully watching the flashing dot on a screen on the dashboard said: "Pull over, they've stopped for some reason." The Mercedes halted at the side of the road, its sidelights flashing. "Right," said the man. "They're off again." The Mercedes purred forward.

An hour later, Kevin said: "We're nearly there. It's just beyond the next bend."

"How long do you think we will have to wait?" asked Thomas, stretching his limbs.

"Ten minutes, max," said Kevin and when he saw Thomas's eyes widen he laughed. "I don't have a clue. However long it takes, I suppose."

As it turned out, they had to wait at the hiding place all day. Concealed in the moorland hills overlooking the loch, they took turns with the binoculars. They ate chocolate and the ham sandwiches they had made in their rooms in the bed and breakfast every night for the past week. Thomas was edgy without his cigarettes and coffee but they could not afford to take the chance.

It was 6.30 in the evening when it came into view. Kevin felt for the tiny electronic device concealed in the lining of his jacket by a master tailor and hoped the third member of the team, who worked as a civilian contractor at the nearby Faslane base, had done his job with the Semtex.

"Bit like the Loch Ness Monster, isn't it?" said Thomas as it began to come nearer. You could not miss it for its size alone. It was accompanied by an odd assortment of tugs and launches and the noise of their engines sent the sheep on the nearby hills running in all directions and brought some curious people from their homes.

Two hours later and it was dark. There was no moon. All they could see were the navigation lights and an orange glow from the Loch.

Kevin knew all the vital statistics off by heart. HMS Vanguard, a 16,000-ton submarine which was the first of Britain's H-bomb fleet, was going out on a short test run before its maiden voyage. It carried 16 Trident rockets with 128 warheads and it was the British Government's proudest military possession, the first of a four-submarine plan costing £25 billion, which it was hoped would put Britain back into the superpower league once again, at least on the high seas. That was why the IRA had decided over a year ago to blow it up. Putting a man on the inside had been relatively easy. Not many wanted to work in that remote area. Their man had skills learned in the Harland and Wolff Belfast shipyards. Being a Protestant and a Rangers' supporter too had helped. Neither Kevin nor Thomas knew who he was and all he had for them was a phone number.

"Another five minutes?" said Thomas. Kevin nodded, and released the safety mechanism on the pocket detonator, feeling the electronic micro-switch.

They watched the lights coming into range and began to see the outline of the giant steel monster.

"Bang, you're dead," whispered Thomas with a giggle. He didn't live long enough to appreciate the irony.

There were two soft cracks in the air and Kevin and Thomas slumped to the ground almost in unison. Behind them, two men rose out of the bushes, walked to the bodies and fired again. The bodies jerked with the shots but both were already dead. One of the men found the micro-switch on the ground and put it in his pocket. They carefully searched the bodies, then lifted them a few hundred yards and gently rolled them into the bottomless loch.

Terry O'Neill wiped what might have been a tear from his eye and said a prayer aloud. Kieran Delaney was not a believer but stood in respectful silence. As they made their way back to the Merc, Terry said bitterly: "I worked with both of them. They were the best. Christ, we shouldn't have to do this. This cease-fire better be worth it. If the British fuck us up this time, we'll never give them another chance." Delaney silently agreed with a nod of his head as they drove towards London.

MI5 HQ, Millbank, London

Thursday 21st April

Being the first woman head of MI5, Britain's internal security service, was no easy job, reflected Stella Rimington, not for the first time, as she sat behind her desk in the new MI5 headquarters in Millbank. Mounted on the wall behind her was the badge of the Service, designed by Arundel Herald of Arms. The winged sea lion denoted MI5's association with the three armed services. The portcullis, badge of Parliament, symbolised the duty to uphold parliamentary democracy. The Latin motto "Defend the Realm" was taken from the 1952 directive issued by the then Home Secretary Sir David Maxwell Fyfe.

After 22 years in the secret service, she had made it to the top of an organisation that the general public, and many journalists, who should know better, associated with either macho lady-killers or stuffy ex-army officers. Many of her best people were recruited directly from university or through headhunters. And it would surprise many people that more than 40 per cent of MI5 personnel were women. Both male and female members of her GI group underwent the same training and she liked to think that the women were following her example and demonstrating they were every bit as tough as the men.

With the Cold War ended and Russia increasingly a basket-case that presented a diminishing threat to the West, three-quarters of MI5's 2,000 personnel were now directed against the IRA. This included almost every member of the General Intelligence Group, the elite force of 340 of the agency's brightest and most experienced operatives.

Defeating the IRA had become a test case of MI5's ability to adapt to the post-Cold War era. If the IRA could not be rendered ineffective, and seen to be broken, serious questions would be asked, budgets would be cut, the whole future of MI5 could be in jeopardy. Opinion in British intelligence had been shifting in the past two years. Until recently, the experts were all devoted believers in General Frank Kitson: guerrilla groups could be destroyed, had been destroyed by British forces in Kenya, Malaya, the Yemen and other places. But Kitson's techniques hadn't worked in Northern Ireland. Even the

SAS had failed. Now, the conventional wisdom had reverted to earlier thinking: a well-led, highly motivated guerrilla army that could draw on significant support from the local populace could be crippled many times but never defeated. Rimington was determined that MI5 would prove the experts wrong.

Operation Fortress Salvo (a computer-generated random two-word combination) was proceeding according to plan and soon MI5 would make certain that the IRA was history. It was now almost a year into the planning and centred on a hand-picked group of fifty top British agents, all experts in assassination. Planning had been carefully compartmentalised and nobody knew the full details yet except herself. M-Day, the start of field operations, was fast approaching.

There was less time than she had anticipated. She let her mind go back to her meeting the previous afternoon at 10 Downing Street.

Stella Rimington didn't think too highly of John Major. It was said that to reach 10 Downing Street a politician required extraordinary levels of personal egotism, ability, ruthlessness and cunning. Major, she believed, had none of these in abundance and the Conservatives had made him Prime Minister because he was the candidate least likely to take any course of action that would split the party. Those who were in regular contact with Major saw, for the most part, what the public saw: a moderately intelligent, decent man, completely lacking in conceit, courteous and friendly in manner. He was ideally suited for upper middle management in the banking world, which is where he would undoubtedly have been if he had not made it into politics. Rimington was reminded of what Churchill had said of his successor Clement Attlee: "A modest man, and one who has much to be modest about."

She wondered if he really enjoyed the job any more. These days, he often gave the impression of holding back anger at finding himself yet again in the middle of intractable difficulties that were not of his own making.

John Major was upset, as she could tell by his arctic politeness as they sat facing each other on comfortable leather armchairs. As always, no civil servants were present when the Prime Minister met with the Director of MI5.

He wasted little time on small talk. "I've just finished a meeting with Sir George Willisden, who is back from a somewhat unsettling meeting in Geneva that was set up by G7. I would like you to read his report." He handed her a folder. It contained a single document of seven pages. He poured tea for both of them as she read it quickly, pausing only twice to re-read a paragraph. When she looked up, he said:

"I would be most interested in your opinion of Sir George's interpretation of what Barry Rosenthal said to him at their private meeting."

"I agree with Sir George," she said promptly. "What the Americans are saying is that if we can succeed in destroying the IRA within the next few months, they won't made any difficulties about the way we do it. They'll make the proper noises to appease the Irish, of course, if we break the rules, but there won't be too much of a fuss from their end. We have been getting a few hints like this in recent weeks. Bill Clinton may be the President, but there are a lot of people well placed in the administration who don't share his enthusiasm for the Irish. We have good friends in State and the Treasury. And both the CIA and FBI are being very co-operative. Langley is still feeding us a lot of hard information on IRA fundraising and arms buying. This overture fits the pattern."

Major was acerbic. "It's most considerate of the Americans to give us permission. No doubt it has occurred to them that the next time there is a Gulf War or its equivalent they can expect little help from the Irish government or its army. They may be giving us their tacit blessing to destroy the IRA, but can we oblige them? It seems to me that we are less capable of handling the IRA now than we were five years ago."

"I wouldn't go that far, Prime Minister."

"I would," he said crisply. "You know, Stella, I had rather hoped that by this time Ireland would no longer be taking up such a disproportionate amount of my time and the taxpayer's money. But here we are. Incredible though it is, the IRA can bring this country to its knees economically. We couldn't survive the kind of outflow of capital that the Arabs are suggesting. Fascinating, isn't it. Two years ago, we stopped Saddam Hussein from taking over Saudi Arabia and most likely the entire Gulf Region. Now, these same Arabs would not think twice about precipitating our economic collapse." He sighed. "Be that as it may, let us get to the point. How real is the IRA threat against the City?"

"Nothing has changed since our last briefing six weeks ago. We know that the IRA has, at most, fifteen terrorists based in the London area. We don't know who they are but we're hopeful of a break on this. We have a huge ongoing security presence in the City of London, much of it unobtrusive at your request. The entire City area and other major parts of London are almost inch-by-inch under constant camera surveillance. Within the perimeter we have established, we can have armed policemen at any point in less than seven minutes. Since you approved our proposal to ease the red tape on the use of the SAS, we have units on 24-hour standby and we can have them in any part of central London within two hours of a request from an authorised police superintendent."

"So are you saying, so that I understand you correctly, that the IRA cannot bomb London?"

"No, I'm not saying that, Prime Minister. We consider it extremely unlikely but we can't rule it out."

Major stood and began to pace the room, hands behind his back. "Then what is the best advice that MI5 can give me in response to what amounts to an ultimatum from the international financial community?"

"We have a plan," began Rimington but the Prime Minister unexpectedly erupted in fury.

"Not another fucking plan!" With an effort, he bit down his anger. "Please forgive my outburst, Director, but I have become very sceptical about plans to defeat the IRA. My predecessor had an unfortunate predilection for such plans, and a seemingly inexhaustible appetite for them. No sooner had one plan failed to deliver on its promise then she was enthusiastically supporting another. I saw very little by way of results from any of them. Are you offering me anything better?"

"Yes, I am. About twelve months ago, we reviewed every possible option for permanently eliminating the IRA as a serious threat to the security of the United Kingdom. We spend four months narrowing options. We eventually decided on a course of action that was based on the well-proven principle that the most effective way to kill a monster is to cut off its head. Too much time has gone into chasing around after the Indians rather than the chiefs. We have been developing and refining our planning since and we are now almost ready. This is a combined operation involving MI5, Special Branch, the SAS, the RUC, Military Intelligence and others. They have all been working on their part of the plan and only a few are aware of its totality."

"Including me, may I say," interjected Major. "What you are telling me now is surely something I am hearing for the first time. I don't recall learning about this at our Security Overview meetings."

"You are quite correct, Prime Minister. Until now, we were not satisfied that the planning was at a sufficiently completed stage to put before you."

Impatiently he asked: "And what results can we expect?"

He's really rattled to ask a question like that, she thought, and said carefully: "As you know, the IRA has been having some internal difficulties. The two men shot dead in Scotland last week were part of a dissident group in the IRA's Belfast Brigade. We have reason to believe that others have been killed and their bodies disposed of in secrecy. It may well be, in the very near future, that this internecine warfare within the IRA will escalate into a bloodbath that will wipe out a large part of the leadership."

Major finally sat down again. "Good lord, are you telling me that the IRA are about to start killing each other off in great numbers?"

"No, Prime Minister, I'm not saying that at all."

Then he got the message. "I see. I don't think we need to go into your plan in any further detail. I shall leave operational matters entirely in your hands. You understand how critical the problem has become in the light of the G7 meeting and that any solution must be comprehensive. I need say no more, I think."

He rose, suddenly anxious to end the meeting. Rimington wanted it over too. The meeting had gone better than expected. So she was stunned by Major's parting words.

"There is one thing I should tell you," he said. "The Government is going to hedge its bets. Through an intermediary, we are sounding out the IRA on the possibility of confidential, informal discussions. I tell you frankly that it is against my every instinct. I find the idea of our people sitting at the same table as these murderous bastards quite sickening. But we may have no choice. I tell you this so that you understand that your window of opportunity is quite short."

Stella Rimington shook his hand as she left. She would have preferred to shake his neck.

New York

Friday 22nd April

Martin Carter is standing in the balcony alcove of the Waldorf Astoria quiet, unmoving. Mack McCarthy is with him, uncomfortable in a business suit and perspiring heavily. McCarthy doesn't know why he is in the hotel and doesn't want to be here but he has his orders. He feels the weight in his jacket pockets of the two parcels Carter has given him and wonders what they are. He wants to ask Carter about them, wants to ask about a lot of things but he says nothing.

As soon as the limousine pulls up outside the hotel, Carter says to McCarthy: "Why don't we clean up that stain on the floor?" When he looks down, Carter clips him behind the ear. McCarthy collapses without a sound. Carter quickly drags him over to the wall and positions him in a half-sitting, half-leaning posture. Then he brings up the rifle. Through the scope, he sees the foyer full of people but almost immediately has Baroness Thatcher in the sight. The police have moved her quickly off the street, but inside she has paused, flashing her familiar smile, acknowledging a greeting from someone in the packed foyer. She is in the crosshairs and Carter fires. He sees her head explode in a cloud of red from the impact of the mercury-tipped bullet. He slides over to McCarthy, leans the rifle against him, straightens up, strolls down the corridor and disappears around the stairwell.

The foyer is a bedlam of screaming, heaving panic. For several seconds, there is complete confusion. But some of the cops and FBI agents have seen where the shot came from and three of them are running up the stairs guns drawn. They see the man prone by the wall, see the rifle. "Get your fucking hands up" screams one of the cops, his gun in front of him trained on the man. They move forward, juiced up and not thinking clearly but starting to notice that there's something odd about the man.

Two floors down, Martin Carter takes the micro-switch out of his pocket, pulls out the aerial and presses the button. The two packs of Semtex in McCarthy's pockets explode with devastating force in the confined space. The cops are flung back against the wall, killed instantly. The whole area is filled with noise, shards of glass, plaster, thousands of bits of Mack McCarthy. There is lots more screaming from the foyer.

Below, Martin Carter walks out of the lavatory and sees two waiters transfixed as the explosion reverberates throughout the hotel, shaking the walls. "What's happening," he shouts. He takes out his security badge, affixes it to his lapel and walks quickly up to the foyer.

In two days, the media has most of the story. Mack McCarthy, a 36-year-old construction worker from Queens, with known IRA associations, assassinated Baroness Margaret Thatcher and then blew himself up, killing two New York policemen, an FBI agent and injuring 28 people in the hotel foyer. He may have been acting alone. Many newspaper cuttings with photographs of the late Margaret Thatcher and hand-drawn maps of the Waldorf Astoria layout have been found in his home. Already the conspiracy buffs are busy raising questions on the Internet, but none of the mainstream media will pay any attention.

And that's how it will go down, thought Carter, sitting at a small desk in his apartment. More or less. Well, it wouldn't be as easy as that. These things never were.

* * *

After he left Sean and Eileen, he had made a conscious effort to put the whole business out of his mind and he went back to the routine of his job at the hotel. He thought briefly about trying to find the source in CIA who had talked to Sean Quinn but he figured it would be a waste of time and might stir things up unnecessarily. Besides, the information given to Quinn had been useless, the outer protective layer of his cover. He wondered idly what it would be like to have two children. It didn't appeal to him.

Ten days later, he got a phone call from his bank in the Cayman Islands to tell him that $450,000 had been deposited to his account. He wasn't really surprised to get the money but he hadn't expected it to come so quickly. His respect for Quinn went up several notches.

The first thing he did was to buy some paperbacks about high profile US assassinations-the two Kennedys, Martin Luther King, Malcolm X, John Lennon. In the main, the books told him what he already knew from his CIA days, that it was comparatively easy to kill any prominent public figure. The problem was getting away. The history of assassination in the twentieth century showed few examples of the killer making good his escape from the scene and not being subsequently caught.

Carter had never taken a contract like this before. Almost always, his targets were largely unknown to the general public and had second-rate bodyguards or none. Escape was not a problem; usually he was hundreds of miles away before even the body was discovered. Thatcher would be a different scale of difficulty.

In his reading, he was reminded of one important fact. Political leaders had highly skilled bodyguards, like the US President's Secret Service, who trained daily to respond instantaneously to attack. But their training was essentially defensive, not offensive. Should their charge come under threat, they would turn inward, shield the person with their bodies, try to rush him out of the line of fire and into safety. They remained with their charge, even when they knew he was dead. They didn't go after the killer, leaving that to others, the FBI and the local police, who were not anything like as well trained to pull instantly out of shock. In the immediate aftermath of an assassination, they would be slow, would not be thinking clearly, could be confused and misled. If they heard gunfire, they would assume that the only danger was from a gun.

A few days later, Carter got a copy of Baroness Thatcher's schedule and saw that she would be delivering a speech in the Grand Ballroom of the Waldorf Astoria. Which was very good news and very bad. The good news was that his job would give him complete access to all the details of Thatcher's security while she was at the hotel. He would even be involved in making the security arrangements. The bad bit was that if Thatcher were assassinated in the hotel, it wouldn't take long for the FBI to become aware that the deputy security officer of the hotel was a former CIA hit-man. It was even possible that the CIA, seeing a huge international scandal looming, would send in a hit team of their own to eliminate their former agent.

So, his gut instinct had been right when he sat in the kitchen in Queens. He needed a fall guy. And he began to put his plan together to give the cops their killer Mack McCarthy. He wondered how Sean would react when he learned that Mack had been set up. Probably he'd like it. Mack would tie the IRA into the killing of Margaret Thatcher without the need for an announcement. It would look good: wherever you go in the world, you can't escape the vengeance of the IRA. And as a bonus, there would be a new martyr for the cause. If Sean didn't like that, to hell with him.

But, with two weeks to go, there was still a lot of meticulous planning to do. He had found a blind spot in the security cordon. There was plenty of time for others to find it also. And the timing was awfully tight. He would have to work on that.

* * *

As these thoughts were running through Carter's mind, Kieran Delaney was in his first class seat on British Airways flight 726 to Kennedy Airport, New York. Admit it, he said to himself, you're scared of this guy Carter. Well, he had every right to be. In his final interrogation, Sean Quinn had a lot to say about Martin Carter, the coldest, meanest-eyed fucking son of a bastard he had ever encountered. This was something coming from Quinn who in one night had personally shot dead a well-armed SAS major in a pub in Newry, then killed the two others who came after him.

What really upset Kieran were his instructions, delivered personally by the Chief. He was to fly to New York and abort the contract on Margaret Thatcher. First, he was to talk to this assassin and try to persuade him to call it off. If that didn't work, Delaney's instructions were to kill him. Bloody great. Once he made himself known to Carter, he was putting the man on his guard. If Carter did not like the idea of stopping the hit, he would expect Delaney to try to kill him and would most likely go for a pre-emptive strike. Delaney could usually take care of himself in a fight, but this guy was a top marksman and a martial arts expert, with all kinds of esoteric skills. Probably pisses curare, he thought mordantly.

To make matters worse, Delaney was alone. He had intended to bring Terry along as back-up but the idiot had gone and broken his leg in a game of Gaelic football and was now hospitalised for several weeks.

Perhaps that's why Delaney was now a little drunk. He looked around him. The first-class cabin was almost empty. One of the most attractive stewardesses had taken a fancy to him. Looking for distraction, he chatted to her. Soon, she told him where she would be with her sister for a few days and let him know between the many glasses of champagne she served him that, if he had a free day, she would be delighted to show him around the Big Apple. He looked at her feline face framed with long black hair, at her large bust and her tight ass and let himself get aroused.

"Eat, drink and be merry," he toasted her. "For tomorrow we die."

"I hope you are not thinking of dying," she said in mock horror.

"Don't deny that many men have pined and died to win your smouldering glance, the toss of your raven hair and the bittersweet caress of your soft hands on their fevered forehead," he replied, letting the champagne do the talking for him.

"A poet, no less," she said, delighted. "Tell me, is there anything else you can do with that tongue of yours?"

Here I go again, thought Delaney happily and resolutely pushed Martin Carter out of his mind.

Tonight they were both staying at the Waldorf so when the plane landed at JFK, Delaney suggested she share his limo instead of the British Airways coach. "I'll just come along for the ride," she agreed, her eyes sparkling. They checked in quickly. He just about had time to call up the champagne on ice when she knocked on his door and was pulling off her clothes as he closed it behind her. He had time to catch her all-over tan and well-trimmed pubis before she hopped into the king-sized bed. Soon they were devouring each other, every part of their naked bodies burning with sensations, first he on top, then her turn, they boxed the compass. At various times, when they came up for air, they downed the champagne and he ordered more. After half-time as he called it, he came alive again and it was an action replay all the way into the night.

At some time in the late night, he awoke and she was gone. "Thank God," he muttered and was immediately back to sleep. Exhausted from the journey in the air and on the bed, he didn't waken until eleven. He felt the blinding headache as soon as he sat up. What was the girl's name? He couldn't remember. Jennifer. He found it written on lipstick on the bathroom mirror with her phone number.

He showered and shaved, cursing at his haggard features in the mirror. What an almighty bloody stupid thing to have done. If the Chief knew about it, he'd face a court martial on the spot. Here he was, about to get into the ring with one of America's top hit men, and instead of getting a healthy night's sleep, he had humped himself into unconsciousness while pouring alcohol into his system at a furious rate. It was the tension, no doubt about it. But was that any excuse. "Oh Jennifer," he said to the mirror. "I wasn't far off when I said you'd be the death of me."

He had a thought. Wasn't this guy Carter a Vietnam veteran? When was Vietnam, 1960s, 1970s? Jesus, maybe Sean was wrong about him. He must be a senior citizen by now, probably went around clobbering people with his Zimmer frame. The idea should have made him feel better but it didn't.

With a bit of luck Carter would be away for the day, and this would give him a chance to recover. He took the elevator to the foyer, feeling fragile, his head throbbing. The first person he saw was Martin Carter. He was standing at the reception desk, leafing through some papers. Sean's description was accurate. The man was in his 40s, Delaney guessed, about his own height of six feet one, short dark hair, slim, elegantly dressed. Sean thought of telling Jennifer about him and going back to bed. Instead, he walked over and said: "Hello, Mr Martin Carter?"

Carter had his back to him and there was an almost imperceptible stiffening of his shoulders at the Irish accent. But when he turned, his face had the bland smile of hotel staff in every well-run hotel in the world.

"I'm Martin Carter. Something I can do for you?"

"My name is Kieran Delaney and I'm over for a few days from Ireland. Some friends of mine asked me to pass on their greetings. Sean and Eileen Quinn."

The bland smile didn't waver. "Oh, yeah, Sean and Eileen Quinn. Sure. Very nice folks. Good of them to think of me." He sounded as though he had no idea who the hell they were but was too polite to say so.

"Could we have a few words in private, Mr Carter?"

"Well, now, Mr Delaney, I'd like nothing better, that's for sure. But the fact is I'm just coming off duty and I'm running late. What you need to do is have a talk with Randy Myers, he's our head of security and I know he'll be thrilled to help you any way he can. Why don't you ask for him at reception and they'll page him straightaway."

Carter stood in front of him expectantly, still smiling helpfully.

"Yeah, well maybe later," muttered Delaney, feeling a fool and realising he had no choice but to walk away.

Bollocks to that, he said to himself as he stood on the sidewalk in Park Avenue. He had really screwed it up. Carter's deliberately phoney politeness had thrown him completely. But how had he expected Carter to react when he mentioned Sean and Eileen? Furtive looks and conspiratorial whispers? Heated denials? Drawing a gun and plugging everyone in sight? Delaney admitted to himself that he hadn't thought it through at all and cursed again his indulgence of the night before.

He found the nearest drugstore and asked for the most powerful headache pills they had. He didn't recognise the brand and his eyes blurred when he tried to read the box. Then he walked across to Third Avenue until he found the shop he was looking for. It was one of those numerous New York newsagents that carried seemingly thousands of magazines and newspapers racked against the walls. His heart sank when he saw that the man behind the counter was a young black man with dreadlocks. But he tried anyway.

"You sell the *Cork Examiner* here?"

To his enormous relief the man said: "No, man. We did have the *Limerick*

Leader once but it didn't sell."

"Then I guess you don't have the *Kerryman*," said Delaney, completing the password.

The man bent down, hair flying like baby snakes and came up with a small parcel in Lucky Strike wrapping and handed it to Delaney without a word. Delaney nodded his thanks and walked out onto the street. At least he now had a gun.

His headache was thumping viciously. He walked slowly back to the hotel, and went into his room. He popped two of the headache pills out of the box and went to the bathroom. When he opened the door, Carter came out fast and punched him short and hard in the ribs.

For a moment, everything went black with flashing multicoloured lights. Delaney fell to the ground, hissing with the pain. Instinctively he scythed with his legs but Carter was no longer where he was supposed to be. Delaney lay on the ground, eyes shut tight, clutching his side, fighting the nausea. Breathing was agony. When he opened his eyes, the room swam and it took a few seconds for things to come into focus. His gun was beside him but it was still in the Lucky Strike wrapping and useless. He saw Carter, sitting on the armchair, knees crossed. He had a gun and was twisting a large silencer onto it. He looked over at Delaney and said:

"I want you to lie on the bed, stretched out, hands back of your head. Do it now, please."

Delaney staggered over to the bed and did as he was told, fighting waves of pain and sickness. If he was going to die, he thought, at least he wouldn't feel as bad. He said weakly:

"Didn't anyone ever tell you not to hit a man with a hangover?"

"What were you drinking?"

Delaney groaned at the memory. "Champagne. Far too much of it."

"I know something good for that. If I don't kill you, I can cure you."

Delaney clenched his teeth to prevent himself moaning. "You don't want to kill me, Carter. If I'm dead, my people will send in ten men to get you. Oh, no doubt you'll kill them all but think of how you'll upset your guests. Then you'll have the police around, news reporters. You'll be a hero, like that subway guy, get your picture on the front of the *Daily News*, an award from the Mayor, book offers, Kevin Costner playing you in the mini series. But your career will be properly fucked."

Carter shook his head. "One thing I don't like with your scenario."

"What's that?"

"Costner's too short."

Delaney was silent. Carter said: "Look, I'd like to stay and chew the breeze but there's something good coming up on television. So tell me what you want."

"I'm here to tell you that the hit is off."

"Which hit did you have in mind?"

Delaney tried to sit up but fell back on the pillow. "You want me to name names? I could be wearing a wire."

"I don't think so. You weren't expecting me. Besides, if you are wired it will be the least of my problems. So who?"

"Margaret Thatcher."

"Heard of her, never met her," said Carter sounding indifferent.

"Oh Bollocks," said Delaney exasperated. "You're the man with the gun, so I have to be polite. But if I had the gun, I'd be shooting now." He paused and went on quietly.

"Last November, you were approached by Sean and Eileen Quinn. You met with them in a house out in Queens and accepted a contract to assassinate Margaret Thatcher when she arrives here on her speaking circus. A fee of $400,000 was agreed and has already been paid to you. Plus $50,000 in expenses, which is a real rip-off, by the way. It was also our money collected here in the States which they used."

Carter held up his gun. "You got any idea how much this alone cost me?"

"I've got a catalogue somewhere. Sean and Eileen told you they were members of the Irish Republican Army. That was true. What they didn't tell you was that they'd gone bad and were in business for themselves. Things are at a critical stage in Ireland. The British government is close to opening negotiations with us in public. For all practical purposes, that's surrender. Unfortunately the Quinns didn't see it that way. They think it's us who are surrendering. They knew that if Thatcher was assassinated, there's no way the British government would sit around the table with the IRA. No kiss-kiss, much bang-bang."

"And so?"

"And so the IRA Army Council sent me over to get to you before you got to Thatcher. Talk you out of it, if I could. Otherwise I have to kill you. Don't make me do it."

"Yeah, I'm sweating. Something else. Maybe you're IRA or maybe you're British Intelligence."

Delaney gave a short laugh, then groaned. " Do be serious, Carter. British

Intelligence wouldn't send a man with a crucifying headache and bloodshot eyes. Only the Irish do stupid things like that. They'd just tip off the FBI. Or more likely they'd fly in a couple of SAS heavies in Mafia suits who wouldn't stop to say hello when they saw you."

"Makes sense," said Carter and grinned. "OK, IRA-man, you want to stop me, it's really very simple. Just give me the abort code word I agreed with Sean."

Delaney said nothing, then swore. "Sean didn't tell us there was an abort code."

Carter was laughing. "That's what I thought." Then he was serious. "Well, it doesn't matter shit. Far as I'm concerned, this job's gone sour and it's off. And it was all going so nice and neat till you came along and reamed it up the ass."

"Glad to be of service. And how I need to go to the bathroom." Without waiting for Carter's permission, Delaney painfully got off the bed and went into the bathroom where he was noisily sick. He turned on the cold tap, filled the sink and plunged his face in. When he next looked in the mirror, Carter was standing beside him, no longer with the gun.

"If there's nothing else..." Carter said.

Delaney towelled his face vigorously. "There is the matter of our money."

"From what you told me, there's a big question mark as to whether it ever was your money. But I don't think we'll be going to law. What happens is you get 50 per cent back. The rest is cancellation fee."

"Agreed." Delaney figured it was as good as he would get. He sat on the edge of the bath and appraised Carter. "How would you feel about keeping all the money?"

Carter raised an eyebrow. "Let's go down to the bar. I said I'd fix that hangover."

* * *

When Delaney went into the bar ten minutes later, Carter was sitting at the counter talking to the barman. Delaney didn't feel up to casual conversation and walked over to a corner table. Carter joined him, carrying two coffees and a glass filled with what looked like cold tar.

Delaney eyed it suspiciously. "What's in it?"

"Don't look at it, taste it, smell it or think about it. Just get it down in one go."

In fact, it wasn't as bad as he'd expected, tasting mostly of herbs and what might have been aniseed. He felt his stomach rebel, then miraculously settle.

"Give it a couple minutes," said Carter. "So what's this job, another winner?"

Delaney thought he could feel the headache beginning to lift. "It's not a hit, nobody gets killed or injured. You simply blow up a place in Britain. Easiest contract you'll ever get."

"I wouldn't be sure. You boys may be kicking shit out of the British Empire, but in my line of work you're amateur hour in Iowa. And customers that aren't professional can get one killed. I'm still listening, though. Talk to me. Where is it? What is it?"

Delaney shook his head. "I can't tell you the specifics. Maybe we're more professional than you think. If I tell you everything and you say no, maybe I have to go up to my room, unwrap my gun, come down and kill you."

Carter laughed. "That's my thanks for nursing you back to health."

"Jesus, the stuff really works. This much I can give you, Carter. We'll want the job done in the next four weeks. It's somewhere in Britain, a government facility, non-military. Very little security because they think it's top secret and nobody knows about it. You don't even have to go into the place, the Semtex will be already laid. By a professional. You fly over to France, take the ferry to England. Two days, three at most and the job's finished. No problem getting out and we can give you any back-up you want."

"Generally I work alone," said Carter. He sat back and thought for a while. "OK, nothing's that easy but I'll do this. Send me the tickets for Paris. I'll come over, you tell me the job and if I think it's like you say, I'll do it."

"Air tickets? What the hell happened to the 50k expenses?"

"What can I tell you. You want receipts, timesheets?"

"OK," sighed Delaney. "We'll send the tickets. But no pocket money."

They sat in silence for a while.

"How is Sean, by the way?" asked Carter.

"Oh, he retired. He spends all his time in the mountains."

"I guess that's the Irish equivalent of sleeping with the fishes. And Eileen?"

"She stays close to him."

Carter had a brief recollection of Eileen in the semi-darkness, her hands caressing her small breasts. He saw that Delaney didn't want to talk about it but he was curious.

"They were a hard pair in their way. You must have had to work to get it out of them."

Delaney looked at him bleakly. "It wasn't like that. Years ago, Sean and

Eileen Quinn watched a group of masked RUC thugs murder their parents in front of them. Both parents were civil rights workers, believed in non-violent protest. Sean was twelve when it happened, Eileen was six. Sean became her big brother, her protector. She was the smarter one but to him she was always the kid sister. He looked after her. When he knew we had Eileen, he told us everything we wanted in exchange for her life."

"And he really believed you'd hold the bargain?"

"Maybe. He was desperate and believed what he wanted to believe. I suppose he thought there was a one per cent chance." Delaney looked at his empty coffee cup morosely. "It was never anything as much as that."

The Channel Tunnel

Sunday 24th April

For Joe Parkinson and his mates, it had been the toughest seven years of their lives working for Transmanche Link digging the tunnel under the English Channel. But now Queen Elizabeth II and President Mitterand of France would soon be doing the official opening. Britain and France were joined again for the first time since the Ice Age.

It was a huge engineering project, costing over £10 billion. Its length, from Britain to France, was over 50km, but with three tunnels, two for rail and a central one for services, it was essentially a 150km tunnel.

For thousands of years, ships and boats were the only means of transport between the island of Britain and the continental mainland of Europe. In 1785, this long tradition was broken with the first successful balloon crossing of the Channel. At about the same time, engineers began seriously talking about a tunnel under the sea. Talk was all they did for the next two hundred years. Then, in 1987, the British put aside their belief that the Channel was their safeguard against the rest of Europe, that only the narrow stretch of the English Channel had saved them from the invasion fleets of the Spanish Armada, Napoleon and Hitler. Work on the tunnel began. The actual removal of material was completed ahead of schedule in 1991 but since then the project had been beset by delays and there was enormous relief, especially from investors, when the postponed opening of what had become known as the Chunnel was finally announced for early 1994.

Joe Parkinson was aware that the IRA were maintaining an interest in the Channel Tunnel and he suspected that at least two of his colleagues were supplying information to an IRA agent in Britain. He decided to mind his own business. He had never taken any part in the Republican movement but he was sympathetic. Two of his cousins had served time in the Maze prison for IRA membership and one of his former school pals had been blown to bits in a Loyalist bomb that exploded in a quiet village one market day. Parkinson was not too surprised when the IRA approached him. He simply wondered why it had taken so long.

In June 1993, the man made contact when Parkinson was having a drink in a pub in London during a weekend break. He was a young man in his early twenties, with a Donegal accent, who sported a heavy black moustache. He dressed and looked like a student with not a lot of spending money. He introduced himself as Eoin MacAnamy and it transpired that he lived within ten miles of Parkinson's home town in Donegal and was, in fact, very distantly related to him by marriage which was a coincidence or maybe was not.

After a lengthy casual conversation, that was also a probing exploration of Parkinson's views and motivations, the IRA man got to the point: would Parkinson be willing to plant Semtex in the Channel Tunnel? He flatly refused. He did not hold with indiscriminate bombing, he said. The thought of someone blowing up the tunnel as trains hurtled along the rails at 160km an hour, packed with hundreds of men, women and children horrified him. That was the reason he gave, but there was something of equal importance to him that he didn't mention. It was not just that he would have all those deaths on his conscience. With a bombing on this scale, the police in Britain and France and other countries would put enormous resources into tracking down the killers. The Irish tunnellers would be prime suspects and he had no desire to spend the rest of his life in Brazil or somewhere, a fugitive constantly looking over his shoulder.

"You've misunderstood me completely, Joe," said MacAnamy softly. "I'm against hitting non-combatant targets and, if you've been reading the papers, you'll surely have seen that our units go to a lot of trouble to make sure that civilians are not harmed."

"Good, good," said Parkinson with forced heartiness. "But then what's the point of rigging the Chunnel if you're not going to make use of it?"

"We're not after the Tunnel as such. It's something else down there that hasn't even been built yet. The British government is going to build a secret extension to the tunnel and it will be their new security headquarters, with the very latest technology and computers. It will be their nerve centre in their war against us and we're not going to let it become operational."

"Never heard anything about that," said Parkinson, rubbing his jaw doubtfully.

"You will and soon. Look, Joe, you don't have to make a decision on this now."

Two weeks later, the elite band of 35 specialist tunnellers were brought to a meeting with the new contractor who offered them double pay, weekly in advance, for a few more weeks' work on a side spur off the main rail link.

A large, grey-bearded man of military bearing introduced himself as Rodney Ferguson, the project manager of DOM Enterprises, contractor for the new project. His voice was clipped, precise but affable. "Our intention is to build a large antechamber off the main tunnel. It will be used for emergency purposes and will house communication facilities, a medical centre and operation theatre and a range of other purposes. Don't mind telling you men that the owners are not very pleased at having to undertake a project like this so late in the day. It means that the opening of the tunnel may not take place right on schedule. Not the best kind of result but can't be helped. Fact is, those Johnnies on the European Commission are throwing many, many sackfuls of money into the Channel project and insist on it. So, that's it. Means we'll all get a share of the extra money at any rate."

He looked hard at the men. "Oh, one important thing, men. Mum's the word on this job. We don't want the travelling public to start reading stuff in their daily comics about enormous emergency facilities down here. We'd just frighten them unnecessarily, OK?"

So Parkinson and his fellow tunnellers worked hard for another few weeks, were brought to and from the site by special carriage during the night, were all kept together in a good bed-and-breakfast near Folkestone. Bed to work and back again was nothing unusual for them but they missed the Guinness and the few half-ones. As usual they were doing the donkey work but, as one of them, Stump Murphy, said: "We are skilled, well-trained, well-paid donkeys and there is nobody in the world who can do it better or faster than us."

Parkinson met Eoin MacAnamy again and agreed to do the job. He liked the idea of personally striking a blow that would force the British to acknowledge that the IRA could beat them at every turn. But he raised no objection to the £50,000 offered by the IRA. Patriotism was fine but dangerous work deserved special payment, he always believed. He got precise instructions on how and where to plant the Semtex and timers. It confirmed his belief that the IRA were using more than one man in the tunnel. Getting the Semtex into the site proved to be the easiest part. Someone had developed a plastic covering that made it undetectable and then manufactured it into lunch boxes. So every day he just brought in a lunchbox that looked exactly the same but was different. The security guards always casually examined what was inside, never the worn-looking box itself. It reminded him of the story his father had told him long ago about the Border back home.

"There was this fellow who, every morning, walked across the Border from the Irish side to the British with a wheelbarrow piled with stones, bags, different odds-and-ends. The British customs man always examined it, found nothing, let him pass but always felt he was being fooled. Years later, when they had both retired, they met in a bar and the customs man asked him:"Now you can tell me, Pat, what were you smuggling across all those years?" Pat puffed on his pipe before replying slowly: "Wheelbarrows."

Rodney Ferguson called every second day to see how the job was progressing, usually accompanied by a retinue of architects and engineers. "How are we doing," he would call to tunnellers as he passed and, without waiting for a response: "Jolly good." They measured the walls, talking about temperature, electronic sockets, computer support systems, air conditioning. Whatever about his other expertise, Ferguson knew nothing about the acoustics of underground chambers and Parkinson heard enough brief snatches of conversation to confirm that the IRA was right about the purpose of the new extension.

Once, he picked up a chilling exchange between Ferguson and another man.

"Tell me Rodney, what do you intend to do with them when they have finished the job. The Germans and the Russians usually buried them?"

Ferguson laughed. "I tell you, there are some people in our shop who would take that seriously. What will I do? Nothing at all. When this job is done, they'll be drunk for a week and after that they'll forget about it. Why should they ever think about it again. Just another job, my boy."

That last evening, Parkinson collected his bonus, said goodbye to the men he had worked with for years, went back to this room, cleaned himself up, put on his new suit, packed his new luggage, pocketed his new passport, took the train and tube to Heathrow, sipped his first-ever champagne in Air Canada's first class and was never seen in Europe again.

May 1994

Roquetas De Mar, Almeria, Spain

Monday 2nd May

Mr Glass crossed the pavement from the Banco de Andalucia and walked along the hot sandy beach in his dark blue tee shirt, faded denim shorts and sandals to the car park where he had left his Range Rover. He was a slightly overweight man in his mid-thirties, long blond hair in a ponytail, wispy beard, wire-framed spectacles, undistinguished features. He was perspiring heavily. He liked living in Spain but he would never get used to the heat. Everything around him shimmered mirage-like in the noonday sun and it occurred to him that that's how he would appear to everyone else-a hazy, indistinct figure. He liked the notion of walking along the crowded beach, unnoticed, almost invisible. Anonymity, essential to his business, had become an obsession. He had given himself the name Mr Glass after G K Chesterton's story about the mysterious, top-hatted stranger about whom a great deal was known but who, as it turned out, didn't exist.

Twenty minutes later, he arrived at his villa and parked in the driveway. It was one of a group of large whitewashed villas in a well-manicured cul-de-sac that seemed to spring up in the middle of nowhere. They had been built as a time-share mini-village, part of an ambitious plan that was to include a hotel, shops and a leisure and sports centre. But the principal investor was an Iranian army general who had mistimed his departure from his country and had ended up in front of an execution squad. The time-share company had gone into liquidation and the ten villas, the only part of the project to be built, had been individually sold off. Mr Glass's neighbours were mostly German business people or wealthy retired couples who visited their holiday home infrequently. He knew none of them to speak with and always kept his distance.

"I'm back, Anna," he called out and when he heard her muffled reply from upstairs he expelled his breath in a long sigh of relief and felt the tension of the past hour wash away. He thought: two years now, goddammit, and every single time he left the villa, he wondered if she would still be there when he came back. They were successful business partners, mutually satisfied lovers, accustomed to each other's routines and quirks. But he could never rid himself of the foreboding that one day she would be gone from his life as abruptly as she had first appeared. It was, he thought, the only real fear in his life any more.

Mr Glass had only two interests in life, Anna and computer technology. He had built his own first computer when he was twelve and sold his first software program a year later. Developing bespoke software packages for small companies had paid his way through college in Berkeley, California. After graduation, he worked for NASA for a year before being approached by the National Security Agency, where he worked on encryption projects intended to protect Government computer networks from both overseas and domestic hackers. In 1988, he decided to capitalise on his expertise and, after a short stint with Microsoft, he set up as a one-man technology security consultancy business in Campbell, right in the heart of Silicon Valley. With the start-up of the Internet, he became one of the few experts who could be picky in choosing their clients and name their own price. As business location became increasingly irrelevant, he made the move to Spain, mainly for tax reasons and personal security, away from the IRS, the FBI and the CIA.

The Internet was already earning him big money, developing methods of encryption that were different and confidential for each client. It was only the beginning.. In June 1993, there had been only 130 World Wide Web pages, now they were multiplying faster than rabbits. He estimated there could be more than a billion by the end of the century.

Many companies, including banks, had been scrambling information for a long time so that nobody could hack into confidential data on the so-called new information superhighway. Security concerns centred on external threats from hackers with transactions from financial institutions being intercepted and unwanted users gaining access to corporate networks. These concerns were usually eased by the use of firewalls, a computer placed between the Internet and the internal corporate system. Simple encryption used a key to scramble and, of course, unscramble data. Authentication was often provided by the use of digital signatures that could help prove that the right person actually signed the documents. The strength of any encryption algorithm was determined by the size of its key, with 56 bits being regarded as secured, although he could now break that code within two hours of the software being available. He was using 128-bit encryption, with special variations and nobody had managed to even get near breaking it. Not yet. There was, he knew, no such thing as an unbreakable code.

* * *

Two years ago, Anna had come into his life. On one of his rare evenings out, he had heard music coming from a café pub with the unlikely name of "Chaplin's Fluffy Duck". It was in his neighbourhood but he usually avoided it when full of tourists. Anna had come to sit beside him as he sipped the local 'wine-with-no-name' as he called it. She was German, a back-packer and after many glasses together, she confessed she had nowhere to stay. She had also let slip that she had just qualified as an electronics engineer which interested him almost as much as her body. So they had gone to bed together. Spent the next day drinking, talking about computers, bombs, detonators, electronic devices and many other items of commerce and war before having sex again. He was exhausted.

Then she got to the point. She wanted to stay with Mr Glass for a minimum of three months to learn everything he knew about computers. In turn, she would give in fair exchange a great deal of information on the manufacture of electronically controlled miniature explosive devices. They both had complementary skills, she suggested, and the combination would benefit both of them considerably in their value to selected customers. There would be no problem with the authorities, in Spain or Germany; officially she was dead and no one was looking for her.

Mr Glass saw himself as a loner and Anna's proposal held no appeal. But he agreed to her proposition with the idea of buying some time to figure out how he would get rid of her. Within a week, he knew that she was correct that a pooling of their knowledge could be highly profitable. Within a month, he first started worrying that she might leave.

* * *

At first, Mr Glass played both sides of the street, providing security advice to some clients, hacking for others. That's how he first became interested in Ireland. In 1990, Rupert Murdoch's new British satellite TV service, BSkyB, developed what it believed was a totally secure encryption decoder system for its subscribers. A swashbuckling Irish businessman approached Mr Glass with a contract for cracking the BSkyB system. It wasn't a difficult challenge. Over the next five years, an agitated BSkyB was forced to issue ten generations of new Smart-cards as he and other expert hackers like himself found ways to unscramble its encrypted signals, creating a market for bootleg cards.

The Irish businessman was funded by the IRA, which was a small but substantial source of venture capital in Ireland for off the beaten track enterprises that promised a quick yield. The businessman made the mistake of skimming the profits and his body was found in his burnt-out Lexus on the outskirts of the border town of Dundalk. But he had mentioned Mr Glass to the IRA and they were keenly interested in the possibilities of intercepting conversations on GSM mobile phones, the system used in Europe and almost everywhere except America.

He told them that GSM, as a method of conducting confidential communications, was a joke and that only the dumbest security people would use it. However, the world was full of dumb people and the IRA, using equipment suggested by Mr Glass, obtained some useful information, mainly from technically naïve politicians and civil servants, before the security shortcomings of GSM became widely known. In time, indiscreet members of the British Royal family, the Ministry of Defence, the Home Office and other government departments, were deeply shocked to discover that their conversations were being intercepted.

In fact, GSM was highly vulnerable. Any amateur electronics or computer enthusiast could track and steal numbers with equipment legally purchased in any of the many specialist telecommunications stores on Tottenham Court Road in London. British Telecom and Mercury estimated that, in one year, over £3 million in revenue was being lost as a result of people with basic electronic scanners picking up the radio signals of mobile phones, transferring the numbers to another phone with connecting leads and then using these phones to make calls world-wide-or selling them privately for that purpose. Mr Glass knew an electronics expert in Hong Kong who went one better by developing a mobile phone that could store a hundred different phone numbers with electronic serial numbers that allowed the user to switch numbers anytime to avoid detection.

Since he had teamed up with Anna, Mr Glass had provided a much expanded service to the IRA.

* * *

Now he asked Anna: "Did they pick up the Channel Tunnel stuff yet?"
She nodded. "It arrived in Paris and was collected by the client. I hope they are able to get into position to use it. It works in theory but I still worry about the distance."

Mr Glass said nothing. They had discussed this many times and there was nothing more to be said. Either it would work or it wouldn't. It was time to resume work on another project from the same client. How do you knock a helicopter out of the sky, without using a bomb or a projectile? This assignment came directly from the person they called the "managing director". He assumed that this was the Chief of Staff of the IRA. Suppliers understood the need. British Army helicopters were proving to be a serious problem. So far, attempts to drop one by high-powered rifle or rocket had come to nothing. It was a difficult assignment but the biggest challenge of his life was on its way to him.

The IRA had managed to take control of a large area of South Armagh around Crossmaglen, wherever that was. All he knew was what he had seen on television: that it was called 'Bandit Country' and that the Irish Tricolour flew there instead of the Union Jack. After many attacks and ambushes the British had to abandon all attempts to reach their heavily fortified barracks by road. Personnel, supplies, etc. were ferried in on a 24-hour basis by helicopter. Now, if the IRA could stop them!

He had talked about it briefly to Anna and they had an idea how it could be done.

New York

Monday 9th

Martin Carter took his post from the hotel porter, flicked through the half dozen envelopes, dumped the junk mail and opened the letter with a Paris postmark. There was an Air France ticket, JFK Orly, departure in three days' time. He read the accompanying letter. It bore the letterhead of a company named Media Publicity Europe and confirmed a non-existent previous letter telling him that he had been awarded a prize of a holiday in France on the strength of the apposite and witty slogan he had submitted in a competition organised by the French Gourmet Food & Wine Association. The letter informed him that, as agreed, his ticket was enclosed, together with a voucher for a week's bed and breakfast accommodation in a hotel near the Jardins de Luxembourg. Media Publicity Europe and the Association once more congratulated him on his win and wished him a holiday of a lifetime. It was signed Nicole Bouchier, associate director.

It was reasonably well done, he considered. If he needed to explain to anyone why he was going to Paris, the letter provided a satisfactory explanation. Some might think that it was unusually mean-spirited of the French Gourmet Food & Wine Association to offer a holiday prize for one rather than two, but since he was not going to explain to anyone where he was going or why, it didn't matter. He assumed that Media Publicity Europe was a real organisation. The letter was on expensive paper, with embossed logo, phone, fax and telex numbers and translation of the company name in five languages on the side. The ticket had an open return and, despite Delaney's jibes about expenses, it was first class.

Sitting in his office with the ticket on the desk in front of him, Carter wondered if he were doing the right thing making this trip. The money was good but it was not his prime motivation. He had already made ample provision for his future. It concerned him that he was breaking two of his cardinal rules. His pattern was to take no more than two jobs a year. Four months previously, he had successfully completed an assignment in Mexico City and he had provisionally accepted a job, details yet unknown, in September.

His second rule was that he always worked alone. But this job meant getting involved with the IRA and he wouldn't be in full control of events. Right now, some IRA asshole in Belfast or London or Paris might be doing something that would indirectly alert British security or set in train a sequence of actions that could ultimately affect him adversely. The thought made him uneasy. His experience with Sean and Eileen had left him with serious doubts about the professionalism of the IRA. Kieran Delaney was better and had the makings of a pro but he had a reckless, impulsive streak that could buy him trouble.

He placed the air ticket in a file, put it in the top drawer of his desk and locked it. He took a stroll through the public areas of the hotel, doing a random security check but his mind was elsewhere. The truth was that in the past year he had become bored between jobs. Four evenings a week, he trained hard at a local gym and a private firearms and martial arts club. Outside of that, he dated and bedded with no great enthusiasm a succession of girls he picked up here and there. It wasn't enough. To stay sharp and alive needed the adrenaline of action, needed the challenge of the hunt, the satisfaction of the kill. There was no substitute. He wondered if he was becoming addicted and that wasn't a good thing because his belief that he was in control would be a dangerous illusion. When he realised that he was going to go to Paris, he stopped thinking about it.

Carter decided it would be a good idea to brush up on his somewhat sketchy knowledge of Northern Ireland and the IRA. For most Americans, IRA was a familiar set of initials and was short for Individual Retirement Account rather than the Irish Republican Army. He had a friend, Pete Gardner, a reporter for *Newsweek*, who was currently based in New York but who did overseas stints from time to time. Carter phoned him and they agreed to meet for lunch in an Indonesian restaurant off Times Square the following day.

Gardner was the kind of person that an insurance salesman would go out of his way to avoid. He was in his early forties but looked at least ten years older, a small, very fat man, bald, face flushed a bright red, constantly perspiring. He was also a chain-smoker and had picked the restaurant because they knew him and would give him a small private room where his smoking would be ignored.

The ashtray on the table already had a couple of butts in it when Carter arrived. The conversation was general as they had a couple of pre-lunch drinks and got through the first courses. When the main course arrived, a heaped bowl of seafood and rice, Carter asked: "What can you tell me about the little war in Northern Ireland, Pete? Weren't you over there last year?"

Gardner piled the food onto his plate. "Northern Ireland? Two years ago since I was there and I'm in no rush to get back. Unpleasant little place. A few years ago, the British appointed a guy called Reggie Maudling as their top man in Northern Ireland. After his first day in the North, he rushed back to Belfast, hopped on a plane and uttered the phrase for which he immediately became famous throughout Northern Ireland: 'What a Godawful bloody country, get me a drink quick.' When I left the place, Martin, I made a point of using those exact words."

Carter laughed. "As bad as that?"

"Worse. I was there four days, doing interviews with articulate, soft-spoken politicians, all of them certifiable lunatics. An hour after I checked into my hotel, right in the centre of Belfast, I was evacuated and stood down the road watching the hotel being blasted by a bomb. Following day, I was lunching in a restaurant when, same thing, cops rush in, tell us get the hell out by the back door. As we stood in a filthy little alley, we heard the bomb go off in the street. Car bomb parked twenty yards from the restaurant. Jeez, I was in Lebanon and I wasn't as scared."

The memory didn't diminish his appetite. He shovelled food into his mouth as he spoke yet, from long experience, managed to talk without spraying any. "What you want to know, anyway?"

"Just a quick backgrounder, Pete."

Gardner paused for a moment to think. "Right. Key thing to remember is that the Irish are slaves to their history. Bit like the Eastern Europeans. Long, long memories. Grudges and supposed injustices that go back hundreds of years. Ancient battles that are like they were fought yesterday. I'll give you a two-minute history lesson. In the twelfth century, thereabouts, the English first invaded Ireland at the invite of a provincial Irish king, and with the blessing of the pope. They beat the shit out of the Irish, conquered everything in sight. Guess the Irish forgave the pope but not the English. It took them seven hundred and fifty years to regain control of their country.

"Read up on any century of Ireland's history and it's the same story. Uprising against the English masters, bloody defeat, hideous reprisals, English end up with a stronger grip than when they started. When Henry VIII persuaded England to go Protestant, the Irish didn't go for it and remained Catholics. The English tried to wipe out Catholicism in Ireland the hard way, massacres, priests hanged in the town square, all land and property owned by Catholics handed over to Protestants brought in from England, general arse kicking. You can work out what happened. Most Irish Catholics became nationalists, most

Irish Protestants wanted the English to stay. You really interested in this?"

Cater nodded.

"In the 1840s, Ireland had its Great Famine when the potato crop failed. That's what the Irish lived on, potatoes. It was a hell of a thing, the Famine. With the potato gone, the British exported every other food in sight over to their own country. Millions of Irish starved to death or fled the country in rags and with empty bellies. That's how we've got so many Irish in the States. Y'know, I've got Irish blood in me. I figure that's why I need to eat so much. It's what Jung called a race memory. Eat now before the Famine comes. But I tell you, the Irish remember that Famine like it was last week. It's deep-etched into their consciousness that the British came damn close to wiping out the entire Irish population by letting them starve."

"Can't say I blame them," said Carter mildly.

"Yeah, I know. But the Irish are wrong. Fact is, the British didn't know any better. Remember, these were the days before governments declared emergencies and disaster areas and poured in the money. No Red Cross, no UNICEF, no televised pop concerts. The Victorians would have been shocked at the suggestion of organising famine relief on a large scale for anyone. Went against the whole economic principle of laissez-faire government. It was considered downright wrong to start interfering in the natural course of events."

He was looking now at his empty plate as though wondering what had happened to his food. Carter prompted him: "But in the end, the Irish got rid of the British?"

"Yeah, sort of." Gardner reached for the menu. "You ever read how it happened? Weirdest thing in its way. It's 1916, World War One is in its record-breaking second year, thousands of Irish boys are in British uniform being mowed down by German boys in the trenches. The British government has promised the Irish home rule as soon as they wrap up the war. Then on Easter Monday, in Main Street Dublin, a few hundred lightly armed men, the volunteers they're called, stage an uprising. They're led by oddballs, a mix of hard-nosed socialists and dreamy mystical poets. It's a balls up, in purely military terms. Some of the leaders only learn about the rising at the last minute and put cryptic cancellation notices in the papers. So half the volunteers never show. Those who do make it, barricade themselves in isolated groups in large public buildings, making themselves an easy target.

"They put up a good fight but it's really no contest. The British have lots more troops plus heavy weapons and artillery, even a damn gunboat. In a few days, the rebels wave the white flag. Guess what? The Irish people are pissed.

They didn't want an uprising. Now, hundreds are dead and half the centre of Dublin is wrecked. When the volunteers are marched into captivity, the British soldiers have their hands full protecting them from angry mobs of Dublin citizens."

The waiter came and Gardner fussed over dessert, finally ordering a combination of several dishes. Carter ordered coffee. "Tell me the rest," he said.

"This is the interesting bit, shows you can't predict people ever. The British military are now on top of things. They don't come down too heavy on the rebels. Most of them are tossed into jail for a few years, only the ringleaders get the firing squad. But the British blunder by stretching it out, one or two executions a day. Big mistake. The Irish go apeshit. Right away, the rebels became patriotic heroes, the leaders are Irish national martyrs. There's a big campaign to free the prisoners and the British intelligentsia jump on the bandwagon. The good old USA, Britain's only hope for winning the world war, starts making sympathetic noises. The British back off. Collapse of stiff upper lip, prisoners released, ticker tape parades for the heroes. Come the next general election, the rebels who are called Sinn Fein, which is Gaelic for 'ourselves alone', something like that, sweep the boards, win most of the Irish seats, announce they won't sit in the British Parliament in Westminster and instead formed their own parliament, The Dáil, in Dublin.

"The British have won the world war and figure they don't have to be Mister Nice Guy any more, so they throw the rebels back in jail. Next thing there's a guerrilla war in Ireland and this is when the IRA makes its debut. The British have thousands of war veterans hanging about the place with nothing to do and they ship them over to Ireland to shoot up the place and cow the natives. It's not that easy. Four years the war goes on. The IRA develops a genius for guerrilla warfare well-planned ambush, hit and run, vanish into the hills. In the end, the British throw their hands at it and give the Irish their independence. And the Irish are overjoyed? Hell, no. Most of the IRA don't like the deal with the British and start a civil war. This time they lose."

Gardner sat back in his chair, breathing heavily from the exertion of talking and eating, wiping the sweat from his face with a large blue handkerchief and reaching for his cigarettes.

"And that's as much as most people will ever want to know about Ireland, Martin, including you. Now tell me why the fuck you're interested at all."

Carter had prepared for this. "I've met this girl, Eileen. She's an illegal, came over from Northern Ireland a few months ago. Her father and brother are in the IRA and she couldn't take the strain and the violence. She wants to get it all behind her but it's not out of her system yet. I'm interested in getting an unbiased version of what she talks about."

"Ah, the Irish colleen," sighed Gardner wistfully. "I could tell you a tale or three. Best thing about Ireland, the women, with their flaming red hair, those green eyes and feline features, utterly enigmatic. 'Cold and passionate as the dawn' as the poet Yeats said, and he knew all about it."

"That's Eileen," agreed Carter comfortably. "Bring me up to date on Northern Ireland, Pete."

Gardner stubbed out his cigarette and reached for his pack. "It's like this. When the British pulled out of Ireland in 1921 or thereabouts, they left a poisoned pill behind them. Most of the Protestants in Ireland are in Northern Ireland, about a fifth of the island in size, more than a million of them. Of course, they weren't happy to see the British go but they would have lived with it if they had no choice. They got a choice. The British started playing political games, egged on the Protestants to set up their own little statelet, keep a corner of Ireland under British rule. Before they left, the British partitioned Ireland, and Northern Ireland got itself a Protestant Parliament, a Protestant state for a Protestant people, as one of their leaders rather tactlessly put it.

"The thing of it is that about a third of the people in Northern Ireland are Catholic and they got the shitty end of the stick. They were treated like Alabama and Mississippi used to treat its blacks. And that's not a bad comparison because Martin Luther King inspired the Northern Ireland Catholics to start their own civil rights movement in the late sixties. The government put Protestant thugs into police uniform and they beat up on the Catholics. And that brought the IRA back into the picture, a new lot, called the Provisional IRA, aka the Provos. They seized the opportunity to repeat history, start another guerrilla war, this time in Northern Ireland, get the last of the British off the island and reunite the country. The rest is what you've been reading about for the last twenty years bombs, killings, atrocities, the lot. See, you can understand why your Eileen wanted out."

Carter watched as Gardner lit a fresh cigarette and plopped half a dozen sugar cubes into his coffee. He said: "One of these days, Pete, you're going to run fresh out of new ways to kill yourself."

Gardner grinned. "Hey, this is life insurance. You ever know of anyone who died simultaneously of lung cancer and diabetes?"

"Until now, no."

"Fuck you, Martin," said Gardner amiably. "You're back in the Waldorf after lunch, you stop some punk burgling one of the bedrooms, he pulls a gun or a knife and gets lucky. That's your job every day, right? And you tell me I'm taking risks?"

Carter suppressed the thought that this massively unhealthy man sitting across the table had a better than fair chance of outliving him and asked the question that most interested him. "As of today, Pete, who's really winning in Northern Ireland, the IRA or the British?"

Gardner shrugged and mimed tossing a coin. "If I had to bet on it, I'd go with the IRA. But, as Al Haig would say, let me caveat that response. I think the British will climb down, it's costing them too much. I saw a story we put together on Northern Ireland a few weeks ago. It never ran for space reasons but it had some interesting stuff. On a body count basis, the Provos are ahead. They've lost 250 but killed 1,750. But we learned in Vietnam, didn't we just, that body counts don't tell the story.

"The IRA had around 1,500 active fighters at one time, now they're down to less than 500 that's the best guess. But what's left is tops. They've organised themselves into small cell units that make it hard for the British to do them major damage. They're well financed and very well armed plenty of AK-47s and Armalite rifles, heavy machine guns, rocket launchers and about three tonnes of Semtex, compliments of the chief camel shagger of Libya. They've got about a dozen of their best fighters working under cover in Britain, and a few in France and Germany. The IRA has discovered Britain's weak spot by bombing financial targets. My guess is that the British are going through their own Vietnam they've got the big battalions but they can't win and they're just about ready to find a face-saving way to quit."

Carter said nothing. The mention of Vietnam, as it usually did, had brought back some memories, an abiding anger and frustration at the way the US had conducted the war. Gardner broke in on his thoughts.

"I suppose this affair with Eileen means that you're not with Jenny any more. I'm sorry to hear that, I thought the pair of you really had something going with each other."

Carter looked blank. "Jenny?"

"Yeah, Jenny. Last time we met, you introduced her, told me she was the best thing that ever happened to you."

"Jenny?" Carter said again. " What did she look like?"

Paris

Friday 20th

Carter was still interested in expanding his knowledge about Ireland. When he got on the Air France flight, he brought with him a copy of Tim Pat Coogan's weighty biography of Michael Collins, the legendary hero of Ireland's war of independence, who helped establish the IRA and shape it into a deadly fighting force and who, ironically, was shot dead in an IRA ambush. Carter never got to open the book and left it behind him on the plane. He found himself sitting next to a well-known American movie actor, who was mildly inebriated but amiable and in the mood to talk.

"You'll never believe in a hundred years how I got to be on this flight," he confided in his famous husky whisper. "My wife, she's big into the Ouija Board. Ever use it? Don't, it will scare the shit out of you sometimes. Anyhow, she's a big believer and she tells me yesterday: 'Honey, I've just had this urgent message for you from Doctor Hobert-he's the medium or the channel or something like that-and he says to avoid any contact with the long-nosed one.' And I immediately think of Barbra Streisand who was sore at me when I had to pass on a movie deal she was pitching to Warner, but I didn't think she was that sore about it. Then my wife says: 'Think about it, the long-nosed one, you're flying Concorde tomorrow.' Long nose, get it? So to keep her quiet, I told them to switch me from Concorde to plain old Boeing. That's the truth. I should be strolling down the Champs Elysees right now."

Carter said: "I guess if this plane goes down, your wife will be awfully pissed with Doctor Hobert."

The actor laughed. "Yeah. All things considered, I'd prefer some other way of weaning her away from the Ouija Board."

They were interrupted by one of the stewardesses, a leggy blonde, trying hard not to appear overawed, looking for an autograph. Carter politely tuned out of the conversation when it became obvious that the stewardess was letting the actor know that she was overnighting in Paris and was available. Phone numbers were exchanged and she moved on happily.

The actor told Carter that he was travelling on to Spain where he was about

107

to do a war movie. "It's the old story. It started out with a great script but they've been fucking around with it for the past six months and now it's looking like a real turkey. If they can't get their act together, I'll be back in the States before the end of the month. It always happens. You get an Oscar nomination, and then all they offer you is garbage."

"World War II?" asked Carter.

"Vietnam," said the actor, his eyes narrowing in the manner that was familiar to millions of moviegoers. "Not the most promising box office, sure. But, hell, I'd like to do it on account of how I missed the real thing. I volunteered for Vietnam, you know that? I was a real dumb kid. They turned me down, said I had a thing wrong with my eyes. Shit, that was news to me, but there it was. I'll never know whether it was good or bad for me, not going. You been over there?"

"Mmm. I was there, tail end of the war. Figure yourself lucky you had an eye problem."

"You're a vet?" he said, a new interest in his voice. "What outfit?"

"Marines, most of the time."

"Jesus, this is something. Do you mind talking about it? Great. I need to know what it was like, I mean what it was really like. But let's get ourselves a drink first, huh?"

Carter talked about his time in Vietnam. The actor made a good audience, companionable, thoughtful, non-judgmental. Carter had volunteered out of a sense of youthful patriotism and too much exposure to war movies. Nothing had prepared him for the realities and, for the first few weeks he thought that he had died and gone to hell. His unit, most of them raw kids like himself, fought in the jungle against an enemy rarely seen but often felt. In his first week, one of the guys he had shipped out with was blown to pieces when he stepped on a mine, taking two others with him.

He remembered seeing a Marine literally cut in two by machine gun fire, both ends thrashing wildly, the bodies of villagers beheaded by the Cong, a helicopter that brought his unit into battle crashing in flames as it tried to fly out. He remembered the blind terror of patrolling in the jungle at night, and the added fear when he realised that many men in his unit went into battle stoned out of their minds and were as likely to kill him as the enemy. He remembered the dreadful stench of the dead, learning that when a man was shot, he usually lost control of his bowels.

And then came the discovery that he had a talent to kill, with his rifle and with explosives. He was encouraged to specialise as a sniper and developed a lethal patience, accuracy and coldness. To his surprise, he felt little emotion the first time he shot and killed an enemy soldier, a kid even younger than himself. After that, he felt nothing at all.

He said nothing to the actor about that afternoon at company headquarters, sitting on an empty gasoline barrel, drinking a beer and listening to a proposition from a thin man in fatigues that carried no identification about joining a special force that would mean he would be working for the CIA. Nor did he mention any of the operations he was involved in subsequently. But he did talk about the frustration, the cynicism, the sour taste in the mouth when it became obvious that the United States had concluded that the war was lost but kept fighting and sacrificing good men through political stupidity. Carter was one of those who always believed, despite the experts, that the war could have been won with better leaders.

He got wrapped up in his story and was brought back to the present abruptly by the pilot's announcement that they would be arriving in Paris shortly. His own candour and garrulity surprised him. "I feel like that guy in the *Airplane* movie who bored everyone to death and had them killing themselves," he said apologetically.

The actor shook his head. "Man, this has been the most fascinating plane trip I've ever made," he said. He had been drinking slowly and steadily during the whole trip but now seemed completely sober. "You've helped me decide about this movie. Fact is, I want to play you. So try this. What I'd really like, if it's possible, is that you take a pass on what you're doing and join me in Spain as my personal military advisor."

Surprised, Carter thought about it briefly and liked the idea. The actor had some business in France and wouldn't be in Spain for ten days. That would be more than enough time to do the job for the IRA if he was going to do it at all. Working at the Waldorf was beginning to lose its appeal as a cover. He didn't need it financially and maybe now was the time to think about some other occupation that left him in control of his own time. A semi-retired investment consultant, something like that.

When they got off the plane, the actor scribbled some phone numbers on a card. "Here, I'm counting on your call." They barely had time to shake hands before the actor was surrounded by an entourage and disappeared in the direction of one of the private lounges. Carter took a cab to his hotel. It was a small, unpretentious hotel in a quiet street near the Jardins de Luxembourg. He had half feared that they would have put him up at the Intercontinental or Hotel Lotti, and he approved their choice of this small family hotel. When he was registering, the receptionist, a young, elegantly dressed black girl, handed him a bulky envelope with his name on it. In his room, comfortable rather than luxurious, he unpacked before opening it.

An unsigned letter on plain paper instructed him to be at a number of places at given times over the next two days and he would be contacted at one of them. They included the Crazy Horse Saloon, the Lido, a night club called Les Bains, the *Mona Lisa* room in the Louvre, and a restaurant, La Coupole in Montparnasse. There were tickets and complimentary drinks vouchers for the clubs. The note concluded by providing a recognition code, response and counter-response Fifth Avenue, Trump, Chrysler.

He shook his head in irritation, noted the time for La Coupole, tore the letter into small pieces and threw it with the rest of the contents of the envelope into the waste basket. Christ, did they really expect him to traipse all over Paris, patiently waiting for them to make contact?

There were people in the CIA who had the same mentality, devoting an inordinate amount of their time to devising elaborate assignations, codes and passwords. More often than not, they were completely unnecessary. Sometimes, the safest and most reliable way to meet a contact was to phone him or her and meet them openly in their office.

Later, he went to a nearby restaurant to eat and returned to his hotel room with a detailed street map of Paris and its environs, which he studied carefully, tracing different routes through and out of Paris. The following day, Sunday, he walked some of the routes, noting the location of several hotels, visiting the railway stations and buying a timetable and making several trips on the Metro. Satisfied that he could find his way around in an emergency, he had a surprisingly excellent meal at the hotel and was in bed early.

Monday lunchtime, he was early when he walked down Rue de Vaugirard, crossing the street to the little bar near the corner, alert for anything unusual or anyone out of place. He had a beer at the bar while surveying the intersection of streets outside, with the main road leading to the Montparnasse Tower Block and the one almost opposite him to the church of St Catherine Labouré. There was nothing out of the ordinary, only Parisians going about their daily business and the occasional tourist.

He went into La Coupole, got a small table, looked over the menu, then looked around him curiously. The place was alive and almost full. He guessed there might be about 500 people there. Its vast art-deco interior was only matched by the variety of its seafood. He saw someone he wished was his contact coming towards him and was surprised. She was a tall, slim blonde, a vision in a Moroccan silk jacket, silk fluted short skirt, long hair framing a stunning face, St Lauren sunglasses shading her eyes. Not what he had been expecting. She came up to him without hesitation and grasped his hand, laughing with pleasure. When she spoke, there was another surprise, because her accent was Irish rather than French.

"Martin, it's great to see you again. You remember me, Nicole Bouchier? Hey, you're really looking great. Gosh, it's almost a year since we met in that bar on Fifth Avenue. How are you?"

He smiled back. "Great. I've just bought myself the Trump Tower and the Chrysler Building. So that gets over the passwords. Now, we can relax and enjoy our meal."

Her smile didn't waver as she sat down. "I suppose we should be grateful that you even memorised them. Aidan is almost speechless with fury."

"Who's Aidan?"

"He's in charge of things in Europe. He's spent the last two days running around town trying to make contact with you. Are you always so cavalier about security?"

He let a waiter take their order before replying. He had a chance to scrutinise her as she studied the menu. She really was one of the most beautiful girls he had ever met. And young, what was she, 22? 23? What the hell was she doing in the IRA?

She looked at him expectantly.

He said: "There's a well-known joke about security. One night in Tel Aviv, Mr Levy hears a knock on the door of his apartment. When he opens it, there's a man in a grey raincoat with a hat pulled low over his face. The man says: 'Red roses are blooming in Vienna.' Levy looks at him and says: 'Pardon?' The man says it again: 'Red roses are blooming in Vienna.' Levy stares at him, then suddenly he understands. 'You got the wrong place,' he tells the man. 'I'm Levy the tailor. You want Levy the spy, next floor, apartment C.'"

She laughed. "I think I'd better keep you well away from Aidan. He takes our security very seriously. He was on active duty in Belfast for five years, was involved in some very hairy operations and the British didn't even know he existed. You would probably call him paranoid. He'd say that's what has kept him alive and free."

She looked casually around the crowded tables. "Speaking of which, I've had this weird feeling today that I'm being followed but I haven't spotted anyone. Maybe Aidan's paranoia is rubbing off on me."

"Maybe," said Carter, letting it go.

Across the street, in Boulevard Montparnasse, the man with the dark blue suit sat patiently in the silver Peugeot reading the previous day's *Daily Mail*. He had followed the girl to the café but decided not to go inside. He had first seen her the previous evening at an OECD reception. She had been pointed out to him by his contact at the British Embassy. She was a striking beauty, surrounded by men, getting envious looks from the dull Embassy wives who were always overdressed, covered with make-up and jewellery. Unbelievable that she was the IRA agent who had been spreading panic in European financial circles by carefully planting information about the vulnerability of the City of London and the upcoming plans by an IRA unit to renew their bombing campaign with even more devastating effect than on previous occasions. He had been sent to Paris to silence her and he intended to kill her that afternoon, in a quiet Paris street before she returned to the small studio apartment off Rue de Rivoli, near the Louvre where she lived alone. This would be his first termination job for MI6 and he was confident that it would be a simple hit, in and out, no fuss.

Inside La Coupole, Carter was saying: "Let's talk about something else. Like, how come a French girl like you speaks perfect English with an Irish accent."

She grinned. "That's because I am Irish. I was born in Derry in Northern Ireland and my family moved to Birmingham when I was three. Then we all moved back to Derry when I was fourteen. I was called Nicole after some actress on television, I believe. We're not all Bridgets and Marys, you know."

"Bouchier isn't an Irish name, surely?" he asked.

"No, my husband is Charles Bouchier. He's head of a merchant bank here in Paris, rich, handsome, elegant. But, as it happens, we're separated. Amicable divorce on the way. I won't bore you with the story."

Carter noted with detached interest his pang of disappointment when she had said she was married and was suddenly aware that his interest in this attractive girl was becoming more than professional. But that was for later. Right now, he wanted to get down to business.

"OK, Nicole Bouchier, Irish and fancy-free, tell me what I'm doing in Paris."

She reached into her bag, took out a pack of Marlboro, still in its cellophane, and a Zippo lighter with a British Airways logo. She placed them casually on the table, halfway between them.

"This is mainly why we wanted you to come to Paris. We need you to bring these with you to London. You'll be meeting a friend of yours, Kieran

Delaney, in the Ritz Café in London at noon tomorrow: He'll take it from there."

Carter looked at the pack of cigarettes. It looked the real thing. "What's in the pack?" he asked.

She hesitated. "Aidan said you didn't need to know," she said, apology in her voice.

Carter controlled his annoyance.

"Then tell Aidan to deliver it himself. Look, right now I'm just your typical American in Paris, doing nothing illegal. That's the way it stays until I decide otherwise. For all I know, if I take that pack, I'm suddenly carrying a bomb. The damn thing might even go off unexpectedly. So tell me, what am I being asked to take to London?"

She thought about it for a few moments, then said: "Yes, I understand. You have a right to know. The lighter is as important as the pack. Inside the pack, there's a small electronics board don't ask me the details, I don't know. But the lighter connects to the board and together they make up what's called a beam bender. I gather that it enables a transmitter to send a signal around corners, that sort of thing. I think it came from some computer guru in Spain but it's only a hunch."

"I know what a beam bender does," said Carter. He looked again at the two objects on the table, then casually picked them up and dropped them into his jacket pocket. "Well, that's our business out of the way. Now, tell me more about how you came to live in Paris."

Two hours later, she looked at her watch. "I've got to leave you now. Thanks for a wonderful lunch. Where did the two hours go? Let me give you a phone number where you can reach me." She wrote the number on a napkin and handed it to him. He noticed the faint blush on her face and an enigmatic look in her eyes. And then she was gone.

Carter stood in the shadows of the restaurant and watched her walk away. He scanned the street scene and almost immediately saw a man in a dark suit get out of a silver Peugeot, lock it and head off in her direction.

Damn, he thought. The IRA may be paranoid, but it looked like their security had been breached. And if so, the operation had been compromised before he even learned the details of it. His choice now was to dump the electronic package, go back to his hotel, pack and get the next plane to New York. Or he could stalk the stalker and see what happened. For all he knew, the man in the blue suit was not really following Nicole. Maybe his interest was sex rather than espionage. Maybe. With a quiet sigh, Carter decided he had better find out. As he passed an empty table on his way out of the café, he stopped for a moment and unobtrusively slipped a small glass salt cellar into his pocket. Then he went in pursuit.

He knew within minutes that the man was definitely following Nicole. After some careful checking, he also established that the man was working alone. That in itself was intriguing. If this were British Intelligence, they would have a team, minimum four, most likely more with back-up vehicles, yet there was nothing like this. Just this one man.

Nicole wandered slowly along Montparnasse, looking in shop windows as she neared the intersection where engines roared waiting for the lights to change, then suddenly almost ran down the steps to the Metro. The man in the dark blue suit followed. When Carter reached the platform, she was getting on the train, while her shadow hung back in the milling crowd. Carter purposefully got onto the train and was not surprised to see the dark blue suit flash into the compartment just before the doors closed. Nicole changed a couple of times but never lost her shadow. So, he was a professional, thought Carter but not experienced in this kind of work. A more seasoned man would be checking carefully that he was not himself being followed.

Blvd St Germain, St Michelle were long gone, Champs-Elysées, Notre Dame, Eiffel Tower, Louvre then on to Montmartre, by Metro, taxi and on foot, then back-tracking again by funicular to the Sacré Coeur. She was like an American doing Paris in one day. She never once looked back, never once lost her tracker. Yet it was obvious that she knew she was being followed and the follower must know that too, thought Carter.

They were in the square near Sacré Coeur made famous by its painters but now mostly inhabited by failed artists, stall holders, and down and outs. They were all three walking fast now and the man in the dark blue suit had closed the gap with Nicole and was now less than a dozen yards behind her. Suddenly, Carter suspected what was going to happen.

. He broke into a run as Nicole and her shadow turned the corner into a deserted side-street. He was in time to see the man, a stiletto knife in his hand, run towards Nicole, who had half turned, her eyes widening. Without breaking stride, he hurled the salt cellar at the man, hitting him high on the forehead. He staggered back, looking confused, his hands falling to his side. Then Carter was beside him and swiftly hit him with the hard outer side of his right hand on the side of the neck. The man immediately collapsed and, as he fell, Carter hit him again. He was dead before he hit the ground.

"I know him, Oh God, I saw him at a party last night. He kept looking at me." Nicole had come up beside Carter who was looking down at the body. She was unnaturally calm. "He was with Masterson, the MI6 man from the British Embassy. He must be MI6 as well. He's awfully young for this sort of thing, isn't he?"

"He was," corrected Carter, aware that she was hardly aware of what she was saying. In a minute, she would realise that he had been about to kill her and her reaction would be unpredictable. They had to get away from this place. Incredibly, no-one had witnessed what had happened, the narrow street was still deserted.

He put his arm over her shoulder and forced her away from the dead MI6 agent. They crossed into another wide and crowded street and he kept walking, not too quickly to attract attention. She stayed with him, unresisting, white-faced, robot-like. He feared she would collapse suddenly. Thankfully, he spotted a passing taxi, half pushed her into the back and gave the address of his hotel to the cab driver, a young North African who was giving most of his attention to the pounding music on his radio.

In the hotel room, Carter poured Nicole a large brandy, loosened her clothes and brought her over to the bed, where she obediently lay down and was unconscious within seconds. He sat on a chair beside the window and looked out at the quiet scene in the park across the street, children playing as their mothers watched and gossiped.

He was annoyed that he had killed the MI6 agent. He didn't care about the man. Already, the dead face was fading from his memory. And he found no fault with the kill itself: it had been fast and efficient, less than ten seconds from her turning into the side-street to seeing the man dead on the ground.

What upset him was that the killing had not been part of his agenda and, to that extent, was purposeless. Only twice in the past ten years had he killed someone without planning it beforehand. In both instances, they were body-guards of his intended victim who had gotten in the way. On both occasions, he was afterwards angry with himself, as he was now. It suggested that his planning had been faulty, that he had permitted events to control his actions and thereby multiplied the risk.

He considered what he had done that afternoon and why he had done it. When he first spotted the man tailing Nicole Bouchier, his first thought had been to walk away, leave her to sort out her own problems. But he needed to know what was happening. If he left it alone and went on to London, it would be like leaving his back unprotected. He needed to know who was following Nicole and what were their intentions. If she was picked up, by French or

British agents or anyone else, it was possible, even likely, that she would be forced to tell them about him. So he had followed.

He looked over at the bed as Nicole whimpered in her sleep. She didn't waken but turned her face into the pillow so that all he could see of her was her mane of long blonde hair.

After a while, he turned back and looked out of the window again. It was evening and the crowd in the park was emptying slowly, with mothers and their children heading unhurriedly towards the exit.

It was when the man turned into the side-street and Carter knew, even without seeing the knife, that he was about to kill Nicole that he acted without thinking, completely impulsively. This was really the moment when he should have done absolutely nothing, just wait at the corner, count off a minute, then walk slowly past the side-street, to confirm that he was right in his surmise, that the girl would be dead on the ground and the man would already be some distance away.

He should not have become involved. He owed nothing to the IRA, in Paris or anywhere, and he had no quarrel with MI6. Nicole's death would be convenient as far as he was concerned, eliminating any link between him and his IRA courier in Paris. The MI6 agent had not seen him, was not even aware of him. Instead, he had intervened and killed the agent. And, as a result, Nicole was still alive. He recognised that he had killed the agent for the sole reason that he was not prepared to see her dead. That was the most dangerous thing of all. He had killed for reasons of sentiment and in his job this kind of emotional response was something he could not afford. If he was starting to let himself think of personal factors like this, he should be getting out of this business.

He was still sitting at the window when, two hours later, Nicole awoke with a gasp, jumped out of bed and rushed into the bathroom, where he heard her being violently sick. He listened carefully but made no move to follow her. In a minute he heard the sound of the shower. She stayed under it for a long time.

When she emerged, she had wrapped herself in one of the large bath towels. Carter was relieved that her face, still very pale, had lost its vacant look.

"I'm sorry," she said and she sounded embarrassed. "I wasn't much help to you back there. I just lost it completely. I've never seen a man, you know..."

Carter went over and put his arms around her. She didn't resist. "You did all right," he said. "We got away safely and right now that's what counts."

She looked at him steadily. "I really don't know you at all, do I, Martin Carter? All I was told is that you were an American expert who would be

116

helping us. I just assumed that you were some sort of technical or computer whiz. I was wrong, though. You've killed people before, haven't you?"

He locked eyes with her.

"Forget about what I do," he said quietly, stepping back from her. "Start thinking about yourself. Your cover is blown. Whatever you've been doing in Paris has been important enough for MI6 to send one of their thugs to kill you. They're going to be sore when they find he's dead. They may well try again and, if they do, they'll send in a team. You're going to have to disappear for a while, you know that?"

"Yes," she said leaning into him, her mind seemingly elsewhere. He saw a sudden sparkle in her eyes. "I feel a cliché coming on. I owe you my life and I'm wondering how I can possibly repay you."

"For a start, you can give me back my towel," said Carter and he reached over and pulled the towel away....

MI5 Headquarters, Millbank, London

Monday 23rd

Stella Rimington looked around the boardroom table at the small group of five people who were to lead Operation Fortress Salvo, which would shortly decapitate the entire leadership of the IRA at one stroke, leaving the organisation running around aimlessly, an easy target for the RUC and the Army.

They were looking at her expectantly, respectful, waiting for her to formally start the meeting. She was aware that outside her presence they nicknamed her Rimington Steel, after the TV detective. She did not know that they also referred to her as Steel Arse.

Three of these five people each headed a unit of sixty operatives, including 25 from her own elite 340-strong General Intelligence Group. In turn, they would be supported in the final stage of the operation by another sixty SAS men who had been specially selected by General Sir Peter de la Billiere, one of the most decorated men in the British Army, who had led the Special Air Services in many wars Malaysia, Borneo, Aden, Oman, the Falklands and in Northern Ireland and knew exactly what was wanted. The SAS men were to be placed temporarily under her command for Fortress Salvo and were currently doing a refresher training course somewhere in the Highlands.

There was a certain tension around the table. One of the problems she had inherited when she became head of MI5 was not just the IRA but the intense rivalry between the various intelligence services. When she took over from the secretive retiring Sir Patrick Walker, she had been thankful for the support of David Bickford, the legal adviser to the intelligence services in simplifying the command structure in the fight against the IRA by putting MI5 clearly in charge.

MI6, of course, wasn't happy with the new arrangement. They had always regarded the whole of Ireland as a foreign country and therefore their patch. The SAS, after failing to get the expected results, were being gradually withdrawn to their barracks in Stirling Lines, Hereford, but it was a much more secret unit which had initially caused her the most trouble.

The 14th Intelligence and Security Company, which few people had ever heard about, had various names during the 25-year war against the IRA. It started in 1970 as the Military Reaction force formed by General Frank Kitson with men drawn from all three armed services. Kitson may have been the acknowledged expert on counter-terrorist activities world-wide but he had failed to deliver in Northern Ireland. Eventually, his unit had added to the management problem rather than providing the solution. After some fierce in-fighting in Whitehall, she had been successful in getting them out of her way, and transferred from their Northern Ireland barracks in Hollywood and Lisburn, back to their headquarters at the Joint Services Intelligence Centre at Ashford in Kent.

Now MI5 had a clear mandate to run the campaign to defeat the IRA and was operating with the direct personal authority of the Prime Minister himself in co-ordinating the security services and planning strategy. The five around the table were her personal choice for making Fortress Salvo go smoothly.

On her immediate left, Chief Inspector Geoffrey Scott from Scotland Yard's Special Branch was the youngest and brightest officer of that rank in the force. A big man, six feet four in height and heavily built, he looked like a profes-sional heavyweight boxer. He fancied himself as a ladies man but his appear-ance and manner tended to intimidate. She knew that, like most of his senior colleagues, he resented MI5's leading role in counter-terrorism. But, so far, he had been extraordinarily co-operative.

On her right, Margaret Blake of the American Central Intelligence Agency was pouring herself another coffee from the pot. She had been recently seconded to the British intelligence services and was acting as liaison with Military Intelligence, MI5 and MI6. Margaret Blake was in her early thirties, small, almost fragile, with long black hair and a face that many men would consider very attractive. She was also, at times, brash and arrogant and did not trouble too much to hide her opinion that what the British security services needed was an injection of CIA know-how.

Rimington was prepared to ignore this. Blake was invaluable in this small circle. She had already helped to increase the flow of useful information from Langley on the IRA in Northern Ireland and the Republic. When Fortress Salvo took place, she would be a vital link in bringing the American govern-ment into line. Rimington was prepared to trust her insofar as she trusted anyone because she knew something that Blake herself never spoke about. Twelve years previously, her father, a US army colonel stationed in Germany, had been killed in a terrorist bomb explosion. Those who planted the bomb were believed to be a small group of German left-wing extremists who were never caught. Margaret Blake had been left with a burning hatred of terrorists of all persuasions, and the IRA were no exception.

Beside her sat Clive Reid of Military Intelligence, dark-suited, starched white shirt and regimental tie, grey thinning hair. He was blinking from behind a pair of what looked like cheap National Health Service plastic spectacles, fiddling with a pipe that he never actually lit. He had been the last to be brought into the group and this was his first meeting. He was the only one who did not have all the details of the operation but Rimington had checked him out carefully and was satisfied that he would be fully supportive.

Sitting directly across from her was Chief Superintendent Ian Taylor of the RUC's Special Branch. He was in his early forties but could pass for ten years younger. Tall, slim, with short blond hair, he was seen as the new wave of progressive RUC man. And he was o rara avis a Roman Catholic, long lapsed, perhaps, but a member of the Catholic community and wise in their ways.

He held a doctorate in criminal law but he was also the man in the frontline of the war against the IRA. Living at the bottom of the Mourne Road, his house had been attacked once, his car blown up twice and he himself almost murdered as he walked into Belfast's City Hall for a charity function. He knew nearly all the top terrorists and where they were to be found.

Sitting at the far end of the table as usual was Commander Trevor Wallace, a top MI6 operative who had seen service in many foreign countries. His appearance was fastidious, almost prissy but he was one of the most ruthless men Rimington had ever met. He would have been surprised and hugely embarrassed to know that everyone else at the table knew he was gay.

Rather like running a coalition government, she reflected. A group of individualists rather than a team, all of them with their own power base, bringing to the meeting their own agenda, but all prepared to work together for a common cause for as long as it seemed that their combined efforts were going to be successful.

Rimington watched her personal assistant fussing with the tea and coffee pots and mineral water on the table before she left. Before she could open the meeting formally, Trevor Wallace cleared his throat and spoke.

"Something I might just bring to your attention," he said almost casually. "I just got a report an hour ago. Yesterday evening, one of our men, Charles Dutting, who was working out of the Embassy in Paris was found murdered in a back street. A karate blow killed him. The French authorities have no witnesses and no clues. They are suggesting that it might be a simple mugging. There was no robbery, though. Dutting's wallet, money, credit cards, watch, were on the body when they found it. The police suggest that the mugger or muggers panicked when they realised that they'd killed their mark. That's the story that will be in tomorrow's papers in any event."

"What do you think happened?" asked Rimington, giving him a searching look.

Wallace shrugged. "Umm. Hard to say. It could be a mugging that went wrong. It's implausible but possible. The world is full of young thugs who have done a martial arts course and don't know how to handle it."

"What was Dutting doing in Paris, anyway?" enquired Margaret Blake.

None of your damn business, thought Wallace. Aloud he said: "I don't have all the details but I understand he was sent over to check out a woman named Nicole Bouchier, whom we have reason to believe is an IRA terrorist engaged in some kind of disinformation campaign, spreading panic among the bankers of Europe, that sort of thing."

"Just checking her out, was he?" asked Margaret sceptically.

Wallace kept his anger under control and, addressing himself to Rimington said carefully: "That's the information I have. But I'll be getting a more detailed briefing later today and I'll advise you if there's anything you should be aware of, Director."

I've no doubt you'll be back to me today with the full story, thought Rimington. I'll bet they're twisting in embarrassment over in MI6 right now, savaging each other to find a scapegoat. They sent over one of their agents to take care of a slip of a girl and he got himself killed. Damn them, the very last thing we need right now is alerting the IRA to the possibilities of assassination. Before this day is out, I'll be carving out a few new assholes over there.

But for now she merely nodded to Wallace. "Let's get down to business, shall we?

"The most important thing I have to say today is that we have somewhat less time at our disposal than we planned. I have met with the Prime Minister and I understand from him that he is about to initiate informal soundings through intermediaries with the IRA leadership in Belfast. This will most likely be direct contact, bypassing the middlemen. In other words, Sinn Fein is out of the loop and so is the Irish government. You know what this means: the British government is considering the possibility that we, the security forces, will not succeed in containing the problem and they are looking at the alternative of a purely political solution."

There were mutterings around the table, but Rimington ignored them. "The decision has been made to take this two-track approach and we have not been invited to comment on it. It's certainly not for discussion here. What it means is that it is imperative now that we win quickly and decisively.

"Outside of this room nobody knows the details of Fortress Salvo and it must remain that way. You have had your best people working under the strictest secrecy gathering the information database. Each of you, Margaret excepted, of course, leads a team of six of the best undercover agents in the Services who themselves do not know the ultimate objective. I would now appreciate a very brief report before we proceed to the next, almost final, stage of the operation. Bear in mind that timing is now critical. To put it in specific terms, the termination phase of the operation must be completed within the next thirty days. More likely within the next week. That's tight but attainable. The Prime Minister demands it, and I demand it."

It was again Wallace who spoke: "From our end, we have had no problems with surveillance on the twenty people targeted. As we agreed, we are concentrating on electronic surveillance rather than people on the ground in order to avoid our targets becoming aware that they are under constant watch. We're operating a system of phone taps, bugging and remotely placed visual devices and the system is working out much better than we had expected. When the time comes, we are totally confident that we will be able to pinpoint the location of all our targets."

"Have you nailed the Chief of Staff yet?" asked Rimington.

Wallace shook his head. "Not yet, but we're pulling out all the stops and I expect we'll crack it very soon."

She frowned. "That's not good enough and you know it. It's now close on a month since we learned that the IRA has a new Chief of Staff and we still haven't put a name to him. He should be right at the top of the list and we've nothing. I want him known and under surveillance before our next meeting. I don't expect to be let down on this any further, you understand?"

Wallace accepted the criticism with a nod of the head. He said nothing but the back of his neck had turned a deep red. It was typical of MI5 to pass the buck to him when it should have been their job, he thought, but said nothing.

Ian Taylor broke the silence, speaking in his carefully neutral accent that had only a hint of his West Belfast origins: "We've got our terrorist leaders eyeballed around the clock. I've got a first-class team of people and they are doing the job as discreetly as possible. In addition, we have been happy to supply back-up to everyone here and, of course, local knowledge. Like everyone else, they are in the dark about the final objective of this exercise and nobody has been told anything more than is necessary. Of course, they all suspect sudden internment and I've been given a few casual reminders that internment was tried in the '70s and failed."

There were a few smiles around the table. Taylor wasn't the only one to hear that internment was the scuttlebutt among the teams. Geoffrey Scott was next to report. "Nothing unusual. We have our boyos under surveillance, day and night and have not had to call on any outside assistance so far. Things are quiet on other fronts at present, incidentally. There are rumours that we haven't yet confirmed of 'dummy-runs' by IRA Active Service Units here in London. Nothing concrete but I'll keep you posted if anything develops. I'm satisfied that our targets do not know they are being watched any more than usual."

Clive Reid coughed and looked like he was about to speak but he just shook his head slightly and said nothing.

Rimington looked around the table, satisfied with what she had heard. "All of us understand what Fortress Salvo is designed to achieve with the exception of Clive, who is joining us for the first time. What we are about is quite simple, Clive. We have identified the fifty men and women who are the key personnel in the Irish Republican Army and we are going to execute all of them at one go. The IRA will be leaderless and will virtually cease to exist after we arrest several hundred of the rank and file in a subsequent round-up. We'll go for internment, though it won't be called that. As Ian has been told, internment didn't work when we tried it previously. That's because we hadn't pinpointed the terrorists who mattered. This time, we know them all. As their leaders will all be dead, it will be easy. The rest will simply disappear to camps here on the mainland."

Reid took the news calmly. He seemed almost indifferent. He carefully removed his spectacles and looked at Rimington as though seeing her for the first time. "Yes, well, that's more or less what I had assumed. I'm glad to hear that it's all moving along nicely. Naturally, my resources are at your disposal and I imagine we'll be able to spread out the burden a bit, relieve the tired and the weary, as it were."

"Thank you, Clive," said Rimington, feeling a surprising sense of huge relief but keeping it to herself.

She paused and looked at the others.

"I'm pleased to know that everything has gone well.

"The next phase begins now. It is perhaps less dangerous but more sensitive. This evening, one of our best agents Jonathan Jones, I think you've all met him, will be flying to Belfast and, with your help, will select fifteen senior people from across the security services operating in the province. He will brief them on Fortress Salvo, at this time in outline only. Each of these officers will concentrate on identifying our primary IRA targets. Specifically, we must establish or re-confirm where they are likely to be found at night, between the hours of 2 a.m. and 5 a.m. over the next thirty days. We will want the complete layout of premises, houses, apartments, hotels, whatever. You know the score.

"The bottom line is that, from tomorrow night, each group will know only his or her own two targets. Each of you will select your best operatives, keeping the top targets as your own responsibility for the moment. That way, the identity of any one target will be known by as few people as possible. We're taking no chances with a security leak. That about sums things up for the present. Are there any questions?"

There was a quiet shaking of heads. She had not expected questions. Everyone was well briefed and knew what they had to do. After quick good-byes, they were gone. Moving forward the deadline was, on balance, a good thing, she decided. It gave an added edge, an incentive to spur things on. She could see it on their faces as they left the sense of seeing the kill in sight.

She picked up the internal phone. "Tell Jonathan and Andrew Manning I'm ready for them now."

Central London

Tuesday 24th

They had booked Carter into the Regent Palace hotel in the centre of London. The place was like a railway station, he thought, watching the hordes of tourists, mostly Japanese and American, clamour around the reception desk. There must be a thousand rooms in the hotel, most of them evidently occupied, to judge by the endless ebb and flow of people. It was big, but it certainly wasn't the Waldorf Astoria, he reflected.

The impression was confirmed when he was shown into a tiny bedroom. Some Palace, he thought. Is this an example of the British sense of humour? If so, like their Queen Victoria, he was not amused. He went over to the single small window and looked out at the bustle of Piccadilly Circus. Curiously, it seemed busier, more crowded than Manhattan. He looked back at his room. Where was the bathroom ? He found a notice on the wall. It advised that, if he wanted a bath, he should ring a bell and someone would arrive with towels and a key to a communal bathroom up the corridor.

He laughed. The IRA must be running low on funds if they were putting him up here. He took his suitcase, left the hotel with relief, hailed a passing cab and directed the driver to the Hilton. An hour later, showered and refreshed, he made his way to the Ritz.

Kieran Delaney was waiting for him at the bar. "Welcome to London," he called cheerily. "I've just ordered a vodka and tonic. What's yours?"

"Oh, whatever the natives drink here."

"That will be Miller or Coors," said Delaney. "Quite true, alas. The bland tastes of American food and drink are conquering England even the Ritz, dammit."

"Either will be fine," Carter smiled.

They found themselves a corner table and Carter looked around the crowded room, taking in the old world elegance of the place. He had visited hotels and restaurants in a number of places in America that were almost identical in appearance. In fact, he could think of several in Las Vegas and Miami that were more opulent. There was a difference, of course. The Ritz was the genuine article, not some ersatz creation of businessmen and decorators who reckoned that money beat style any day.

"Had a good trip over?" asked Delaney. "I heard reports of some bad weather over the Atlantic last night."

He doesn't know I've come through Paris, Carter realised and saw no reason to set him straight. He liked Kieran Delaney but, over the years, had acquired the habit of talking about himself as little as possible.

"No problems," he said. "When am I going to find out what you guys are planning? And tell me, Kieran, who's idea was it to meet here in the Ritz? Not the usual hang-out for your outfit."

"Very soon now," agreed Delaney, signalling the waiter for another round of drinks. "Fact is, despite what I may have implied in New York, I don't have all the details either. We're both going to get the whole story this afternoon. The Ritz? They are always searching for us in spit-and-sawdust pubs in Kilburn."

Carter took out the cigarette pack and lighter and placed them casually on the table. "These are yours. I guess, like they say on the pack, they're likely to seriously damage someone's health."

"Bloody good," said Delaney, eyeing them with interest. "Where there's smokes, there's fire, I always say. Where are you staying?"

"The London Hilton," replied Carter. "Not quite up to the standard of the Waldorf Astoria, but it gives Americans what they want the illusion of being right at home anywhere in the world."

Delaney whistled and said in mock disgust: "The bloody Hilton, no less. If we fail to win this war it's because we've run out of money paying your fees and expenses."

Carter smiled and shook his head. "So why are we in the Ritz? Kieran. Not the cheapest in London, I'd guess."

"Touché, mon ami. In real life, I'm quiet, mild-mannered Kieran Delaney, respectable, even stuffy, editor of a monthly journal of great fascination to those who work in procurement and logistics. I'm also the owner, publisher, advertising director and chief reporter of the rag and I have to do a fair volume of interviews and advertising solicitations. This is my favourite watering hole and trough. Usually impresses the hell out of people. The Queen Mother herself has afternoon tea and gin sandwiches here once a fortnight with her old friends who are specially disinterred for the occasion. Besides, it's the last place in the realm where anyone would expect those of evil intent to congregate-other than the normal run of politicians and big businessmen. We're absolutely safe, here."

In this, he was wrong.

In a corner of the room, just several tables away, Chief Inspector Geoffrey Scott of Scotland Yard and Margaret Blake of the US Central Intelligence Agency were cautiously taking stock of Jonathan Jones of MI5. It was all very awkward, thought Scott in irritation. After leaving the meeting with Rimington, they were in the front hallway of the building heading out when they got a message at the reception desk asking them to meet with Jonathan Jones at noon in the Ritz on Piccadilly.

"What the hell is this all about?" growled a disgruntled Scott as they walked over to the Ritz. "I guess it must be important," murmured Blake. "It's not as though we haven't got a full agenda."

It wasn't at all important. In fact, it was something of a misunderstanding. Rimington had wanted Jones to get a first-hand briefing from Scott and Blake before going to Belfast. Jones had been asked to meet with the two, but inexplicably had not been given the reason for it. Assuming it was some unnecessary courtesy meeting, and busy arranging his flight, he had gone there as a favour to show hospitality to the man from Scotland Yard and the woman from the CIA.

As a result, the three of them were sitting at a table in the Ritz, having pre-lunch drinks and wondering why they were meeting. Scott was especially irked, and trying hard not to show it, because he had no idea where Jones fitted into the MI5 pecking order. Was he, like Manning, a trusted agent who worked directly to Rimington? Did he know anything at all about Fortress Salvo? It was most awkward and he inwardly cursed Stella Rimington for wasting his time.

Blake, on the other hand, was quite happy to spend a few hours socialising with Jonathan Jones, who was the first member of the international espionage community she had ever met who resembled a movie producer's idea of a spy. He was in his mid-thirties, was just over six feet in height and his slim figure was expensively tailored. His dark good looks complemented a general air of confident ruthlessness. Many women would gaze once into those intelligent brown eyes and would be lost forever, she thought. Careful, now Maggie!

They were discussing the continued fear that the IRA was planning another attack in the capital soon and had the resources to do it.

"The situation is not a happy one," said Scott, with a heavy grimace. "My lads tell me that the IRA now has active service cells in the London area, all operating separately. If we could locate even one of them we would quietly send them over to the RUC in Castlereagh where they know how to give them the treatment and keep it out of the public eye. The RUC would get them talking all right, and one thing might lead to another. As it is, we've been putting all our best assets into this final do-or-die operation."

He sighed deeply with frustration.

"We're trying everything. All known suspects are being followed not only here but in Paris, Belfast and Dublin. GCHQ is paying special attention to all phone calls. We have taps on all the known houses. Our lads are drinking pints of Guinness and joining in the chorus of rebel Irish ballads in Kilburn every Saturday and Sunday. The truth is, we have no idea who they are or where they are."

Jones nodded sympathetically. "We're due a lucky break," he said. "If you slog at it hard enough, something always turns up, usually in the most unlikely place."

Several tables away, Delaney spotted Tara Barry coming towards them. "Here's the person we've been waiting for." He watched Carter's expression expectantly and was rewarded with a look of complete surprise, before becoming impassive again. "Equal opportunity employers, that's us."

Another one straight off the catwalks, thought Carter. Where is the IRA getting them, and what draws these incredibly beautiful young girls into a terrorist organisation?

Delaney was so intent on seeing Carter's reaction that he was slow to notice that Tara Barry's personality had undergone a considerable change from the day before. She let Delaney introduce her to Carter and sat down without a word.

"What can I get you to drink, Tara?" enquired Delaney jovially. She ignored him and looked at Carter with a frown.

"I tried to phone you in the Regent Palace hotel a few minutes ago. I was told you had checked in and then checked out within the hour."

There was no mistaking the coldness in her tone. Carter decided to let her play her hand. "Right," he said. "I didn't take to the Regency."

She smiled, trying to be friendly and not succeeding. "You really shouldn't do that, Mr Carter. We booked you into the Regent Palace for good reasons. You are being paid an awful lot of money, and it upsets some of our people to think that you are taking a casual approach to their carefully thought out plans."

Carter let it pass and she seemed almost relieved that he didn't comment. He saw that she was nervous, anxious to assert herself, steeling herself for confrontation and at the same time hoping it wouldn't happen.

128

She continued to smile, but with an effort. "I think I should tell you that the project we are working on has evolved considerably in the past few days. In many ways it has become more straightforward and less risky. We will still need your assistance, you'll be glad to hear, but it looks as though we won't need to make use of your more specialist talents, so to speak." She laughed. "Maybe we should be renegotiating your fee, Mr Carter."

Carter returned her smile. "I love your Irish sense of humour."

Delaney looked at the two of them, sensing the hostility and not understanding. He felt himself getting angry with Tara, wanted to snap at her but couldn't take sides against her. Frustrated, he said nothing.

Tara said quietly: "I don't want any misunderstanding between us, Mr Carter. I have been given total responsibility for ensuring that this project is carried out smoothly and efficiently and successfully."

She saw Delaney's eyes widen in shock and he stiffened.

She went on. "An enormous amount of time and money has been invested in this project and I am satisfied that we can bring it off. It has immense strategic importance for us. To put it bluntly, I can't allow any mavericks on the job. You will have to keep in mind at all times that you are under orders here. I've heard from Paris earlier this morning that your freelancing activities over there have all but wrecked a very delicate and extremely valuable operation. Well, I'm not going to allow that to happen here. Do we understand each other?"

"Paris?" broke in Delaney, utterly bewildered and seizing on anything. Too many things were confusing him. Tara had completely changed personality, from the companionable girl of their previous meeting at the London bombing into some sort of harridan. She, rather than as he had assumed himself, was in charge of the operation and to hear it this way was humiliating. Her hostility to Carter, whom she had just met, was palpable. He felt as though he had somehow missed a large part of the conversation.

"Paris?" he asked again into the silence.

Carter got up suddenly. He had a lazy smile on his face but it didn't reach his eyes, which were expressionless. He said to Kieran:

"I've done what I said I'd do, come over and look at your operation. I can tell now it's not for me. I'm out."

He turned to Tara. "Interesting to meet with you, Miss Barry." And he was gone.

Delaney said in as friendly a tone as he could manage: "I think our operation has just gone down the tubes, Tara, my dear."

She looked stricken. All the arrogance and authority had gone out of her. "I

129

didn't intend-"

"No time for that," Delaney interrupted. "Are you going after him or do you want me to?"

"I'll go," she said firmly getting up and hastened after Carter.

Delaney quickly finished his drink, pocketed the cigarette pack and the lighter and followed her.

Margaret Blake had watched the little drama unfold with mild curiosity. Geoffrey Scott had been explaining, in tedious detail, how a new computer system co-ordinated every piece of information about the IRA in Britain known to Scotland Yard, to no effective end that she could see, and had tuned out of the conversation.

The cool beauty of the girl as she walked across the room had caught her attention. She idly watched her sit down with the two men, sensed the instant quarrel, saw one of the men rise, make a curt remark and depart. Moments later, the girl was all but running after him, followed by the other man. Interesting little slice of life. She tried to put a storyline on it. Girl arrives late for date. Impatient male gets sniffy. She puts him down and he walks off in a huff. Remorsefully, the girl follows her man to apologise, with mutual friend tagging behind, no doubt mortified.

But there was something nagging at her about this lover's spat in the Ritz, something familiar but elusive. Her instinct told her it was something important, relevant to her job.

Scott and Jones were still immersed in their shoptalk. She got up and said: "Excuse me for a few seconds, guys. Carry on and I'll be back."

She went to the main entrance. The first man was nowhere to be seen but the girl and the second man were standing on the pavement, having an animated but apparently friendly conversation. The girl leaned forward suddenly and kissed the man on the cheek. He patted her on the shoulder. They walked off in opposite directions.

Margaret Blake examined them both carefully but was satisfied that she had never seen them before. What about the other man? She tried to recall him, recalled him striding out of the restaurant and immediately an almost duplicate memory superimposed itself, the same man walking purposefully out of one of the staff restaurants. Was it? Christ, what was he doing here? It could not be. Surely he was dead?

She had seen him several times at Langley, and they had even exchanged some innocuous small talk in the restaurant. He had changed, of course. There was grey in his hair and he seemed more relaxed, less of a coiled spring than she remembered. But was it still the same man? It looked like him. Maybe a double? Maybe her vivid imagination again?

One of her colleagues had once spoken about him: the infamous Black Knight, he had called him, one of the CIA's most effective killers. Knight was one of the people on the elite little group that formed Jay Trander's team. Trander himself was a CIA legend, a former marine brigadier who served with distinction in World War II and Korea and who had been brought out of early enforced retirement by John F Kennedy. A Georgian, who looked a little like Colonel Sanders, Trander seemed to run his own little empire within the CIA, answerable to nobody except for end results. His group, so the rumours went, were specialists in surgical assassination of political figures hostile to the United States. Inevitably, any highly publicised killing abroad was attributed to them.

About five years ago, at the time when Congressional investigations were focusing on some of the less savoury aspects of CIA activity, it was abruptly announced that Trander had taken retirement again. His department was closed down and its personnel were let go. The rumours were rife that Trander had simply privatised his operation and now ran an assassination bureau, with the CIA as his sole client.

Still following her instinct, Blake shadowed the second man as he walked down Regent Street, turned into a side street, got into an open red MG sports car and slumped into the driver's seat, making no move to drive off. She quickly memorised the registration and returned to the Ritz.

Jones was standing in the foyer and brightened when he saw her.

"How nice to see you again. I was beginning to think that there was something wrong with my deodorant. First you do a vanishing act, then Geoff Scott looks at his watch, utters a fierce oath, mutters something about an urgent appointment and rushes off in all directions."

Margaret laughed apologetically. "I'm really very sorry, Jonathan. I had a call of nature to make and, on my way back, I saw someone I thought I knew that I hadn't seen for years. I ran after them but they got away. Just give me a second. I want to write something down before it goes out of my mind."

She opened her handbag, took out a pocket diary and scribbled down the registration number of the red sports car. She tore off the page and handed it to Jones.

"I shouldn't ask this because it's personal rather than business, but do you think you could check out this motor registration for me? If I can get this guy's address, I'd like to look him up. It shouldn't be too difficult. It's a red sports convertible."

Jones glanced at the registration number idly and put the paper in his pocket. "No problem. I should be able to track down the owner in a couple of hours. I'm heading back to the office now. Want to share a taxi?"

When the taxi stopped at the American Embassy in Grosvenor Square, Jonathan asked her: "If you are free this evening, Margaret, I thought we might have a spot of dinner."

"Should be good, " she replied. "Why don't you come around to my place in St John's Wood and I'll fix us something. Around eight OK?"

He look a note of her address and, as she watched from the Embassy steps as the taxi turned towards Millbank, she was thinking: let's see if this sexy British gentleman spy can live up to his James Bond looks, Maggie!"

LONDON

Same day

Carter was lying on the bed in his room at the Hilton. He had taken off his jacket, shoes and tie and was reading a copy of *Newsweek* when there was a knock on the door, soft and tentative.

"It's open," he called, not moving from his position. Tara Barry walked in, closed the door behind her and stood with her back to it.

"Sit down, relax," he said, letting the magazine fall to the floor. She didn't move. For a few moments neither spoke. Again, he was struck by her resemblance to Nicole Bouchier and he had a brief mental flash of the other hotel room, in Paris, Nicole standing nude in front of him, her body showing an all-over tan, her pubis shaved, moving towards him.

Then Tara began hesitantly. "I'm afraid we got off on the wrong foot," she said.

Carter nodded. " A lot more than that, I'd say."

She held out her palms, yielding the point and took a few steps over to the bed, near enough that he caught a whiff of perfume. "Whatever you think about me, I deserve it. I was unpardonably rude to you and I want you to forgive me. Put it down to the fact that this is a big responsibility I've been given, the biggest job I've ever had and I don't want it to fail. I suppose I'm a bit of a control freak but I wasn't quite sure how to deal with someone like you, a freelance agent. I just pressed the wrong buttons. Can we put it behind us and start afresh. Please?"

She was evidently aware of her attractiveness and was used to getting her way. Her tone was sincere and serious and yet there was a hint of the seductress. She probably wasn't aware of it at a conscious level, thought Carter.

"You came at me with an attitude but I don't care about that," he said flatly. "It's bigger than that. Since I first got involved with the IRA, I've had one screw-up after another. The first approach was straight out of a bad made-for-TV movie. A job was set up, then it was called off. The IRA guys I met were more interested in killing each other than the enemy. Against my better judgement, I agreed to look over a job here in Britain. I was sent to Paris and asked to do something else. It seems that your people in Paris are paranoid about security to a crazy extent and yet they've got British agents on their asses. I finally get to London and, instead of dealing with a guy I know, who's halfway OK, I find the operation's being run by a prima donna. Everyone tells me that the IRA is the best outfit of its kind in the world but, you know, I don't see it."

She went over to a chair against the wall and sat stiffly, primly, her legs together, her arms folded.

"I haven't been briefed on the background to our contacts with you, and there's no reason why I should." She talked and looked more businesslike as though she had realised that this was the best way with Carter. "So when you talk about screw-ups, I can't offer an argument. But few organisations are even close to being perfect, Carter. You were in the US army, supposedly the best there is in the world and I'll bet you didn't find it to be a model of efficiency. 'Snafu' that's an American military expression for 'situation normal, all fucked up', isn't it?"

"You got that right," said Carter, amused. "My man's army was only one of the most fucked up in the history of warfare. And we lost that war, remember?"

"But we are winning our war," said Tara firmly.

"So they tell me," he acknowledged. Now that she was all business, he found himself wondering, paradoxically, how she would look with her clothes off. He changed tack. "Why are you in the IRA?" he asked.

She looked startled, then said with sarcasm: "Do you mean, what's a beautiful thing like me doing in an ugly job like this?"

"No. I mean why are you in the IRA?"

She seemed to draw into herself for a moment, then inclined her head. "I'll tell you. And I don't want to sound patronising but I'm not sure if you can fully understand. You're not from Northern Ireland. We are mostly young people in the IRA, Protestant as well as Catholic in spite of what you may hear."

She stopped as though expecting an objection. When he said nothing, she went on.

"We all want peace, not war. We are ready to give up anything, everything, except the right to the freedom and independence of our 32-county Irish Republic, to gain this peace. We want to live in the same harmony with Britain as we do with all the other nations of the world. Consistently, down through the years, the ordinary English people, in many opinion polls, agree with us, but the government, the establishment, the military and secret service machines refuse to listen to us, or even to their own people.

"They still want to hold onto six of our 32 counties against the wishes of the great majority of the Irish people at home and abroad. We are willing to give the Unionists, Loyalists, Orangemen, Protestants, or whatever they want to call themselves, equal rights with everyone else in the new Republic. But the history of Ireland and of almost every country in the world once occupied by Britain, shows they have never left without violence, or the threat of violence."

She was leaning towards him intently, face flushed, speaking rapidly, gesturing with her hands to emphasise her argument.

"So here we are, in the middle of another chapter of the same old story which will go on until the inevitable happy ending, when the last British soldier leaves the island of Ireland forever, and all the people can determine their own destiny through the ballot box in a 32-county Irish Republic. That's how it's been for hundreds of years. The objective remains the same in my generation and in every generation to come until victory is achieved."

She looked at him, defiant. "Can you really understand this?"

"In a way," said Carter. He had heard much the same thing before, from other people in other countries. Always, they thought that they were making a reasoned and logical case for their cause. Always, they sounded like zealots, reciting by rote from someone else's speeches and pamphlets. He was disappointed with her and annoyed with himself for having asked the question. What the hell had he been hoping to hear? A persuasive argument that would strip away his layers of cynicism and make him a believer in her cause? A personal set of reasons that would help him to understand and get some sort of rapport with her? He hadn't really expected any such things, so why bother asking? Maybe he was just politely giving her an opportunity to talk about her zeal and distract her from the feelings of humiliation that she had been forced to come here to plead with him to continue working for them.

Tara could see that she had made no impression on him. He sees me as one of those naïve, airhead young things spouting mindless propaganda, she thought. Well, the hell with him if he had been expecting her to bare her soul. How would he react if she said: "I joined the IRA to get revenge. My only brother aged sixteen was shot in the back by soldiers from a British parachute regiment on Bloody Sunday, 1972 in Derry, within sight of his own doorstep, 'trying to escape', as they put it. Michael, who loved people and animals and had never cared for politics, much less handled a gun in his life. I want revenge for my sister who was raped and beaten before my eyes by British squaddies, as I hid in a dark corner of the bedroom. This was a nationalist family's life in Belfast. Almost every week, the soldiers had returned, sometimes accompanied by the police, wrecking their little home, even taking up the floorboards, smashing everything in sight. I want them to pay for what they did to my family and my friends and me." She could imagine his polite feigned expressions of sympathy masking his indifference.

She remembered why she had come here and let the anger and bitterness seep out of her. There was one thing she had to say to him. She deliberately softened her voice: "I'm one of many people who believe completely in what we're fighting for. For almost all of them, there has been a high cost. Some are in jail and some are dead. To be truthful, when I was first told about you, when I heard that you were working strictly for money, I disliked the thought of having to work with you."

"And?" asked Carter.

She looked at him steadily. "It takes all kinds to win a war. You don't have to be committed to what we're trying to achieve. Just so you help us get results. I've been told that you are the best at what you do. I need you we need you. I can promise you that there will be no more difficulties."

Carter got off the bed and began putting on his shoes. "Right. We start all over, Tara. Now, tell me about this job."

She didn't try to hide her relief. She grinned at him. "I shall lay the whole thing out for you very shortly. I know you think we're paranoid about security but I don't want to go into specifics here." She took a Yale key out of her pocket and tossed it on the bed. "We've got a very secure place not too far from here. It's number 10 St Christopher's Place, a small, almost hidden alleyway off the very busy Oxford Street. You'll have no trouble finding it, just stand at the Bond Street tube entrance and look around you. It's, what, just after four now. Can you meet me there at seven o'clock? Kieran will be along, too. I need to contact our intelligence people in about an hour to see if there are any developments. Then we can go over the whole plan together."

"I'll be there," said Carter, pocketing the key.

"See you, then." She stood awkwardly for a moment, as though there was something else she wanted to say. If I ask her to go to bed with me, thought Carter, she could start pulling off her clothes or she could come clawing at my face. I don't have the measure of her at all.

As though she had read his thoughts, she gave a Mona Lisa smile, then turned and left the room.

* * *

136

Carter took a cab to Marble Arch and got there shortly after six. He walked through the crowds of one of the busiest shopping streets in Europe, with its mixture of elegant department stores and restaurants, alongside huckster shops selling cheap souvenirs and quick service franchise cafes. Near the Bond Street junction, he found that there were a number of underground entrances. He crossed the street at a peculiar-looking bar called the Pig in the Pound and saw a tiny sign on a lamp post pointing to St Christopher's Place. He went down a very narrow passage, and found himself in a little oasis in the heart of London, with cafes, boutiques, antique shops, restaurants, all hidden from the thousands bustling in nearby Oxford Street.

There were apartments over some of the tiny shops and business premises and he soon found number 10, a green door with neither bell nor knocker and nothing to indicate who, if anyone, lived there.

He retraced his steps back to Oxford Street, went down the steps of the Underground and studied a wall map of the train lines. He watched people buy tickets at a booking office and at automated machines. He came back into Oxford Street and walked through St Christopher's Place, checking its various entrance and exit points. He browsed some of the shops and had a coffee in one of the cafes.

It was a good location for the business, busy enough that a person visiting number 10 was unlikely to attract notice. He hadn't been able to find a rear entrance to the place but otherwise it was well suited for a quick escape if it ever came to that. There were numerous side streets that would take one within seconds onto a crowded street, with passing cabs and an underground station. Most important, number 10 was not under observation. There were no casual watchers, no parked utility vehicles, no shaded windows opposite the apartment, nothing that indicated surveillance.

At five minutes to seven, Kieran Delaney strolled into St Christopher's Place. His pace was unhurried. He paused to look into shop windows, stopped to examine a menu in the window of an upmarket Japanese restaurant, shook his head at either the food or the prices. Unobtrusively, he was giving the area a careful scrutiny before going near the door of number 10. He saw Carter but ignored him for a minute and then walked over to him. Delaney was his usual ebullient self. He made no comment on what had occurred earlier in the day except to say ironically: "As you know, Martin, the struggle for ould Ireland's freedom takes place in a bed of manure and thorns." He smiled impishly. "Mind you, with a bit of luck, you usually find a fine scented rose at the end of the thorns."

"I'll keep my nose clean in case I miss it," said Carter.

Delaney, grinning, took out a key, opened the green door and they both went in. The door was obviously heavier than it looked because the sounds of London abruptly vanished and the house was silent. They were in a short hallway leading to a flight of bare wooden stairs. The place had a neglected look and a dry, musty smell and was obviously unoccupied. The faded wallpaper was damp and peeling and there were bare wires on the ceiling where the lights had been removed.

Delaney looked around him happily then climbed the stairs, saying to Carter who followed: "You'd never believe just how much money this place is worth. Millions, I'm told. Bought by a man from county Kerry in the south of Ireland five years ago. He came over to England as a teenager and started as a helper on a dustbin cart. Then he bought a second-hand van for fifty quid and started buying and selling the fixtures and fittings from buildings that were being demolished. After that, he got into property development and he's one of the wealthiest Irishmen alive. Married an actress who's a third of his age and is reportedly barely able to keep up with her sexual demands."

At the only door on the first floor landing, Delaney turned to Carter. "This place is a fine box of tricks. You're going to like this."

He unlocked the door and led Carter into an apartment. It was empty of furniture and, like the rest of the house, down to bare boards on the floor. Someone had made a half-hearted attempt to strip the wallpaper and much of the wall showed the dull blue paintwork. What looked like a fireplace had been removed, leaving a gaping hole. Delaney walked across the room, Carter behind him, through an entranceway, along a narrow corridor with small rooms on either side, to a door at the end. He unlocked this and they were on the first floor landing of the next house.

"There's more." Delaney happily walked over to a door opposite, unlocked it and waved Carter in. They were in an apartment room that was as bare and empty as the one they had just passed through. There were several piles of yellowing newspapers on the floor in the centre of the room. Again, the fireplace and any fittings had been taken away. They walked through the apartment, to the door at the end and once more were on the landing, facing another door.

"End of the line," said Delaney, opening it and, with a mock bow, ushering Carter into a small sitting room.

Inside, it was almost a surprise to see carpet on the floor, an intact fireplace, furniture. There was a heavy oak table, several kitchen chairs, a three-piece suite with a blue floral design, a battered filing cabinet and, on a smaller table, a large and new television set and a transistor radio. Two Renoir reproductions in cheap plastic frames hung on the walls. It all looked like it had been bought sight unseen from a warehouse. Carter checked the rest of the apartment. There was a toilet with a washhand basin and shower, a small kitchen, with a gas cooker and a humming fridge that was empty, and a bedroom that had a made-up double bed, a battered bedside table and a built-in wardrobe press, doors open and showing an assortment of plastic and metal hangers. Everything in the apartment was cheap but clean.

In the main room, Delaney was sprawled on one of the sofas, his feet on the table. Carter went over to the window and looked through the net curtains without moving them. Directly below him, across the street, was the café where he had sat drinking a coffee a few minutes earlier.

"You see the beauty of it," said Delaney. "We're in number 8 but no-one has seen us come in. Anyone watching the place will have their attention on number 10, two doors down. They won't know what's happening. We walk in and disappear, just like something in Sherlock Holmes. You noticed the one key opens everything? Anyone making a raid on the place will have to break down the door of number 10 which, incidentally, has been reinforced and will trip a number of alarms getting here, if they think of looking here, and they'll find us long gone."

"Back exit?" asked Carter.

"Yeah, but not obvious. You climb out the window in the bedroom onto the roof of a shed, drop to the ground, go into the shed and there's a door, always unlocked, that gets you through the hallway of a house across the way and out through the front door."

"It's good," conceded Carter.

"What do you mean good. It's a bloody marvellous example of the ingenuity, painstaking attention to detail and appalling sense of interior design that has the IRA feared throughout the British Empire."

Carter threw himself down on one of the other sofas. "All this is courtesy of your sex-crazed property developer?"

"Um, sort of. You know, I think he's forgotten he owns this place. Owns the whole street as a matter of fact. Had plans to pull it all down and build a great big office block. The local planning office looked at his plans and told him to piss off. So he put it on hold. Meantime, the property value of the place goes up and up. Plus he got all the fireplaces and fittings to keep him happy, flogged them for thousands of pounds or so, I'd imagine. Anyway, he hired an agent to look after it who farmed out the job to a friend of ours."

He glanced at his watch. "Where's the royal Tara, I wonder. She's running late."

"Royal?" queried Carter.

"Tara, don't you know, is named after the hill of Tara, once the great palace of the ancient high kings of Ireland. You really ought to take a greater interest in the traditions and heritage of your clients, Martin."

"You're right. Just knowing she's named for a hill in Ireland makes me feel on top of things already."

The transistor radio came alive with a low buzzing sound.

"Talk of the devil and she doth appear," said Delaney. "This, by the way, is our alarm system. Sounds off as soon as anything bigger than a rat moves anywhere between here and the front door of number 10." He went over and pressed a button on the radio and the noise cut off.

A minute later, Tara came through the door. A second person was with her, a thin sallow young man with untidy black hair and a thick moustache. He wore a black anorak and faded brown corduroy pants and he had a battered brown document case under his arm. The bottoms of his pants were tucked into his socks and he wore bicycle clips. MacAnamy greeted Delaney with a raised thumb.

Tara made the introduction: "Eoin MacAnamy, this is Martin Carter and vice versa." She didn't elaborate. She was dressed in a bright blue tracksuit, a red sweatband and Nike runners and carried two filled shopping bags. She looked like she'd just had a shower.

"Sorry I'm late," she said, sounding breathless. "I picked up some beer, tea, coffee, things like that. Also, I've come straight from the gym, as you've probably noticed."

"Healthy mind, healthy body. It's important to make the choice," said Delaney cheerfully, blowing her a kiss.

She laughed. "Wasn't it Nietzsche who said, 'Men never make passes at girls with fat asses'?"

"Nietzsche? Isn't he the chap who drew the Superman comics?"

"You're probably thinking about Schopenhauer," she responded, taking a six-pack of Budweiser out of one of the bags and putting it on the table. "This OK for everyone?"

"Better than OK," said Delaney, opening a can. "Not Schopenhauer. He did Batman."

Carter waited for them to stop clowning and get down to business. MacAnamy also looked impatient as he sat down at the table and took out a pack of cigarettes. "Anyone mind if I smoke?"

Tara frowned. "Well, actually-"

He had already struck a match and lit up.

"Rhetorical question," she said.

"We ready to start?" he asked.

They all sat around the table. Tara led off.

"The four of us constitute what amounts to an ad hoc special unit of the IRA. It's the first time that a unit like this has been brought together. Three of us belong to different active units, and our coming together is in itself a pretty flagrant breach of standard security. Martin is not even a member of the organisation. Only the Army Council at the very top of the organisation in Belfast know that we exist as a group and know what we intend to do. That tells you just how important this job is. It may well be the most important operation ever carried out by the IRA in terms of the damage and humiliation it will cause to the British. It will show them that nothing is safe and that they had better recognise the reality of cutting their losses and sitting down around a table with us.

"Our target is the Channel Tunnel."

She paused dramatically.

"Judas Iscariot Murphy!" exclaimed Delaney, leaning forward and staring at her.

Carter swore to himself. Since arriving in London, it had occurred to him that the IRA was planning something outlandishly bizarre like blowing up the British Parliament or kidnapping the Queen. The Channel Tunnel fitted right into that category. He had a quick mental flash from some TV disaster movie. Train rushing through a tunnel. Passenger compartment packed with happy families. Cut to train driver, goggle-eyed. Enormous wave of water appears in tunnel, smashes into train. Engine, carriages swept of the tracks, engulfed. BRUCE WILLIS MEETS HARRISON FORD! What a load of crap!

The IRA obviously assumed he was a homicidal maniac, ready to kill anyone for the money. He would hear them out before walking. Expressionless, he opened a can of beer.

MacAnamy obviously knew about the job because he showed no surprise and was gazing at the lengthening ash on his cigarette. But Delaney was sitting bolt upright, looking from one to the other with an incredulous expression. Finally he said quietly but with an edge in his voice, "I'm so sorry, Tara m'dear, but for one extraordinary moment I thought you said the Channel Tunnel."

She had a faint smile. "Yes, but it's not what you think. The target is not the tunnel itself but something else that's down there. Don't worry, Kieran," she chided. "You know our policy is to avoid civilian casualties."

Carter remembered newspaper photographs showing bodies in the street after IRA car bombs in Northern Ireland and Britain. "That's something new, right?" he asked her.

Immediately she got angry. "We did what had to be done to wake the public out of their indifference and make them aware that we had just grievances and demands and we weren't going to stop until they were met. We're a small people's army. We don't have the resources to take the British armed forces head on. The British understand all about killing civilians, they've been at it in Ireland for hundreds of years. Their Paratroops massacred the innocent in Derry, their agents planted bombs that wiped out dozens of people in Dublin. Remember, we're talking about the same people who first invented concentration camps during the Boer War to"

Carter cut her off. "Forget that. I don't care about the morality of war. It was a straight question, OK? Why switch to a policy of no civilian casualties?"

Tara looked flushed and embarrassed at her outburst. She dropped her tone but still sounded defiant.

"It's a reasonable question. Earlier this year, the Army Council made the decision that all future operations would be organised so as to avoid non-combatant casualties. The reason, frankly, was tactical. We have won the war against the British in that they know we cannot be beaten no matter what they do. Now the British government must declare a truce and formally open negotiations about when and how they hand back the six counties of Ireland to the Irish people. As always, they are stubborn about recognising reality even when it is staring them in the face. Our operations are designed to force their decision."

She was speaking quietly now but still sounded like she was quoting from something. "We are giving the British an opportunity to save face. Civilian casualties just give them an excuse to make propaganda about so-called atrocities. And their own propaganda then makes it difficult for them to publicly do a U-turn and announce that they are prepared to talk to us. Personally, I think we're being too clever. The British government and the British people have already seen the writing on the wall where Ireland is concerned. They can talk about atrocities as much as they want but they'll be coming to talk to us pretty soon, no matter what happens."

"Aye," said MacAnamy with a sigh that could have meant anything. He unzipped his document case, took out a large sheet of paper and unfolded it on the table. Carter saw what looked like a random, confusing mass of overlapping lines drawn in multicoloured pen, something a child would do.

"Sorry about the messy look," said MacAnamy. "It's a basic precaution. I don't go around London with what is clearly and obviously a sketch of the Channel Tunnel. Look hard at the red lines only and ignore everything else."

Carter stared at the multiplicity of lines, concentrating on the red and he began to see it. It wasn't a detailed blueprint, more a rough outline of the tunnel, with its main tracks and service areas.

Tara looked relieved that they were getting down to specifics. She leaned over the table and began talking, now cool and all professional.

"Early this year, the British made an addition to the Channel Tunnel that wasn't in the original plans. They built a large underground chamber just off the main tunnel. It has just been equipped with the latest computer, telecommunications and electronic equipment. It's not my area of expertise, but I understand that the hardware and software is the best and most expensive available and that the cost of all this technology is close to one billion pounds."

Delaney whistled softly and happily.

She went on, "It is a multipurpose security communications centre. For example, it will take over the co-ordination of all surveillance of Ireland North and South by the security forces, with a direct feed into about fifty surveillance posts around the country. In addition, it will also be used to get improved intelligence on a whole range of things, drugs, money laundering, international espionage and what not. But its primary purpose, where most of the money and effort has been spent, is to provide a communications mirror of financial transactions in the City of London. Our last attack on the City destroyed and disrupted the flow of information to the City to such an extent that it came awfully close to eliminating London as a world centre of finance. They don't want that to happen again. They know that we know that the City is where we can do most damage to the Brits. If we strike again, they want to be ready with a back-up system that keeps the financial information flowing without a break.

She snorted. "What they've done, in fact, is to give us an even bigger target."

"Don't the French know about this?" asked Delaney. "Surely the Tunnel is a joint venture."

Tara shrugged. "I'm sure they were told something by the British but I imagine it was some sort of cover story. Anyway, it's not an issue. Here's the important thing. We found out about this new underground centre even before they started building it. And, during its construction, we were able to smuggle in enough explosives to completely destroy the place. They're planted under the floor and within the walls and, right now, they're ready to be set off by a remote electronic signal. The explosive force will reduce every piece of equipment in the centre to smithereens and collapse the entire chamber. They can kiss their billion goodbye."

Carter frowned. "The security people must have been asleep on the job and are still out. They let the stuff in and they still haven't detected it. Jesus! What is it, Semtex?"

Tara nodded. "It's a Semtex derivative, something new, custom-made for us. We've used it only once before and it's more powerful and harder to detect than anything we've ever had.

"The centre is set back about one hundred yards from the main tunnel-92 yards to be precise. Initially, it looked easy. One of our people would detonate the bomb from a train at the moment it passed the entrance to the centre. Too easy, right? As it's turned out, we hit a few problems."

"There are no such things as opportunities, only problems," intoned Delaney.

"Shut up, Kieran," said Tara without rancour. Her emotionalism was gone for the present and she was in business mode. "First problem was the door opening from the centre into the tunnel. This is not a main entrance. It's really an emergency exit door that leads from the centre itself to the small spur that, in turn, gives access to the main Channel Tunnel. The real entrance to the centre is above ground, a two-story converted factory. Staff go in through the main gates, into the factory, pass through security and use elevators to get down. We can forget about getting in that way. It has very heavy security and they can call in a lot of reinforcements within minutes. It's no go.

"That's why we've concentrated on this back door. It's a massive steel affair that can only be opened electronically from above ground. No matter, we don't need to get in. We do, however, need to get close to it, fifty yards line of sight so as to trigger the bomb."

She leaned forward and tapped the map. "Here's the snag. The location of the door was changed. In the original plans, it opened directly into the spur that ran in a straight line to the main Tunnel. In other words, if there was enough light, the door would be visible from the Tunnel. Somewhere along the way, they did a redesign, changing the spur from a straight line to a curve. This meant that the position of the door was shifted about thirty yards to the right in relation to the Tunnel. See?"

Her finger traced along the thick red lines of the main Tunnel shaft, then moved along a single, thinner red line of the spur that arched to the right before ending at a red X.

"We understand that the change was made simply to place the door out of sight of the Tunnel. An added security precaution, no more. All anyone can see now, is a little black tunnel that turns a corner, and looks like a shunting siding or something. But it gave us a lot of planning headaches. We put together a dozen different plans for getting our people into that little spur so that they could get within sight of the door and detonate. In every case, there was a high risk of failure and a strong likelihood that our people would be captured or killed. We're not Islamic so we don't have suicide volunteers."

She got up and went over to the filing cabinet, pulled open the top drawer and took out a small corrugated cardboard box, the size of a shoebox. She brought it over to the table and opened it. Inside were what looked like two packs of Marlboro cigarettes. Carter supposed that one of them was the pack he had brought from Paris. He was mildly surprised. He had supposed that he was the only courier.

"We finally hit on the answer." There was undisguised pride, even triumph, in her voice. "You'll recognise the packs, Martin. One was yours. They are miracles of miniaturisation, by far the most sophisticated pieces of ordnance we have ever used in an operation. We have been calling them beam benders, but in fact they are MMDS microwave amplifiers. Essentially, they extend the range of an electronic signal by relaying it along a line of sight."

Delaney took one of the packs from the box and hefted it in his hand. "Amazing. First thing I noticed today when I picked up Martin's pack is that its weight is just about right for a cigarette pack." He looked at it and laughed. "It gets to me every time I see the warning on the sides about 'serious risks to your health'. Talk about unconscious irony."

At a sharp glance from Tara, he sobered up. "Sorry. Serious business. So, the idea is we somehow plant these beam benders or whatever they are in a line from the entrance to the spur right up to the door of the centre, then detonate from a passing train, right?"

Tara shook her head. "The train is out for two reasons. First, we're no longer talking about a mobile-phone-sized trigger. The electronic signal needed to interact with the MMDS relays is the size of a briefcase. It needs to be quite powerful. And it requires approximately five minutes to fully power up, lock and hold the nearest relay, send a stream of data that bounce along the other relays and retain enough strength to get through the door of the centre and set off the explosives. And that can't be done from a train flashing past."

"What then?" asked Carter. "Whatever the power, it won't be enough to send the signal from above ground down to the tunnel and into the spur." He tried not to show his impatience with Tara's drawn-out explanation, her desire to go through all the problems and difficulties before proudly showing how they were resolved. He didn't give a damn about all that. He was still waiting for the plan.

"You're right," she agreed. "We can't do it overground. This is where the French are going to help us, believe it or not. Under the Channel Tunnel deal, the French have jurisdiction over a small part of Folkestone. It's just a small building, surrounded by importers' offices and warehouses. It's a nondescript place, just two offices and facilities. There is a staff of five French customs officers on a rota, with three on duty at any given time. Mostly, they spend their time on paperwork."

Again, the irritating, teasing pause before she went on.

"Inside that building, there is another entrance into the Channel Tunnel. A locked-off area has a flight of steps that goes straight down to an emergency exit. The Tunnel is full of these emergency ways out but this one is the most accessible for our purposes. And it's also in direct line of the spur tunnel that leads to the centre."

"And it's guarded by a couple of French customs penpushers?" asked Delaney, dubiously. "Are they armed?"

She shook her head. "They don't have to be. The door to the Tunnel is one-way only. It can be opened remotely from a safety control centre in the Tunnel and manually from the Tunnel itself. It can't be opened from the customs office and it's too powerful to blow. But we don't need the door open. All we need to do is get right up beside the door with our transmitter, switch it on, wait five or six minutes ten maximum and get out."

She sat back and looked expectantly at Carter and Delaney, inviting them to put it together now that she had laid out all the pieces. MacAnamy was looking across at the window, seemed to be preoccupied with his own thoughts. Carter had most of the plan figured but waited for Tara to lay it out.

After a few moments, she went on, "The operation has two parts planting the relays and later transmitting the signal. The first part is where you come in, Martin. Every Wednesday afternoon, the Foreign Press Association in London organises a group tour of the Channel Tunnel for visiting journalists. By good fortune, the tour actually gets close to the spur entrance. You sign in as an American journalist and make the trip. Once you're down there, you slip away from the group and place the relays inside the spur."

She waited for him to say something and, when he just nodded, she went on. "The second part takes place the next day. We have a group of four reliable volunteers on stand-by. They don't know the target but they know what to do and we've simulated the layout of the customs offices and they've been rehearsing for the past week. They arrive in one car, take out the customs officers, tie them up and make sure that we have access to the stairway. When they give the all-clear, Martin and Kieran, who have been waiting in another car, take the transmitter in, go down to the Tunnel door and trigger the explosives. It's in and out in twenty minutes."

"Now give us the rest," said Carter. "You want to go this week."

Her eyes widened. MacAnamy pulled out of his reverie and looked at him thoughtfully.

"How did you know that?" she asked, surprised.

"It's obvious. If you've been rehearsing your guys for a week, it means they're ready to go now."

She made a grimace. "Yes, it has to be this week. We've had information that the centre is being staffed up this weekend and will be fully operational next week. There will be seventy-five people in there. Thursday of this week is the very last day when we can count on the place to have all the equipment but no personnel."

She went on quickly to pre-empt any interruption. "I know the time sounds short, but that's because you're just coming into the picture now. We've been working on this operation for six months. All the planning is done. Yes, we've moved up our schedule but that doesn't affect anything. Maybe it's for the best that we do it now before the security people do something that sends us back to the drawing board."

Delaney slowly nodded. "Makes sense. Besides, any one of these days, they could accidentally find the explosives."

He looked questioningly at Carter who asked, "Why me?"

Tara was thrown by the question. She had been expecting vociferous objections from Carter to the timing. "How do you mean?" she asked.

"It's another straight question. You want me to pose as a reporter and drop a couple of items in a tunnel. Then you want me to go down a stairway and switch on a transmitter. There's no expertise in that. You've got fifty guys who've done tougher jobs. Instead, you bring me over from the States like I'm John Rambo and you're paying me big money to do it. Why?"

"There are a few reasons," replied Tara. "The money you're getting is neither here nor there when we put it against the cost to the British when this operation comes off. There are some other things. First, there's the timing. We have only one shot at this and we need the best person we can get. That's you. Nothing should go wrong but, if it does, you've got the experience to think on your feet. Second, there's the press tour. We're not going to risk sending an Irish person. Just the name might get security people checking. You're an American with no Irish connections and nobody is going to question your credentials."

Delaney broke in, "Plus you look like a respectable journalist. You remind me of that news announcer I saw on TV in New York, Tom Brokaw. You even sound like him. You'll pass easily. Of course, ideally we would have preferred if you were a black American. Obviously no Irish connections."

It was the first time Carter had ever been told he resembled Tom Brokaw and figured it was something only Delaney saw. "What do we know about this press tour? What's the security like? Are they searched, patted down, walked through an x-ray screen?"

MacAnamy said, "Nothing like that. We got someone on the tour two weeks ago. He was Irish, but raised in England, no accent like me." He smiled briefly. "And he's a bona fide journalist. We had him as a Brit now living in America, over freelancing for *US News & World Report*. Naturally, we can't use him again. I can go over his report with you. Security is gearing up but it's still minimal. Like, they have cameras all over the place but most of them are not connected up yet."

He spoke with a heavy North of Ireland accent, so that Carter had mentally to scan what he said a couple of times before getting the sense of it. He was the IRA's intelligence man for the operation, Carter realised, and spoke only when his end of things came up. He asked him, "How good is your information on this?"

MacAnamy thought for a few moments, then said: "It could be better that's true of everything, I suppose but it's a lot more than we usually have for a big operation. We had someone with the tunnelling crew, of course, to place the explosives. He's long gone by now but he gave us a lot of useful material on the chamber. We had a contact among the engineering inspectors for the Tunnel proper and again we got good background, blueprints, that sort of thing. Right now, we have a contact on the Eurotunnel security staff. And we also have a line into British Intelligence in Cheltenham. Unfortunately, these are low-level people. Sometimes, when important decisions are made, they're not in the loop or they get the information late or they get just part of it."

He shrugged dismissively. "We always want more intelligence than we get. But we've been getting some hard information lately. We've learned that they've advanced the schedule for moving into the centre. We also know why they're doing this. It seems that we've been more effective than we expected with a disinformation campaign we've been running in Europe. MI5 is convinced that we're about to launch another strike on the City real soon." He gave a short, barking laugh that had little humour in it.

There was a pause, then Tara asked Carter, "Well, Martin, are you happy with the plan, despite the tight deadline?" She tried to sound light but it came out edgy.

The room was getting uncomfortably hot and MacAnamy's cigarette smoke hung in the air. Carter stood and removed his jacket before replying. "I don't know that you have a plan, yet," he said bluntly. "Timing's not a worry. The reconnaissance bit is done. We got a couple days. So what? If we had a month, we'd just sit around playing poker. We know that we do two things put the amplifiers in place, then trigger the explosives. The press trip and the customs office sound good. Now we need to get the details right?"

"Which details did you have in mind?" asked Tara warily.

Carter said, "The numbers are wrong. You'll want two people on the press trip, not one. I don't go down there with the hope that I can somehow slip away from the rest of the reporters. Suppose I can't? No, I'll need a well-planned diversion, something small that distracts people but doesn't get the security guys worked up. That means someone goes with me."

"We can't get anyone at this short notice," objected Tara.

"Sure you can. Kieran goes with me."

Delaney started, then smiled broadly. "And why not. Bloody good idea."

Tara shook her head and said obstinately, "We're not going to risk an Irish person, remember?"

"Are you calling me a damn Paddy?" demanded Kieran. He had changed his voice only slightly, was speaking with a lazy drawl. Any hint of an Irish accent was gone and he sounded maybe like an Australian who had lived a long time in England. "I happen to be Charles De Laney, London correspondent for the Pittsburgh-based *Project Equipment News*. As it happens, Charles is my middle name and I am an occasional writer for the selfsame magazine. I'll have all the necessary credentials by this time tomorrow."

Carter spoke before Tara could jump in again. "Good, if you can hold that accent. The other thing is the customs office. We don't need your special team for three unarmed clerks. We go with two, me and Kieran, same as the press trip. We go in, tie up the clerks, one of us watches them, the other sets the bomb. That's all it takes."

Tara was starting to get upset again. "No, no. We can't change the plan at this late hour, it's too risky. Besides the Army Council has approved it as it is."

"You make them sound like General Motors, everything going up to a plans board for the nod," said Carter. "They just want the job done right. Two is all it's going to take."

He could see that Tara was getting upset at losing control. Questioning the plan was questioning her role as the team leader. Well, he couldn't do anything about it. He wasn't walking into something he didn't like just to keep her happy.

She was saying nothing but shaking her head vigorously. MacAnamy intervened. "What else?" he asked Carter, indicating that he had bought the point about dropping the special team. Tara looked sharply at him but said nothing.

"We go through everything now. I've a lot of questions. I want to be clear about everything we know, everything we don't know. I want to see it step by step until we're all satisfied that we've put the best plan together."

Kieran said, "And if we're all happy, that means you're in?"

"Yes. That means I'm in," confirmed Carter. "Now, let's get down to it."

* * *

They broke up two hours later, leaving one by one at ten-minute intervals. Carter left first, figuring that they would want to talk about him, compare notes. The smoke-filled room had given him a slight headache so he decided to walk back to the hotel. It was still a bright evening and warm. He strolled down Oxford Street, now much less crowded on the pavements, though the traffic was still heavy with red double-deck buses and black taxis seeming to make up most of it. Twice he detoured down a side street and paralleled Oxford Street before coming back onto it. He was satisfied that he wasn't under observation.

He thought about the job. He was feeling good about it, it was finally starting to get the adrenaline going. All things considered, it was nothing like as difficult as he had been expecting. Blowing up part of the famous Channel Tunnel would be one of the all-time top terrorist actions but, as far as he was concerned, the operation was one of the least complex jobs he had ever taken, which made him suspicious in view of the money he had been offered. He had overstated things back there when he had said that there was no plan. Apart from a few changes here and there, some fine-tuning, some specifics that needed to be worked out, the plan was actually very well put together. MacAnamy's work mostly, he guessed. He had a lot of respect for the man, liked his unemotional approach, his refusal to become involved in anything that didn't directly affect his intelligence function. And he was happy to work with Delaney. Sure, he liked to play the fool and could be a pain in the ass if you weren't in the mood for it. But he would be solid and reliable enough for the job.

He reached Marble Arch and turned down Park Lane. He thought of crossing over and taking a stroll in Hyde Park but didn't. He thought about Tara Barry and was glad that her team leader role kept her out of the action. Otherwise, he would have dropped out. He no longer thought about her sexually. Tara was insecure, quick to feel threatened whenever she felt her authority was being questioned. She was one of those girls who knew that she was highly attractive to men and wavered between trying to use the fact and resenting it as a weakness. If a man whistled at her in the street, she might smile and flash a bit of leg. Or she might drop him with a sudden kick to the groin. But it went beyond that. Tara was volatile, unpredictable. She had the capability of turning a good operation sour without either intention or effort.

He put her out of his mind and went back to the key question: why did they want him for this job? The fact was, he had never previously been given anything approaching this payout, and for such comparatively little effort. He already had $400,000 in his account and, so far, he had done nothing for it. OK, half the money was a cancellation fee. And maybe the IRA wasn't convinced that he'd hand over the other half, with good reason. It was a fine point as to whether it was ever their money and he was not sure that he would have given it to them. So, it wasn't really costing them to hire him, and it solved what might have become an awkward issue.

But, that aside, the IRA didn't need *him*. They could get what they wanted from their own ranks, despite what they said, or could hire an acceptable free-lancer for a tenth of what they were paying him. The reasons they gave were spurious. It was revealing how they couldn't send an Irish person on the press trip to the Tunnel, then agreed that Delaney could go with almost no argument.

He saw the Hilton up ahead and slowed down to think it through. What had he got that made him so important in the eyes of the IRA? Basically, he was a professional hitman. He was also, they believed, an explosives expert, though they seemed to have an idea that he was some sort of Semtex genius, which he certainly was not. But neither of these skills were on call here.

151

Come to think of it, the IRA really knew very little about him. Somehow, they had got hold of an old CIA file, but they had taken the top layer of his cover story at face value, had swallowed it whole. Some Irish-American ex-CIA clerk, most likely, had conned Sean Quinn out of a fat payment by giving him dud information. Stuff so out of date that Quinn assumed that Carter was still on the Langley payroll.

The thought stopped him cold. Yes, that was it. Quinn had believed that Carter was a CIA agent. It didn't really matter to him except that CIA was an OK brand name that validated the expertise he was buying. Quinn would have been equally satisfied with a KGB or Mossad agent or even a proven hitman from the mob. But Quinn had obviously told his torturers that Carter was CIA and this had opened up interesting horizons for the IRA.

Blowing up Britain's spanking new multimillion-pound intelligence centre before it even commenced business was a helluva coup. Having a bona fide member of the American Central Intelligence Agency on the team was marzipan on the cake. There were a dozen ways for them to leverage it. Discreet blackmail of the US Government: silence about the CIA connection in exchange for putting extra pressure on the British. Or, getting the word to the British Government and have their confidence utterly undermined at the thought that the US Government was covertly assisting the IRA. Or well, there was a dazzling range of opportunities for playing what they believed was their CIA card. It all made perfect sense.

Later, in his room, as he sipped a whisky and watched a World War II movie on the TV without taking it in, he began to think about his own endgame. It would not be enough for the IRA to have him taking part in the Tunnel operation, or even ensure that it was his hand that triggered the bomb. Afterwards, they had to be able to prove it. They would want to be able to produce hard evidence of his involvement. And that also suggested that they would be stupid to let him get back to the States, back to the CIA, where elaborate alibis could be concocted and where he would be available to produce convincing denials. The interesting question was what suited the IRA's purpose best keeping him alive under their control or using his dead body to get their message across?

US EMBASSY, GROSVENOR SQUARE

Margaret Blake spent the rest of the afternoon and into the evening tediously in the company of several men whose expressions and body language ran the gamut from polite uneasiness to deep unhappiness and who clearly wished that she and they were elsewhere. It was her weekly briefing session with C. Sylvester Clote III, her CIA liaison at the Embassy. He was a small, spare, balding man in his late 50s who seemed to have a wardrobe of light grey suits and striped bow ties and who could have made a good living as a character actor playing henpecked accountants. How he got himself into the CIA, she would never understand. He had probably been counting the days to his pension from the day he started work and was horrified to be linked with Margaret Blake in any way.

When she came into his office, he rose, formally shook her hand and gave her a sour smile that was gone so quickly it was hard to be sure that it hadn't been an optical illusion. She smiled inwardly at the three other men who had gathered in the office, obviously at Clote's request to give him cover in numbers. Their politeness did not hide the fact that they would have preferred the company of a paedophile. She couldn't blame them. If Anthony Lake, President Clinton's national security advisor, or any of the pro-Irish Republican people at the White House discovered that CIA had set up a direct liaison with MI5 who were planning a mass extermination of Irish patriots, a lot of careers would be going down the toilet in one quick flush.

They sat around a table and she brought them up to date. As always, she was circumspect, using a lot of euphemisms and circumlocutions but leaving everyone clear about what was developing. Clote took spidery notes on a yellow pad, the others concentrated on avoiding eye contact with her. One, a youngish man with large spectacles on a remarkably small head kept asking, "And this is approved?" No one answered him.

If they were all that unhappy having to meet with her, they should have been anxious to end the session, she thought. Instead, they wasted time, each feeling the need to make statements about the "complexity and sensitivity" of the Northern Ireland situation, and the need to maintain "appropriate distance" and "await developments and direction." She didn't know why they were scrambling to get on the record since there was no record. Their vapid comments were hardly likely to be passed onto Langley for information and even an asshole like Clote wouldn't tape the meeting.

She thought about finding a way to casually bring up Peter Knight, to check if Clote or any of the others knew about CIA agents currently active in London. She wanted badly to know if the Black Knight was still with the CIA. "Hey, know who I bumped into at lunch?" No, that wouldn't do. It was a waste of time in any event. She doubted if these people knew anything relevant. If they did, they were unlikely to tell her.

The meeting finally ended when everyone ran out of things to say. The goodbyes verged on the hostile. She forgot about them as soon as she was out the door. She found herself an empty office, switched on the computer terminal, bypassed the password in less than thirty seconds and tried to call up information on Knight. The computer didn't even ask for her clearance level. NO SUCH RECORD EXISTS, said the computer. She tried Jay Trander. The screen went blank then a single cursor blinked. Nothing else happened and she was about to try something else when the message came up: INFORMATION UNAVAILABLE. YOUR ENQUIRY HAS BEEN LOGGED.

Margaret switched off. An appointment book on the desk had the name P. Fantoni. She felt briefly sorry for P. Fantoni who was going to be asked a lot of questions shortly. She looked at her watch. It was 7.20. "Jonathan! Damn, damn, damn," she muttered and hastily made her way out.

It was a late shopping evening and it occurred to her that it was going to be difficult to get a cab. But she was in luck. As she walked out of the Embassy, a black taxi was dropping someone off and she was soon heading to her quiet cul de sac apartment in St John's Wood. The taxi driver was a voluble middle-aged Jew from Slovakia who had little else on his mind but the kosher restaurant he had set up in Manchester and which had gone bust. He waited outside Marks and Spencer while she picked up a three-course meal for two and spent the rest of the ride offering her esoteric culinary advice in barely comprehensible English. Like almost everything else in England, the cab service was turning into American pastiche, she reflected. It was time to rush back to St John's Wood.

* * *

Inside her apartment, she did a quick tidy, a quicker shower, changed into black lace underwear and favourite short black dress, splashed on some

154

'Impulse', put an early Sinatra on the CD player and was pouring herself a large gin and tonic when the bell rang.

Jones had flowers in one hand and wine in the other. He looked relaxed in an eight-button navy blazer, dark grey slacks, black tasselled loafers and a pale blue shirt with a subdued club tie. As he kissed her lightly, she felt the first tingle of anticipation and caught a mild whiff of Kouros aftershave. He tossed out the usual compliments about her apartment and was soon seated beside her on the soft couch with its big floral cushions, sipping his gin and tonic and chatting comfortably.

They talked mostly about her experiences of working in London, her impressions of the capital, the differences between English and American lifestyles. He was surprised that she had seen so little of London's attractions, but he didn't make the conventional offer to show her around the "real" London, for which she was grateful. She asked him about himself and, from his self-deprecating responses, got the impression that he was a quietly ambitious workaholic but who had recently been making a determined effort to broaden his limited social life. All work and no sex is making Jonathan an unhappy boy, she thought.

As she was refreshing their drinks, he said, "By the way, I'm afraid I didn't make any headway in tracking down your chap from the Ritz. My contact was out of the office today. I'll get onto it tomorrow."

"Don't go to a lot of trouble," she said as though it were of little interest. "I feel bad about using official resources to check out a personal thing." That's how she would play it until she could be sure that she hadn't stumbled onto a CIA operation.

"No trouble at all," he assured her, but shot her a quick, speculative look.

Wanting to move on quickly, she broke her mental resolve to keep the evening away from shop talk and asked: "What kind of a guy is Trevor Wallace? I thought he was going to have a coronary today when Stella Rimington jerked his chain."

Jones looked disdainful. "It really ruins his day having to sit around a table when Stella is calling the shots. Trevor's problem is that he can't cope with the very idea of any woman telling him what to do. He finds it terribly demeaning. Oddly enough, he thinks that Margaret Thatcher was the greatest Prime Minister we ever had. But, then, I don't think he ever saw her as a woman."

Margaret laughed. "He's gay, isn't he?"

"Oh, indeed. Trevor is a fully paid-up member of Shirtlifters and Chocolate Stabbers Amalgamated. Um, sorry, if I'm crude. I did not mean to shock."

She chuckled. "It's refreshing to hear some colloquial vulgarity from a Britisher. I am just taken aback by your utter lack of political correctness in referring to a member of the gay community. I'd advise you not to say anything like that if you visit the States. And, whatever you do, stay well away from the State of California."

"Oh, I'm not homophobic. Human diversity is the spice of life, and all that rubbish. I suppose it's just my antipathy to Trevor Wallace. I can't for the life of me figure out how he keeps rising steadily up the ranks of MI6 like rancid cream."

"He seems a bright sort of guy," she hazarded.

"Oh yes, he's clever, and more important, he's smart," he admitted. He pursed his lips disdainfully and she had a momentary thought that he was glad not to be a subordinate of his. "But he's also treacherous, untrustworthy and on the take."

"You know that for a fact, that he can be bought?"

He hesitated. "I shouldn't tell tales out of school. In fact, I won't. Let's just say that I am satisfied in my own mind that friend Trevor has turned a blind eye to certain things in the past and has not suffered financially as a result."

He suddenly moved closer to her on the couch. "Let's forget the unsavoury for this evening and talk of pleasant, beautiful things instead. Now, what were you telling me about yourself?"

Dinner was a success. She still marvelled at the wonderful range of prepared meals at Marks & Sparks, as locals called the store. His bottle of Muscadet nicely chilled had disappeared and, at the end of the meal, they were comfortably sipping a reasonable Côte du Rhône. She reached across the table to refill their glasses just as he had the same thought. Their hands touched and he saw the animal desire in her eyes.

He was kissing her gently at first, their lips touching, then parting, and then touching again. She felt his hand move to her breasts where her nipples were now straining against the soft black silk. He was fumbling a bit with her bra so she helped him and then she ran her left hand down his leg and into the centre and felt the pulsating part of him push against her. She opened her legs just a little and could feel the dampness between them. Without a word, they rose from the table, he knocking over his chair, and headed for the bedroom, casually dropping clothes as they went.

Later, as they lay together in exhausted tranquillity, the bedclothes in a heap on the floor, she said: "Well, I guess my friend was right on the button."

"How so?" he asked lazily, a finger tracing intricate patterns on her breasts.

"I have this girlfriend back in the States and when she heard that I was coming over to England, her reaction was, 'viva la difference'. She said, 'You know, darling, how American men are invariably circumcised. Well, Englishmen, they like to let their dicks grow long."

He burst out laughing. "Ouch, no pinching. Actually, your girlfriend was talking through her no doubt elegant ass. Most of the best type of Englishman gets his wick trimmed as a baby. I was at boarding school on a scholarship and, in the showers, it was very evident that I was definitely lower middle class. Circumcision is an upper-class fancy. They take their lead from the Royals. Soon as Prince Charles was born, Elizabeth was on the phone setting up an appointment for a mohel."

"What's the reason?" she asked interested.

"I've no idea, except," he paused and said deadpan, "except they want to be a cut above the rest of us. Dammit, no more pinching."

"So your handsome Prince Willie has had his willie doctored?"

"Willie?" he asked. "Where did you pick up that English word? But, as it happens, Prince William is intact. Charles was keen to pass on the legacy but Diana raised such a stink that he had to retire foiled."

His finger and her hand were working them both up to slow, delicious arousal. She tried to see him in the dark but saw only a pale outline. "Incidentally, Jonathan, how come you're such an expert on circumcision?"

"I'm not," he said and his voice was thickening. "In our business, as you know, you fill your mind with trivia that just might come in useful some day. All I really know is what I read in a magazine once. It said that where sensitivity is concerned, being circumcised is like going around all day with your tongue hanging out. Eventually, you can't taste much."

She moved onto him and he watched passively as her head moved down his chest. "Speaking of tongues hanging out," she murmured.

EDGWARE ROAD, LONDON

When the two large men walked into the crowded pub on the Edgware Road shortly before closing time, the buzz of conversation didn't come to an abrupt stop, like in the movies, but it dropped down to something less animated and more subdued. The cops usually stayed out of this pub and their presence now could mean trouble for just about anyone in the place. No-one looked to be paying them any notice as they sauntered to the bar, but everyone was tensely aware of them. They were both in their mid-thirties, one in a brown summer suit, the other in a sports jacket and jeans. The suit ordered two Scotches and the barman placed large measures in front of them and moved off, not asking for payment nor expecting it.

Drinks in hand and expressionless, they stood with backs to the bar, let their eyes wander the smoke-filled saloon to finally fix on the pair in the corner at a table near the side door. They stared stolidly at the small, well-dressed man, white haired and with a neatly trimmed grey goatee who seemed to be completely preoccupied with the glass of ruby port on the table in front of him. He was probably in his sixties but held it well. He was with a muscular kid just out of his teens, red hair in a tight crew cut, broken nose, wearing a T-shirt and leather jacket and drinking a Coca-Cola. The young man looked at the two policemen and held their gaze until the older man said something to him quietly and then he looked away.

After a minute, the bearded man looked regretfully at his drink, sighed, got up and made slowly towards the back door. The young man jumped up and got there first, holding the door open. The two men at the bar sipped their drinks and watched them go, indifferent.

It was turning dark outside but there was still enough light for the man and the kid to see the three heavies, cold and confident as the two inside, in the narrow alleyway, waiting. All three were dressed in heavy sports jackets, at odds with the warm evening. The older man put a hand on the kid's elbow, a warning gesture.

One of the heavies, sweaty and running to fat, walked over to the kid and leaned his pockmarked face into him. "Tell me something Columbo," he said, taunting. "I'm trying to remember, when did you last leave the ring under your own power? Four, five years, was it, back in the juniors? How punchbags like you get to work as a minder when you can't do more than two rounds anymore?"

The kid said nothing, watching as the other two moved in closer. The fat man grinned at the others. "What d'you think, Columbo is a minder? Or maybe something else, hey? You selling your arse, Columbo? Want to take care, laddy. AIDS, whoa, a desperate way to go. Don't have to tell you, do I? Runs in your family. Pity about"

It was quick. The kid didn't change expression, didn't seem to move, but suddenly his right fist smashed into the fat man's mouth, knocking him to the ground with a scream of pain. He was not quick enough for the others, both of whom had taken iron bars from inside their jackets. The first swing connected with the young man's arm with a sickening crack. The other man feinted with his iron bar and snapped a kick into the kid's shinbone. As he went down with a grunt, the bar was jabbed hard into his ribcage. He twisted on the ground, pushing himself against the wall, hands on his head and legs up against his groin to give them less of a target.

The fat man was up on his feet, swearing profusely, a stream of dark blood pouring from his mouth. He kicked out at the figure on the ground, trying for his crotch and getting a kneecap. He pulled out his iron bar.

"Right, that's enough, thank you." A fourth man appeared out of the shadows, big like the others but better dressed, wearing a light grey three-piece suit and red velvet bow tie. Immediately, the three stopped and looked at him, like well-trained rottweilers, panting a little. They were equally ready to beat the kid senseless or walk away.

"Much obliged, gentlemen," he said. He looked over at the older man, who had remained all the while standing against the wall as though detached from what was happening, and nodded towards the kid, who was rocking and moaning on the ground. "Send him home, Barry."

Barry McGrath leaned down and tried to help the kid to get up. It took a bit of effort but he finally got him unsteadily to his feet, eyes closed in pain, clutching his side and breathing hard.

"I'm very sorry about this, John," he said softly. "Can you make your way to Doctor Russell and get yourself seen to. I'll be all right, don't worry about me."

"That's good advice," the man in the bow tie said in a fatherly tone. "Get thee hence, my son, and sin no more, if you don't want to find yourself in the nick charged with assaulting a police officer."

John opened his eyes and looked questioningly at McGrath. He was humiliated and hurting but was still ready to have a go. McGrath shook his head and patted him on the shoulder. After a few seconds, John limped down the alley and out of sight. The heavies walked to the top of the alley and remained there, talking quietly, already bored.

"Game lad, your John, but that's part of his problem," remarked the man in the bow tie. "He still doesn't know when to stay down, in the ring or out of it. Takes a few too many punches to the head."

"There really wasn't any need for all that, Mr Wilson," said McGrath sadly. The man in the bow tie believed that McGrath knew him as Superintendent Ted Wilson of the CID. In fact, McGrath had long been aware that he was Trevor Wallace, a senior MI6 agent, whose IRA code name happened to be Trousers. Prudence suggested that he mention neither item of knowledge to Wallace.

"Ah, maybe you're right, Barry. But I must use the tools they give and these are the best that the local shop had on offer. Animals every one of them, scum of the earth, without the finer sensitivities of you and me." Wallace dismissed the fight with a wave of his well-manicured hand. "Well, it's been quite some time since we had the pleasure of a friendly chat, a bit of gossip, a few laughs. How's trade, these days?"

McGrath shrugged. "Oh, dragging the devil by the tail, as always."

"Better than that, Barry, I would say, much better than that. If the sole supplier of booze to every blasted Republican Club in Ulster can't earn himself a nice penny, who can? Especially when half your bottles of premium spirits are filled with that junk you get in from Tokyo. And all the ciggies come from warehouse jobs up and down England. Of course, it's a big help when your first cousin is Chief of Staff of the IRA. You'll grant me that?"

"I run a clean business, as you know," said McGrath, for the want of something to say, "and don't know anything about the IRA."

"And speaking of warehouses, Barry, I was very sorry to hear that Brian's been nicked. Not exactly a chip off the old block when it comes to brains, that son of yours. What I want to know is how was he able to move around that tiny flat of his with four hundred laptop computers piled up around him."

"This is a true miscarriage of justice, Mr Wilson," said McGrath earnestly. "You are right. Brian was just plain stupid. He was going to start working for me, a nice respectable sales job. But he wanted to clear off some debts, too embarrassed to tell me. He thought he was getting a bargain, just selling on. I've talked to him. I swear he didn't know they were from the factory job."

"Maybe so, but is anyone going to believe him? Two security guards dead, very improper. Lot of pressure to get this gang banged to rights. And within two days they find Brian babysitting the merchandise. You know, of course, they'll throw everything at him. He's going to be a lot older than you before he gets out in the world again. Sad times for you, Barry, with your first grandchild just weeks away."

Barry nodded sombrely.

"Well, such is life," said Wallace, as though closing the subject. Then he added, as though it had just occurred to him, "Chief inspector Harry Wrixon is running this one. Know him? Big feather in his cap, this. Certain promotion. No one deserves it better than Harry. He's a very good mate, we go back. I'd do a lot for Harry, he'd do a lot for me."

Barry came alert. "You could maybe put in a good word, Mr Wilson?" He tried to make it casual but failed utterly

Wallace looked like he was considering the idea. Then he shook his head. "I don't know how we got talking about this. I really wanted to have a wee chat about something else. Tell me, how is Gearoid these days, eh?"

Barry hesitated. "Poorly. The truth is I haven't seen him for a couple of weeks but his health has taken a turn for the worst. The fact is, he's over in Switzerland, at the moment, attending some private clinic. It's supposed to be the best in the world for heart disease, better than anything in America. Big Middle East clientele. I'm told they've got some miracle cure, so we're all hoping they can do something for him."

"Switzerland, aye, that's what I heard. Expensive place, but what's money when it's the health of the Chief of Staff? Or is he still the Chief?"

"I don't know much about that side of things," replied Barry levelly. "But I was told that Gearoid retired a few weeks ago as Chief and then he quit the Council altogether. He's not a player now and even if his health recovers I don't believe he'll be involved. He's earned a peaceful retirement."

"Oh, without a doubt, though there are many widows and orphans in these islands who might not agree with you. But I hope it isn't bad news for you, Barry, losing such an influential contact in the topmost ranks of the IRA. It would be a shame if that lucrative contract of yours is put at risk and unsentimental competitors start breathing down your neck. Hard times looming, perhaps?"

"I've no worries on that score." He wondered if Wallace had heard anything. The truth was that worrying efforts were being made to muscle in on his contract with the Republican Clubs. In fact, at this very moment, that thug

Mosse was in a hotel suite in London trying to wheel and deal with some of Barry's prime suppliers.

But Wallace had only been making talk. Now he came to the business. "I suppose, then, that you're on good terms with the new Chief of Staff?"

So that's what this is all about, thought Barry. He said, "I don't know the new Chief at all, I'm afraid."

Wallace acted like he hadn't heard him.

"He sees himself as a bit of a mystery man, this new Chief. Something of a Scarlet Pimpernel they seek him here, seek him there. Likes to think his identity is a bloody great secret, which is a new angle for the IRA. Well, they'll be very upset to learn that we know quite a lot about Sam the man."

McGrath, who had just been made aware that British Intelligence knew almost nothing about the new IRA Chief of Staff, stayed quiet.

"So, what's your own impression of Sam?" asked Wallace amicably.

"It's like I said, Mr Wilson, I don't know a thing about him. Never met him or seen him. I wouldn't have direct contact at that level, anyway."

An airplane flew low overhead, the noise of the engines almost deafening in the alley. They looked up and waited for it to pass, lights flashing in the darkening sky.

Wallace sighed. "Well, I'm sorry that we can't seem to be able to help each other, Barry."

McGrath had to do some fast thinking. He had no intention of telling Wallace anything about Sam, not that he knew anything. Only the idle rumours in the pub in Camden Town after a good few pints of Guinness that a new man had taken over at the top. But he could lie. The thing was not just to make the lies plausible but to give them enough substance for Wallace to decide that he had got enough value to put in a word for Brian. At the same time, anything he said would have to stand the test of time. If Wallace later decided that he'd been messed around, the consequences would be unpleasant.

"Wait, now. I've heard a few things," he said tentatively. "But I don't think there's anything that would be of any use to you. I'm just not privy to the Council."

"So you keep saying. So what are the few things you've heard?" Wallace showed an edge of impatience.

The idea came to McGrath in a flash, fully formed in all its beauty and ramifications, like a chess grandmaster initiating inevitable mate a dozen moves ahead. Oh yes, this was rich in its potential. And, best of all, he would tell Wallace everything he wanted to hear and nothing.

"My understanding is that Sam is a leading figure in Sinn Fein," he began.

Wallace snorted. "Is he, now? What else is new? Every top dog in the IRA is a Shinner, for Chrissakes."

"What I mean is that he's an elected councillor. Someone said to me that some speech Sam had made in the council chamber nearly led to a fist-fight."

Wallace gave a barking laugh. "That doesn't narrow it down much. You get that every day of the week." But he had dropped the pretence of having any detailed knowledge of Sam.

"He's not from the Belfast area."

"How do you know?"

"Last time I met Joe, we had planned to have an early dinner together, but it was nearly midnight before he showed. He said that the Council meeting had started nearly five hours late because of Sam. His usual driver had taken sick and they'd had to send him a car and driver from Belfast. For some reason, I got the impression that Sam was coming from Derry. But that's just a guess."

Wallace shrugged. "Londonderry? Still doesn't tell me much."

McGrath let him mull it over, knowing that Wallace would pick up on oddity.

"Funny business, though," murmured Wallace, as though talking to himself. "Why would he need a driver from Belfast? He could have got any of the local boys in Londonderry, or wherever, to drive him. More likely, he would have just driven over himself. Since when have the IRA top brass insisted on a chauffeur-driven service, eh?"

Here goes, thought McGrath. "Ah, no, it's nothing like that. Fact is, Sam can't drive himself, I'm told. Well, not at present, anyway. Someone, can't remember who it was, said to me that it's a nuisance for Sam not being able to drive but that'd he'd be back behind the wheel in a couple of months. I thought maybe he'd had an accident of some kind, you know, and was incapacitated."

At first, McGrath thought that Wallace would miss it. He was beginning to look like the conversation was going nowhere for him.

Abruptly, Wallace got it. He said nothing and tried to remain nonchalant, but couldn't hide an intake of breath, a new sharpness in his eyes. He was hesitating, wanting to probe further, yet not wishing to let McGrath realise the importance of what he had said.

With studied casualness, he remarked, "So, what it amounts to, Barry, is sweet damn all. You've never actually met Sam, wouldn't know him if he came up to you and gave your vandyke a trim?"

"That's about the truth of it," assented McGrath.

"Well, listen, I'd like nothing better than to freeze my arse off in this stinking alley chewing the breeze with you, but I've got a few things to do before I can call it a day."

As he moved off, McGrath asked, trying not to make it sound like a whine, "Any chance of a word for Brian?"

Wallace gave a tight little smile. "You know my motto: get a favour, do a favour. The thing of it is, I haven't got any favours from you, now have I?"

McGrath swore to himself. So far, he had been too clever by half. He had appeared to hand Wallace the identity of Sam on a plate, but in such a way that both of them, for their own reasons, could deny that anything had been said. One more lie, then. Wallace was already halfway up the lane when he called after him, "There is one other thing, Mr Wilson."

Wallace turned and came back. "I thought you were holding out on me, you bastard," he said without rancour.

McGrath didn't have to put on an act of looking nervous. He said solemnly: "I want two things: no mention of me to anyone as the source, and a serious word for Brian in the right place."

Wallace looked at him curiously. "Agreed, depending. I most sincerely hope you're not about to waste my time further."

McGrath licked his upper lip. "The IRA has a big job coming off in London sometime over the next few days. I don't know the details, I swear to you. Except this: Sam is running the operation personally and is here in London right now."

There was no longer a reason for Wallace it play cool. "Where?" he demanded hoarsely.

McGrath shook his head. "I heard mention of the City. And I swear to you that is everything I know. I was on the phone yesterday to someone in Belfast and he let it slip indirectly. I don't think he even realised what he'd said. But Sam is here and it's going to happen before the end of the week."

"Dammit, that's bugger all use to me," snapped Wallace. "You're not still keeping secrets to your bosom, are you? Because if you are"

McGrath just about restrained himself from making the sign of the cross on his chest. "Nothing. There's nothing else I know. If I did, I'd tell you. For Brian's sake. A favour done, as you say."

Wallace stared at him, then gave a menacing smile. "A favour given," he agreed. "But God save your balls if this is some cock and bull story because I won't."

McGrath watched him vanish around the corner of the lane. He hadn't noticed the heavies depart, but they were long gone. He felt the perspiration ooze out of his pores and the energy drain out of him. His whole body went into a shaking spasm. He wanted to lie down on the ground and close his eyes. His triumph at what he knew he had just achieved was something he wasn't ready to think about and savour. Not just yet.

* * *

Wallace walked to his car, which he had parked two streets away. He got in the dark blue Rover 800 and placed his hands on the steering wheel but made no move to start the engine. He was in a high state of euphoria, feeling waves of heat course through his body. A dozen thoughts were whirling in his brain like lightning flashes, and, for a few moments, he couldn't focus on any one. "Christ, slow down, slow down" he muttered to himself. He forced himself to take long, deep breaths and calm the whirlwind in his mind. He had to start thinking logically, reviewing and analysing what McGrath had told him. The implications were huge, incredible. It was the single most important piece of intelligence he had ever acquired. And the staggering thing was that McGrath was in utter ignorance of just how much he had unwittingly given away. Incredible!

Wallace looked down at his white knuckles and forced himself to loosen his clench on the steering wheel.

Sam, according to McGrath, was a Sinn Fein councillor, most likely from Londonderry, who was temporarily unable to drive a car, probably due to an injury or accident of some sort. But there was an alternative reason that would stop a man from driving a car. Yes. He wouldn't risk it if he happened to be well known locally and had been banned from driving. Wallace remembered reading about the court case four months previously. A Sinn Fein Councillor, prosecuted for being drunk behind the wheel when he had knocked down and killed a cyclist. The Councillor had a good barrister who made much of the fact that the cyclist, too, was drunk and produced three witnesses who testified that the cyclist had actually fallen off his bike into the path of the Councillor's car. Two of the witnesses happened to be Sinn Fein members. The Councillor was treated leniently: barred from driving for six months.

Well, well, thought Wallace. Councillor Sean Anthony Mosse. It was almost a case of hiding in plain sight. S.A.M. Even his bloody nightclub was a giveaway: Sambo. It was as though the bastard didn't give a damn whether or not the security forces knew he was Chief of Staff of the IRA.

It all fit so well that Wallace wondered why they hadn't tumbled to Sam's identity straightaway.

He leaned back in the seat, now more relaxed, his mind ice sharp. Just an hour ago identifying Sam would have been a sweet intelligence coup all by itself. And so it was. But it was far bigger than that. He could *prove* that Sean Mosse was Sam, because Mosse was on the surveillance list. Which meant that Wallace could find out Mosse's present whereabouts in a matter of hours. And if Mosse was in London...

Once Sam had been located in London, surveillance would be intensified. The big operation planned by the IRA would be discovered. The publicity bonus alone would be stunning: BRITISH AGENT FOILS IRA BOMB PLOT TOP TERRORIST CAPTURED. And for him personally? Promotion, a living legend in the intelligence community, a knighthood surely.

He frowned as he caught himself daydreaming. Enough. He had a lot of work to do. The IRA operation could be anytime in the next couple of days. But he was not yet ready to make an official report. First, he wanted to be certain, to have the whole package put together. He would personally check and double-check everything in the files on Sam and on Mosse and see if he could find anything that would tend to point to the two being the same person. He would check the watchers' reports on Mosse's movement for the past few weeks and fine-comb them for anything relevant. He would get a present location for Mosse and, if it was anywhere in the vicinity of London, then he was ready to call it in.

He would request a priority meeting with the Director of MI6 and brief him fully. He did not doubt the response. MI6 would formulate a plan, weave a net around Mosse and then inform Rimington, who would have no option but to play second fiddle on this. He recalled with a throb of anger how Rimington had tried to humiliate him at the last meeting of the group. Soon, she would be forced to retract her words.

With a decisive nod of his head, he started the car and headed for his office. He had a long night ahead but, Christ, he had energy to spare.

US EMBASSY, GROSVENOR SQUARE

Margaret Blake sat in a small cubicle office in the American Embassy in Grosvenor Square and watched as the digital clock on the wall clicked to 14.28. It was twelve years ago on this day and at this time that US Army Colonel Frank Blake, a widower with one daughter at college in the States, having arrived home early on a Friday afternoon to his rented house in a Cologne suburb, began unwrapping the small, gaily wrapped package that had arrived in the post during the morning and was virtually decapitated when the small but powerful bomb it contained exploded.

Back in the US, Margaret had been watching an early Woody Allen movie on TV with her then boyfriend, and the story was top of the news programme that followed. No name was mentioned, but she knew immediately. She had called the Army press office in Cologne and, by the time the local cops tracked her down to her boyfriend's home to officially tell her, she was already in the guest bedroom, having been sedated by a doctor called by the horrified parents.

The worst moment came after the funeral, when she was interviewed by two American Army intelligence officers and a security man from Germany and learned that the package had been sent from the US and carried her name with a gaudy 'Happy Birthday' message. Colonel Blake had turned 52 the previous day. She had sent him a birthday card with her weekly letter and had spent half an hour chatting with him on the phone, making plans. His tour of duty had only two months left to run and then he would be back home. He had obviously assumed that the package was a surprise gift.

Her bitterness at the outcome of the investigation of her father's death still remained with her. She had been puzzled, then enraged when the security authorities failed to discover who was responsible for her father's violent death. The killer or killers had gone to a lot of trouble to send Colonel Blake a package that he would open unthinkingly. They had found out his date of birth, established that he had a daughter in the States and had arranged for the package to be posted from there.

But, try as they did, Army investigators could come up with no particular reason why Colonel Blake had been so specifically selected for murder.

Reluctantly, but unsatisfactorily, they could only speculate that he had been selected at random as an American military officer based in Germany, and a comparatively easy target. The forensic experts concluded that the timer used in the bomb was similar to those used by a small group of German left-wing extremists, who were believed responsible for the death of a Frankfurt banker in similar circumstances. But, despite intensive activity, the investigation had come to nothing.

With the passage of time, her deep grief and loss had abated. She could recall her father and her mother, who had died of cancer when she was ten, fondly but without sadness. She guessed that any competent shrink would tell her that she was suppressing her memories of them, subconsciously blaming them for so abruptly and traumatically abandoning her. But she honoured her father's memory in her own way. His death had started her on the career path that had brought her into the CIA. Her hatred of terrorism in any form was the reason she was now putting her job at serious hazard by acting as a quasi liaison officer with British intelligence in an operation of mass assassination of the entire IRA leadership.

She looked again at the clock. 14.30. Two brief minutes of remembrance. With a sigh, she turned her mind to other things.

Peter Knight. The name kept coming back to her. For what seemed like the hundredth time, she replayed in her mind the scene in the Ritz, saw him again get up from the table and stride towards the door and out of sight. She thought about the two who remained. The man had been looking at the girl, with an expression that had both exasperation and something like sympathy. He had briefly put his hand on hers, patted it, then took it away. A gesture of friendliness, but with no special intimacy. She had simply looked utterly bewildered.

Blake stopped thinking of them and again followed the man in her mind's eye as he walked across the room. It was Peter Knight, no doubt about it. But, so what? Was he still with the Agency? Even if he was, he might be simply taking a holiday in London, or was over on business, or now lived in England. What she had witnessed could have been anything from a lovers' spat to a business deal going sour.

Right. Yet some instinct was telling her that there was something more to it than that. There was something about Knight's presence as he walked across the room that didn't jibe with the notion of tourist or businessman, seemingly relaxed but controlled, taut, a faint whiff of sulphur wafting about him. Was this all in her imagination? Was her knowledge that the man had almost certainly been one of the Agency's elite group of professional assassins making her imagination run wild? Perhaps. But she was going to run with her feelings and see if she could check him out.

Her starting point was the unlikely one of seeing if she could get anything out of C. Sylvester Clote III. He was a prize asshole but he would know about all CIA activities currently taking place in England. She was searching her mind for some plausible reason for dropping in on Clote when the phone on her desk rang.

"Margaret, glad I caught you," said Clote. "You got a couple of minutes free? Now in my office if you can."

He was alone when she walked into his office, which was something of a rarity in her dealings with him. Usually he went for the committee approach, giving him the benefit of witnesses and the comfort of sharing responsibility for any decision that might have to be made. He got up from his desk when she came in and gestured her towards a pair of black leather armchairs in a corner of the room, another first in his approach with her. Blake became wary.

Making small talk wasn't one of his strengths and he came to the point, inasmuch as he was able.

"Margaret," he said with a curious twist of his mouth that might have been his best effort at a smile. "We had a great deal of discussion and, ah, debate as we reviewed the intelligence you gave us yesterday. As you might expect, some of what you were able to tell us was pretty startling material. The drastic actions planned by the Director of MI5, working through a special executive committee of which you now appear to be at the very least an ex officio member, are without a doubt going to raise an almighty firestorm of controversy. We wonder if it is prudent or politic for us to maintain the Agency's direct association with this committee. Qui tacit consentit, our silence amounts to consent. Are we not giving hostages to fortune, perhaps?"

Blake realised what he was getting at. And she wasn't going to help him. Strictly speaking, this was none of his business. He was her senior in rank but not her direct superior. His job was to debrief agents and pass on relevant information through previously agreed channels. He had no function in second-guessing whether a particular Agency activity was good or bad.

At the same time, he was seeing the risk to himself. If Operation Fortress Salvo went ahead, as looked likely, and the top echelon of the IRA was taken out in a British intelligence version of the Night of the Long Knives, there would indeed be hell to play. The Irish-American lobby would be laying siege to the White House, and how would President Clinton react when he discovered, as he would through the British, that the CIA had actually sat on the assassination planning committee? The careers of anyone associated with aiding British intelligence in their massacre of Irish leaders would be flushed down the toilet with abandon, with no time for niceties about whether Clote and his fellow penpushers in the London Embassy were just passing on information.

Tough shit, she thought. She said nothing, just raised an eyebrow quizzically.

Her lack of response disconcerted him and he continued to look at her expectantly. But he had no talent for playing the silence game and soon resumed.

"I realise that, under ordinary circumstances, ours is not to reason why. The decision to establish a direct relationship with MI5 was made at a very high level in Langley and it is for them to decide whether or not it is wise to continue this liaison. Nevertheless, it could surely be argued that the potentially devastating fallout that could result from our involvement requires us, as the people on the ground, to at least put our concerns on record regarding MI5's acaphelic intentions."

He emphasised the exotic word and paused, but she was not going to give him the satisfaction of asking what it meant. She said, "I know what you mean. The words 'rock' and 'hard place' come to mind, but that's often the way of it in the wonderful world of espionage."

He frowned and drummed his fingers on the desk. He would have liked to make an acid comment on her frivolity but he was trying to get her on side. "What you say is all too true," he responded mournfully. "But I feel strongly that we cannot simply let things take their course. And I think that, between us, we can and should articulate our concerns.

"What I would like you to do, Margaret, as the person most directly involved in this business, is to prepare a memorandum quite short, I think giving your evaluation of the situation in terms of its possible consequences for the agency, and offering your own assessment as to whether or not our continued liaison, even partnership, with MI5 is really worth the candle. If you would you do this as a matter of some urgency, I can take it from there."

You must be joking, Punch, she thought. That was about as blatant an attempt to pass the buck as ever she had met. "No," she said firmly. "I don't think it's a good idea to tell them back home how to do their business. It's not my job, nor," she added pointedly, "is it yours. We could both expect a swift kick in the ass for our trouble."

He looked decidedly pained, both at her language and her decision. He sighed unhappily. "You must admit, if the Ambassador received the slightest inkling of all this"

"But he won't," interrupted Blake impatiently. This was all a waste of time and, knowing Clote, he was quite capable of spinning it out for another hour in the hope of finding a way out of the dilemma that he obviously saw as bringing his career to a shuddering halt, to take the most benign scenario. Time to change tack and get to what she wanted to know about Knight.

"By the way," she remarked. "The concerns are not all on one side. MI5 is worried that we in the CIA are playing some sort of a double game with them."

"What is that supposed to mean?"

She had given some thought to how she would run it. "I had an informal approach from Jonathan Jones, who works directly to Stella Rimington. He claims that he, and some other British intelligence officers, were attending some function in the Ritz during the past few days, and discovered that they were being monitored by an agent of the CIA. He wanted to know the purpose of this surveillance."

"That's a load of crap," spluttered Clote, dropping his official voice in astonishment. "You are the only member of the Agency who is currently involved in any way with British intelligence. If there were anyone else, I'd know all about it and I'm telling you now that there isn't anyone else. This is paranoia gone mad."

"For sure," Blake agreed. "But he gave us a tentative ID on the agent from their files. They believe his name is," she hesitated, "Tony Regula."

"I've never even heard that name," he protested.

"According to Jones, he works for Jay Trander."

Clote turned very pale. He swallowed and glanced hastily at the door as though expecting to see Trander come smashing through it. "Mr Trander doesn't work for the Agency, he's long retired. Both he and his entire section were disbanded some years ago. MI5 are well aware that that is a fact and their files seem to be woefully out of date. You can categorically guarantee him that he's way out of line with his accusations. Jeezus."

Blake got up. "OK, I'll give him the word. Did you have anything else?"

Clote shook his head, still bewildered. For the moment, Jay Trander's name had replaced his earlier worries with a new and potentially more ominous one.

Back in her cubicle, Blake reviewed the meeting. She had got as much as Clote had. He had given her a small part of the answer. Peter Knight was not in London on official CIA business. So what was he doing?

After a few minutes, the phone on her desk rang. It was Clote.

"You can tell your friend Jones that Tony Regula died two years ago in a drowning accident off the Florida Coast. If they say they saw him in London last week, it was a different kind of spook they saw." He chuckled, or maybe just cleared his throat, and hung up.

So he had checked promptly with Langley, as she had expected. She was glad that she had not brought up Peter Knight's name with Clote. For no particular reason, she wanted to keep it to herself for the present. It was time for a spot of networking.

She checked her personal organiser for Doug Hill's number. Doug had been a good friend of hers when she worked in Langley. A handsome, prematurely bald man in his mid-forties, he had slipped into the CIA on the strength of an uncle who was a US Congressman of some importance and, over the years, had moved several rungs up the promotional ladder without making much of an effort. He was laid-back and tended to be lazy, not working too hard or showing much of an interest in any of his assignments or desk work. But he was an inveterate gossip, regarding the agency as one big village, and took an almost obsessive interest in office politics and the careers and private lives of Agency personnel at all levels, most of whom he had never met.

The previous year, he had succeeded in parlaying a minor accident at home, falling off a ladder while adjusting a rooftop TV aerial, into a medical condition that enabled him to get out of the Agency with a satisfactory disability pension. He now lived with his wife and three children in a large, pleasant farmhouse on the outskirts of Wilmington, North Carolina, where he was engaged, in a desultory fashion, in writing a biography of a distant ancestor, the brilliant but irascible Civil War Confederate general, Daniel Harvey Hill.

She hadn't spoken with him for almost a year but, when he picked up the phone, he greeted her casually as though they were in daily contact and almost immediately launched into an excited story of how he had stumbled upon a set of original letters from President Jefferson Davis relating to the Battle of Chickamauga that represented a complete vindication of General Hill's conduct on the night before the battle.

Blake more or less agreed with Henry Ford's observation that history was bunk and did not in any way share the fascination of millions of Americans in the events of the Civil War. She was not surprised that Doug Hill assumed as a matter of course that she shared his passion for the subject and understood its intricacies and she let him chatter on, without her doing much more than inject the occasional murmur of interest.

Finally, he began to run down and realise that there might be some other reaon for her call than Civil War minutiae.

"How are you shaping up over in London, England?" he asked, offering her the opening.

"It's not a bad place," she allowed. "Nothing too strenuous for me, mainly being nice to our British cousins. We mostly exchange secrets both of us know already. But, yeah, what I wanted to ask you about was someone I bumped into here a few days ago: Peter Knight."

A short whistle came over the line. "The Dark Knight, no less," he said, interest in his voice.

"I thought he was known as Black Knight," Blake queried.

"That, too," confirmed Hill with a laugh. "And more. Tell me, what is he doing in London, apart from scaring the natives?"

"Dunno," she admitted. "The circumstances were a bit peculiar. It's what I wanted to check with you. Is he still with our operation? I thought he was enjoying blissful retirement like you."

Again his easy laugh. "Well, now, there's retirement and retirement and they're not necessarily the same thing, as the fella said. Men like Knight don't take well to retirement. You know his section got a lot of people all atwitter and it was closed down, lock, stock and high-powered barrel? However, these people had certain ways of bringing a difference of opinion to a speedy conclusion and their skills continue to be in demand. So the agency outsourced. Jay you know who I mean now makes a lot of money from a single client providing the same kind of services he did as an underpaid civil servant like you. And Jay's team is still more or less what it was, a new face here, an old face fading there."

"What about Knight, is he still on the old team?" she queried.

"Oh, indeedy. He's one of their very best, always has been. Tops with a scope and an awesome demolition man. Quality bang for your buck. Gets the plum assignments, works couple of times a year, I'm told. Matter of fact, he's not Peter Knight any more, they all got new makeovers. These days, he answers to Martin Carter."

"Tell me this," asked Blake cautiously. "Apart from their main client, are any of these guys in the freelance end of the market?"

"There's a rule against it and if they got caught, they'd be in deep doo-doo, as George Bush would put it. But it happens. You heard of Barry Weinstein? One of Jay's top notchers, with many notches to his credit. Seems he took an assignment from his chosen people to finalise a business in Milan. When Jay found out, he went ape, fired Barry out on his tush. Maybe it was the freelancing, then again, who could help speculating, right?"

Hill was never especially security conscious but was going through the motions of being oblique on an open phone line. Blake understood what he was saying. Weinstein had carried out an assassination in Milan at the behest of the Israelis. Jay didn't approve, plus he had to think that the Mossad were among the last people in the world to need a hired gun. Therefore, Weinstein could well be a double agent and was dumped.

"So, you reckon the occasional freelance job may prove too tempting?" she asked.

"Anything is possible, Margaret, as you notice every day of the week. But, unless you've got something more, holidays and business trips are also possible."

"Yeah," she agreed. It was quite on the cards that Knight/Carter was in London for wholly legitimate business. Why did she feel so strongly otherwise?

"Yo, I just remembered," said Hill. "Martin Carter has a day job in New York. He's on the security staff of the Waldorf Astoria in Manhattan. Nice pay and conditions, not too taxing, I hear. Takes a few days off a few times a year for the big bucks. Nice if you can get it?"

Blake switched the conversation by mentioning Clote. Hill was shrewd enough to know that she had got the information she wanted. But he was happy to add a few titbits to his store of gossip and the conversation went on for another few minutes, ending with an invitation to her to come over to North Carolina in the near future to watch a re-enactment of some battle or other.

She thought for a few minutes about her next step, then looked up the phone number of the Waldorf Astoria in New York. When she got though, she asked for the security office. A girl, smooth voice with a hint of Spanish accent, took the call. "Security, Mr Myers' office. Maria Gonzalez speaking. Can I help you?"

Blake said, "Good day, Ms Gonzalez. I'm Doctor Fine calling from London in England and I'm trying to contact Mr Martin Carter."

"Mr Carter's on leave right now," Gonzalez replied. "Could we have somebody else assist you?"

Blake pushed concern into her voice. "It's Mr Carter I need. Look, I'm calling from the American Mercy Hospital here in London and his sister is ill, very gravely ill. It's so important that I reach Mr Carter kind of quickly."

"Oh my, that's sad news. I'm truly very sorry." She sounded genuinely upset.

174

"But fact is that Mr Carter is right now over in Paris for the week. That's in France." She had a question mark about the last bit as though she was not altogether sure.

"Well, it would be a great help to us here if you had an address or phone number in Paris."

"Just hold on, please."

Blake crossed her fingers, hoping she was not going to be passed to someone more senior. Ms Gonzalez had unhesitatingly accepted her story. A more experienced member of the security staff might have doubts, questions.

But the girl was back in less than a minute, breathless and excited. "Dr Fine, Mr Carter is actually in London. He called in yesterday and said he was staying at the Hilton Hotel in Park Lane. Told us we could get him there in an emergency. And, heck, that's what this is, right?"

"Absolutely," confirmed Blake warmly. "And Mr Carter will thank you for it. And so do I."

"OK, then. You have a nice day."

Blake smiled as she put the phone down. She looked at it and wondered if anyone had been monitoring the call. It was possible that some third party had listened in, but she doubted it. As best she knew, neither the agency nor the State Department monitored the calls of Embassy personnel. The British may well listen in to the Embassy's phone traffic but it would be on a keyword or voice recognition basis.

She figured it was the least of her problems if someone was listening. Thinking back on her meeting with Clote, she knew that he was right to fret his heart out about the outcome of the CIA's involvement with British Intelligence on this operation. She despised the dyspeptic bureaucrat but he had sense enough to see that, when shit hit the fan in any government operation, the people at the top devoted all their resources and expertise to finding the goats at the bottom to sacrifice.

Clote had hoped to make her an ally in an attempt to disentangle the CIA from Stella Rimington's Operation Fortress Salvo before the bullets started flying. He didn't reckon with the fact that Blake fully supported the operation and had, in fact, somewhat exceeded her mandate by indicating to Rimington's group that the CIA would use their influence to ensure that the US response would be as muted as possible.

Blake wanted it to work. This would be the first time that one of the leading terrorist organisations in the world would be effectively and visibly destroyed. It would send out a message to other groups of bombers, murderers and kidnappers around the world that the forces of law had changed the rules and that they could be taken out at any time.

She accepted realistically that her contribution in this particular theatre of war was nearly over. Her days in the CIA were numbered whichever way it went. She would have to start making future plans. In her short time with the agency, she had developed some useful contacts and knew she would have little trouble picking up another job where she could still be in the frontline against terrorism. She wanted nothing else, saw no other future. Out of nowhere, the thought "Mrs Jonathan Jones" came into her mind. She laughed, surprised at the idea.

It reminded her that it was time to level with Jonathan about Martin Carter. Inadvertently exposing some other CIA business in London was no longer an issue. Carter was playing his own game. If he was playing anything, of course. She was still playing her hunch with little to back it up.

She called Jonathan at MI5 but was told that he would be unavailable until the following afternoon. Unless it was a matter of some urgency? No, it wasn't, she admitted reluctantly, she would wait.

Before she left the Embassy, Blake checked "acaphelic" in a dictionary. It meant headless. She couldn't decide whether Clote had been referring to the intention to remove the IRA leadership or was inferring that the British were running around like decapitated chickens.

IRA Meeting, Dundalk

Same day

"I fear that this is going to prove to be a terrible mistake," said the Deputy Chief of Staff of the IRA. "If it goes wrong, not only do we lose our Chief of Staff in the most embarrassing of circumstances but the British might, as a result, ratchet up their security and place the Channel Tunnel job in jeopardy." He spoke quietly and unemotionally, which gave his words a greater force.

"I agree with everything you say, Brendan," said Sam, matching his tone. "Let me put it in even stronger terms: what I propose is audacity to the point of recklessness. But what is the alternative? Answer me that."

Brendan grimaced. "I can't. We've been through all the options and they amount to nothing. And I agree that we can't just sit here and wait to find out what happens. But this...I can't escape the feeling of hopping with alacrity from the frying pan into the fire."

They said nothing for a while. They were sitting in the lounge of the Deputy's home in a middle-class suburb of Dundalk, just on the Republic side of the Border. Outside, the sun shone fitfully between light rain showers. Children were playing noisily on the street. Next door, a neighbour was busy polishing his already gleaming new Toyota Corolla. It's like living in a TV advertisement, reflected the Deputy, not unhappily.

He was pleasantly surprised that Sam was here in his home, sitting in one of the armchairs of a worn but comfortable three-piece suite. Joe, shortly after becoming Chief of Staff, had appointed him as Deputy Chief. No one had voiced an objection. The two of them had been close for many years.

When Joe had retired, Brendan had intended to also slip away quietly after a few weeks, giving the new Chief a chance to name a Deputy who was in the same age group. But Sam had anticipated him and had asked him to stay on, saying that the movement could not afford right now to lose the knowledge and experience of both him and Joe. Flattered, he had accepted, doubtful if Sam really wanted an old 'un like him. And it was working extremely well, better, if he were honest with himself, than in the past. Where Joe regarded him as a trusted assistant who would faithfully carry out whatever tasks Joe set him, Sam treated him almost like a Mafia consigliore. Sam had a definite agenda for ending the IRA's long struggle on winning terms and Brendan found himself at one with the new Chief's approach.

Sam jumped up from the armchair abruptly and began pacing. "Let's just recap on where we are. Over the past few weeks, the Brits have stepped up their observation of just about every senior person in the movement. We've had a flood of reports from our people saying that they're being tailed everywhere they go. British surveillance teams have been strengthened fourfold, more. On two occasions, when we tried to run off the tails, our boys were nabbed. What does it mean?"

"And we don't think they're bringing back internment," Brendan said flatly.

"No," agreed Sam. "We don't think it's that. Internment requires a lot of preparation and we would have heard. Our sources in the Prison Service tell us it's not on the cards. What then? The Brits have got something big in the pipeline and we don't have a clue about it. We can't afford to press the panic button and tell our people to disappear for a while. That might only postpone whatever is in the offing. So, as of now, we're all walking around feeling like we've got targets pinned on our backs."

"A succinct summary," adjudged the Deputy.

Sam stopped pacing and gazed unseeing out of the window. "And last night I get this call from Barry McGrath. He tells me that he was hassled by our friend Trousers, who was very much interested in establishing the identity of the new Chief of Staff of the IRA. It figures. I'm quite sure that they haven't got a tail on me. I've worked very hard at staying in the shadows since back when I became Director of Intelligence.

"Anyways, Barry spins him a yarn and sends Trousers off looking in the wrong direction apparently. It so happens that Barry was very coy about the exact nature of the false trail he set but I have my suspicions. But now comes the rather unfortunate part. In order to get Trousers off his back, Barry tells him a great big lie that we've got an operation that is about to take place, with the City of London as the target. Only what Barry doesn't know is that it's the great big truth. Barry's tip-off is vague enough to be useless to British Intelligence and, with just a wee bit of luck, it may cause them to concentrate in the wrong place. But it's all too close for comfort, agreed?"

The Deputy nodded. "I've known Barry for years. He has a very strong sense of family and I imagine he sees us as one big extension of Gearoid's family, and therefore we are his family. He can be trusted. Pity about what he told Wallace but he couldn't know that he was, ironically, telling the truth. The damage is done and it's limited. I'm inclined to agree that it really won't do the British much good."

"So, let's move on. Since the beginning of this year, we've been planning to take care of Trousers aka Trevor Wallace. And when we heard about Paulo in the Dunmurry Hotel, we started to think that there were better uses for Wallace than killing him."

"Pity about the fiasco with Paulo," remarked the Deputy, then laughed. Sam turned from the window and grinned.

The IRA had learned about Paulo, an Italian teenager who was living with relatives in Belfast and who had taken a temporary job as a junior waiter at the Dunmurry hotel. Here, one evening, he had served Wallace in the restaurant. Later, Wallace had taken him out to the car park and accused him of stealing his American Express Card. He ignored the boy's tearful denials. He told him that he was a senior police officer and showed him a laminated RUC identity card. He gave him a choice: the certainty of a year in prison, sucking cock every night, followed by deportation. Or he could enjoy a few hours in Wallace's company, doing it for just one night.

Frightened out of his wits, the boy followed Wallace to a bedroom in the hotel and was told to take off his clothes. When he protested, Wallace grabbed one of his hands and painfully demonstrated how he was going to break several of his fingers. The boy yielded. Later, he said he guessed that a few broken fingers would have been less painful than enduring sex with Wallace, who was heavily into a number of sadistic techniques.

When the IRA learned about this, they sensed a dramatic publicity coup. But when Paulo, who had never gone back to his hotel job after that night, heard that the IRA wanted to meet up with him, he completely misinterpreted their interest and, in a panic, took the first plane he could get back to Italy and vanished.

Sam waved a hand, brushing the memory aside. "We learned from our mistake. This time, we're providing Wallace with his fleshy pleasures. The whole thing was set up by Kieran Delaney and we've been ready to run with it for a month. We've got a fix on Wallace's movements, we know where he parks his car, where he walks to his house, the boy Charles is on tap. The hotel has been fixed up, Danno has his camera and Feargal is on standby. The only reason it's been on hold is that we switched Kieran into the Channel Tunnel job. Although only fifteen, poor Charles is already a pro and will do anything for what we are paying him."

"The Tunnel is a higher priority," reminded the Deputy.

"No argument," answered Sam. "But the two operations are not mutually exclusive. We can run both, and we need to run both and do it now. Remember that Kieran has been kept very busy lately. When he's done the Channel job, we can't push another one on him for at least a few weeks. We just can't wait."

"So, you've decided to personally run it." It was a statement rather than a question.

Sam returned to the armchair and sat down with a sigh. "I know the risks and, yes, I'm going to take it on. I'm flying over to London early tomorrow. It's the best, maybe the only opportunity, to discover what the Brits are planning for us."

There was a long silence between them. Then the Deputy said, "Right, then. Discussion over, decision made. Time to give it our best. Shall I start activating our people in London?"

"Thanks, Brendan, do that." said Sam. "Let's give it up the arse to Wallace."

FPA, Carlton House Terrace, Central London

The next day

Delaney picked up Carter at the Hilton late the following morning and they drove to the imposing building, 11 Carlton House Terrace, where the Foreign Press Association was located. There was no difficulty in signing in for temporary membership. Delaney immediately went into his role as an Englishman working for an American trade magazine and much pleased to be back home for a short stint. He had on a stylish but rumpled tweed suit and sported what looked like a regimental tie. Carter had dressed in a blue summer blazer and light grey slacks. He had decided that he was a feature writer for the *Philadelphia Bulletin*. He had attended a week-long hotel security seminar in Philadelphia some months previously and was familiar with the paper. He also thought that it was an obscure enough US big city daily to arouse little interest from anyone.

There were several journalists drinking at the bar or standing around chatting. Carter and Delaney stayed together as they moved around, pausing occasionally when someone wanted to strike up a brief conversation. Most of the journalists were from the Continent, mainly German and French, and looked like club regulars, casually interested in newcomers. There were only a couple of Americans, which was predictable. They had their own association in London.

"Marvellous bloody place," exclaimed Delaney at one point. "I heard, you know, that the grand old man himself, Gladstone, was wont to bring ladies of the night here for earnest discussion about why they should abandon their profession and lead new and better lives. It was a consuming passion of his, chatting up good-looking harlots. It should have caused great scandal but, in fact, he was much applauded for his missionary zeal. Those were the days before Freud, of course."

"Naturally," agreed Carter, who had no idea who Gladstone was but didn't feel the loss. He looked around with interest at the magnificent, well-maintained interior. Tara had warned them to be careful. "The place is worth millions and the government leases it to the FPA for a nominal sum. So, it's a reasonable assumption that the intelligence services have planted some people on the staff or posing as journalists or both to keep tabs on the foreign media," remarked Delaney.

Carter didn't think it was a reasonable assumption at all. He doubted very much that MI5 and MI6 were so overstaffed that they could afford to assign agents to spy on the shop talk of journalists who, if they came into the possession of information of any importance, were unlikely to share it here with their colleagues.

They lunched in the elegant dining room on the roast beef for which it was famous, sharing the table with a young French reporter, who looked like he was on his first real assignment and whose English was poor and a portly, affable writer for a German glossy magazine who was researching a feature on the Duke of Edinburgh, the Queen's husband. The story was clearly going to be heavy on the alleged lascivious private life of 'Phil the Greek', as the German referred to him. He kept up a non-stop stream of mostly salacious anecdotes about the Duke during the lunch.

Delaney, taking to his role as a true blue Britisher, kept up a huffy, disapproving silence. This only spurred the German to add even more lurid details.

"Good LORD," said Delaney loudly as they exited the dining room. "That man was talking the most utter balderdash. Why do we allow people like that swinish, sewer-minded Hun into this country? Sometimes, I wonder just who won the war."

"We did," reminded Carter.

Delaney sniffed. "If I'd brought along me monocle, I'd peer down disdainfully at you."

"Fate worse than death, sounds like."

* * *

They went out to the hall, checked the noticeboard and saw the prominent announcement that the weekly press visit to the Channel Tunnel would take place the following day. They went over to the desk and put their names down. They had a drink at the bar with the London correspondent of the *Times of India* and left soon after.

"No problems?" asked Tara when they met her half an hour later in a pub in Knightsbridge. She wore a tight pastel blue velvet trouser suit that was guaranteed to turn heads.

"None whatever, m'dear," replied Delaney, still in character.

She was carrying a Virgin Records shopping bag which she placed casually on the floor between herself and Delaney.

"I'm going to leave this behind. These are the beam benders. They're still in their Marlboro packs. Strip the packaging away before you place them. Just remember where they go. One as near to the spur entrance as possible, without it being in view, of course, one as close to the door of the Centre, and the third more or less equidistant."

They had already been over this several times but Carter saw no harm going over it again. A thought occurred to him.

"How robust are these things?" he asked her.

"I don't really know. Why?"

"I may have very little time to do this and I wondered about tossing the last one towards the door instead of having to walk right up to it."

"I'm sorry. I just don't know if they could take a shock like that. But I can find out later tonight and let you know."

"Fine," he said.

Delaney asked, "Still minimum security at the Tunnel, as far as we know?"

"I got word from our man there this morning," she told him. " They're fairly relaxed at present. The trains are not running. Their security is tight enough to ensure that no unauthorised person can get in. But there are a lot of VIP and press trips going on right through the week and they've got used to them. They are not seen as a problem. The PR office has been telling security to stay in the background."

She looked at her watch. "I'm running late as usual. If there's nothing else, I'll be off." She stood and looked at Delaney, then Carter. "Good luck, both of you. Get back safe to us," she said softly, then quickly turned and left.

Delaney's eyes followed her. "A sweetheart bids farewell to her loved ones as they leave for the front. Makes you feel like we're in a real war.

"Let me tell you," he went on, "I never thought the day would come when I'd look at my boss and think, I want a piece of your ass in the worst possible way. Oh my God, she's the most incredible-looking girl I've ever come across. 'Cold and passionate as the dawn', as Yeats said. Aren't you ready to die for her, Martin?"

"I'm not planning to die for anyone just yet, least of all Ms Barry."

Delaney looked at him curiously. "I keep forgetting. You don't really like her, do you. Hell, I know the two of you got off to a bad start but"

"That's history," said Delaney dismissively. "But you're right. I'm not comfortable with her. She is a looker but there are lots of them. But she's one of those true believers who is too much in love with their hatreds. In my book, Tara is a powder keg looking for someone to light her fuse. If you're too close to her at the wrong time, you get blown up as well."

Delaney signalled the barman for a round and said thoughtfully, "I suppose it's true that Tara keeps her feelings up near the surface most of the time. But we're all of us true believers in this particular cause. Otherwise we would be doing other things with our time. Darling Tara doesn't pull her punches and she's more forthcoming in her political views than I would be, but, dammit, I agree with every word she says."

Carter looked at him curiously. "You would have fooled me. No offence, but I had you pegged as the kind of bright guy who didn't buy any political crap."

"Thanks for the compliment lurking in the undergrowth of those words," laughed Delaney. "The way I see it, all politicians are crap but politics isn't. The distinction is subtle, I admit, but it gives me hope. I've got all of Tara's abhorrence of the Brits but I usually manage to keep it on the back burner. For more than seven hundred years, they have tried to destroy the Irish and that's not putting it too strongly. Even after we got our independence, the bastards still won't let go of part of the country. Northern Ireland is of no use to them. It's like a loss-making subsidiary that keeps draining away the cash. But they're still trying to hold onto it in spite of all the bloody noses we've been giving them. Well, it won't be much longer."

"And then?" asked Carter.

"We get a united Ireland, sooner than anyone thinks, twenty years tops. And that's when we begin to come into our own. Blend together the genius of the Celt and the work ethic of the Northern Protestant into one nation and there'll be no stopping us. It's just like the United States, in a way. It was the same kind of mix that got your nation started. And we've got far more justification. We want to take our country back. Your founding fathers did a rip-off. The colonies really belonged to King George and you stole them at gunpoint. Same way you took California away from the Mexicans. And I say nothing about the unfortunate injuns."

"That's what made America great," agreed Carter comfortably. "When we couldn't buy it, we just went in and grabbed it. Of course, nowadays, we actively discourage anyone else doing the same sort of thing. That's progress."

They sat silent for a while. Then Delaney said in a more serious tone, "This job we're doing, it's my swan song. After this, I'm off the active list."

"They'll let you?"

"Oh, yeah, there won't be a problem. We're all volunteers and there's no conscription in this outfit. Anyway, I have to get out. I've taken part in a lot of things over the past few years and I've been lucky. Never caught, never even close. It can't go on like that forever. Sooner or later, Lady Luck decides you've had your quota of her attention."

He paused, lost in a train of thought for a few moments.

"There's another thing that freaks me. I get an unbelievable charge out of what I'm doing. Not when I have to kill, that's a downer. I mean, the excitement, the rush of adrenaline, even the fear and the panic. It's a totally different plane of existence and there's nothing that compares with it, not even sex. The trouble is, it becomes addictive and, worse, it becomes the end and not the means, you know?"

Carter said, "Someone once said: 'It's a good thing that war is so terrible, else we would grow to like it too much.'"

"Jesus, I know exactly what he means," said Delaney.

Carter wasn't surprised at Delaney's burst of candour. He had seen it in the past, a reaction just prior to the big jobs. As far back as Vietnam, a friendly Captain had told him to watch out for confession time. Before a major action, there was often a strong urge to unburden one's soul to others who were also going into battle. "Keep your lip under control," growled the captain. "Otherwise, when the fight's over, you can be pretty pissed off with yourself for having blurted out too much."

Next, Delaney would expect reciprocal confidences. To head him off, Carter asked, "You've got plans for the future?"

"Betcha." Delaney was suddenly animated. "I'm getting out of publishing trade rags. I've got a buyer offering a handsome price for the business. My plan is to move back to Ireland and start up an Internet software company. The Internet is going to be the biggest thing since cavemen learned to grunt their first words. I'll be getting in almost at the start of it. Believe me, the Internet is the best place where you can make a million, even tens of millions, legit, with just a few years of smart work."

"I didn't know you were a computer geek at heart," said Carter, smiling at Delaney's manic mood changes.

"I probably know as little about the technical side as you do. But I've met a man, an American living on this side of the water, who is maybe the world's top Internet genius. Does some work for us, on and off. I figure I can persuade him to team up with me."

He leaned across and patted Carter on the shoulder. "You know, Martin, you should be thinking of getting out, too. Maybe you and me could work out something. The way I'm planning things, we'll very quickly need the right person to head up our American operations. Listen, give it some thought."

Carter promised to give it a lot of thought and immediately forgot about it. A few months back, there had been an IBM conference at the Waldorf and he had seen the kind of delegates who had attended. If ever he did retire, and he had no plans yet, he didn't intend to become a computer software salesman.

* * *

Later, when he got back to his room in the Hilton, the message light on his telephone was flashing. He checked with the hotel switchboard and was told that a Mr Myers had called from New York. He rang the Waldorf and got through to his boss, Randy Myers.

"Hey, Lou, how's it going over in London," said Myers cheerfully. He was an ex-captain of detectives with NYPD. He had an increasingly bad memory for names and solved the problem by calling everyone 'Chief', except for his security team, all of whom were 'Lou' or lieutenant.

"Big Ben still swinging and all that? Lou, just thought I'd update you about a call we got today. I was out and young Gonzalez took it. A medic from the American Mercy Hospital in London wanted to reach you urgently about your sister who was ill. Seeing as how there's no American Mercy Hospital in London and you don't have a sister anyway, I thought you'd want to know. Ah, Gonzalez wasn't on the ball and she gave out your hotel."

"Glad she did, Randy," said Carter. "I was expecting the message."

"Thought as much." Myers assumed it was some CIA code message. He believed that Carter was still on the CIA payroll and that his occasional absences from the hotel were on the official business of the US government, which he was happy to accommodate.

As soon as he put the phone down, Carter got his suitcase and began packing. Ten minutes later, he was at the hotel reception, checking out. He walked into the restaurant, went through the kitchen, no one paying him any attention, and walked out of service entrance.

He spent ten minutes walking rapidly away from the hotel, ignoring the weight of his suitcase, checking that there was no tail. Eventually, he hailed the third passing black taxi he saw and asked to be taken to Waterloo Station. He sat sideways on the back, watching the traffic around him. When he got to the station, he told the driver he'd changed his mind and gave new directions.

Half an hour later, he lay on the bed in his room in the Adams Hotel in

Gloucester Place. It was one of three hotels he had checked out the previous day. It wasn't the Hilton and didn't try to be, favouring an English turn of the century style. But it was comfortable and Carter would have settled for the grittiest bed & breakfast establishment if that's what it took to get out of sight.

Who the hell was looking him up, he wondered. He thought about it for some time but there were too many possibilities for useful speculation. He was annoyed with himself for having phoned his location to the Waldorf the previous day. He had been thinking that maybe his actor friend might have been in touch. But it was a stupid and uncharacteristic security lapse on his part. He was going to have to avoid any more sloppiness, especially during the next few days.

The Channel Tunnel

Friday 27th

The Channel Tunnel had garnered much favourable publicity the previous month when it had been officially opened by Queen Elizabeth II and President Mitterrand in a carefully orchestrated display of Anglo-French accord, a suitable curtain raiser to the D-Day 50th anniversary celebrations. Despite the substantial international media turn-out for the event, press interest continued to run at a high level and the series of Tunnel junkets organised by the Foreign Press Association attracted a good attendance. This was the third such trip since the opening and, on Carter's quick headcount, there were about 40 journalists in the reserved first-class compartment of the yellow and white special Eurotrain that pulled out of Waterloo Station at 11 a.m.

Delaney was again in tweeds. Carter had on a dark grey casual jacket, black slacks, a blue polo neck and black moccasins. Discreet camouflage for what he had to do.

The organisers had laid on the expected VIP treatment for the press. Half a dozen professionally cheerful hostesses in blue uniform were dancing attendance, offering the day's newspapers, trays of buffet fingerfood, plentiful champagne and full bar service. Press kits, with a lavishly illustrated booklet and a collection of news releases and background features, were distributed and, after a quick flick through, were mostly ignored.

Carter and Delaney sat together, across from a matronly woman in old-fashioned horn-rimmed glasses, assiduously reading the London *Daily Telegraph*, and whose badge said she was from *Du* magazine of Switzerland, and a pink, plump young man with grey crew-cut and clipped moustache from *Hamburger Morgenpost*, who was looking out the window at the passing countryside.

"We are not travelling very fast, I think," he observed to nobody in particular. The train was rolling along smoothly, but at nothing like the speed promised when the passenger service went into operation later in the year.

Delaney, who had been sitting silent and withdrawn, got up and made his way to one of the toilets at the end of the carriage.

The man from *Hamburger Morgenpost* looked at Carter's name badge and suddenly exclaimed, "You are from the *Philadelphia Bulletin*, I notice."

"Right," confirmed Carter, noticing that the German's name was, improbably, Otto Schwinghammer.

"This is most remarkable," said Schwinghammer happily. "You see, I have a very close friend who is the editor of the same *Philadelphia Bulletin*. His name is Frank Obell. I suppose you know him?" Great, thought Carter. More than 1,500 dailies in the States and I pick the one with this guy's pal at the helm. More proof that coincidence happens more than we think.

Aloud, he said, "What kind of editor is he?"

Schwinghammer looked puzzled. "How do you mean?"

"Well, there's a whole bunch of editors on the paper, a news editor, a metropolitan editor, a State news editor, a national news editor, a night editor. It's a big paper."

"Yes, of course. We have that, too. But Frank, he is the editor. You know, the man at the top, as I understand it. He is a very distinctive person, a big bear of a man with a great white beard. He looks like God."

Carter smiled. "We've got lots like that in Philadelphia. And, I'll tell you, if Frank is that high up the chain of command, I wouldn't know him. I work from home and mostly I deal with the features people. I don't have much to do with the brass."

"Ah, you are freelance."

"You got it."

"So, you think your readers in Philadelphia are interested in the Channel Tunnel?"

Carter shot him a quick look, but the German was simply making conversation.

"I doubt it," he answered. "A lot of them come to Europe but I don't do the holiday stuff. I don't know if I'll get an angle, maybe it's part of a bigger story I'm looking at. We'll see."

Delaney came back from his somewhat lengthy visit to the toilet and flopped into his seat. The woman from *Du* glanced up from her paper, then gave him a searching look.

"Are you perhaps feeling unwell?" she asked hesitantly.

Delaney looked terrible. His face was ashen and he was breathing heavily. There were beads of perspiration on his forehead. He looked as though he were in considerable discomfort.

"Thank you most kindly, ma'am," he said with a ghastly grin. "I expect that

I shall be fine."

Carter studied him critically. "You look like you've been on an all-night bender." Delaney opened his mouth to reply, then shut it with a grimace.

Schwinghammer got into the act. "Pardon, but you do look quite ill. Are you sure you wouldn't like us to get an attendant?" He was about to get the attention of one of the uniformed girls who was chatting to a group two seats away, but Delaney leaned over swiftly and grabbed his arm.

"No need for that, I assure you, old chap. I don't want to be a bally nuisance and it's really not as serious as it may seem." The effort seemed to take something out of him and he fell back in his seat. The two journalists looked at him with uncertainty.

"I'll tell you what it's all about," said Delaney with an effort. "It's a kind of claustrophobia. Can't stand going into tunnels. Look here, I don't know if any of you ever heard of the Moorgate disaster in the London Underground?"

The woman nodded

"There was a big fire, yes?"

"No, no. That was King's Cross in '87. Moorgate happened in 1975. It was the worst accident ever on the Underground. The driver crashed a train full of people into a dead-end tunnel at full speed, no one knows why. Dozens of people killed. I was just a school kid at the time. I was lucky that I was in one of the end carriages. No serious injuries thank Heaven, but I was trapped under a ton of twisted wreckage and it took them thirty-six hours to get me out. All that time in total darkness, hearing the screams and prayers and curses, and the metal grinding and groaning around me. I could feel something wet soaking into my clothes and I didn't know if it was water or blood. I truly believed that I might not be found, that I was going to die in that godawful place."

"Oh, dear God," murmured the woman in sympathy. Suddenly, she yelped as it went dark outside as the train entered a tunnel. In less than half a minute, they were back in sunshine.

Delaney said nothing, but his eyes were staring and his face was shiny with sweat as he went on. "Two years ago, I started having these terrible nightmares of being buried alive, night after night. Straight out of Edgar Allen Poe. A doctor told me that I should try to confront my fears, and I did. I've made a few journeys on the New York subway. Last week, I took the tube from Euston to Knightsbridge. Now, I'm doing the Channel Tunnel."

He sighed heavily. "Each time I go through this. But, you know, it gets easier all the time. It's something I have to do so, please, say nothing about it to anyone. Don't any of you worry."

"If you say so," said Carter unsympathetically. "But with your heart condition, I think you're crazy."

"Say nothing to anyone," repeated Delaney fiercely. Then he deliberately turned away and stared out of the window.

The others looked at each other and then at Carter, who shrugged.

"Forget about him and think happy thoughts. He'll be all right."

After a minute, the woman went back to her paper with an uncertain expression. Schwinghammer seemed anxious to distance himself and quickly struck up a conversation with a fellow German seated across the aisle.

In a few minutes, the train slowed then halted at the Shuttle terminal. The attendants ushered out the passengers and the group straggled their way along the platform, past the half-finished toll booths and terminal area. They were brought into a large reception room, the only part of the complex that seemed to be finished. One half of the room had a series of promotional display panels, a free-standing movie screen, a rostrum and several rows of yellow plastic seats. The other side had a long trestle table laden with a lavish cold buffet and the inevitable free bar.

Most of the journalists went straight for the bar and were soon in loud conversation. After a few minutes, a PR man for Eurotunnel, smart grey suit, tanned, coiffed hair, mounted the rostrum and invited everyone to sit. He waited patiently as the journalists dragged themselves away from the bar area and took their seats. Carter and Delaney sat at opposite ends of the back row.

After the expected welcoming words, the PR man announced that a special film would be shown, then suffered ten minutes of embarrassment when the equipment didn't work. Making a bland apology, he hastily improvised a speech on the wonders of the Channel Tunnel, unleashing a torrent of facts and statistics. The Tunnel was 31 miles in length, 23 miles underwater, 150 feet under the seabed. The 95 miles of tunnels had been dug by 13,000 workers, removing earth and rubble that was three times greater than the Pyramid of Cheops. Britain and the Continent were physically joined for the first time since the Ice Age. The crossing would take just twenty minutes.

His audience had heard all this many times. They became impatient and began interrupting him with questions. Would the passenger service really start on schedule? Any truth in reports of water leakage in the Tunnel? What about stories of a phantom train appearing on the main control panel? Was Eurotunnel in serious financial difficulties again?

This last question was raised by a Swedish journalist who, with two of his colleagues, were laying an ambush and were soon peppering the PR man with intricate financial questions and ignored his broad hints that perhaps it was time to wrap up and enjoy the lunch. Other journalists, bored, took up the invitation and drifted over to the buffet area. Delaney made his way to the toilets. After a minute, Carter followed him.

Delaney was leaning over one of the sinks, dry retching. He didn't turn round when Carter came in, but raised his head and stared at him balefully in the mirror. Carter looked back at the image of Delaney's bloodless features and red-rimmed eyes.

"Congratulations," he said. "You look like crap."

"That's me. Oh Jaysus, Mary and Joseph, if this isn't patriotism of the very highest order. And bollix to Tara Barry, while I think of it. She swore that the pill would make me look terrible but I'd only be feeling some mild nausea. Mild like fuck.

"At least I'm getting noticed. A couple of people have been asking if I'm OK, including that delicious little blondie hostess. Annie, it says on her bosom. Anytime, Annie, but not today, m'girl."

He grimaced. He had already unbuttoned his collar and now pulled down his tie with a vicious jerk.

Carter said, "Just so long as you're well enough to be ill enough to distract everyone for a few minutes."

"Yeah, yeah," muttered Delaney absently. "So far, everything has gone as we thought it would, hasn't it. Remarkable, as these things go. If our luck holds, the train will put us right next door to the Centre."

He reached into his pocket and lobbed a Marlboro pack to Carter. "Now you've got all three. Tara says that they can take mucho rough handling, so toss 'em if you have to, old man."

"Glad to hear you haven't dropped the accent. You sure you're not really British, Delaney?"

"Talk about adding insult to injury," he said sorrowfully. "I don't have to take any more of this." He waved feebly and went out the door.

Carter went into one of the cubicles and locked the door. He ripped off the Marlboro pack, tore it into small pieces and tossed them in the lavatory bowl. He looked at the device, a hard but lightweight rectangle of dull grey plastic-type material, pocked with several dozen small holes through which he could see multiple strands of wire. Then he took the other two from his jacket pocket and shredded the packaging, which also went into the lavatory bowl. He flushed, using a toilet brush to make sure that all the pieces went round the bend. He pocketed the three devices and left the cubicle. Two journalists were at the urinal but they paid him no notice as he went out.

The formal briefing was over and the PR man had disappeared. Already, the attendants were politely but firmly guiding the journalists back to the train, tactfully persuading some of them to leave their drinks behind.

The train started up and glided slowly on the tracks for less than five minutes and then it was inside the Tunnel. It travelled a couple of hundred yards, then came to a stop, just past the point where the Tunnel was under the seabed. Everyone was ushered out again, this time to see the Tunnel close up, with construction almost finished. As they disembarked, Carter was first onto the platform and Delaney was last, so that they were at either end of the group, standing alone.

Suddenly, Delaney gave a loud cry of pain and staggered along the platform, which took him a few further paces from the group. They watched with consternation as he grabbed at his chest, gasped out some incoherent words and abruptly keeled over onto the platform.

The moment he heard Delaney cry out, Carter started walking down the platform towards a turn in the tunnel. Within a minute, he was out of everyone's sight.

The North Tunnel, with its single track, stretched out in front of him. He felt a stream of air on his face, but the Tunnel was hot and clammy, with pervasive damp smell. It was lit intermittently, with patches of light, then shadow. On the right, the doors to the service tunnel were spaced every few hundred yards. A distance away, a group of workmen were working around some scaffolding. Otherwise, he was alone.

Almost immediately he saw the entrance he was looking for. He walked unhurriedly up to it and looked into the large cavern. It was not, in fact, a spur; there was no rail line. The lighting in the Tunnel gave visibility for just a few feet into the cavern, revealing a heap of rubble, a tar barrel and an upended wheelbarrow on the ground. The rest was blackness and it was impossible to see how far back it extended. It had a musty odour as though it had not been visited for a long time.

Carter moved quickly. From his inside pocket, he took out a pen flashlight and switched it on. The narrow beam bounced off the walls, showing the angle to the right about forty yards ahead, he guessed. He took out a pair of surgical gloves and slipped his fingers through with practised ease. He placed the first device among the rubble. When he stepped back, he could barely see it.

He walked quickly but carefully up the cavern, watching for obstacles until he got to the turn, then placed the second device a foot away from the wall. If security men checked the tunnel by flashlight, it was just possible that they would miss it. He shone the torch ahead of him but couldn't see to the end where the door to the Centre was located. He flung the final device forward as far as he could, and heard it thud not too far ahead, and again when it hit the ground.

He walked back towards the tunnel, slipping gloves and flashlight back into his pocket. He was alert and heard the footsteps a second or two before he saw the figure appear at the entrance and peer in. A man's voice snapped, "What the hell do you think you're doing in there?"

Coming out from the darkness, Carter was still a silhouette but could see the other clearly. He was a small but muscular man, dark hair shaven close to the skull. He had on an informal uniform of navy blue pullover with black leather patches, grey pants tucked into short leggings and trainer shoes. A cloth patch on the breast of the pullover said that he was Eurotunnel Security.

Carter, as he came into the light, made a show of fumbling with the zip of his pants. "I'm with the Foreign Press Association," he said loftily.

The security guard stood with hands hanging by his sides as though readying for an expected attack. He looked at Carter with deep distrust. "I asked you what you were doing here. Why aren't you with your press party?"

"Caught short. Had to take a piss," answered Carter, speaking with deliberate slowness and slurring his words slightly.

The guard looked disgusted. "That's one sure way to get electrocuted down here."

"They've really been pouring the booze into us today. Why don't they have a john down here?"

"Don't know anything about that," replied the guard. "But I'm going to have to ask you to come with me."

"Give yourself a break, pal, " said Carter impatiently. "You don't want to be playing the heavy in front of the world's press. That shower would have you on the front page. They're just around the corner and I don't need any help to get back to them."

He walked past the guard, who muttered "bloody arsehole" and glared at him but made no move to stop him. When he reached the bend, Carter turned and saw the guard walking back down the tunnel. Evidently, he hadn't bothered to look into the cavern.

He saw that Delaney was still the centre of attention. Someone had taken off his jacket and put it on his lap like a blanket. He was sitting propped against the platform wall, in animated discussion with two of the hostesses and a journalist who seemed to be taking his pulse. The rest were standing a few feet away, uncertain what to do or maybe not wanting to crowd him. Carter looked at his watch. He had been away less than ten minutes. He went over to Delaney, nodded briefly and said, "You feeling better now?"

At the nod, Delaney began to recover rapidly. He took his hand away from the journalist, pulled himself to his feet, picked up his jacket and put it on. He said to Carter, "There is really nothing wrong with me, as I've been trying to explain to these good people. Just a regrettable failure of nerve, bad show and all that. I'll be right as rain in a few minutes, ready to go on with the show, full steam ahead."

Both hostesses looked horrified at the thought of Delaney rejoining the trip and doubtless having an even more spectacular collapse. They showed enormous relief when Carter persuaded him to get back on the train and the two of them, together with Annie the blonde hostess, were shunted back out of the Tunnel to the terminal. A doctor and a nurse with a wheelchair were waiting for them. Delaney's feeble protests were ignored and he was wheeled away for examination. Carter remained on the platform and watched the train head back into the Tunnel.

CENTRAL LONDON

The meeting with Tara Barry later that evening was a short one. They came together in a quiet pub off Leicester Square. Delaney was in high spirits, insisting that he was fully recovered from the effects of the pill, but his face was still pale and he opted to have nothing stronger than a cup of tea.

"I was afraid that the idiot doctor would insist on sending me to hospital for overnight observation. With hindsight, I wished we hadn't iced the cake by saying I had a dodgy heart. He took the best part of an hour inspecting all my vitals before I could persuade him to let me go. Meantime, Carter here was down in reception stuffing himself full of buffet food and drink."

"Well, that's all behind us. What counts is that everything is in place," said Tara with satisfaction. "And we go tomorrow. The more I think about it, the more I'm happy with the timing. If we wait, there's always the risk that a security inspection will find the amplifiers. This way, we're in and out before anyone has the slightest idea where we came from or how we did it."

Carter wondered if she believed that. British intelligence would piece it all together quickly. They would find the devices, the security guard would remember him, and they would start checking the press party. Delaney's illness would be identified as an out of the ordinary event. Soon enough, they would have two prime named suspects. Carter had already concluded that his career in hotel security was over.

Tara was saying, "We meet tomorrow at eleven in St Christopher's Place and have a final run through. The guns will be delivered there. Then both of you are driven down to Folkestone and do the job. The triggering box will be already in the car. Martin, are you still staying at the Hilton?"

"No," he replied but didn't volunteer anything.

She gave him a mildly irritated look but only said, "Then check out of wherever you are tomorrow morning and drop your suitcase into the luggage office at Charing Cross. It can be picked up later."

"I'm going to make a brief visit to the FPA tomorrow morning," announced Delaney.

"Why?" asked Tara.

"Two reasons. First, I want to check that everything is normal on that front,

196

no strange men nosing around asking questions. Second, my presence on the trip today was highly conspicuous, to put it mildly. I don't want to just vanish people may start to wonder. So I make a brief appearance in the club after the trip. That way, there's nothing to excite suspicion."

Tara thought about it. "Fine, it can do no harm and possibly a lot of good. But don't be late for our meeting or we'll start drawing conclusions."

"Don't worry," said Delaney reverting to his British accent. "It will be a piece of cake, m'dear."

"I've been meaning to ask you," said Carter. "Where did you come up with that weird and wonderful idea about being trapped in a subway crash?"

Delaney chuckled, then went serious. "True story, except it wasn't me. I dated a girl once who was on the Moorgate tube that day. What I told you today was how she told it to me. Actually, she lost a leg. They had to amputate it on the spot. I left that out. And those two journalists were so enthralled that I found it hard to resist telling them that, by the time the emergency services got to me, I had unfortunately died."

"Har har," said Tara.

"Could have happened that way," said Delaney.

US EMBASSY

Margaret Blake had a hangover and was late getting to the Embassy. For her CIA cover, she was on the Trade Attaché's staff, with a special interest in developing tourism links between the US and Europe. As a result, she occasionally had to file a report to the Commerce Department in Washington and, about once a fortnight, attend meetings with British travel organisations and the European Travel Commission. Almost always she went with two of the Trade staff who were genuine tourism specialists and she let them do the talking. There was also a seemingly endless round of freebee receptions, lunches and dinners that she tried to avoid. Lately, she had been neglecting her cover and, feeling the need for a token gesture, had gone along to a reception hosted by British Airways for some visiting executives from the American Association of Travel Agents.

It turned into an unexpectedly pleasant occasion that had ended with a group of them swilling champagne and behaving indecorously in the Câfé de Paris in Swallow Street.

Forcing herself out of bed, she belatedly remembered that she was due to have an early meeting with Sylvester Clote to get a sign-off on two months' worth of expenses that she had finally got around to writing up. Clote would take offence at her lateness, and this would almost certainly result in a lengthy and acrimonious examination of her expense sheets. It was a total waste of time, she reflected, in that he was authorised to query them but not to disallow them. It was yet another example of the mind-numbing and pointless bureaucratic system that was familiar to those who worked for the US Government in general and the CIA in particular.

But Clote wasn't there. His secretary, Charlene Sanchez, a well-stacked blonde who was known behind her back as Forty Watt in reference to the extent of her intellectual brightness, informed Blake that Mr Clote had phoned her the previous evening, a tremor in his voice, to say that he had been called back to Langley urgently. He was, even now, winging his way across the Atlantic.

Blake went to her office entertained at the thought of Clote, slouched in his business class seat, paralysed with fear by the sudden summons. The message light on her telephone was flashing. The voice message said tersely that there was an eyes-only message for her in the communications centre.

She went down to the centre, underground in the Embassy, where a young black man in Marine uniform carefully checked her identity though they had passed often in the Embassy corridors and handed her a newsprint page with the decoded message. It was brief. With immediate effect and until further notice she would have no further dealings with Sylvester Clote. All future contact would be only by coded messages sent via the Embassy communications centre to an address in Langley. The address was a meaningless mix of twelve letters and digits.

Back in her office, Blake's first, incongruous, thought was to wonder who was now going to clear her expense sheets. She imagined the reaction in Langley if she sent them in code to her new contact. Then she starting thinking about the implications of Clote's sudden recall and the message she had received. She pondered two possibilities, neither of them especially good from her point of view.

First, Clote had either lost or found his nerve, depending on how you looked at it, and had decided to cover himself by sending a communication to Langley stating his doubts about the wisdom of CIA involvement with British Intelligence's intention to dispose of the IRA leadership. That would almost certainly have precipitated a demand for his immediate presence back home, either to elaborate on his views in more detail or, if they didn't want to hear what he was saying, to reassign him to some obscure administrative backwater with unsubtle threats about learning to keep his mouth shut. The second possibility, more benign for Clote, was that, somewhere up the CIA chain of command, he had friends who were prepared to extend a helping hand and were doing him the considerable favour of pulling him out of London so that he would be out of it if and when things went sour.

Either way, it put her personally that bit further out on a limb, she reflected. On the one hand, maybe her bosses had decided to take Clote out of play in order to give her a freer hand in dealing with the British. Or, they were laying the groundwork for offering her up as the fatted calf if the need arose. Well, the hell with it. She had already figured out that she might not have a long-term career with the CIA. Like Scarlett O'Hara, she'd think about that tomorrow.

Then Blake had another worry. Was Clote's recall an indication that maybe the CIA was having second thoughts about working with British Intelligence and all but concurring in the plan to wipe out the IRA leadership? She knew that the top echelon at Langley was highly politicised and that a lot of senior people had got their present positions thanks to Bush and Reagan. They owed zip to the Clinton White House. Also, in their global perspective, they were pro-British and anti-terrorist and the Irish didn't count for diddly squat.

But operation Fortress Salvo was going to have many consequences, many of them unforeseeable and some possibly threatening to the Agency because of its tacit complicity with the Brits. Was someone in Langley now experiencing doubts, misgivings, fear? Perhaps the next confidential message she'd get would be an instruction to emphatically suggest to the British that they postpone and rethink the operation. She didn't want that to happen.

Once again, she tried to get Jonathan on the phone and again was told without explanation that he was unavailable. As she slammed down the phone, she reluctantly admitted to herself that she was kind of pissed off with Jonathan Jones. She hadn't been sure what would follow from their night of lovemaking. She had entertained a vague notion of Jonathan, in his awkward, English romantic way, sending flowers the following day. Certainly, she had expected a warm, intimate phone call. Sure, she was a big girl and was the first to say and had, in fact, said it several times in the past that going to bed with someone did not imply obligations. But she had to admit that it wasn't nice to be treated like a one-night stand.

She had to get out of the office, get some fresh air and clear her head of the lingering effects of her hangover. Earlier it had been raining but the clouds had cleared and it was starting to be a hot summer day. She left the Embassy and began an aimless walkabout, along the Square, past the liveried doormen outside Claridge's Hotel on Brook Street and on into the small, elegant Hanover Square, with its famous St George's Church, where Teddy Roosevelt had got married.

She didn't notice any of it. She was now occupied with a new and alarming reason for Clote's abrupt departure. Yesterday afternoon, after she left the meeting with him, he had evidently made a phone call to someone at Langley to check out the whereabouts of one of Jay Trander's people. Within hours, he was summoned home. Cause and effect? Did his casual question mentioning Trander's name cause a flurry? But then, did Clote, the asshole, just drop an off-hand enquiry, or did he blurt out the line she had given him that MI5 believed they had spotted one of Trander's men? And what if Clote's recall had been precipitated by the fact that the CIA was, after all, running one of Trander's men in London. Not the late waterlogged Tony Regula but Martin Carter?

Dammit, she thought, I'm back to the Dark Knight or the Black Knight or whatever the hell his name is. He just won't go away. Right, let's suppose Carter is in London in some quasi-official role. What would call for the services of an assassin or an explosives expert? It still made no sense. She wondered if Jonathan had bothered to run down the licence plate. And that brought Jonathan back to her mind. She sighed.

A street sign told her that she was in Conduit Street. She was tired and was relieved to see one of the many small coffee shops that seemed to be everywhere in London. She went in, ordered a cappuccino at the counter, passed on the rich display of cream cakes and pastries and took a seat at a table in the corner. The place was almost empty. A black man and woman were in quiet, animated conversation at one table and an elderly man was occupied with a newspaper crossword at another. A young couple had come in and were ordering a pot of tea. To take her mind off her confused thoughts, Blake picked up the menu and read it without interest.

"Do you mind if we join you?"

Blake looked up. The two who had just come into the cafe were standing at her table, smiling expectantly. It was the woman who had spoken, a soft, educated voice. She was holding the pot of tea on a plate, while the man carried the two cups and saucers. Seeing them at the counter, Blake had put them in their early twenties, a pair of good-looking college students maybe. Up close, she saw that they were older, in their mid-thirties. They were smartly but not expensively dressed. He had a blue pinstriped suit, white shirt and muted striped tie. She had a red blouse with a cravat and a tartan skirt. Around her neck, she wore a silver Star of David at the end of a chain.

"Why?" asked Blake bluntly. There were at least half a dozen empty tables in the cafe.

The man answered, "Because we hoped we could have a chat with you, Ms Blake."

She hid her surprise. "You bastards have been following me, right?"

As though taking turns, the woman spoke. "We were actually outside your Embassy for about half an hour, trying to get the courage to go in and ask for you. Then we saw you come out. It didn't seem right to stop you on the street so, well, we couldn't think of anything else to do but walk after you. We agreed that it was a stroke of luck to meet you unofficially, so to speak, outside the Embassy."

Blake gestured and they sat down, relieved, and began to busy themselves pouring their tea. She didn't take them as a threat but, just in case, she quietly moved her chair back and hooked her foot around one of the table legs. If they were not what they seemed, they would soon be on the floor pinned by the table and with scalding tea pouring on them.

The man said, "Let me introduce ourselves. My name is Simon Slater and this is Sharon Green. We both work with MI5 in Millbank. We are, neither of us, in senior positions nor are we what you would term agents. More on the administrative side of things, I suppose."

Blake just nodded. He didn't seem to know what to say next. The woman, Sharon, took over.

"We want to make certain information known to the Central Intelligence Agency."

Blake raised a hand. "I guess you've got the wrong person, folks. I'm with the Commercial Attaché's office and I'm not even remotely interested in spying on anyone."

Simon smiled. "Yes, we understand that, of course. We're not asking you to say anything at all, just hear us out, please."

"It's your show," she said shortly.

"There is a special committee that is chaired by our Director, Stella Rimington. It consists of Chief Inspector Scott from Scotland Yard, Chief Superintendent Taylor of the RUC, Commander Trevor Wallace of MI6, Brigadier Clive Reid of Army Intelligence and, ah, Margaret Blake of the American Central Intelligence Agency. It has three other members but they do not usually attend meetings Jonathan Jones, Andrew Manning and Richard Sterwood, all senior MI5 operatives. The committee has only one purpose, to implement an operation that is codenamed Fortress Salvo. The target date for this operation has been moved forward very recently in response to a course of action being taken by 10 Downing Street."

He paused as though expecting Blake to confirm or deny what he had said.

"Like you asked, I'm listening," she said.

"We know the full details of Fortress Salvo. I would rather not discuss it here beyond saying that the first part, Fortress, involves fifty targets."

Blake took a sip of her cappuccino and looked at them with polite interest. If they had expected her to be reeling with surprise or dismay, they would be disappointed. She knew that knowledge of the operation extended beyond the committee itself and that, of necessity, quite a number of people in MI5 would have been involved in the planning and logistics. But it was unusual, even surreal, to be talking about it in a Mayfair coffee shop with two of MI5's personnel if they were who they said they were.

Abruptly she said, "You say that you're not senior personnel. But you claim to know a lot about what's going on at the top in MI5."

"Between us, yes," said Simon with a glance to Sharon.

"So you say. Before we take this any further, I'm going to ask you three questions that may go to your credibility. The first is this: Rimington always insists on being served a certain brand of tea. What is it?"

Simon looked puzzled but Sharon smiled. "She doesn't. Her tea comes up from our restaurant. She would have no idea what brand it is. The same goes for the coffee you drink at committee meetings."

"Second question: What is the name of Andrew Manning's current secretary?"

Sharon answered again. "Another trick question. He doesn't have one. Mrs Rascombe was his secretary earlier this year but she retired and he didn't replace her."

"Third question: Where is Jonathan Jones right now?"

"Right now, I couldn't be sure," said Simon. "But he went over to Belfast yesterday morning and he's due back later this afternoon. He's probably on his way to Belfast Airport right now." He smiled. "Do we pass?"

"Thank you," said Blake gravely. "Please continue if you wish." The news about Jonathan explained why he hadn't phoned and she felt good about that. She was reasonably satisfied that Simon and Sharon worked in Millbank. Simon's next words jerked her back.

"The full name of the operation is Lilac Fortress Salvo," said Simon. "There are three parts to the operation and we believe you are aware of only two. That's why we are here. Fortress concerns the fifty, as I said. Salvo is the follow-up, mopping-up phase. But Lilac comes first and is intended to pre-empt criticism and influence public opinion in advance."

He hesitated, looked at Sharon who nodded encouragement, then went on.

"We found out about it by accident. A file was left open on a desk instead of being put in the safe. The information in the file showed us where to get other information, and we've now more or less got the full picture.

"Lilac will be carried out by three special teams of four men, all ex-SAS, all of them with a proven track record under fire. They are part of a small group of 25 highly trained specialists in what is called Extreme Response Situations. Officially they don't exist, of course.

"Most of their work is overseas but they've been active in Northern Ireland and have carried out at least one operation in Britain that was attributed to the IRA. That was at Heathrow Airport, some years ago. They are headed by a

203

colonel and are answerable only to three Brigadier Generals in Army Intelligence. One of those is Brigadier Clive Reid."

Blake recalled the stiffly dressed man from Army Intelligence, playing around with his pipe, listening keenly and saying almost nothing.

Simon went on, "Four days before Fortress begins, each team will undertake a bombing operation, in Belfast, Dublin and in London. The bombings will look like the work of the IRA, or a faction within the IRA. Fingerprints will be found, a bomber will apparently blow himself up, that sort of thing. Public opinion will be outraged. There will be faked admissions from the IRA, with all the right code words. The genuine IRA denials will be discounted. A careful campaign of disinformation will suggest that civil war is about to break out within the IRA. When Fortress happens, public opinion, both here and internationally, will be either utterly confused or will welcome it."

Blake's first thought was: what a brilliant idea. And why didn't we think of it? With the right kind of targets, the public could be panicked. Whole sections of the media would be screaming out for action. The assassination of IRA leaders would be seen and reported initially as confirmation that the movement was engaged in internecine warfare, not for the first time. The assassinations carried out by British agents could be attributable to IRA blood-lust. It would fully justify the SAS being called in to round up the rank and file. It might take days, even weeks, before any suspicion of British Intelligence involvement surfaced. And, by then, the chances were that it wouldn't matter.

Selecting the targets would be crucial high news value, impressive damage, no serious casualties.

"What are the targets?" she asked.

"That's the thing," said Simon softly. "The Belfast bomb will be placed outside the offices of the *Newsletter*, right in the City centre and will be exploded at midday. The result will be carnage. Dozens will die or will be maimed. In Dublin, the bomb will go off during the official opening of an electronics trade show in the Royal Dublin Society hall. The Industrial Development Board of Northern Ireland has a big stand. Another high body count is certain. In London..."

He broke off and was silent. It was Sharon who said, "The London bomb will explode in Kensington and will blow the Princess of Wales to bits."

Blake shot back in her chair. She stared at them both in total disbelief. "You're talking about Princess Diana?"

They returned her stare and nodded in confirmation.

"Where are you coming from with this shit?" snapped Blake angrily. "You know, right up to this point, I was starting to believe you guys. But Princess Di? Jeez, get away with you."

Simon smiled grimly. "Amazing, is it not? I tell you that agents of the British Government are going to cold-bloodedly murder scores of innocent people and you're ready to accept it without raising an eyebrow. I mention the Princess of Wales, and suddenly you are so shocked you cannot accept it. You Americans think more of the Royals than we do."

Blake reddened. "Don't hand me that crap. Listen to yourselves. You sound like you've been writing scripts for Oliver Stone. Yeah, maybe the Belfast and Dublin bombs are just about possible. British Intelligence has organised more than one bombing in Dublin before now. But you're seriously asking me to believe that they're gonna take out a member of their own Royal family? You're shitting me."

"I rather wish that we were," retorted Simon sharply. "No offence, Ms Blake, but I suspect that most of what you know about the Royal family comes from *People* magazine and CBS. You haven't been keeping up to date on your own CIA files. It's pretty well known that, within the British Establishment, many are convinced that the Princess represents the greatest possible danger to the future of the British Monarchy, which is steadily falling in popularity year by year. She makes them look anachronistic, makes Charles sound like a loony or a retard. Worse, she's regarded as emotionally unstable and utterly unpredictable, a loose cannon. And, her greatest crime, the Princess is the most popular woman in Britain. The most influential person in the Royal Household, I don't need to mention his name, has been dropping quiet hints for some time now that something needs to be done about her."

Sharon added, "Blowing her up with a supposed IRA bomb is actually the least incredible thing we've told you. It kills two birds with the one stone and it ensures that Army Intelligence has the highest protectors in the Establishment."

There was a long silence. Then Blake asked, "Either of you guys smoke?"

Simon took out a pack of Rothmans and a box of Swan Vesta matches and lit a cigarette for her. She took a deep drag, looked at the two of them, shook her head incredulously and asked, "Can you prove any of this?"

"All of it," said Simon.

"You got documents, files, signatures?"

He nodded.

"Got them with you?"

He shook his head.

"Ok, when can I see something?"

He kept shaking his head. "I'm afraid we don't intend to let you see or give you anything. It isn't necessary."

"I don't get you."

Sharon put her hand across the table and placed it on Simon's. "I have no doubt that many people would regard our decision to talk to you today as treason. But we are not betraying our country, Ms Blake," her voice quivered and Simon grasped her hand tightly. "Operation Fortress Salvo is part of our war to rid the United Kingdom of the IRA terror. We're eliminating a gang of organised killers in our midst and that's a good thing. The other part of it, the bombs in Belfast and Dublin and London that's murder plain and simple. And it has got to be stopped."

She was calm again. "We talked about what we had to do. Our obvious course was to take everything we had to the Director. We don't believe that Ms Rimington would countenance these things. But could we be absolutely, one hundred per cent sure? And if not her, who else could we trust in MI6 or anywhere in Intelligence? We thought of going to John Major. But there is no direct way of getting to him and there is every risk that we could be intercepted along the way. Just as important, if this information got to the PM, the fallout would destroy MI6, and we don't want that either."

Simon cued in again. "It was my idea to tell you. Your agency is the only one that we can be sure is not involved. Ironic, is it not? We have decided not to give you any documents. If the CIA had them, sooner or later, they'd use them to blackmail our Intelligence services. If things were the other way round, we'd do the same."

"But what do you expect me to do?" asked Blake puzzled.

"Tell your Agency, of course. The CIA will have no proof but you can't ignore it and you can't afford to be involved with it. We expect that your Agency will most likely ask our Director about it. And that, of itself, will be the end of it."

"You do realise," said Blake slowly, "that if we mention our source to your Director, you could both be looking at twenty years apiece in the slammer?"

"Forty years each is the more likely sentence for treason," responded Simon. "But I don't believe that the CIA will mention us. You'll start thinking how you can blackmail us. Well, best of luck to you."

He got up from the table and Sharon immediately rose also.

"As I said, best of luck, Ms Blake," he said.

They both walked out of the café without looking back. Blake looked after them and thought: if you're able to organise something that's seriously unethical, don't let an intellectual Jew get into the loop, and especially not two intellectual Jews in love. They're always the ones with the conscience and guts to go whistle-blowing.

She wished that Simon had left his cigarettes on the table.

* * *

Jonathan rang her at home around six o'clock. He was sincere in his apologies that he hadn't been able to call before, without patronising her by making too big a deal of it. He asked lightly, "How has your day been?"

"Oh, the usual," she replied, thinking back on it. After leaving the café, she had found herself at a loose end, not wanting to go back to the Embassy. She had continued her aimless wandering for a while.

A movie house in Piccadilly was showing an Ingmar Bergman retrospective and it seemed as good a place as any to pass a few hours. In an almost empty cinema, she sat through the second half of *The Face*, the whole of *The Hour of the Wolf* and the first half of *Winter Night* without really seeing them. Later, she browsed in Foyle's enormous bookshop on Charing Cross Road but couldn't find anything she wanted to buy. Eventually, she took a taxi to where her car was parked off Grosvenor Square and drove to her apartment, where she took a long shower, gradually switching the water from hot to almost icy cold. She poured herself a Jack Daniels, switched the television to CNN and dozed in front of it.

Jonathan said, "I hope you didn't spend all day in that dreadful Embassy building. This was a day for working on your sun tan."

She found herself getting impatient and irritated with the chit-chat, and said, "Jonathan, some things have come up and we need to talk. Like, right away if you can make it."

He picked up on her mood and said briskly, "Absolutely. I could meet with you in, um, an hour hence, if that suits." He named a bar restaurant in Chancery Lane.

He was already there when she arrived and waved to her from a small table in an alcove of the bar. She had been expecting, for no particular reason, a chic, trendy place, with bright lights, garish paintwork, packed with people from marketing and finance. In fact, it was dark and dowdy, with several groups of middle-aged men in subdued and serious conversation.

"An excellent place to have a quiet chat," he remarked as if an explanation was needed. He had waited for her before ordering a drink and now motioned a waiter. Blake decided to stick with Jack Daniels and Jonathan asked for a pint of the bar's special beer.

She had a moment of awkwardness, remembering the intimacies of the other night and was unsure how to set the tone. His amused smile suggested that he understood, but was going to let her make the running. He had a small plastic shopping bag from the HMV record store on the seat beside him and she asked, "Been buying some CDs? Mind if I look see?"

He handed her the bag and she took out half a dozen CDs, curious to know about his taste in music as though it would reveal some insight into his character.

She looked at the labels, bemused. Symphony No 4 by Sir Arnold Bax, Piano Concerto No 2 by Sir Charles Villiers Stanford, Symphony No 1 by Sir C Hubert H Parry, A Solway Symphony by Sir John Blackwood McEwan, the String Quartets of Edmund Rubbra. She realised that she really knew very little about Jonathan Jones.

She pointed to the Rubbra and said, "I'm surprised you bought that one."

"Oh, why so?"

"All the other guys got knighthoods. He didn't rate. So I guess his music can't be up to much."

He laughed. "Rubbra's actually the best of them, as it happens."

The waiter came with their drinks. Jonathan took a tentative sip of the yellow-brown liquid, sighed happily and, without change of expression, said, "Tell me about Kieran Delaney."

She was puzzled. "Name doesn't ring a bell, sorry."

"He's the chap whose car licence plate you asked me to check."

"Oh, him? Yeah, well, I don't know him and I'm really not interested in him." She said, preoccupied with other things.

Jonathan kept his smile with an effort. Noticing, she said quickly, "Hey, sorry, Jonathan. I didn't mean to sound off-hand, but it's the truth. I don't care about Kieran whatsit. I wanted to get a lead on the guy who was with him in the Ritz and it was the only way I could think of at the time. As happens, I don't anymore need Kieran whoever."

"Delaney," prompted Jonathan. "And who was the other chap, as a matter of interest?"

"I'm about to tell you everything I know about him. But, first, do me a big favour, please. Give me the spiel on Delaney and why you are now interested

208

in him. You've got something, right?"

He held up his glass and studied it while he considered. He took a long swallow and said, "OK, I'll show you mine first. After we left the Ritz, I went back to Millbank and had Kieran Delaney's name within ten minutes. He was Irish, a mild point of interest, but I was intrigued as to why CIA was checking him. I got someone to do a quick and dirty computer check to see if we had anything.

"Our records are better than I thought and we got a hit. It went back nearly fifteen years, when Delaney was a student at Queen's University of Belfast. His family was IRA two uncles and a brother were interned at the height of the troubles. At different times, he himself had three arrests taking part in an illegal march, assaulting an RUC constable by wilfully smashing his nose into the constable's fist and he was suspected of throwing a Molotov cocktail. He was lucky each time, got away with warnings, and a small fine in one instance.

"After that, he falls off the map. Got his degree, worked in Belfast for five years, came over to London. Advertising sales rep with Haymarket Publishing and EMAP, set up his own magazine and has prospered quietly, as far as we know. Hasn't been seen back in Belfast, no problems with the law, and we've nothing on his personal life except that he never took out a marriage licence. And there you have him. A typical profile of yesterday's rebellious student who has metamorphosed into today's respectable businessman."

"Or the typical profile of an IRA sleeper," said Blake thoughtfully.

Jonathan signalled the waiter for another round. "The thought did occur to me. And that's why, just for the hell of it, I had a bag job done on his home yesterday. I hadn't enough to make it official so I got two of our people to do it for me as a personal favour."

"And?"

"He was completely clean, which was his mistake. He has what an aunt of mine calls a lapdog computer a laptop, in other words with an Internet connection. One of our men accessed his mail and found it empty. Everything had been wiped. But nothing, as you know, is ever really wiped off a computer, so our man did his magic tricks. Nothing. It seems that when Delaney gets e-mail, it comes equipped with some sort of self-destruct programme that wipes it just like *Mission Impossible*. Better than anything we've got. Very sophisticated security for the publisher of a trade mag.

"There was something else. Our men discovered that a number of little traps had been set to show up the presence of an intruder. Basic things like a desk drawer left slightly open at a particular angle, talc on the white carpet in the study, a small piece of thread wetted and placed across the top of a closed door."

"Definitely an IRA sleeper," said Blake firmly.

Jonathan shook his head. "He's not the usual type of IRA terrorist. Mostly they turn out to be fairly low level stockroom workers, tradesmen or students. It's possible, maybe even probable, that he's part of an IRA cell in London. But it's far too thin for me to take to the Director. I'd be shot down in flames and told to go and get some hard proof. She would be right, of course."

"So you're doing nothing?" she asked doubtfully.

"Not at all. I'm doing, er, next to nothing. I've called in another favour and put a tail on him. Just one watcher, which means it won't be easy, and I'll have to drop it if there's nothing worthwhile within a few days."

Blake sipped her drink slowly. She saw that Jonathan had scarcely touched his second pint, which had lost its froth and was looking flat.

"Your turn, I think, Margaret," he said.

"OK. The man I saw with Kieran Delaney in the Ritz is Andrew Knight, but he now uses the name Martin Carter. He's ex-Agency, I came across him a couple of times briefly in Langley. He was attached to a special covert unit headed by a guy called Jay Trander, which took care of the Agency's wet work. They were active in South America and, to a lesser extent, in the Middle East and Eastern Europe."

"I've heard of Jay Trander," said Jonathan.

"Well, then, maybe you'll know that his outfit was wound up just before a major Congressional investigation of the Agency. Trander set up his own private security firm, offering the same services as formerly on an exclusive basis to one client."

"Yes, it's not too much of a secret in the Intelligence community," he confirmed.

"Martin Carter, as I'll call him, was and is one of Trander's best operatives. He apparently did extremely well with the Agency in Vietnam. He's a specialist in assassination, as well as being an explosives expert. My information is that he is one of the most dangerous professional assassins in the business. Now, factor in what we know OK, what we think we know about Delaney being an IRA sleeper, and add in the vibes we've been getting about the IRA planning a major bombing here, and we're maybe looking at a very lethal combination.

"I've spent the past few days trying to get a track on Martin Carter. The Agency here in England knows nothing of him. I'm not sure about Langley.

It's just about possible that someone back there is running him. But I don't think so. I've located Carter, incidentally. He's staying in the Hilton Hotel."

"That well-known enclave of assassins and terrorists," said Jonathan sardonically.

"You don't think this is serious?" she said piqued.

"I'm sorry for that fatuous comment. Yes, I do take it seriously. The link between Delaney and Carter is significant. Take either man by himself and we are chasing shadows. Put the two together, and it's far more likely that we're onto something. What it may be is difficult to imagine just now. Of all the terrorist groups in the world, I would have said that the IRA would be the last one to buy in the services of a sniper or bomber. Their in-house capability in those areas is second to none as we have, alas, found out the hard way."

"So what do we do next?" she asked.

He thought for a few moments, tapping his glass with his fingers.

"I can make some informal enquiries about Carter. We have some good friends in Langley."

"No," she responded vehemently.

His eyebrows shot up. "Go on."

"This entire conversation is between the two of us, Jonathan. I still have this fear that I might be compromising some ultra-confidential Agency operation. I want your word that, for the present, you keep everything to yourself. Not a word to anyone in MI5 or 6 or anywhere else in British Intelligence or CIA."

He was in the act of raising his glass. He put it down and looked at her with a puzzled frown. "Margaret, you, above all, must know I can't promise any such thing. If I did, I'd be lying to you and I don't want to do that."

"I think you'll promise," she said confidently. "I've got something to trade."

She paused, then asked, "Were you aware that Fortress Salvo is really Lilac Fortress Salvo?"

His frown deepened. "Did you say Lilac? What the hell are you talking about?"

He clearly knew nothing. She had never believed that he was involved but still felt a great surge of relief coursing through her.

"Let me tell you about Lilac." And she related most everything that Simon and Sharon had told her in the café in Conduit Street. He leaned back in his seat and regarded her with half-closed eyes, motionless, showing no reaction to any part of the story. For a long time after she had finished, he stayed like that, as though frozen in place.

Then he murmured almost to himself, "Clive Reid, eh?"

"I know it all sounds like something out of Tom Clancy" she began, but he broke in. "Oh, I believe it."

"You do?" she said surprised. "I thought you might tell me to see a shrink when I mentioned Princess Diana."

"No, I've no problem with that. There are people, in the Palace and outside it, who have been actively canvassing if there is some convenient way to get rid of her before she brings down the monarchy.

"Actually, I've no real problem believing everything you've just said. Maybe I should have guessed. It fits exactly with a number of things I've picked up in the last week. Yesterday, I was in Ulster and I had a very peculiar conversation with a senior RUC officer. I had no idea what he was talking about and, when he realised that, he shut up and changed the subject awfully quickly. With what you've told me, it now makes a lot of sense."

He wasn't looking laid-back any more and was getting more upset by the minute as implications struck him.

"How did you find out about this, Margaret?" he asked, then held up a hand. "Sorry, I shouldn't have asked. Question withdrawn. But may I ask who else have you told?"

"Just you."

"No one in the Embassy or the Agency?" he said, surprised.

"Only you," she repeated.

"I'm very grateful, needless to say."

He thought for a moment. "Y'know, naming Clive Reid clinches it for me. He was foisted on us a fortnight ago by a very senior chap in the Home Office. We didn't want him or need him but we were told that the SAS, no less, insisted he had to be on our committee. Since when did the SAS make that kind of demand? And, when I briefed him on Fortress Salvo, I got the distinct impression that I was telling him what he already knew."

He stood up abruptly. "Will you please excuse me, Margaret? I want to make a phone call. I shouldn't be long."

He walked over to the bar and used their phone. Blake couldn't hear the conversation but it was brief. As he walked back to their table, Blake tried to imagine what her reaction would be if she were seeing him now for the first time average height, handsome in a languid way, elegantly dressed. She dropped it. With the business in hand, their relationship was now professional and the fact that they had recently been in bed together seemed unreal and almost an irrelevance.

He told her, "The Director is at a dinner party and is expected home at around eleven. She'll be told that I'll be waiting for her. I don't expect it to be an especially pleasant session for either of us."

She laughed. "British understatement is absolutely unique. You really should bottle it and export it."

He smiled ruefully. "Perhaps. I'll say it in case it needs to be said, Margaret. This conversation, everything we've spoken about, remains between us until we both agree otherwise. I won't give the Director the source of my information and I know she won't press me. And, naturally, I intend to say nothing about your Martin Carter."

"What are we going to do about him?" queried Blake.

He shook his head as if to clear it. "I'm afraid he's rather taken a tumble in my priorities. It's difficult to concentrate on the ifs and buts of Carter when I see the best part of a year's work about to unravel."

He looked at his watch. "Very well, I've got a suggestion. I have maybe two hours free right now. Why don't we discreetly check out this Mr Carter. We'll go across to the Hilton and make some enquiries. If he's out, we'll have a quiet look around his room. Even better, we'll toss his room and see how he reacts. If he really is an innocent businessman, he'll go hotfoot with a complaint to the management. His response, or lack of it, will tell us something."

They drove over to the Hilton in his car, a ten-year-old but impeccably maintained Jaguar 3.4. They said little. Blake wondered if they were making the right moves. Jonathan's spur of the moment decision seemed like he was looking for action, any action, for its own sake to pass the time before he met with Stella Rimington.

She stayed in the car and let him go in alone. They both decided against the risk of her accidentally bumping into Carter, who would likely remember her. After a minute or two, she got out of the car and paced up and down the side street where he had parked, regretting now that she hadn't gone in with him.

He returned after half an hour and they sat in the car.

"The bird has flown," he said briefly. "Carter came in on Tuesday and was booked through to Sunday but checked out suddenly last evening. Paid with Amex. One small lead, though. I took a look at his bill and there were three phone calls to the Waldorf Astoria Hotel in New York, and one local number, to the FPA the Foreign Press Association in Carlton House Terrace. The FPA is a sort of club for overseas journalists, some London-based, others passing through."

"Two possibilities, I think," said Margaret. "Either he has a contact there or he's posing as a journalist. Are we going to check it out?"

213

"Indeed, but not tonight, I fancy. I want to be early for the Director. And I need to think carefully about what I'm going to say to her. I'll drive you back to your car and let you go home."

On the way back, he said, "I forgot to mention another curious little item. Carter's Amex is a gold company card, a new one, in the name of Media Publicity Europe, an outfit in Paris. Do you make anything of that?"

Paris? What was important about Paris? Then she remembered.

"Listen, this is interesting. Carter got into London on Tuesday, so he may well have been in Paris on Monday. Wasn't that the day that Charles Dutting of MI6 was murdered by a martial arts expert or a professional assassin?"

He considered it. "It's a stretch," he said sceptically.

"Jonathan," she said impatiently. "It's all a stretch. Like you said, take anything we know about Carter or Delaney in isolation and it amounts to shit. Start putting it together and we've got hold of some really weird stuff."

"You're right," he sighed. "It's just that I'm finding it hard to take my focus away from Clive Reid and his merry men."

"Yeah, I hear you. You've got your priorities right. So go get 'em. You'll let me know how it goes down?"

"Expect my call, partner," he confirmed. She looked out of the side window to hide an unexpected flush of pleasure.

Central London

Saturday 28th

She had expected a late night call from Jonathan to report on his meeting with Stella Rimington but her phone was silent. The following morning, she phoned the Embassy, and told them she had a heavy dentist's appointment and wouldn't get in until much later in the day, if at all. She asked for the communications centre and relaxed when she was told that there was nothing for her from Langley. She had just put the phone down when it rang.

Without preliminaries, Jonathan said, "I'll be driving by your place in half an hour, Margaret. Can you be ready?"

It was going to be another hot, cloudless May day and she waited for him outside. The Jaguar pulled up beside her almost precisely 30 minutes later. "I've had a hell of a late night," he remarked as she got in. But there was no tiredness about him and he looked freshly groomed and bright eyed.

He went on, "If I had hoped to shock and amaze the Director, I was more than gratified. She's pretty good at taking bad news in her stride but this time she was knocked for six. At least, she was generous with the brandy. It was a bit of a bother that I didn't feel free to tell her my source, or your source although I've a fairly good idea about who gave it to you.

"In any event, we spent a long time taking the story apart and examining the pieces and we both came to the reluctant conclusion that it was more than credible. Then, we put an emergency plan together, which involved getting a lot of people out of bed in the wee hours. The upshot of it all is that the Director is right now on an RAF transport plane en route to Scotland, accompanied by a substantial entourage of grim-faced senior civil servants and security bods. Before the day is out, I expect that there will be blood on the floor, though not in the literal sense of course. Project Lilac is dead and, though your contribution remains secret, you have the grateful thanks of at least one of Her Majesty's humble servants."

"All part of the service. What's going to happen to Clive Reid?"

"Very little, I'm sorry to say. It will all happen behind closed doors, as you would expect. This business is far too embarrassing for even an internal

Inquiry. But he has his protectors in high places and they'll take care of him. I wouldn't be at all surprised to see him a Major General in the next Army list."

"I thought at the very least he'd be tossed into the Tower of London."

"No, London is not all that different from Washington when it comes to covering up. Let's just be glad we were able to stop them, Margaret."

"Anything on Delaney?"

"No. My watcher lost him early on, which often happens on a solo surveillance. He went out to Delaney's home but he didn't show last night. We'll pick him up at his office today, I'd imagine."

She looked at the unfamiliar streets they were passing. "Are we going somewhere specific?"

He was already manoeuvring the Jaguar into a vacant parking space. "Bit of luck getting a place to park here. The answer to your question is that we are in Carlton House Terrace. I thought we might pop in and see if we can get a lead on the mysterious Mr Carter."

They both went into the Foreign Press Association building. Jonathan made straight for the porter's desk, while Blake had a look around. At this time in the morning, there were not many people there. In the lounge, were perhaps a dozen men and women sitting in groups or alone reading a newspaper. Three men were at the bar and one of them affably waved her to join them. She shook her head with a smile and tapped her watch to indicate that she didn't have time.

She was standing at the noticeboard, idly reading the circulars and flysheets when a voice said, "Nothing much of interest today, is there?"

She turned and found Kieran Delaney standing beside her. In the Ritz, she had seen him only at a distance. Up close, she noted his rugged good looks and impish expression. He also had a tightness in his face that suggested he was nursing a hangover. In his well-cut light brown three-piece suit, he didn't look like a journalist.

"I'm sorry," he said, in a cultured English voice. "I didn't mean to startle you."

Blake recovered. "Oh no. I was lost in thought for a minute."

"You're American."

"I guess that's not hard to tell. Not many of us in this place, I'm told."

"There are a few," he said easily. "I presume you are of the journalistic persuasion yourself?"

"No. But my friend is with the *Christian Science Monitor*." She said the first newspaper that popped into her head.

"Ah, that's something like *Scientific American,* isn't it?"

Blake found herself enjoying the amused, mildly flirtatious Irishman. She wondered what would happen if Jonathan appeared, what he would make of the conversation.

"Nearly right," she said.

"Or maybe not. Christian Scientists, now. They're the people that have themselves four wives, right?"

"You're thinking about Mormons, and they don't practise polygamy any more. It's illegal."

"What a shame to see such fine cultural customs becoming extinct through the ravages of modern civilisation."

"Have you ever been told that you are a fine cultural example of a male chauvinist pig?" she asked amiably.

"At least once a week, more often on a good week."

"And how do you defend yourself?"

"With a non-committal grunt."

They both laughed. She thought: this happy go lucky guy is almost certainly a murderous IRA terrorist. He could have been giving the same line of chat to a young waitress in a restaurant, then sauntering out, leaving his bomb ticking under a table.

Delaney glanced at his watch and gave a mocking half bow. "And now, to my sweet sorrow, I must away to satisfy my insatiable readers."

He was barely out of sight before Jonathan was back. He said, "I've got something"

"Me, too. I've been chatted up by Kieran Delaney."

"What?"

"He's just gone out the front door. Hope you still know how to tail someone."

"Good Lord, I haven't done that in years. Let's get out to the car."

They sat in the car and watched Delaney walk unhurriedly northwards on towards Piccadilly Circus. He looked at his watch again, stopped, placed a foot on a railing and ostensibly tied his shoelace, glancing casually around.

"That's one advantage of a tinted windscreen," remarked Jonathan. "Let me bring you up to speed quickly. The day after he arrived in London, Martin Carter signed into the FPA as a representative of the *Philadelphia Bulletin.* Make of that what you will. But, for now, Delaney is our quarry. We'll follow him and, twenty minutes from now, when he gets to where he is going, I'll call in for some help. Here we go, he's finished fiddling with his shoe and checking his back. We'll give him more distance and go after him."

"Do I have to ask how you know he's twenty minutes away from some-where?"

"I'm guessing from that quick peek at his watch. You know what they say: a man who looks at his watch is a man who doesn't know the time. He wants to know where he'll be at a later time. It's twenty to eleven and my bet is that Delaney has an appointment at eleven, not too far away because he's in no rush. The game is afoot."

"What?"

"Haven't you ever read Sherlock Holmes?"

They got out of the car and began to follow Delaney in the distance. Blake said, "I'm a liability, here. If he sees me, he'll know he's being tailed."

"Good point," agreed Jonathan. "Why don't you tail me instead of Delaney. Keep the same distance and you'll be too far away for him to spot you."

"You got it, Sherlock."

She gave Jonathan a lead of a hundred yards and set off after him. As they headed into Lower Regent Street, there was a gradual increase in people and traffic. At the Eros statue in Piccadilly Circus, she could no longer see Delaney and at times even Jonathan's figure seemed to vanish in the crowd, and then reappear again, like some mirage, shimmering in the heat of the morning.

As they continued along the circular sweep of Regent Street, almost passing the Ritz on their left, the crowds were even thicker. They were in the heart of London's shopping centre and there was a non-stop stream of people flowing in and out of every store entrance. As she passed a side street, she looked up and saw that it was Conduit Street. She glanced down it but couldn't spot the café where she had sat with cold coffee, listening to serious Simon and sad Sharon. London was really a small world. The Ritz and the Conduit Street café, and weren't Grosvenor Square and the Embassy, what, five minutes away?

They were now in Oxford Street, heading towards Marble Arch, two pave-ments packed with people, separated by a constant stream of red double-deck buses and black taxis. At the first intersection, she saw that Jonathan had stopped and seemed to be window shopping. Getting no stay away sign, she went up to him. She was feeling sweaty and out of breath but he looked like he had made the journey in an air-conditioned limo.

He nodded towards the underground entrance. "He just went down there. I didn't go after him, it's an ideal place for him to check if he's being followed.

I expect him to appear somewhere on Oxford Street any second now."

"Unless he's taken the subway," she said, looking at the red and blue Underground sign.

"No, there he goes," exclaimed Jonathan. "The chase resumes." She glimpsed Delaney on the far side of the street before he was lost in the crowds.

They went down the steps and across the underground concourse. Blake stopped and let him take the lead again.

Out onto the far side of Oxford Street, Jonathan said, "Why don't you wait here. I suspect he's almost at his destination. She was near a strange-looking pub called "The Pig in the Pound".

She stood at the corner and Jonathan headed down a side street. In a couple of minutes, he was back.

"He's gone to ground. There's a narrow street about a hundred yards up. He let himself into what looked like an office building, although there's no name-plate or any other indication of what it is. It's this way."

She followed him up the side street. He stopped at the first crossing and indicated the narrow, busy little street just ahead. She looked up at the street sign. It said St Christopher's Place.

St Christopher's Place, off Oxford Street

They stood at the corner for a few moments, looking up the street. Jonathan remarked, "It's full of little shops and cafes and plenty of passing traffic ideal for keeping him under observation. There's a wine bar a few doors up from him on the far side of the road that should give us a good vantage. Let's do a quick detour around the block so that we don't need to pass his place, OK?" They went right down the side street, and swung left into a street that ran parallel with St Christopher's Place. A few hundred yards up, they turned left again down another narrow lane until they were at the far end of St Christopher's Place.

They went into a bustling Italian wine bar just as a couple were vacating a table near the window. Jonathan made an undignified scamper for it and Blake sat beside him, ignoring the indignant looks from two young women who had been sitting at the bar, evidently waiting for the table to be free. The restaurant was small, but busy, with a heavy aroma of fresh baking. A tape recorder at the bar was playing Nino Rota movie themes. It had about a dozen tables, all occupied by groups of tourists and office workers taking a morning break. More coffee and croissants than wine being consumed.

Jonathan lifted the large sized menu and held it so that it hid his face from outside. Blake did likewise. "What more could we ask for," he said jovially. "A comfortable seat, a spot-on view of the doorway, where we can't be seen and a nice cold beer. This surveillance business is not half as bad as I seem to remember it."

"We've never had it so good," agreed Blake, recalling the last time she had been on surveillance, huddled against a tiny alcove in a street in Washington, shivering in an intense and bitterly cold rain. "Which doorway?"

"See the green one, three doors down, number 10? That's the one. He had a key so I don't know if anyone else is in there. Seems to be apartments or offices but it looks deserted, don't you think?"

There was no waiter service, only a fat bearded man in a red and blue striped apron who stood behind the bar, pouring drinks or coffee and occasionally shouting an order into a curtained-off area behind him. Jonathan went over to him and was back surprisingly quickly with an Italian beer and a glass of

Chianti.

"How long do we give him?" she asked.

"Not long. For us, anyway. I'm going to call my man to take over so that we can put our time to more productive use. I don't want to sound pompous but it's ludicrous, really, for people at our level to be chasing around London, tailing God knows who, for reasons we don't know what. Forgive my English."

He kept the menu in front of him, pulled out his mobile phone and keyed in a number. He took a quick gulp of his beer while he waited.

"Peter? Jonathan. I've got Delaney under observation right now so you're wasting your time hanging around his office. Oh, where are you, then? Yes, I understand, no problem. No, that's fine. I'm in an Italian bar in St Christopher's Place, just off Oxford Street, near the New Bond Street corner. OK, look it up and come in from the opposite direction. When can you get here? Damn, no that's fine, I'll wait."

He hung up. "Damn again. He was called back to Millbank this morning, never even got started on trying to find Delaney. Not that it matters the way things have turned out. But I was hoping he was only ten minutes away. In fact, it's going to be the guts of an hour."

"Oh, dear. You figure we'll be able to take each other's company that long?" she said, smiling.

He grinned back, glanced across the road and went serious. "Well, well. I think they've got a customer. Caller at the door."

She waited a moment then casually moved her head.

There was a man at the door of number 10. He was tall and heavily built with a ruddy face and a mop of black hair streaked with grey. He was perspiring heavily. He looked out of place on this hot summer morning in dark blue woollen suit, a tie and wing-tip shoes. Under one arm he awkwardly carried a long rectangular package in blue and red wrapping, with a yellow ribbon that had a logo 'Floral Fancies'. He also had a black expanding briefcase that, from his stance, was heavy. But he kept them both firmly in his hand when he might have been expected to put them down while he waited.

"He looks like a prosperous farmer on a rare visit to London," observed Jonathan. "But I suspect that his appearance is deceptive."

"You really believe flowers?" she asked.

"Maybe it's someone's birthday."

The door of number 10 opened and a girl appeared briefly, smiling. The man quickly entered and the door closed behind him.

"That's her," exclaimed Blake.

"Huh, who?"

"The girl I saw with Delaney and Carter in the Ritz. Wanna bet that Carter is in there, too?"

"The plot thickens," he said thoughtfully. "Always assuming there is a plot."

* * *

In the sitting room on the first floor in number 8, Carter and Delaney waited for Tara to bring up the man with the weapons. Delaney, hot and breathing heavily, was lolling back in the armchair, drinking a bottle of Carlsberg lager.

"God, but I've been looking forward to this for the past ten minutes. It's an oven of a day to be tramping around London."

"You walked over from the FPA?"

"That I did. I spent last night in the delightful company of a young lady friend out Hampstead way. I stashed my car at her place, took the tube to the FPA and walked over here. Soon as we get back, I plan to spend a few days in her place, out of harm's way."

"Makes sense," agreed Carter. "So, all quiet at the FPA?"

"Yeah." There was a trace of hesitation.

"What?"

Again a hesitation. "I dunno. There was nothing out of place at Carlton House. Just a few people around, working off hangovers or starting the next one. One discreet enquiry after my health. No furtive looks or exaggerated bonhomie, no strange men sitting in corner armchairs, peering over their newspapers. But when I was leaving, there was a very attractive girl hanging around in the hall. I've seen her somewhere else recently but I'm damned if I can place her. We had a few words. She's American, New Yorkish accent, said her boyfriend was with the *Christian Science Monitor*, seemed OK, a fun-loving gal, I'd say. But, when she laughed, I knew immediately that I'd already seen her laugh in just the same way and not all that long ago. Sounds romantic, doesn't it? But it's bloody infuriating that I can't recall where I saw her."

"If she's American, you likely saw her in New York, or on the plane. Or could be she was in the FPA first time we went."

"Maybe." Delaney sounded dubious.

Just then, Tara came into the room with a heavy, red-faced man who was carrying a large expanding briefcase. She introduced him to Carter as Douglas King and didn't elaborate.

"What ho, Douglas," said Delaney cheerfully. "Fabulous day for a leisurely stroll around London town."

"As you can see, I've been having a ball," said King, heaving package and briefcase onto the table. "I was just about to tie this briefcase to my bollix in case I felt like breaking into a trot."

Delaney laughed, went into the kitchen and came back with a bottle of Carlsberg, which he tossed to King. "Take a delicate sip of this magic potion and let's unwrap our presents."

He slipped off the ribbon, opened the box and whistled appreciatively. "God, it's a while since I've had an Uzi in my hands. Excellent."

Tara was unzipping the briefcase. "Leave the Uzi in the box for the moment, Kieran. You can assemble it later. These are the handguns." She took out four packages and unwrapped them: three Smith &Wessons, two .38 Specials, a .44 Magnum and a Glock 357 semi-automatic.

She motioned to Carter. "Take your pick. Kieran will be backing you up so I suggest we give him the Uzi. Take one or two of the handguns, if you want." She peered into the briefcase. "There are belt clip holsters and plenty of ammunition."

"Lot of firepower," observed Carter.

"Well," retorted Tara. "We were planning a bigger team."

Carter took up one of the S&W Specials and inspected it. "I'll settle for this one."

"They're all new," said Tara, "but they've been well tested and they're ready for action."

He nodded and put the gun back on the table. He would have time to check it out in more detail later. Delaney examined the other guns with evident pleasure. "I'll take along a spare just in case. I've used a Glock a couple of times and I've been happy with it."

King, who had been sitting at the table watching them quietly, said, "This brings back a lot of memories. To tell the truth, I wouldn't mind being in on the action again, whatever it is."

Tara smiled at him. "For as long as you're willing to help, you're far more valuable to us where you are, Colum."

"Better get used to calling me Douglas. I'm long used to the name."

Delaney looked over at him. "How did you come to pick Douglas King as a name?"

King replied, "I was holed up for a few weeks in a basement flat in Liverpool with nothing else to do, and I got through a power of reading. I had this book about the First World War and it had a picture of Field Marshal Douglas Haig with King George V. I thought, Hey, Douglas King, now that's a good, respectable English name. So I baptised myself on the spot."

Delaney looked at him critically. "Y'know, if you grew yourself one of them handlebar moustaches, I reckon you'd even look like Haig. Or grow a beard, too, and look like King George."

"Maybe I'll have my arse transplanted to my face and look like you," and he guffawed.

"Behave yourselves, kiddies," said Tara. She went over to Carter, who was standing close to the window, looking through the slatted venetian blinds at the busy street below. She looked out, too.

Tara said softly, "Whenever I'm involved in an operation, I find myself watching people as they pass by, going about their business, worrying mostly about trivia. I know it's a conceit, but it's almost as though I'm an alien from another planet trying to work out how people can live ordinary, routine lives and find some purpose to their existence. I look at them and wonder what is going on in their minds. Do you ever wonder that?"

Carter was silent for a few moments, then he said, "Hmm. I was just wondering what's going on in the mind of that CIA agent across the street."

She shot him a puzzled look and smiled tentatively, expecting a joke. "What do you mean?"

"Directly across, sitting by the window in that cafe, watching our doorway. Her name is Blake, can't recall her first name. She's a field operative with the Agency and what the hell is she doing here?"

Tara looked and suddenly put her hand to her mouth. "Oh Christ," she gasped. "The man with her is MI5. It's Jonathan Jones, Stella Rimington's right-hand man, he co-ordinates their anti-IRA campaign, along with Andrew Manning?"

"Is that a fact?"

"Yes it is. He's in and out of Belfast all the time. A few months ago, we very nearly took him out. I had him under observation for two days. Look's like we've got trouble. See how they're holding those menus so they can't be seen from number 10. Unlucky for them we're not in number 10."

Behind her, Delaney remained seated and took a box of ammunition from the briefcase and loaded the Glock. He asked casually, "Dear me, am I to understand that we may be surrounded like rats in a trap?"

King, too, kept his seat but said something to Tara in Gaelic, his voice angry. She replied in Gaelic. Carter looked at the two of them, then went over behind Delaney, leaned over him and took a box of ammunition from the briefcase for the S&W. He said, "No, I don't think we're surrounded. Look outside. There are lots of people walking around. Looks like families, children, dogs. If they were coming after us, first thing they'd do is get the civilians out of harm's way."

Delaney got up and walked unhurried to the window. He glanced out and suddenly recoiled. "Jaysus and Mary," he exclaimed. "That's her. The girl from the FPA, I was telling you about. She followed me here."

He looked at the others sheepishly. "Sorry about that, folks. I was looking out for a tail on the way over but I obviously didn't look too well. Christian Science, my bollix."

He asked Carter, "She's one of yours, CIA?"

"She's with the Agency."

Delaney shook his head and smiled. "Looks like we've each got us a CIA agent. What the hell are the Yankee imperialist running dogs doing getting involved in our little war? Don't they have enough problems of their own?"

"The old story," said Carter. "Everyone calls on us for help and then starts whining as soon as we arrive."

Delaney took another look out the window. "Well, now, what have we here? So that's Jonathan Jones. Now I remember where I saw that girl previously. I saw them together in the Ritz on Tuesday. They were with a group of people in a corner away from us."

"You sure of that?" demanded Tara. "I didn't notice them." She looked at Carter who shook his head.

Delaney said, "You two had, ah, other preoccupations. But I got there first that day, remember, and had nothing better to do than look around while I was waiting but watch the passing parade. She caught my eye because she was an attractive girl with a group of men, and I noticed that she was giving one of them the eye your lad, Jones, matter of fact."

Tara looked grim. "If they were onto us at the Ritz, the chances are they know about this operation. It could mean that we're blown."

"Maybe not," said Carter slowly. "Look, this doesn't add up. You really think that the number two in British Intelligence spends his time pounding the sidewalks doing surveillance? And would they put a CIA agent right in the front line? Not their style. I don't know what's going on but these two birds seem to be doing some sort of solo run."

Tara took a mobile phone out of her bag and speed-dialled a number. She listened for a moment and said, "Tara. I think we've got company out front.

What's it like your end? Two of them? OK, no, do nothing, just stay in place."

She clicked off. "I've got someone watching our back. He says that it looks quiet except for two Telecom vans that pulled into the street about ten minutes ago. The drivers parked and went off. Maybe they're Telecom vans, maybe not. Otherwise, no activity." She looked at Carter doubtfully. "You may be right and there are just the two of them down there. On the other hand..."

He was back at the window. "You're not the only one using a cellular phone."

* * *

In the restaurant, Blake heard a low repeated buzzing. Jonathan frowned, reached into his inside pocket and took out his mobile phone. "Who is it? Peter, I hope you're on the way. No, go ahead." He listened intently for a minute and said, "No, I want you here anyway to take charge. Hurry it up, Peter."

He looked pleased as he put the mobile on the table, then took it in his hand again. "Remember what you said last night about Carter being in Paris on Monday? Look's like you may be right. I got MI6 to run a check on Media Publicity Europe, the outfit that gave him his Amex. Bingo. Media Publicity Europe is a front for an IRA propaganda cell in Europe. One of their employees, a girl called Nicole Bouchier who is originally from Ulster, despite the name is believed to be responsible for spreading the word in financial circles that the IRA is about to launch another wave of bombing in the City. Charles Dutting had her under observation when he was killed. She's gone to ground and the offices are empty. Incidentally, I suspect that Dutting's assignment was more than just surveillance, but that's neither here nor there. What matters is that we've got a hard link between Carter and the IRA."

"So I was right all along about him."

He heard the surprise in her voice and raised an eyebrow.

She shrugged. "You know what it's like when you're following a hunch with little to back it up. You believe it and yet you don't. So, what now?"

"We're pulling out, Margaret." he said decisively. "I'm ordering up a full-scale surveillance on this lot across the road. Within the hour, this area is going to be saturated with watchers. I've no doubt that it's an IRA cell and my guess is that chummy was bringing in arms and maybe bomb equipment. Carter may well be in there, too. If he's not, they'll lead us to him and we'll snaffle the lot of them."

"Jonathan, that girl who answered the door, you think maybe she's Nicole Bouchier?"

"I thought of that. We'll find out soon enough. Time to get things moving."

He had started pressing buttons when the mobile started buzzing. He looked at it startled, put it to his ear and snapped impatiently, "Yes, who is it?"

"Geoffrey Scott," he mouthed to Blake. "Geoffrey, can I get back to you, I'm involved...fine, go ahead. Sorry, you're fading. OK, I've got you. You mean, now? What's so important about...You what?" He looked at Blake, astonishment on his features. "When? I'm losing you again. You're back but it's a bad connection. I'm actually sitting in a restaurant in St Christopher's Place, just off Oxford Street. No, No. Don't do that! Repeat, don't approach...Hello? Hello?"

He looked like he was going to slam the mobile on the table but stopped himself. "Lost him, dammit. These bloody mobiles," he said in exasperation. Then his bemused expression returned.

"That was Geoffrey Scott. He's got Trevor Wallace with him and they're heading over to Knightsbridge police station. He says that MI6 has just captured the IRA Chief of Staff in a Knightsbridge Hotel."

"You mean they've finally got Sam the mystery man? Here in London?"

"So they say. Geoffrey was saying more, but I lost him. Y'know, Stella is going to blow her top when she hears. This should have been a joint operation. Still, if Six have taken Sam in flagrante, it will be brownie stars all round. I'd better make that call and get us out of here fast."

He speed dialled. "Jonathan Jones here," he snapped. "Get Andrew Manning on the line within the next ten seconds wherever he is. I'll hold." He said to Blake, with a nod across the road, "It will be interesting to see how this lot react when they learn that Sam is taken. We need Manning here now."

* * *

Delaney looked down at them. "Looks like he's calling in the cavalry. I reckon it's time for us to make a swift advance to the rear."

King asked, "What about those Telecom vans?"

Delaney bared his teeth. "We'll be ready for that. If it's a trap, they'll be at a disadvantage when they try to get out of the vans."

Tara shook her head. "No. We can't walk away and leave things up in the air like this, Kieran. We need to know what those two are doing down there, what it means."

"The hell with them. If we don't move now, this could turn into a siege. And if that happens, they'll call in the SAS. And we sure as hell don't have anything like the firepower to take them on. Let's get out while we can."

"Listen to me," she said, speaking urgently. "It's vital that we focus on our mission"

"Jaysus, that's blown," he interrupted.

"No, it's not," she said fiercely. "Least we don't know that it is. Look, there are three possibilities. There's the obvious one, that the Brits are onto us, have been tailing us for a week, maybe longer, and they know what we're planning. But that doesn't make sense. If they had made all of us, we would have been picked up, one by one, before now. You two wouldn't have made it back from the Tunnel yesterday.

"So, number two possibility is that they've been tracking just one of us. The fact that one of your CIA colleagues is outside means that it's most likely you, Martin. And the reason they haven't taken you is that they've been waiting for you to lead them to the rest of the unit. If that's the case, we're going to be grabbed as soon as we set foot outside the door. And they haven't cleared the area of civilians because they're counting on taking us by surprise."

"If it's Martin," said Delaney slowly. "Then they've also made me. What's worse is that they had their people on us yesterday. They saw where we went, what we did. They've probably got the bloody amplifiers in their lab by this time."

She nodded. "Yes, but the third possibility and the most likely is that there's a lot less than it seems to Jones and the CIA woman being here. I'm thinking this: somehow, Jones stumbled onto Martin. He finds out that he's CIA. He calls in a CIA agent for confirmation. They've followed you here, Martin, but they don't know about the rest of us and don't know what's going on. That's why Jones himself is here. He's not expecting trouble.

"Now he's seen Douglas arrive, maybe saw me at the door. But he still has nothing much to go on. If this is the right scenario, what we saw a minute ago was Jones calling in agents to start tailing us all."

Delaney went back by the window. "You could be right," he admitted. "Nothing's changed down there. They're still studying the damn menu. So, you're thinking we can walk out of here, let them follow us, lose our tails and regroup later?" He sounded sceptical.

"I don't know. But we need to find out."

"How?"

"Simple. I walk out the front door, no weapon, and I stroll past the restaurant, going about my business. I head into Oxford Street, see if I'm being followed, lose the tail in one of the department stores and call you on the mobile."

Delaney wasn't happy with that. "I don't like it, Tara. Even if we get an all clear, we're going to have to leave the guns behind us and we'll need them later. Besides, you're not the one to take risks. You're the planner on this operation. The way it's already shaping up, all sorts of things can still go wrong. We're going to need you to cover us."

Tara was getting her stubborn, angry look. "As you say, I'm running this operation and"

"I think Tara is right," said Carter. She looked at him, grateful but taken aback. She had assumed that he would react when she had laid it on him for attracting the attention of MI5. She had been expecting angry protestations, vehement denials, sarcastic jibes about IRA security. Instead, he had remained at the window, arms folded, apparently ignoring the argument.

He said, "We need to know if the job is still on. I don't think they know about it and someone has to go out there and see what happens."

King was still sitting at the table, the forgotten man. He had been listening intently but saying nothing. Now he cleared his throat. "I'll be the goat," he said diffidently.

They turned to him in surprise.

"Why not?" he said. "I'm a respectable businessman with a good reputation back home, a pillar of the community." He smiled, ironic and proud at the same time. "I'm clean as they come and I've done nothing incriminating. I don't have any problems about stepping outside. If they take me, I've got a damn good firm of solicitors in London who'll come running."

Delaney stared at him. "Don't kid yourself, er, Douglas. Fact is, you're the only one here with a record. If they haul you in, the first thing they'll do is print you, and that will be the end of Douglas King."

"Yeah, I suppose. But the way I see it, this is a big operation, right?"

"The biggest," confirmed Tara.

He gestured impatiently. "Then it's clear cut. Near as I can make out, you three are essential to getting the job done. I'm the only one here that's expendable. Besides, I agree with how Tara sees it, I don't think they're ready to grab any of us. And, if they are, I'm the only one who definitely can't be made to talk because I know nothing about the operation."

It wasn't quite true. He had heard Tara mention 'the Tunnel'. But he mentally buried that.

There was a moment of uncertainty. Then Carter spoke again. "Do it or don't do it. But it's time to stop talking."

"Right, then," King got to his feet and smoothed down his jacket.

Delaney slipped the Glock into his belt. "C'mon, I'll walk you down."

Tara moved over to King and touched his arm. "Thanks, Colum," she said gently.

He grinned at her. "Up the Republic," he said lightly and went out the door, Delaney at his heels.

Carter was putting ammunition into the S&Ws. He asked, "The door directly below us, is it locked?"

She nodded. "But only from the outside. From the inside, you don't need a key, just slide back the bolts."

He put one gun in his belt, and grabbed another one. "I'll be downstairs," he said and left the room. Tara picked up the Uzi and went to the window. St Christopher's Place was still full of people, most of them walking by unhurriedly, some stopping to window shop. She had no intention of starting a massacre but, then, neither would MI5, and, if they were intending to make a move, a few quick bursts in the air from the Uzi would scatter their plans. She watched as a long black Rover came into view, driving slowly. Uh, uh, she thought, looks like trouble.

* * *

In the restaurant, Blake asked, "Jonathan, you sure Geoffrey heard you tell him to stay away?"

"Huh?" He looked out and saw the Rover. "Damn and double damn," he exclaimed, jumping up and running out to the street. Scott and Taylor of the RUC were in the back, with a plain-clothes driver and Andrew Manning in front. Jonathan rapped at the window, gestured to the driver and shouted, "Keep moving, we'll meet you round the corner."

Evidently the driver didn't hear him because he stopped the car. Scott immediately hopped out.

"Get back in the car, please, Geoffrey and drive around the corner," said Jonathan sharply. Then Andrew Manning also jumped out.

But Scott got distracted when he saw Blake coming out of the restaurant. "Margaret, you're the very person I've been trying to reach. Have you heard?"

Meantime, Ian Taylor got out on his side and smiled a greeting at Blake.

This couldn't be worse, reflected Jonathan, and was immediately proved wrong. In his peripheral vision, he saw the door of number 10 open and the heavily built, ruddy man emerge. He started walking towards them and suddenly stopped as he almost drew abreast, staring at Taylor. At the same moment, Taylor saw him. An astounded look came over his face and he shouted, "Colum McRory!"

For a moment, the man seemed rooted to the spot, then he turned and hastily walked away.

Taylor went after him and bellowed, "Stop right where you are, McRory."

The man walked a few more paces, then stopped and faced Taylor. He reached inside his jacket. Taylor had learned on the streets of Belfast to respond quickly when confronted with someone reaching inside his jacket. Almost instantly, he had his gun in his hand. "Don't make a fucking move," he screamed. But the man kept fumbling.

Delaney had the door opened a few inches and swore, surprised. He hadn't really believed that anything was going to happen and had fully expected King to stroll away unhindered. Instead, the moment he had walked onto the street, a car had appeared from nowhere, with men jumping out and going for him. King had almost reached the doorway and had turned, his back momentarily blocking Delaney's view. Then, without warning, there was a loud bang and a cry from King who staggered, then toppled onto the pavement where he lay still.

Delaney flung the door open and stepped out. The man who had fired the gun was looking at King on the ground, as though stupefied by what he had done. "You murdering bastard," snarled Delaney and fired. A man's face exploded in a crimson haze and he was flung to the ground. Delaney immediately turned his gun on the group at the car. He fired and saw one of the men fall against the bonnet of the car. MI5's Andrew Manning was dead.

There was a few seconds of total silence in St Christopher's Place as people tried to absorb what was happening. Then there was sudden pandemonium, with screaming and shouting, people running and diving to the ground. A few had been sipping drinks at tables on the pavement outside a cafe and they scrambled inside. Tables and chairs were overturned, glasses smashed on the pavement and then an even louder smash as a large sun umbrella crashed through the front plate glass window of the cafe. A middle-aged woman in a bright yellow dress stood outside a shop and was saying in a sharp, loud voice, "Stop this at once, please." A man pulled her to the ground, she resisting angrily.

Blake had watched it happen with disbelief. She had felt a moment of indignation when she heard Taylor shout at the man, thinking, the asshole has screwed up the surveillance. She saw the man walk away with Taylor after him and then, incredibly, Taylor had shot him without warning in a busy public street. Next moment, Delaney was standing there and Taylor was falling to the ground. Then an agonised yelp from Scott and he was falling across the hood of the car. Taylor had taken cover, the bullet meant for him had hit Manning instead.

She saw Jonathan pull a gun from his shoulder holster and fire at Delaney, who fell back into the doorway. Scott, still half leaning on the hood of the car, had got out his gun and was swivelling from Delaney's direction to directly across the street.

She looked over. The front door was open and Carter was standing there, firing fast. His first bullet took Scott on the crown of his head and he slid off, almost into Jonathan, who was forced to step back. The move probably saved him because Carter's next shot took out the front window of the restaurant behind him. The front-seat detective was half out of the car when Carter took him in the chest, then shot the driver through the windscreen. Carter swung the gun onto Blake, held his aim for a second then stepped back and closed the door behind him.

Blake suddenly realised that she was in the line of fire and dived for the ground, falling onto Scott's body. She wriggled away, trying to blot out the picture of his bloody shattered skull and leaking brains. She saw Scott's revolver on the ground, picked it up and crouched behind the car. Delaney stepped out of his doorway and fired two quick shots. She heard Jonathan mutter a curse and drop to the ground behind her. She fired at Delaney and hit him. He stumbled back into the building.

"You OK, Jonathan?" she yelled without turning around.

"Indeed." He sounded cool. "Damn good shooting Margaret but let's get off the street before our luck runs out."

She looked back and he was on his haunches, scuttling back into the restaurant. She fired another shot in Delaney's direction and another at the closed door opposite, then followed him. She was barely through the door when she heard a smashing of glass, followed by the staccato roar of a sub-machine gun. The car shuddered with the impact, its windows exploding in fragments of glass. There were further screams of terror from the dozen or so people who were still in the street, all of them lying prone on the ground, fearful of moving.

"Christ, there's a whole mob of them and they've got Uzis," said Jonathan.

He looked around and found himself staring at a score of frightened faces. Everyone was on the floor, some lying flat, others peering apprehensively over the table. All except the fat man behind the bar. He was leaning on the counter, swaying slightly to the Godfather theme on the tape and contemplating Jonathan and Blake with lively interest, as though they were a pair of minor celebrities who had walked into his restaurant.

"We are police," said Jonathan, in a calming tone, putting his gun away. "There's been trouble outside but you have nothing to worry about. Just relax." He asked the barman, "Is there an exit out back?"

The man stood away from the counter and regarded him sceptically. " 'Ere, pal, how do I know you're a copper?"

Jonathan looked at him incredulously, then strode behind the bar, put his arm around the man's shoulder, tightened his hold and said in a low menacing voice, "You'd better believe I'm a copper because if I'm not you're going to get your fucking head blown off in two seconds if you don't get your customers out of here."

The fat man pulled away, his eyes wide. "Awlright, pal, no need for the heavy stuff." He came out from behind the counter and said loudly, "Awlright, ladies and gents, show's over. Time to go home. Just make your way out through the curtains into the back."

The customers were quickly on their feet, scrambling for the kitchen.

"Take your time, ladies and gents, pul-eese. No pushing there, Missus. Plenny of room, plenny of time. Don't knock over anything in the kitchen, now." The restaurant emptied quickly, leaving only the fat man, standing at the curtain, glaring at Jonathan.

"Want anything else, copper?" he asked, with heavy sarcasm.

"No, you did well, thanks. Better get out yourself."

The fat man wasn't mollified. He waved a hand. "Don't you go nicking anything, copper. Everything here is counted." Satisfied with this parting sally, he vanished behind the curtain.

"Can you believe that guy?" said Blake, amused despite herself.

Jonathan just shook his head. He was dialling on his mobile. "The police are going to be pouring in. We'd better let them know what to expect." He snapped into the phone, "Scotland Yard? This is an emergency. Put me onto Commander Jim Percival. No delays."

* * *

Carter had slammed and bolted the door and was halfway up the stairs when he heard the distinctive machine-gun fire. When he got to the sitting room, Tara was sitting below the window, the Uzi on the floor beside her. "I gave the car a few bursts. That should keep their heads down for a while." She gave a mirthless smile.

"Delaney's down," he announced.

She scrambled to her feet, careful to avoid the window. "How bad?"

"Couldn't tell. Not too bad, I guess. He's still shooting. I'd better go see."

"We'll both go."

They made their way swiftly across the intervening rooms to number 10, glad that Delaney had left the doors open when he had brought King downstairs. Tara said, "We're going to have to pull Kieran out and make a run for the back."

Not how I expected you to go, thought Carter. He had, in truth, reckoned that Tara would behave badly in a crisis, would be hysterical or reckless or both. When he had heard the Uzi being fired, he had briefly imagined people in the street outside being mown down at random. He had misjudged her. Under fire, she was cool, focused, professional. She wasn't wasting time by starting a discussion on what had gone wrong.

As they ran down the stairs of number 10, they heard a single shot below them. Then they saw Delaney, propped up against the wall beside the door, which was open a few inches. His face was blood streaked and both his jacket and pants had ominously large dark bloody patches. His tie was wrapped around his thigh in a makeshift tourniquet. He fired another shot at random out onto the street, then lay back against the wall, closed his eyes and groaned.

When he heard them, he opened his eyes. "Are we winning?" he asked, with a grin that became a grimace.

"How bad are you?" asked Carter, kneeling beside him. "Let me have a look."

Delaney waved him off and wiped his hand across his forehead. "Forget it," he said, his voice firmer than Carter had expected. "I've been hit twice, in the leg and in my left side, and I don't want to know how bad. Maybe a few ribs are banjaxed, feels like that anyway. It was your CIA friend who did that. Dangerous woman that, but I'll bet she's a tiger in bed."

"Lot of blood on your face," observed Carter.

"Is there? Maybe a splinter." He looked at his bloodstained hand. "Actually, I think I've been rubbing blood on my face without knowing it. Oh Jaysus." His face contorted with pain.

234

Tara said, "Kieran, we're going to break out. Now. Are you up to it?"

He thought about it. "No, you'll have to go without me."

"We won't leave you like this. Can you stand? Maybe we can support you between us." But her tone was dubious.

"Much obliged for the thought but no way. You may have a fight getting out and the last thing you need is to be dragging around my dead weight. You go and I'll hold them off here as long as I can."

She hesitated. "I don't know"

"He's right, we can't take him with us," said Carter, standing up. He handed both of his S&Ws to Delaney. "You'll need these. Good luck, Delaney."

Delaney winked, then lay back. His eyes closed, he said weakly, "I'll be alright. I just need to rest for a moment or two." He sighed. "Ah, join the IRA for the good life."

"Let's go," said Carter, and headed back up the stairs. Tara followed him, then turned and said to Delaney, "I'm going to take care of the files, OK? There's going to be a lot of confusion outside. Might give you an opportunity."

Delaney nodded but she wasn't sure if he had heard. She ran up the stairs after Carter and caught up with him in the sitting room of number 8.

"Which way out?" he asked.

"Hold on. There's something I have to do first."

She went over to the filing cabinet in the corner and, with a quick heave, pushed it over. It fell onto the floor with a noisy clatter. Where the cabinet had been, there was a square stainless steel plate screwed into the floor, about six inches square, with a metal lid. She squatted down and lifted the lid. Underneath, there was a blank LCD display and two plastic buttons, green and red.

For the first time, there was the sound of police sirens and the bells of ambulances. They ignored them. Carter looked on as she pressed the green button. The number 3600 appeared on the screen in red letters. She pressed the green again and it changed to 3300. She kept hitting the green button, stopping when it was 600. Then she pressed the red button. The number started flashing and began counting down 599, 598, 597, 596.

"Ten minutes," she said briefly.

"How big a bomb?"

She watched the numbers until she was satisfied, replaced the lid and stood up.

"Enough to blow this room apart," she said. " I'm counting on it to cause maximum confusion, especially if there's anyone out back. OK, I'm ready."

She grabbed the Uzi and went to the bedroom. He picked up the remaining gun, the S&W, fished in the briefcase and found two boxes of ammunition and followed her. It occurred to him that MI5 and the police were fortunate that she had decided on the bomb as a quick distraction. Otherwise, she could have set it to go off in thirty minutes, when the room might be crowded with police and other security people all legitimate targets as far as the IRA was concerned.

She had let herself out through the window and was balancing on her elbows. "It's only about six feet to the top of the shed. You probably won't even have to drop." She nodded her head towards the Uzi on the bed. "Pass it to me when I'm down."

Then her face vanished and he saw only her fingernails clinging to the sill, noticed, which he hadn't previously, that she wore them short as a man, and then they were gone and he heard her land lightly. He looked out and she was standing on what looked like a reinforced tarpaulin roof, looking up at him. He handed her down the Uzi and she walked to the edge of the roof. He climbed out of the window and lowered himself. Before he was at full stretch, his feet touched the roof. He looked across at the back windows of the row of buildings in the next street. He saw no faces looking out, not that it mattered. He could hear the overlapping sirens and bells, sounding much closer.

They both climbed off the shed and were in a narrow yard that looked like it was used as a depository for hundreds of small wooden fruit boxes, which were piled in rows along one side. They made their way to the rear door of the building. She turned the door handle and pushed. It was unlocked and creaked open. They walked up a short flight of stairs, past empty rooms on either side, their doors missing, broken furniture and rubble on the floors. They came to a small return area with, on one side, a toilet with a broken lavatory bowl and a washbasin. Carter glimpsed himself and Tara in a mirror on the wall as they went past. They hastened through an archway of well-gouged plaster and were in a narrow hall that led to the front door. Everywhere, the place was in a state of rot, with peeling plaster walls and a strong odour of decay.

Tara glanced at her watch. "About three minutes before it goes up. We'll give it another two minutes after the explosion, then we move, OK?"

She looked at him, as she did sometimes, expecting him to be taking offence that she was giving orders. But he just nodded, took off his jacket and handed it to her. "Better cover the Uzi."

The clamour of police sirens and emergency services were now a loud cacophony but when Tara stood close to the door and listened, it seemed to be quiet on the street outside.

"Nothing."

"Or everything."

* * *

In the doorway of number 10, Delaney opened his eyes with a start. The noise had brought him to. There must be half the cop cars in London heading towards St Christopher's Place, and it sounded like there were dozens of ambulances on the way as well. He had blacked out, he guessed. But how long had he been out of it? A few seconds? Several minutes? Christ, and he was supposed to keep the bastards outside busy so that Tara and Carter could get away.

He leaned over to look out the doorway and saw a uniformed policeman on the ground less than ten feet away and crawling steadily towards him. Delaney grabbed one of the S&Ws that Carter had left. The policeman's eyes widened and he stopped moving when he saw Delaney looking at him, pointing the gun. He was young, looked barely out of his teens, with a broken nose and wispy yellow moustache. "I'm not armed." He had a Scottish accident. "Why don't you put down your gun and let's talk."

Delaney was disgusted. "You stupid bollocky fool of an imbecile. You want me to blow your head off? You want to be a hero, kid? Don't say another word, just get the fuck away from me."

The policeman started to say something and Delaney shot him in the hand. He screamed and immediately wriggled back, turning and twisting, until he was out of sight. From somewhere across the road there was a fusillade of gunshots and bullets which thumped into the door.

Then he heard a loud crackling and a voice boomed out. "This is the police. This is the police. Stop shooting and throw out your weapons. Your position is hopeless. I say again"

The voice stopped abruptly as Delaney fired off a few shots through the doorway. This time, there was no return fire. He sat back and tried to decide on a course of action. He realised at once, with surprise, that the pain was less acute that it had been. There was a dull throbbing in his side and leg but he could take it. The blotches of blood on his clothes were not getting any larger. And he felt like he was getting a second wind. Must be all this adrenaline bubbling through me, he thought.

237

He tried to imagine the scene outside: police cars and Landrovers clogging both ends of the street, jostling crowds of the curious being pushed back, TV cameras arriving, police marksmen in flak jackets waiting behind cover. Maybe some were already darting from door to door, heading towards him. How long before the bomb upstairs went off?

Suddenly, he thought of Cathal Brugha, the legendary Republican leader of the Irish Civil War in the early 1920s. Caught in the blazing inferno of a hotel in Dublin's O'Connell Street, and surrounded by Free State Government troops, he had ignored pleas to surrender and came charging out of the flames, both guns firing, into a hail of bullets. Butch Cassidy in real life.

Maybe this was the way to go. He had a flash of himself, staggering through the doorway, bloody but defiant, firing away until they brought him down. He could see the live TV coverage, the page one pictures around the world. His death would electrify the Republican movement everywhere, his heroism would be the stuff of verse and song. Was this the way to go?

He thought about it for a moment, then said aloud, "I will in my arse!"

Carefully, he got to his feet and took a couple of steps. "Mother, I can walk," he said. He thought quickly, relieved that his mind was alert. He had done as much as he could do for the others. Time to look after himself. There was no escape out front. So, his choices were to stay here and be captured or shot by panicky, trigger-happy cops neither option a pleasant one or follow Tara and Carter to the back. But, had he the strength to make a run for it? Only one way to find out.

He stepped over, slammed the door closed and pushed the bolts into place. Then, he headed up the stairs. Every step seemed to hurt a bit more, and his side and leg sent out sparks of pain. He was at the top of the stairs and heading across to the sitting room in number 8. He felt dizzy and his vision seemed to blur at the edges. A cold perspiration was breaking out all over his body. But he would make it, he thought. He would make it if he didn't pass out first.

He tried not to think about the bomb, but his mind was making frantic calculations. How long since Tara had left him? Five minutes, more? And how much time had she allowed when she set the timer? What would he have given it, fifteen minutes? Five? No, more than five for God's sake, more than five.

He hobbled into the sitting room, saw the overturned filing cabinet, the metal plate on the floor. He fought the impulse to go over and lift the lid and see what time was left. In his mind, he could see the red numerals clicking down...3,2,1 and then imagined the room erupt around him. But it wouldn't be like that, he wouldn't see or hear anything. He kept moving, into the bedroom, saw the open window. An incredible burst of agonised pain swept over him as he clambered awkwardly onto the small windowsill. He was gingerly lowering his body onto the roof of the shed, when the bomb went off.

* * *

Jonathan saw the door of number 10 close. "They're pulling back from the doorway," he said to Blake. They were in the restaurant squatting behind the temporary cover of upended tables and other furniture that they had hastily dragged into position. "I think they're going to make a stand upstairs, probably in that room right over there."

"No way we'll get that door open," said Blake. The police sirens were echoing loudly on the street and they were shouting at each other. "You thinking the window?"

"Exactly. You start firing at the room up there, and I'll run across. Doubt if they'll hear me smash the window in this din. There's a chance I can hit them before they know it."

"I'll follow you."

He shook his head quickly. "No, Margaret. Better you stay here and keep firing at them, keep them occupied. How are you on ammunition?"

They were interrupted by a loud male voice. "Police. Freeze where you are and drop your guns on the floor."

They both looked to the side. A policeman in helmet and flak jacket had materialised on the pavement at the restaurant door. He was lying prone beside the Rover and had a rifle aimed at them.

"It's OK," said Jonathan, not making a move. "We're the good guys. MI5."

The policeman might not have heard. "Put your fucking guns down," he commanded, his rifle steady on Jonathan.

Just then, a second policeman came into view, crawling on hands and knees, the flak jacket looking out of place over his smart uniform and braided cap. "You Jonathan Jones?" he demanded crisply.

"Yes."

"Right, Stevens, take the rifle off them. I know who they are." The policeman lowered the rifle slowly but kept cold eyes on Jonathan and Blake.

"Can you get over here?" called the senior policeman and then, "Great God almighty!" when he saw Scott's mangled head.

"On our way," said Jonathan. "But you stay where you are. We think they're holed up on the first floor directly above you." Both he and Blake made their

239

way in an ungainly crouch to the relative shelter of the car. "Chief Superintendent Ted Boudren," he said, extending a gloved hand to Jonathan, who shook it. He looked in his early 50s, tall and slim, with cropped salt and pepper hair and a thin moustache.

Jonathan glanced back up the road. It was mostly deserted. The police were keeping everyone well back. The flashing lights of police cars were reflected on the windows of buildings at the end of the street. Three policemen were in doorways across the road, a few yards up. Two were in uniform and one was plainclothes, all had flak jackets. They must be feeling the heat, thought Jonathan.

Boudren looked uncertainly at Blake.

"She's part of our team," said Jonathan briefly.

Boudren looked at her curiously as they shook hands and said nothing. He turned to Jonathan. "You've talked to Commander Percival and he's been briefing me by phone. I'm taking over now, OK?"

He said it with authority, but with the slightest hint of a question mark. It was his responsibility, but one could never be sure about getting into a turf war with these intelligence bods.

"It's your show," Jonathan agreed immediately. "But keep me in the loop. Right, let me bring you up to speed. We suspect an IRA cell and I estimate that there are four of them, maybe more. One is shot up, don't know how bad. They've got submachine-guns and hand pistols that I know of. They took us from three points, the window right across from here, number 8; the door of number 10, the green one down there; and the first-floor room directly above us, right? Within the last couple of minutes, I believe they have abandoned the ground floor and are on the first, very probably in the room above. I was just about to get in through a ground-floor window and go for them."

"Negative on that, said Boudren sharply. "If anyone goes in after them, it's going to be the SAS. Commander Percival already has them on stand-by. I don't have all my resources here just yet. Most of our people are still over at that Kensington shoot-out. But I'll be up to strength within the next ten minutes. We'll put a cordon around the entire area, then see if we can persuade them to give themselves up." He looked down at Scott's body. "They seem to be a bloodthirsty crowd of buggers so my gut feeling is that the SAS will be going in. We'll see."

Jonathan resisted the temptation to ask for details about Kensington. It was the first he had heard of a shoot-out.

"Now, then," said Boudren, all business. "We're going to take the casualties out. Are they all your people?"

"No. they're mostly yours, I'm sorry to say. That's Chief Inspector Geoffrey Scott," he nodded towards him. "The man on the other side of the car is my friend and colleague Andrew Manning. I don't know the other two by name but I believe they're from the Yard. One was Geoffrey's driver, the other I don't know. Taylor of RUC is over there very lucky to be alive."

Boudren looked grim. "I know of Geoffrey Scott, but I never met him. This is a terrible thing. I didn't realise it was so bad."

No worse than if they had all been MI5 agents, thought Jonathan bitterly. Aloud he said, "The fifth body is a member of the IRA cell. He brought in the guns."

"What fifth body?" demanded Boudren.

"Just across the road," said Jonathan, looking over the car bonnet. To his astonishment, the body of the heavily built man was gone. He stared at the spot for several moments, speechless. He slowly lowered himself back into a crouch, and said to Blake and Boudren, "He's vanished."

At that moment, as though it had been timed dramatically, there was a deafening thunderclap and, a moment later, a rain of glass, bricks and other debris was falling onto St Christopher's Place.

* * *

Carter and Tara were both watching the second hand of his watch as it swept jerkily around. "Should be anytime now," she said, and a moment later, it went off. The whole building shuddered violently and a loud roaring resonated in their ears. The floor beneath them vibrated and bits of plaster were dropping from the ceiling like the start of a snowfall. The roar intensified for a few moments, then slowly subsided.

As soon as the noise faded, Carter said, "The hell with waiting." He opened the front door a fraction and looked out. First thing he noticed was the tumult of sound. The police sirens had been joined by a clamour of ringing, blaring and wailing alarms from buildings and parked cars in the vicinity that had been set off by the blast. There were people outside, but they were all running towards one or other end of the street. There was no sign of the British Telecom vans.

He opened the door wider. "This is our best chance. Everyone's gonna to be in shock for the next couple of minutes."

Tara followed him, the Uzi at the ready under Carter's jacket. She looked quickly up the street. It was now deserted except for a man who was getting out of a Toyota Corolla a few yards away, who wasn't paying them any attention. A black taxi was pulling out of a car space at the end of the street and Tara waved to get the driver's attention. As they waited for it to pull up beside them, the man from the Toyota gave them a disinterested glance and turned back to lock the car door. He was young, with sharp features and a receding hairline with an untidy clump of curly hair. He had on a grey summer jacket, open white shirt and blue jeans.

Suddenly, Carter took two paces over to him, grabbed his shoulder, spun him around and kicked him hard in the kneecap. The man shrieked and went down. As he hit the ground, Carter grasped the back of his neck and slammed his head into the pavement. His body jerked and he went still.

"What are you doing?" shouted Tara, staring wide-eyed at Carter as though he had gone berserk. He leaned down and turned the man onto his back. He reached a hand inside the man's jacket and pulled out an automatic.

"If you're going to carry, wear a jacket that doesn't show the bulge," he said. He clasped the man by the lapels of his jacket, dragged him over to the doorway, and propped him in a seated position, his head lolling on his chest.

Carter was surprised that the cab had not taken off but stayed beside them, its engine running. The driver, a small, white-haired man with craggy, lived-in features who looked to be about a hundred and ten years old, was looking at them phlegmatically. Carter pointed the automatic at him and said, "This will be aimed at the back of your head till we get out of here. Don't do anything stupid, and you'll come to no harm." The driver's mouth twitched but he said nothing.

As soon as they were both in the cab, the driver took off without a word. He turned left at the end of the street, away from St Christopher's Place. Carter looked to the right as they passed but could see nothing except a huge and noisy crowd of people who had obviously not been deterred by the bomb blast from trying to see what was happening. The taxi had to mount the pavement to get past a trio of parked ambulances. At the next crossing, a policeman stopped the traffic and impatiently waved them through.

Within minutes, they were in normal traffic and Carter felt himself relax. "That was a hell of a lot easier than I thought," he confessed.

Tara said to the driver, "Take us a few miles from here, it doesn't matter where." Then she said to Carter, "Do me a favour and stop pointing that gun at my Uncle Paddy."

In the mirror, the driver bared his yellow teeth in a wide grin.

* * *

When the bomb went off, surprise, rather than the force of the explosion, caused Delaney to let go his hold on the windowsill. As he landed on his feet, an excruciating jolt of pain shot up his leg, and he fell over, his hand out instinctively to protect his side. He managed to fall on his right side but that didn't stop an incredible surge of pain that suffused his whole body. He was blinded by the agony, his whole being centred on the pain. He could feel himself tumbling into a kaleidoscope of vivid yellows and reds, like a succession of erupting suns. For a second, he thought that he had taken the force of the bomb. He fought wildly to retain consciousness. His vision returned but seemed to be betraying him because, as he looked up, he saw the buildings opposite, with every window bursting out in slow motion and the falling glass form into a sparkling, twisting, tinkling waterfall. Then he was on his hands and knees on the roof, vomiting violently, every heave bringing another stab of agony.

When he stopped, he could hear someone sobbing loudly, and realised it was himself. He wanted to lie down on the roof, wait for unconsciousness to overtake him and somehow get away from the pain. It was a whiff of the acrid smell of his own vomit that got him moving. Slowly, he crawled to the edge of the roof. He had no recollection of lowering himself down, of weaving and staggering up the path, of opening the door and walking through a building.

He caught a brief glimpse of himself in a mirror as he went past one of the rooms. He took a few more paces, stopped, went back to the mirror and stared at his image, horrified. He couldn't believe what he saw. His face, from forehead to chin, was grotesquely buried in a layer of blood and dirt. Bits of vomit clung to his chin. His hair was plastered to his skull like a helmet. His clothes had big dark patches and he saw that a fresh line of bright blood was wending its way from his side. Oddly, it all looked utterly artificial, like he was an extra in a cheapo horror movie that couldn't afford a good make-up man.

He turned on the tap in the sink. A dribble of dirty liquid came out. He leaned down painfully, scooped up some debris from the floor and poured it onto the plughole as a makeshift stopper. He began scooping handfuls of water and splashing them onto his face. He leaned over the sink, ladling more water on his face, rubbing furiously. Soon, the water was rust coloured, but he kept sloshing more and more water and massaging it into his face. Eventually, he stopped, took out a handkerchief, dried his face and looked in the mirror again. His face had gone a peculiar shade of brown. He wondered if he would pass for an Asian.

He took out his comb and tried to get his hair into some sort of shape, without much success. Finally, he scooped up handfuls of water and poured them all over his clothes until he looked like someone who had been caught in a shower. The darker bloodstains were still visible but stood out less against the wet clothes. It was the best he could do.

The hasty clean-up had temporarily revived and invigorated him, but he didn't fool himself. Every breath, now, was more painful, he was getting weak and dizzy. He had very little time and had no idea what he was going to do.

Moving slowly, he left the washroom, walked through an archway and was at the front door. Without pausing, he opened it, half expecting to see a circle of police, guns pointing at him. Instead, he was astonished when a man, who had apparently been lying against the door, tumbled into the hallway and fell motionless onto his back, his grey jacket falling open. He was unconscious and breathing noisily. Delaney noted the ugly purple swelling, oozing blood, on his forehead, and the leather arm holster and thought, "Carter was here."

The man's feet were sticking out of the door but Delaney wasn't going to waste his strength pulling him in. He stepped out onto the street and found it completely deserted. Faintly in the background, he could hear a lot of noise, but he couldn't make much sense of it. Close by, all was silent and he realised with a shock that his world had been silent for the past few minutes. The bomb had deafened him. He tried not to think about it. It was just another problem and far from the most serious.

When he saw the Corolla with its keys hanging from the open door, he could have shouted with joy. "Oh, thank you God," he mumbled. "Just kidding when I doubted you. Always knew you were around. Well done, God. Oh, well done yourself, man."

He hobbled over, took the keys out of the door, climbed painfully into the driver's seat and felt another burst of pleasure when he turned the key in the ignition and the car started up immediately. He pulled out onto the street. It wasn't easy. He could use only one hand on the steering wheel and felt a jolt of pain every time he put his foot on the clutch. But he was grimly determined, having come this close, not to fall at what he hoped was the final hurdle.

There was a small lane way halfway along the road and he turned into it, hoping it wasn't a blind alley. To his relief, it came out into a small street.

There was a further alley in front of him, so he continued across. He came to another street, turned right, passed several crossings and found himself in a flow of traffic. He saw Welbeck Street, then Cavendish Square, then Oxford Street again.

He looked around, recognised where he was and did a quick mental calculation. Driving slowly, with no hold-ups, he could get to Doc Russell in about twenty minutes. It seemed an awful long time and he wondered if he could hold out. Then, it would be to the girlfreind's flat and lie low there until the next time. Carter and Tara, if they had escaped, would manage without him.

OUTSIDE LONDON

Douglas King, once known and feared as Colum McRory, sat in his BMW in a service area carpark off the M25, a few miles from his home in Rickmansworth and cried like a kid, sobbing and keening to himself and occasionally wiping away the flow of tears. He had parked in an unobtrusive spot between two trucks, so nobody noticed the burly man with the tomato-red face and wearing a suit and tie on this sweltering day, rocking back and forth in the driver's seat or heard his moaning. The trucks gave some shelter from the sun, but not much. He felt that he was being slowly broiled alive, despite the open sunroof, but couldn't summon the energy to wind down the car windows or turn on the cold air blower.

He was overcome by the enormity of his humiliation, the scalding realisation that he was not anything like the person he had believed he was until a few hours ago. His mortification was all the greater when he recalled what had been running through his mind, almost right up to the time he had stepped confidently out onto St Christopher's Place.

It was more than three years since that day when Kieran Delaney and Terry had walked up to him outside his factory and he learned that his IRA comrades had rediscovered him. He had told them, then, that he was no longer the man he once had been. Now he thought, what a great bloody pity that I hadn't listened to myself. After that encounter, the IRA had used him again, but sparingly, no more than once every six months or so. It was always the same kind of thing: letting a van park at his premises, or holding onto a sealed wooden crate for a few days. He was taking relatively big risks, he knew, but he didn't mind. It was worth it for the feeling that he was back in action and part of the armed struggle, even though it was at the periphery.

Gradually, he became less satisfied with this marginal role, and dropped the occasional hint that he'd be interested in something more active. But they were content to have him as a reliable and safe distribution point. When he was asked to deliver the guns to the active service unit in the centre of London, he was initially excited that they were maybe starting to make better use of his capabilities. But, driving up to London, it occurred to him that he was no more than a courier, lowest on the totem pole, and he felt a renewed sense of frustration.

Meeting the unit in St Christopher's Place deepened his dissatisfaction. He frankly didn't think much of them, especially when set against the men he had worked with-had-commanded-,OK?-in years past. Tara Barry, who headed the unit, was too young and raw. She struck him as edgy and giddy, and rather too anxious to make clear that she was in charge. Delaney had fallen in his estimation. The first time he had met him, he looked tough and professional. Now, he behaved like he was the lead character in a James Bond movie, all debonair and full of quips.

As for the American, King just couldn't figure him. Carter was a cold, ruthless killing machine he had met the type before and their air of icy detachment could be scarier than all the tough talk in the world. But why in Heaven's name did the movement need a hired thug from the US of A? Mercenaries, he had learned, were almost always overrated and were never reliable. Indeed, his first thought, when the surveillance outside had been spotted, was that the American was playing a double game.

He had seized the opportunity to volunteer to be the one to run the gauntlet in St Christopher's Place. He had two reasons. He had picked up Tara's reference to 'the tunnel', and realised that the unit's target was the Channel Tunnel. He was astounded and delighted with the audacity of it damaging and perhaps destroying this symbol of British pride within a month of Queen Elizabeth opening it. This was an IRA mission that could not be permitted to fail.

More importantly, he saw a possibility of finally taking a more active role. If, as he expected, he made it to Oxford Street, giving any pursuers the slip, the unit might well be persuaded to involve him in the actual operation.

His first flash of doubt came as Delaney was opening the front door to let him out. What if he were stopped? He had to remind himself that his cover was solid and authentic. He was a respected businessman of many years standing in his community, past president of the Chamber of Commerce, a committee member of the local branch of the Confederation of British Industry, prominent in the golf club and the school PTA. He instinctively patted his breast to feel his wallet, with his business cards, and array of gold charge cards. Restrained indignation would be the right tone, he felt.

He was striding confidently up the street, trying to look like a busy man lost in thought, when he came face to face with Ian Taylor and the whole world he had spent twelve years creating dissolved in an instant. Inspector Taylor, who had come close to breaking him under interrogation, always taking the bad cop role with a relish, an expert in the agonising punch that didn't leave a permanent mark. Now, Taylor made him without a hesitation. "Colum

McRory," he shouted, fully as astonished as King.

At the sound of his name in Taylor's distinctive guttural, Douglas King had panicked. Without thinking, he had made an about face and walked rapidly away. But Taylor came after him, bellowing his name again. That's not me, King had screamed to himself and had turned to face Taylor, reaching for his wallet, for his business cards and Gold Visa and Platinum Master Charge and all the others to show him that he was really mistaken.

And then Taylor had pulled out his gun and was levelling at him and saying something that King didn't catch. He had understood, though, that Taylor was automatically responding to a perceived threat, that reaching inside his jacket had been a stupid mistake. But his mind wasn't working rationally and, instead of slowly withdrawing his hand, he fumbled all the more eagerly to get out his wallet, and swore when a corner of it caught in his fountain pen.

The shot had taken him utterly by surprise, its sound amplified in the narrow street. He jumped back, stumbled on the kerb and felt himself falling. In a moment of clarity, he saw that the barrel of Taylor's gun was pointed upward and that he had fired only a warning shot. Then he hit the ground painfully.

And there he stayed, paralysed with fear, a frozen witness to everything. He had seen Delaney jump out of the doorway and fire, saw Taylor fall, Delaney shot, the American killer dropping everyone in sight, the black car shuddering under the chatter of the Uzi. Delaney reappeared and was shot again.

King's nostrils were filled with the smell of cordite and the distinctive coppery stench of blood. Someone lay a few feet away and it was like every drop of blood in his body was oozing out into a spreading crimson pool around his head. He was acutely aware of the heat of the sun and had a sudden raging thirst. He had an impulse to crawl over to a bar that was just across the road, and pour himself an ice-cold beer.

He remembered noticing a gun on the ground, almost within stretching distance. Down the road, the man from MI5 and the woman from the CIA were crouched behind the black car. It would have been so easy to go for the gun and shoot them both before they were even aware of him. He had thought about it, imagining himself with the gun, imagined firing it, watching them fall. But he couldn't do it.

Across the road, a young black man with a neatly trimmed beard was lying prone, just like him. He reminded him of the boxer, Thomas Hearns. Thomas "The Hit Man" Hearns. Oh, let me take you by the hand and lead you through the streets of London and show you what a fucking Hit Man is all about,

248

Thomas!

The nightmare seemed to go on forever, but then there was a lull in the shooting. The black man was scrambling up and was shouting to him, "Hey, let's go for it, man." And King at last found himself able to move and the two of them were running, bent double and weaving until they were into the crowd at the end of the street.

There were just two uniformed policemen, bewildered and harried, trying to keep the crowd back. One of them glanced at the two men.

"You OK?"

When they nodded he said, "Go to the back of these people and make yourselves comfortable. There's an ambulance on its way."

They passed through the throng, ignoring the questions thrown at them. When they got to the rear of the crowd, the man had clapped King on the shoulder and said, "Man, I ain't waitin' for no doctors and nurses. Got my business to take care of, y'know what I mean?" And he was gone at a fast lope down the side street.

King walked down Oxford Street, only half aware of the stream of howling police sirens and honking ambulances as they flashed past and the rising buzz from the crowded pavements. Ten minutes later, he was in a pub in Wardour Street, his knees shaking uncontrollably and gulping down his ice-cold beer, with a large brandy waiting as a chaser. At least he had kept his head and not got drunk before he headed for his car.

Slowly, alone in the corner of the car park, he began to calm down and he stopped crying and moaning to himself. He looked out at the rows of parked cars and, for a few moments, lost track of where he was. It was most strange. He couldn't remember anything after walking out of the pub, no recollection of driving here and parking. He noticed how hot the interior of the car was, despite the shelter of the trucks. One was a brewery truck and had an advertising slogan in big red letters on the side: Be the Best You Are. It seemed to mock him.

He accepted that the entire fiasco in St Christopher's Place was entirely his fault and, with that recognition, and the full acknowledgement of his own limitations, he felt curiously at ease about what had happened and slowly his mind started functioning properly. He took stock. Taylor, the only one who could identify him, should be dead. The others, RUC or MI5 or whoever might have heard Taylor call out his name, well, he'd seen most of them go down as well. Delaney might be dead and he suspected that Tara and the New York gangster were, too. There would be some witnesses, sure, who could give a description of him. But, most likely it would be vague, imprecise. By tomorrow, there would be a police photofit in the papers and on TV. He could live with that. He knew that his features were average and undistinguished. And yet, how did Taylor remember him so quickly after all those years?

Never mind, what now? He looked at the car radio, but couldn't bring himself to switch it on and get a news bulletin. He didn't want to know, not just yet, maybe in a few minutes. He reckoned he was through with the IRA. They wouldn't want to risk using him any more. No one in Rickmansworth would dream of connecting him to the sensational shoot-out in London. Still, better play safe. First thing to do was to get away for a few days, give the story time to get out of the headlines, find out if he was the subject of any enquiries. One of his suppliers in Milan, Dino, had invited him several times to visit, to see his plant, and enjoy his hospitality. That would do it. He would tell the office that he had been suddenly called to Italy to discuss a joint contract. He would spin some story for Dino, that wouldn't be difficult.

What would he tell his wife? Hell, he would bring Josie with him. Her mother could take care of the kids. She deserved the break and, he admitted, it would ease some of his guilt at having told her nothing about his IRA involvement. She knew about his past but he had told her nothing about his more recent activities nor would he. What if, he thought, what if he had been gunned down or captured. Until then, it hadn't really occurred to him that he had been putting his family at risk as well as himself. Trusting, faithful Josie! If he had not miraculously escaped, her whole world would now be shattered into tiny pieces that could never be put back together again. He shuddered. A few minutes later, he started the car and headed for home.

* * *

Tara and the ancient taxi driver had an animated exchange in what Carter presumed was Gaelic and then she said, "Martin, I'd like to introduce you to my uncle, Paddy Flynn. This is Martin Carter, Uncle Paddy, the American specialist I told you about."

"Hi," said Carter shortly. He didn't much like the idea of Tara dropping his name to relatives and friends. Flynn returned the greeting with a grunt and a wave of his hand, fingers dark brown with nicotine.

Tara said, "Uncle Paddy is both a member of our unit and my personal guardian angel. He watches my back wherever I go and I can always count on him to get me out of scrapes like this. Isn't that right, Uncle Paddy?"

250

He answered with another non-committal grunt, evidently his preferred mode of communication-which suited Carter just fine.

"We really gave MI5 a bloody nose today," she went on, her voice excited and gleeful. Unconsciously, she put a hand on Carter's arm and left it there. She looked aroused, her face flushed and eyes sparkling. It occurred to him that if it had been Delaney in the cab with her instead of him, she would probably be tearing off her clothes now and to hell with Uncle Paddy.

"I want to thank you, Martin, for all you did for us back there." Her voice held a tremor. "It was fantastic having you as part of the team."

"Well," he said. She was gushing, offering him her highest praise. But, had she been trying for a way to goad him, she couldn't have done better. Carter had been unsettled at St Christopher's Place, watching the situation escalate without being able to control anything. He was not used to a secondary role, letting others dictate the action. But leaving Tara in charge gave him the best chance to get out of what he saw as a largely self-made trap. He had gone along, throwing his support to Tara only because he saw that it was necessary to maintain someone in the leadership role.

He had briefly considered abandoning them. When he had opened the door and shot the group clustered around the car, it was in his mind to walk rapidly away. But he had failed to hit Jones, and had decided that he would be buying too much long-term trouble by shooting the CIA girl, Blake. He couldn't leave the doorway with those two at his back. So he had stayed.

She was asking, "Who was that man with the gun, the one you took down?"

He shrugged. "Someone who got in the way."

She gave him an odd look. He said, "Yeah, that came out sounding like bad movie dialogue. I don't know who he was, probably an off-duty cop who heard something on his radio. We had to get him before he took notice of us, and we didn't have time to go talking with him."

When she spoke again, it was clear that she was rapidly coming down from her high. Her tone was matter of fact.

"We need to review what has happened and what it means. We're going to have to plan our next moves very carefully."

"Right."

"Why don't we stop and have something to eat. I don't know about you but I'm absolutely starving."

He wasn't especially hungry but reckoned it was right to eat when there was time. Besides, he wanted to talk with Tara one-to-one, without any other member of the team, especially the gnomic Paddy Flynn.

251

"OK, where are we?" He hadn't been watching where they were going. Once out of the centre of London, all the streets had the same look to him newsagents, video shops, fast food places and laundromats, with blocks of apartments hovering in the background.

"Highgate," she said. The name was vaguely familiar. Wasn't Karl Marx buried in a cemetery in Highgate?

They stopped at the first restaurant they saw. Flynn declined Tara's invitation to join them, saying that he had made his own sandwiches and didn't feel like wasting them. He let them out and drove down a side street where he parked.

The restaurant was one of those salad bars where customers were invited to fill their plates from a large assortment of trays of cold meats, vegetables and salads. Tara's mood was swinging again and she heaped her plate with little *ooohs* of pleasure. Carter, who would have preferred a steak and fries, scooped an assortment onto his plate without much interest. They took a bottle of house wine and went to a corner booth in the almost empty restaurant.

"Poor Paddy," she murmured, as she surveyed the array of titbits on her plate. "I hope he is enjoying his sandwiches. He always makes his own sandwiches last thing at night for the next day."

"I guess the IRA isn't big into retirement benefits," Carter observed, his mind on other things.

She took it as a criticism of Flynn and spoke with vehemence. "Paddy is an old man, yes, but he's still able to pull his weight where it's needed. He's in the movement because he is committed, not because he needs to be. You wouldn't know, of course, but Paddy Flynn is something of a legend in Ireland. His name scared the hell out of the RUC back in the 1950s, when there were precious few freedom fighters. In fact, if you had been around in those days, Martin Carter, I wouldn't give much for your chances if you'd come up against Paddy in his prime."

"Wouldn't have happened," he responded mildly. "If he was as good as you say, I'd have stayed clear of him. No matter how good you think you are, there's a whole bunch of guys out there who are better and faster and deadlier. The thing of it is to spot them early enough and keep out of their way."

Mollified, she said, "If MI5 had the same attitude, the ones we met today would still be alive. I wish we had some idea what they know, how they got onto us. The more I think about it, the more it seems to me that they had to have been trailing you, especially with that CIA girl around. Maybe they got onto you in Paris. No offence, Martin, I'm just trying to get the right answers."

"None taken, kid. But you've got it wrong. I haven't been under surveillance here in London."

"Can you be one hundred per cent sure?" she demanded. "I've done surveillance and it's been difficult because we've never had enough people to do the job effectively. But the Brits can lay on the full works a dozen or more people at any one time, cars, vans, trucks, even helicopters. They can be almost impossible to spot if they're doing it right."

"Sure. I might not have spotted a tail once, maybe twice. But not over several days. If they were onto me from the time I got into London, I'd have picked them up at some point. No one is that good. Besides, it just doesn't add up."

"What doesn't?"

"Figure it out. I arrived in London at around ten in the morning. I went to the hotel, got the phone message that we were meeting in the third of the three places that I'd been given by Nicole in Paris that morning. I switched hotels and came straight to the Ritz. Now, according to Kieran, both Jones of MI5 and Blake of the CIA were already in place before I arrived. If they were following me, how did they get there before me?"

"Good point. I hadn't thought of it that way," she admitted.

He nodded. "There's something else. Night before last, I took a call from the Waldorf. Someone was going to a lot of trouble to track down where I was staying in London. That's why I moved out of the Hilton. But, if they were tailing me, they would have known where I was."

"Then how did they find us in St Christopher's Place?"

"Dunno for certain. My guess is that our two groups coming together in the Ritz was a coincidence. Not too much of one. From what I understand, the Ritz is an establishment place. So, maybe you'd expect the top guys from MI5 and whatever to eat there. The big mistake was, what were we doing there? I think Kieran's idea is that it was the last place that MI5 would go looking. But that turned out to be asshole thinking because they weren't looking. Not until we showed ourselves."

"Dear old Kieran," she said sadly. "Is he alive or dead?"

Carter stayed on the point. "My guess is that Blake Margaret! Just remembered her first name, Margaret Blake. She was probably just visiting London and the MI5 guys decided to give the VIP treatment to a CIA operative. She saw me in the Ritz, said something to the others, got them interested. They lost me because I was gone in five minutes. Instead, they put a tail on you or Kieran or both. It was fairly low-level surveillance because they didn't really know what they were after."

She mulled this over. "It had to be Kieran because he saw Margaret Blake at the Foreign Press Association this morning. But, oh God, that means they know that you and Kieran made the trip to the Tunnel, yesterday." She looked at him with dismay.

"Could be. But I don't think so. If they knew we'd been inside the Tunnel, they would have grabbed us. It's too big a thing for them to take chances. They couldn't chance losing us. For all they knew, we were carrying remote detonators and might press the button at any time."

She nodded. "Just like Gibraltar."

"What about Gibraltar?"

"Six years ago, three of our volunteers were shot dead by the SAS in broad daylight on a street in Gibraltar. The SAS said that there was a possibility that one of them might have been carrying a remote control detonator that would set off a car bomb in the centre of town."

"And the SAS took them out? Sure, it's what I'd have done if I was with the SAS."

"It was cold-blooded murder," protested Tara, hotly. "Our people were unarmed and could have been arrested. They didn't even get a warning and were just gunned down on the street. A shoot-to-kill policy. Just like today, in fact. I saw them shoot Douglas in the street. He wasn't armed."

"That's my point," he said impatiently. "If the Brits believed yesterday that Kieran and I were capable of blowing up the Channel Tunnel, we wouldn't have gotten to St Christopher's Place this morning."

She seemed to be brooding on Gibraltar. Then she came out of it.

"So, you think they still don't know what we're planning?"

"We can't be sure. But my hunch is that they don't know about the Tunnel."

She looked at him intently and said, "Then we can still do it, essentially the way we planned it?"

"Yes."

Her relief was obvious. She let out a long breath and, for a moment, he thought she might come around the table and hug him.

"When? Today? There's time," she said eagerly.

"Today, like we planned. If we're guessing right, MI5 have all their attention now on London, not Folkestone."

"That's right. The longer we wait, the greater the danger that someone will stumble on those beam benders." She hesitated, then said, almost defiantly, "You'll need me with you to take Kieran's place."

She expected him to reject the idea and was getting ready to argue. But he surprised her by saying, "Yeah, it's going to need the two of us."

"Right." Suddenly she was all business, confidently in charge again. "We're going to have to split up. They're less likely to be looking for us singly and, if the worst happens, there's a better chance that one of us will get through."

She glanced at her watch. "There's a train to Folkestone from Waterloo station in forty-five minutes. I'll take that. There's a direct connection from the Highgate tube down the street to Waterloo. Meantime, Paddy will take you down in the taxi. You can be the American tourist out for a day's sightseeing on the East Coast."

He shook his head. "We split, that's good. But you take the cab and I'll take the train."

Annoyed, she began, "No, no. The way I see it"

He interrupted. "Why don't you shut the hell up and do what you're told," he said harshly.

Her face went scarlet. She opened her mouth but was speechless.

"It's like this," he said in a more conversational tone. "You want me to do this job, I'll do it. But we do it my way, which means I call the shots. Back there, it was your show and I didn't get in your way. Now, we're getting to my part of the operation and I'll be running it. You'll do exactly what I tell you to do, or you're a liability. We may run into problems and I won't have time to give you explanations or get into a debate. That's how it is and if you've got a problem, we call it off right now."

She blinked rapidly and tried to swallow her anger. "Very well, I accept what you're saying and I agree we'll do it your way. But there was no need to be so bloody boorish about it."

He had little patience for smoothing down hurt feelings. It was why he chose to work alone. But, if Tara was going to be backing him up, he needed to have her on side. He made an effort to get her to understand.

"Tara, I had to say it as strong as I did so there would be no possible misunderstanding. The fact is that I operate as a loner. I haven't worked as part of a team since Vietnam, and even then I was never comfortable with it. I've become used to relying on just me, it's the only way I operate. Now, we both want to get this job done and if you want me to do well what you're paying me to do, you'll go along."

She gave a tiny smile. "I've never really met anyone like you, Carter. Fine,

I'm with you. Before we go, let me ask you just one thing that's got me puzzled. What is Blake, a CIA agent, doing working for British security? I mean, the American Government is on our side."

"You're confusing Bill Clinton with the US government."

"It's the same thing, surely?"

He sighed. "That's the trouble with news soundbites. People are told that the President of the United States is the most powerful man in the world and they swallow it whole. He's not. The President is part of the most powerful ruling system in the world. But he doesn't control it.

"Your pal Clinton has a very limited ability to call the shots with the CIA, the FBI, the State Department and the Pentagon. If they don't like his policies, they'll go their own way. And there's a whole lot of very influential people in CIA and State who see more strategic sense in being pro-British than pro-Irish."

"But, come on. They can't just ignore their President."

He sat back in his chair with a wry smile. "Let me tell you a true story. Back in '75, when Saigon fell, there was a hell of a scramble to get out of Vietnam. You've probably seen the TV footage of the helicopters airlifting out the last Americans from the roof of the Embassy. The Americans got off, but there were thousands of Vietnamese, who had been loyal to America, left stranded in the Embassy compound. Gerry Ford was the President then and when he saw all those people being abandoned, he ordered the helicopters to go back in and pull out as many of them as possible.

"It never happened. A few days later, when Ford checked, he learned that when his Presidential Order arrived in the Pentagon, they didn't like the idea so they binned it."

"You're kidding. What did he do?"

"Being Gerry Ford, he probably stomped up and down the Oval office in a temper until he fell over something."

"I don't know," she said doubtfully.

"That's what Gerry said, too."

As they got up from the table, he asked, "I nearly forgot. When we first saw Jones and Blake down there in that café, Douglas King said something to you in Gaelic and you answered him. What was it about?"

Her smile was wicked. "When he heard that there was another CIA agent outside, he asked me if I was sure you were not working for the Brits. I told him that I didn't think so but that I'd know soon enough and, if you were, you'd be the first to die."

Carter said, "That's more or less how I figure it went."

* * *

Carter came out of the restaurant alone, Tara having given an unlikely undertaking that she would need less than two minutes to freshen up. The brightness of the day hit him immediately, but it was no longer oppressively hot and the sky was no longer cloudless. He could see the front of the black cab parked in the side street and he walked over to it. Paddy Flynn wasn't in the driver's seat. He was a few yards away on the far side of the road, leaning against a wall and vomiting. Carter hurried across. Flynn looked up and saw him and tried to wave him away, then turned and retched again. Carter saw a pool of dark blood on the pavement.

After a minute, Flynn straightened and walked back to his cab, passing Carter without a glance. Carter slowly followed him. He was sitting in the driver's seat and he looked like a corpse. His face was a dreadful bluish white and was shining with sweat. He was gulping air rapidly and wheezing with the effort, while he daubed his mouth with a none-too-clean handkerchief. Carter saw dried bloodstains on it.

Flynn fixed him with his bloodshot, watery eyes. "Say nothing about this to Tara, not a word," he said in a croaking whisper. "She's got enough on her mind without having to worry about me."

"I'm not going to tell her, but maybe you should. Are you getting treatment?"

Flynn considered before answering. "Aye, I've been to the doctor, had some tests in the hospital. Too late for them to do anything, they said. I've maybe six months left if I'm lucky. That was in March, three months ago, right? The big C, that's what they call it, y'know."

He fished in the dashboard and took out a pack of Silk Cut cigarettes. He took one out and lit it with a plastic lighter. He waved the pack at Carter. "Them's the lads that have done for me. Sixty a day since I was fifteen years old and what else can you expect?" He went into a brief coughing fit. " Know what we used to call them when I was a kid? Nailers. Meaning nails in your coffin. A pack of nailers, please, here's ten pennies, that's what I'd say. Ah Jesus, I still can't do without them. Not that it matters any more, like."

"The cigarettes will do for you, sure enough," agreed Carter.

The cigarette, perversely, seemed to be doing Flynn good. Some colour came back into his face. He gave Carter a crafty look. "Come here and let me show you something."

He reached over to his radio and pressed three of the buttons at the side, paused, then pressed them in a different sequence. Then he leaned over and, with an effort, unscrewed the interior door panel.

"If anyone ever tries to open this without hitting the buttons in exactly the right way, then 'Boom'." A chuckle rattled in his throat.

Carter leaned over and looked. Inside the door panel were two revolvers and half a dozen packages in thick plastic wrapping. Wires connected them to a small metal box.

"Semtex," said Flynn with satisfaction, rescrewing the panel back in place. He fiddled with the buttons on the radio again. "If I get the chance, I'll use these, take some of the bastards with me. I'm thinking it will be a far easier way to die, am I right?"

Carter was appalled. He was immediately vastly relieved that he had opted not to take the trip to Folkestone in Paddy's cab. Last thing he wanted was to be driven around England by an IRA kamikaze.

When Tara came out of the restaurant, Flynn grabbed Carter's sleeve. "Now remember, Mr Carter. Not a word to Tara." He added, "I can see that you two have something going between you, if you don't mind me saying. I can tell you you're a lucky man. I'm glad that there's going to be someone to look after her when I'm gone."

Carter thought, if that's what the old man wanted to believe, he was welcome to his illusions. When Tara came across to them, he said, "You two better head off. I'll find my way to Waterloo. Wait for me outside the rail station in Folkestone. Don't come inside."

He watched the cab drive out of sight but made no move towards the underground. After a minute, he hailed another passing cab and asked to be taken to the Savoy Hotel in the Strand, one of several hotels he had noted in a guidebook earlier in the week. Inside the ornate Art Deco hotel, a relic of Britain's palmier days, he went to the shop and bought a bundle of papers and magazines. In the foyer, he slipped a porter twenty pounds to order him a chauffeur-driven limousine to Dover and, half an hour later, was sitting in the back of a comfortable stretch Mercedes as it sped along the M20 motorway for Folkestone.

It was highly unlikely that British security or the police would yet be organising a manhunt. But, if they were, they would be covering the main rail stations and it wasn't worth the risk. He had seen no reason to explain this to Tara. He felt more comfortable about making his own decisions and, for the first time since he had arrived in Europe, he had the relaxed feeling of depending on no one.

He glanced at his watch. It was 3.15 in the afternoon. It struck him that time was passing incredibly slowly this day.

CENTRAL LONDON

Margaret Blake looked at her watch again. 3.15. She found it unbelievable that the day was crawling so slowly. She sat in Jonathan's car in Carlton House Terrace, waiting for him and wondering if his black mood would have improved any. Probably not.

The sound of the bomb exploding in St Christopher's Place had been enormous. It felt like an earthquake, with the ground beneath them shaking and every building shuddering as though they were all going to collapse into the street. For the first few moments, it seemed that this was in fact happening, as bricks and glass and other debris showered onto the street. Two of the policemen, cut by flying glass, fell screaming. The roar of the blast was immediately followed by the ringing and wailing of every alarm bell in the vicinity.

Boudren was shouting, "The buggers have blown themselves up, godammit."

Jonathan was beside her and, not too gently, pushed her back into the café. "Watch where you go," he said. "There's glass and sharp edges everywhere."

They leaned against one of the walls. "What now?" she asked.

"We stay out of it. I've got to let Boudren run things, it's his show." He sounded tired, defeated.

"Put that gun in your purse, Margaret," he ordered. "Listen, in a few minutes, as soon as he sorts things out, Boudren will be back with a lot of questions. I'm glad it's someone like him in charge. He's a professional, but he's going to be feeling the pressure. That's when I'm going to tell you to go, and I want you to vamoose immediately."

She started to object, but he cut her off. "Head back to my car and wait for me there. Christ, it's bad enough that MI5 is in the middle of this. We cannot afford to have the CIA mentioned as well. Do what I say, Margaret, please, and don't even open your mouth and let him know you're an American."

She saw his point and nodded.

He tossed her his keys and said wearily, "Christ, what a screw up."

From their vantage point, they watched as a dozen black-clad policemen, heavily armed and armoured, and wearing breathing apparatus, entered the building through the broken windows, some of which were billowing smoke.

They could hear muffled shouts ringing out and figures in black appeared through the smoke at the upstairs windows. They saw two of them look down from the roof. A few minutes later, two fire engines came onto the street. One of the policemen opened the front door of number eight and several firemen entered pulling hoses with them.

"They've gotten away," said Jonathan mournfully.

She didn't need to ask. The firemen would not have been allowed in unless the police were certain that there was no shooting threat.

Ambulance medics arrived and carefully examined the bodies of Scott, Manning and their two detectives. They made no attempt to move them but signalled to the ambulance crew who placed blankets over the corpses.

It was half an hour before Boudren came back to them. Jonathan immediately said to Margaret, "Right-ho, you'd better be off."

"Before you go, would you mind giving me your name?" said Boudren, to Blake, stiffly polite.

"You don't need her name," responded Jonathan. "This is my colleague and is part of my team."

Boudren frowned. "I'm sorry, but that's really not good enough."

Jonathan said quietly but with a terrible menace in his voice, "Are you really absolutely sure that you want to get into a pissing contest with me, Chief Superintendent? The way I feel right now, I'd welcome the opportunity to fuck someone over, and you're welcome to apply for the job."

Unfazed, Boudren regarded him thoughtfully. "We're on the same side, remember?" He glanced at Blake. "You'd better be off then." He called over a uniformed policeman. "Assist this young lady to go to wherever she's going and do it discreetly, mind."

She didn't wait but walked quickly towards the back door of the café, followed by a curious but silent young policeman. Behind her, she heard Jonathan making apologies.

She walked mechanically back to Carlton House Terrace. In contrast to her journey to St Christopher's Place, the streets were now almost empty and quite a number of shops were closed and shuttered. The unmistakable sound of a bomb going off had cleared the crowds out of the centre of London.

She sat in the car and waited for Jonathan. He had parked in the shade and some of the heat had gone out of the day, so it was tolerable sitting there. She felt tired and switched on his radio to see if she could get a news bulletin. It seemed to be locked onto a classical music channel. She liked the occasional light classical stuff but what they were playing grated on her ears and she switched it off. She pushed the seat back, rested her head on the headrest and closed her eyes.

She dreamed that she was in a children's park, rather like one in New Jersey she had visited with her parents when she was a toddler. It had a miniature railway, and she was sitting in a small wooden turn-of-the-century train engine that moved slowly along a circular track, emitting artificial puffs of smoke. But there was another train some yards behind, a real full-sized train, bearing down fast, and Martin Carter was leaning out of the engine box, a gun in his hand, firing at her. Delaney was beside him, grinning mischievously at her and yanking on the train's whistle, which strangely made no sound. Bullets, fiery and yellow, whizzing by her.

She wasn't afraid for herself but for her father, who sat beside her in the little engine, dressed in dungarees, with a train driver's cap and looking like he was having fun. She kept telling him to keep his head down, tried to explain to him that Carter was a killer. He was pointing to a tunnel up ahead. "If we reach the tunnel, we'll be safe. He can't get in after us." But then, as they got nearer, she saw that it wasn't a real tunnel, just a black shape that had been painted on a wall. Her father saw it also and said with a smile, "I'm going to have to take on this man. You don't really have to worry about me, of course." She knew that he was referring to the fact that his death was already decided, at some other time in some other way.

Jonathan was tapping lightly on the side window of the car. For a moment she was disoriented, then she was wide-awake and was filled with an immense sadness. With an effort, she shook it off.

"I can't believe I just fell asleep," she said hurriedly. "I've been having the strangest dream."

"Yes? I could do with a bit of kip myself," he admitted. "For choice, I'd like to go into hibernation for a few months until this business blows over. Oh boy, I've really ballsed this one up. Move across so I can drive."

But he made no immediate move to start the car. "They really did get away, all of them," he said, shaking his head in wonder.

"I still don't believe it," she exclaimed, "I saw Taylor shoot the courier and Delaney was hit twice once by me."

"True," he agreed. "And yet every damn one of them is gone. There was a back way out into the next street. Boudren finally lost his well-cultivated imperturbability when he found out. Seems he ordered the back street covered but, in the confusion when the bomb went off, someone forgot. Maybe it's just as well. He didn't have many armed men and if unarmed police had met up with that gang, there would have been another massacre."

"It sounds awful, Jonathan, but you know, I haven't really thought much about poor Geoffrey and Andrew. I can't really take it in that they're both dead."

"I know what you mean. We're both in denial somewhat." He paused. "They got Peter Rhodes, too."

"Who?"

"One of my best men and a good friend. Peter was the one tailing Delaney. I'd ordered him over to relieve us, remember? The police found him unconscious in a doorway at the back. He's got a fractured skull, possibly brain damage. It's not looking good for him."

"I'm sorry," she said, putting her hand on his.

"It's a monumental cock-up for MI5. When the Director gets back from Scotland, there's going to be an awesome reckoning. It's a toss-up if I'm still going to have a job by the end of the week and, if I do, I'll probably be deputy assistant spycatcher in the Outer Hebrides."

That's unfair, she almost cried out, but wisely didn't. Instead, she said, "Sorry for bringing this up, but did you tell them about Martin Carter?"

He looked at her bleakly. "That's another thorn in my flesh. No, I didn't mention Martin bloody Carter for the reason we both agreed to keep your bosses in Langley from getting their drawers in a twist if they learn that one of their subcontract assassins is on the payroll of the IRA.

"Actually, I was rather embarrassed by the paucity of information on the gang that I was able to give. I had chapter and verse on Delaney, of course. But Chief Superintendent Boudren's well-groomed moustache fairly quivered with indignation when I told them I got only a quick glimpse of the girl and a rear view of the courier. The best I could offer was that he resembled George Baker, an actor who plays Inspector Wexford on TV, except that Baker is taller and heavier. Oh dear."

"I guess maybe we've lost Carter," she said. Despite everything, she still had a tiny question in her mind about Carter. Was he really making a solo run or was US Intelligence pulling his strings somewhere in the murky background?

"Certainly not, " said Jonathan, savagely. "Soon as I get back to the office, I'm going to set it up with Scotland Yard to put Carter in the frame as a murder suspect. We'll attach him to some recent killing, something that has rape and violence in it. We'll keep it out of the media for as long as possible and concentrate on a heavy police manhunt. That way, Langley will still be in a panic but they won't be looking at MI5. We'll find him, I reckon."

He turned the key in the ignition and drove out. They were both silent with their own thoughts. Margaret was thinking about the dream. Something was nagging at her, something that it was important to remember. She saw her father's wind-blown hair, Carter, the false tunnel, Delaney's playful grin.

She suddenly shouted, "Stop the car!"

Jonathan, who was lost in his brooding, acted instinctively, slamming on the brakes and pulling out his gun.

"What? What is it?" he demanded, his eyes swivelling left and right.

"Oh Christ, I'm sorry," she said contritely. "Take it easy. It's not that kind of emergency, OK?"

He shot her a pained look and slowly replaced his gun. "Damn fortunate that there was no one directly behind us," he grumbled. "Well, what is it?"

"I think I know why the IRA are using Carter and what their target is. They're going to blow up the Channel Tunnel."

He stared at her. "Now, how did you suddenly come up with that idea?" he asked incredulously.

She decided to say nothing about her dream. "Something I've just remembered. In the Foreign Press Association, in the hall, just before Delaney came up to me, I was scanning the noticeboard. They had a big notice on it inviting members to take press trips to visit the Channel Tunnel. There was a trip yesterday, in fact."

"And so?" he asked.

She felt slightly annoyed that he didn't get it. "Think about it, Jonathan. What the hell were Carter and Delaney doing in the Foreign Press Association?"

"Meeting a contact? Establishing their press credentials for any one of a number of reasons? Planting a bomb in the FPA? Who knows?"

"You're right. It could be any of those. But it would be interesting to know, don't you think, if they took the Tunnel trip, or have their names down for it."

He came to a sudden decision. "You're right. It would be worth knowing." He made a U-turn in the street, ignoring angry car horns, and headed back the way they had come.

"Has it occurred to you," she asked, "that the IRA may be targeting your brand-new communications centre in the Tunnel?"

He considered it briefly, then shook his head. "I think not. For one thing, the centre is still going through its test phase and it's not operational yet. If the IRA even knows about it which I doubt and were planning to target it which I doubt they would wait a few weeks when it's up and running. In any event, while the centre was built during the Tunnel dig, it's not really part of the Channel Tunnel, you know, and you can't access the centre from the Tunnel. It has its own entrance about half a mile away and it would take more than what the IRA has got to break in."

"Just a thought," she said.

He pulled up outside the FPA. "No point in us both going in. I'll be back as soon as I can."

She watched him stride into the building and thought that there was every point in both of them going in, rather than leaving her again waiting around in his car. She wasn't going to make an issue of it. But if her relationship with Jonathan were to develop much further, he'd need to bring himself up to speed on current thinking about the role of women. So far, he was running things but she was coming up with all the answers. Anyway, did one night in the sack mean that they had a relationship? She decided not to think about it right now.

Within ten minutes, Jonathan came out of the front door, talking animatedly into his mobile phone. He finished the call and got into the car. He grinned at her, a touch sheepishly. "Well, you're right again. Martin Carter and Kieran Delaney calling himself DeLaney, for some reason went down to the Channel Tunnel yesterday. I'm told it was a routine event, except for the fact that Mr DeLaney, it transpired, was a claustrophobic and collapsed. He, er, very rapidly recovered after medical attention."

"Creating a distraction for Carter," she snorted.

He started the car and pulled away. "Yes, but a distraction for Carter to do what? If he were planting explosives, how did he get them into the Tunnel? Security is rather lax on those press trips, I gather, but anyone bringing along a rucksack or large bag or a briefcase would have had it searched. And to do any serious damage in the Tunnel, Carter and Delaney would have had to be carrying several large and very heavy suitcases each, which wouldn't have gone unnoticed."

She mulled that over. "Yeah, OK. But how about a small, powerful explosive, enough, say, to rip up a few metres of track. It could derail a train and cause a lot of damage. You could carry a bomb like that in your pocket." She held up a hand. "Don't tell me, that doesn't add up either. If they use a timing device, they know that it's likely to be discovered within a few hours. Plus they don't know when a train is going to pass. Plus, if it was remote controlled instead of a timer, they couldn't get a signal down to the tunnel. Plus..."

"Plus," he took up. "It's not the IRA's style to go to a lot of trouble just to let off a tiny explosion that might not even make page one. Plus, the Channel

Tunnel is not just ours, it's an Anglo-French project. And I don't think they'd go out of their way to piss off the French. Enough plusses?"

She laughed. "Except for maybe the biggest one. Why would the IRA hire Martin Carter for such a shitty little bomb blast. But the fact is that he was down there yesterday with Delaney, so what were they up to? Some sort of reconnaissance? I've got another one of my hunches about this."

"What could they possibly learn from a bog standard PR press trip? They don't show the media reptiles anything that really matters."

"Yeah." She looked out at unfamiliar streets, unable to work out where they were. "Mind my asking where we're going?"

"Battersea."

"And what's in Battersea?"

"The Battersea heliport. Quickest way for us to get down to Folkestone. I phoned the office and had it set up."

"Hey, cool. I've always wanted to see England by helicopter." She leaned over and gave him a nudge. "I'm not arguing, but I thought we were doing a good job of convincing ourselves that the Tunnel was a dead end. Oops, I didn't mean that as a pun."

Jonathan said, his voice very serious, "I'm going down there for two reasons. The first is that it's your hunch and, so far, you've been guessing right about everything and I haven't been listening enough to you. That's not a compliment, Margaret, just a fact."

Don't for Chrissakes blush, she warned herself.

"But I'll be totally honest about it," he continued. "I'm going to Folkestone for self-preservation. Oh, I don't really expect to be fired or demoted after today's fiasco but I won't be the most popular boy around for some time. Right now, the two of us should be in MI5's interrogation suite going through the process of a lengthy and not very pleasant debriefing and grilling. The only reason we're not is that I have a small window of opportunity, a few hours before Stella Rimington gets back from Scotland.

"I've briefed no-one in MI5 yet about Carter. I'm hoping that when we get there, we'll find something, anything, that will give us a track on Carter and what the IRA are up to. I don't expect we'll foil a dastardly plot to blow up the Tunnel. But I'm happy to settle for a damn sight less to show the Director that I'm not a write-off yet."

There was nothing to say to that. MI5 wasn't very different from CIA or possibly any security service in the world. A good part of the job was watching your own back and making sure that you weren't the one left twisting in the wind. She knew all about it.

A few minutes later, they lifted off in a small twin-engined chopper and rapidly left London behind. They had earphones with mikes so that they could talk over the roar of the engines but there wasn't much to say. Blake looked down, marvelling at the abrupt change of scenery, modern bustling motorways and clinical industrial estates giving way to small villages that didn't look like they had changed much in centuries. Soon she glimpsed the sea on the far horizon.

The flight was under half an hour and they landed in a small airfield outside Folkestone. Jonathan had arranged for a car to be waiting, a silver Honda Accord. After checking directions, they drove off, Jonathan driving. His office had set up an urgent appointment with the head of security for Eurotunnel.

THE CHANNEL TUNNEL

From inside a video shop, Carter casually browsed the titles on the rack and kept watch on the black cab, parked down the road from Folkestone railway station. After fifteen minutes, he was satisfied that he was the only one paying any attention to it. He left the shop, walked down to the cab, approaching it from the rear. He saw Tara in the front, chatting with Paddy Flynn, looking relaxed. She jumped and gave a small scream when he opened the rear door and got in.

"Martin," she cried. "Don't you know better than to sneak up on people like that? You frightened me half to death. Where have you been? We've been watching the station entrance for ages, and were starting to get worried."

"Guess you missed me. I took a short walk, needed to stretch my legs."

"We couldn't have missed you," she said, suspicious. Then her expression cleared.

"Have you been listening to the news bulletins on the BBC? Kieran got clean away and, would you believe it, Douglas got away, too. Douglas! He isn't dead after all. Isn't it just fantastic?"

"Fantastic is the word for it," he agreed. He was surprised that Delaney had made it, another reminder never to underrate people. "What else was on the news?"

"It's all a bit sketchy. There was to have been a press conference but apparently it's been put off. I can just imagine them trying to think up excuses for letting us all escape." She giggled.

"What about the guys we killed?"

She winced at his bluntness and said, "Four dead, according to the BBC. Well, we knew that. Something odd, though. They're reporting that all four were Scotland Yard detectives, one of them a senior officer."

"Now that's interesting," he said thoughtfully. "If the guys we shot were police, it means that they may have accidentally blundered into Intelligence surveillance. And that suggests, like we thought, that MI5 were trying to find out who we were or what we were up to. And they don't know about this operation."

"You think so? Yes, that's what I think, too. Oh, another thing. We just heard a few minutes ago that there is a quote unconfirmed report unquote, that the IRA chief of staff has been arrested in London." She sneered. "That's rubbish and I know that for a fact. I think the Brits are going to try anything to hide the fact that they tried to take on an IRA unit on their home ground and took a beating."

"Bloody right," said Flynn hoarsely, speaking for the first time.

"Well, thanks for the news update," said Carter, looking meaningfully at his watch. "Are we ready to move?"

"OK, Uncle Paddy, let's move off," she said, her voice brisk. "We're less than fifteen minutes away from the French customs office. Want to have a final run through on everything?"

* * *

Margaret suddenly shouted, "Stop the car!"

"Not again," bellowed Jonathan, but he slowed down and eased the car into the kerbside. "What now?"

She was twisted around in the front seat, looking behind her. "Didn't you see them, Carter and that girl?"

"What? Here in Folkestone? Are you absolutely sure?"

"Yes, yes, yes," she cried impatiently. "It was them. They're in a black London cab. I noticed it because it's the first one I've seen down here. Then I saw the girl in front and Antichrist Carter in the back, I swear to God, I saw them, Jonathan."

"Take it easy, I believe you," he assured her. "There's a roundabout just ahead. Hang on and put on your seat belt. Have your gun ready."

He slammed his foot on the accelerator, shot around the roundabout with a screech of tyres and roared down the road. The traffic was light and the powerful silver Accord whipped by the few cars on the road. After a couple of minutes, he slowed and said, "Nothing. We should have caught up with them by now and there's no black taxi ahead of us."

"Then they turned off."

"Yes. Near as I can figure it, any of those turns are in the general direction of the Tunnel. I'm taking this next right and we'll probably parallel them. It's a small enough place, this." He added grimly, "if they're in the area, we'll find them."

* * *

"There it is," said Tara, pointing. They had just passed through an industrial estate outside the town and Flynn had stopped in a lay-by. A hundred yards ahead, there was a small, squat, one-storey building, painted white that had the look of something that had been erected the previous day and might be demolished tomorrow. It was surrounded by a small grass verge, with a wide gravel path. There was a row of windows with untidy venetian blinds and a wooden door in the centre. Two small saloon cars were parked near the door, one of them a battered-looking Citroen 2CV. That, and the tricolour that hung limply from a flagstaff on the roof, were the only things that gave the place a French identity.

"It's pretty well isolated, just like we were told," she noted. "This whole area is deserted."

Carter studied the building for a minute, then said, "Let's do it."

Tara got out of the front seat and got in the back with Carter. They sat on the pull-down seats and Tara clicked a button under the back seat and lifted up the top. Inside, most of the space was taken up by a medium-sized burgundy Samsonite suitcase. They ignored it and first unwrapped the guns, which were bundled in cloth. They each selected a Smith & Wesson, checked them carefully and slipped them into their belt holsters. Tara opened a large plain plastic shopping bag, looked inside and started laughing.

"This is Kieran's doing," she chuckled, taking out two plaster facemasks in the image of John Major. "If he knew I would be here, he would surely have added a Maggie Thatcher."

Carter said nothing. At a time like this, he found Delaney's sense of humour irking. Balaclavas would have been more functional and more comfortable. He put on the mask. Visibility was limited through the small eye-holes but it would be all right. Tara looked bizarre in hers, John Major with long blonde hair. She looked like a druggie. They both donned thin surgical gloves. Tara took several pairs of manacles and gags and put them in her jacket.

"Right," he said to Tara and Flynn, who seemed to be completely indifferent to what was going on. "We do it exactly as we planned it. You ready, Paddy?"

He started the taxi without a word and drove slowly down to the French customs office and turned onto the drive, stopping outside the door. Carter got out, Tara directly behind him, and rang the bell. Almost immediately, it was opened by a pale young man with glasses in a dark blue suit and blue shirt. He looked in astonishment at the two figures in front of him, frowned and opened his mouth to speak. Then he saw the guns pointing at him and he clamped his mouth shut.

"Good thinking," said Carter harshly in French. "Don't open your mouth again or I'll shoot you dead without a moment's hesitation. This gun is designed to make great big holes in things. Put your hands on the back of your head and walk inside." When the man just stared at them, he jabbed the gun in his ribs and snarled, "Now. Do it now, you turd."

That got his attention and he immediately put his hands around the back of his neck and stepped slowly back. Tara closed and bolted the front door.

"Go to the front office where the others are," Carter instructed. He didn't need to make further threats. The man almost trotted off in his anxiety to show that he would not cause trouble. Up the corridor, he came to a door, stopped and looked at Carter to know if he should take his hands away from his head to open the door. Carter shook his head, turned the handle and flung the door open.

The room was crowded with untidy, paper-strewn desks, a scattering of chairs and half a dozen grey and dark green filing cabinets. A fat man, with a goatee beard and no moustache, also in blue shirt and suit, was leaning back in a chair, his feet on the desk, reading *Le Monde*. When he saw Carter and Tara, his reaction was instantaneous. His newspaper flew into the air, he tumbled off his chair and fell onto the floor behind the desk, his feet swinging in the air.

Tara burst out laughing and the young man started grinning. In a minute, he'd stop being scared, thought Carter. He strode behind the desk, reached down, grabbed the fat man around the neck and squeezed. His face turned red and he began choking and squirming ineffectually.

Carter heaved him onto his feet, slammed him heavily against a wall and then knocked him to the ground, where he lay without moving. The younger man stopped smiling. Carter pointed the gun at him. "Joke over. Where are the others?"

"There's just the two of us today." His voice was high and trembling. "Sometimes there are three of us but André, he's the boss, he's out today."

"OK, get down on the floor beside your fat friend. Hands behind your back."

He hesitated, then got down on the floor. As Tara was cuffing his hands and feet, he turned his face around to her and said, pleadingly, "I'm getting married next month, really. You don't have to shoot me. I'm not going to cause you any trouble."

Carter said to him, "Listen, friend, there's one way you can save your life, guaranteed. Where is the key to the door that goes down to the Tunnel?"

"It's in that filing cabinet beside the window. Third drawer, in the metal box."

Carter found it immediately. "Guess what, you get to live," he told the man.

While Tara was cuffing and gagging the two officials, Carter went away. He came back a minute later and said, "There's a broom closet down the corridor with a key in it. Help me haul them in there."

For some reason, he immediately felt the Frenchman was not hostile towards him, so smiled and treated him as gently as he could in the circumstances, which he saw was appreciated.

"Will they have enough air?" she asked.

"I don't know. If it worries you, shoot some holes in the door."

She wondered if he was serious.

"I'm going out for the case," he said.

* * *

Margaret and Jonathan spotted the black London taxi stopped outside the building at the same time. "Act like we haven't seen it," said Jonathan. He didn't slacken speed until they were out of sight. He took a right turn, sped up an empty lane, and took the next two rights. He stopped the car in a lay-by and they both looked up the road.

"Is that a French flag? What is that place?" she asked.

"I'm not sure. It may be a French customs office. It's their Tunnel, too, and they've set up all sorts of facilities around here. Question is, what is Carter doing in there? Let's get into the back seats, and keep a low profile."

They made the switch and crouched low in the back.

"Shouldn't we call for back-up?"

He shook his head. "Not just yet. Let's give it a few minutes and see if we can get something more solid."

Margaret said nothing but got a sudden foreboding. More solid? Shit, they had trapped a couple of cop killers. This was becoming all too reminiscent of their vigil outside St Christopher's Place a few hours earlier. It occurred to her than there was an indecisive side to Jonathan, combined with a reluctance to delegate. If this were a CIA operation, dozens of agents in cars, communication trucks and choppers would already be moving in to surround the place.

As though reading her thoughts, he turned to her and said, "You understand, of course, that I'd much prefer that we quietly took Carter ourselves, if we can. It will solve a lot of potential problems."

"Of course," she replied. "What else?"
They smiled at each other. Touché, she thought.
Then he stiffened. "There's Carter."

* * *

Carter gave a brief nod to Flynn and climbed into the back of the cab. He hefted the suitcase out of the space in the back. It was lighter than he had expected. He looked at the Uzi, now wrapped in an old beach towel, thought about it, then left it there. He got out of the cab and said to Flynn, "I'd like you to pull across the road and park to the side of that warehouse. Have the cab out of sight but keep your eyes on the front door here. When we next come out, be ready to pick us up immediately."

Flynn nodded slowly, a wide grin on his face. It puzzled Carter until he remembered his John Major mask. "Paddy, this is important. Don't react to anything and don't move until you see us coming out. You got that?"

Flynn dropped his grin. "Oh, for sure," he said confidently.

Carter went back inside the building and said to Tara, "We may have a problem. You got a vanity mirror in your bag?"

"Sure." She took a small compact out of her bag and held it out. "What kind of trouble?"

"Use it to look up the road," he said. " Keep your back to the window."

"What am I looking for?"

"Silver car in the same lay-by where we stopped."

"Got it. It's either an unbelievable coincidence or we're being watched again. Oh, Damn. They're onto us, they know everything."

"If they knew everything, we'd be dead now. I'm going down now to finish this job. You'll have to play things as you see them until I get back. Whatever you do, don't come down after me or we'll both be trapped. By the way, Paddy is just across the road."

She heard his footsteps down the corridor, heard him unlock the door, then silence. She felt she should be grateful that he was treating her as an equal, with cold professionalism and no false platitudes. And yet she found herself wishing perversely for an affectionate pat on the shoulder, a conspiratorial wink, a gruff, "Here's looking at you, kid." A promise of things to come if they both got out of this alive.

Mother of God, will you act your age, Tara, she admonished herself. She stood well back from the window and cautiously looked out. Uncle Paddy was well hidden; she couldn't see the taxi. She looked towards the silver car and saw the back door open.

* * *

They watched Carter go back into the building with the French tricolour and saw the taxi back out of the driveway and disappear up the road.

"He's got on a mask of some sort," said Margaret. "And what's in that case?"

"It could be anything. Could be a bomb," responded Jonathan thoughtfully. "Time to call the cavalry?" she asked.

"I'm ahead of you." He already had his mobile out and was speed dialling. He swore and tossed it on the seat. "Battery's dead. I don't suppose you've got yours with you?"

"Sorry. It's sitting on my desk in the Embassy. I was trying to avoid calls."

He grunted. "Never mind. We actually have a spot of luck on our side. There's a phone box back up the road, two minutes away. I'll make the call and you keep an eye on things. Don't take chances, OK?"

"Fat chance."

He opened the door and slipped out. She watched him in the rear mirror as he trotted off, thought she could see the phone box in the distance. Ahead, nothing moved in the French building. She rolled down the window. All was silent except for a distant rumbling of heavy traffic somewhere. Her stomach was empty and she realised that she was hungry. She carefully reached into the front and rummaged in the glove compartment. Under a pile of travel brochures, she found half a pack of Polo mints and crammed a couple into her mouth. Better than nothing but not by much.

She saw Jonathan returning and a moment later he slipped into the back. He had a harassed look.

"Trouble?" she asked.

"No, just a slight delay. I talked to Head of Security at the Centre, guy called Ajax Cox-Heather, believe it or not. I know him. He's OK, willing to help, but has to cut through some red tape. Centre Security is not fully staffed yet and his operational orders are to keep all security personnel inside the Centre at all times. That makes sense. However, by sheer good fortune, there's an MI5 team in place at the moment, a dozen of our chaps, well armed. Ajax is prepared to send them over and put them under my command. But first he needs written faxed approval from Millbank. He expects to have this within fifteen minutes at most."

He opened the car door and got out.

"Hey, where are you going?" she asked. "Wouldn't it be better to wait for your guys?"

He shook his head. "Look, as soon as the chaps arrive and surround that place, anything can happen. We might have to shoot our way in. Even worse, Carter may have hostages over there and we'll find ourselves in a siege situation. If that happens, the SAS will be called in. Either way, Carter and whoever is with him will die. I want him alive and answering a lot of questions."

"So what are you going to do, sweet talk him into surrendering?"

He gave a wry grin. "More or less. I'm counting on the fact that he's a professional. If he knows what he's up against, I think he'll see sense. Don't worry, Margaret, I'll be careful. You stay here and brief the team when they arrive. If you hear shooting or if I'm not back by"

"Forget it," she said sharply, getting out of the car and facing him. "I'm going in with you. And let's not waste time arguing. I know Carter and he knows me. If we're going to try for a deal of some sort, I might just be able to give us an edge."

Jonathan hesitated briefly, then shrugged and said, "You have a point. Let's do it. We've got fifteen minutes at most."

They walked openly towards the French building. Blake was reminded of Gary Cooper loping up the Main Street in *High Noon*. She resisted a temptation to giggle and realised that she was nervous. She looked at Jonathan, who seemed lost in thought.

She asked, "When they get the all clear, how long will it take your guys to get here? How far away is the Centre?"

"Um, not more than one mile, I would guess. Think of it like a triangle. We're at one point, the Centre is at another and the Channel Tunnel entrance is at the third."

"We're that near the Tunnel?"

"Oh yes. See where the ground rises over there? Those are the famous Cliffs of Dover. Can't you smell that bracing sea breeze?"

She breathed in the tangy smell of the sea. She hadn't noticed it until he mentioned it. I'm more tensed up than I know, she thought.

When they walked up the gravel pathway, they found the front door ajar.

"I think we're expected," said Jonathan with a grimace, taking out his gun. Margaret followed suit. Cautiously, he pushed the door and entered. They made their way along the corridor. Ahead of them, on the left, was an open door and they stopped.

Jonathan said loudly but conversationally, "Martin Carter? I'm Jonathan Jones from British Intelligence and I'm with Margaret Blake of the Central Intelligence Agency. We're both armed but we don't want any shooting. It's not necessary, believe me. We need to talk to you, in your own interest."

After a few seconds' pause, a woman's voice answered. "Come on in and we'll talk. I've got a gun, too, and I'm prepared to use it but only if I have to. Please come in slowly and carefully, OK?" She sounded calm and relaxed.

Jonathan licked his lips and looked at Margaret. They both nodded. They stepped up to the open door, guns extended and were facing the girl from St Christopher's Place. She was standing, feet apart, both arms extended in a shooter's grip on her gun. When they appeared, she moved her aim slightly to midway between Jonathan and Margaret.

They faced each other for a few moments, then Jonathan said, "Let's not do anything foolish. We need to talk. You'll want to hear what I'm going to tell you."

She said nothing and seemed to regard him with mild amusement.

"You know," he said. "If we start shooting, you will die for sure. There are two of us, one of you."

She laughed pleasantly. "But I'm more ready to die, isn't that so? I'm the fanatical terrorist, ready to die for my cause. I don't think either of you are ready to die right here and now."

"You got that right," affirmed Margaret. "I want to live to collect my pension and, right now, I'm scared shitless that with all these guns pointed at each other, one of us is going to read the signals wrong and start shooting."

Tara nodded, still with that half-mocking smile. "I agree. So, let's show a small act of faith and stop pointing our guns at each other. We'll hold onto our guns but keep them by our side. And I'll listen to what you want to say to me. Agreed?"

Jonathan would have preferred if they all put their guns away. But her proposal was better than nothing. Slowly, he lowered his gun until it was resting at his side, pointing down. Margaret and Tara followed his example almost in unison. None of them audibly breathed a sigh of relief, but the tension eased palpably.

"Where's Carter?" asked Margaret.

"Down in the basement, getting some blueprints we need. He'll be back up in a few minutes."

It sounded plausible and it provided the reason why the IRA were in the building. But something in her tone suggested to Jonathan that this was not the truth. He let it go and, gesturing around the room, asked, "Where is everyone else?"

"In a little room up the corridor. There are only two of them. They're tied up but quite healthy. Now, why don't you tell me why you're here."

Jonathan said, "To save your life-and Carter's."

He caught her sceptical expression and went on, "Oh yes, I want you both alive. The fact is that the place is surrounded, by a lot of heavy security boys. We're not playing by any rules and there won't be any negotiations. They won't give a damn about your hostages and that includes us, incidentally. Once the first shot is fired, they won't take your surrender. And, you can't escape by the back door this time. The only way you and Carter will be alive an hour from now is to give yourself up to me."

Tara laughed and, to Jonathan and Margaret, there was something disquietingly manic about her mood.

"And what would you have in mind for us? A show trial and a murder conviction? I can't see you getting on the witness stand and admitting that your side fired first without warning."

"You would go on trial, certainly. And I think the evidence would convict you. But I rather imagine you could get yourself a lot of propaganda value out of it. And you'd still be alive."

She laughed again. "I'm curious. How did you find us here?"

He grinned. "Our team was tailing you and Carter all the way from London. It's not very difficult to keep a London taxi under observation on a motorway."

Tara recognised the lie but didn't change expression. Carter had not been in the taxi. Therefore, there was no MI5 team tailing her in the taxi. And this meant that, perhaps, these two were running a bluff and they were not surrounded.

She said, "Why don't we wait for Martin and see if he's ready to surrender?"

* * *

Carter unlocked the steel door and saw a circular flight of stairs leading down to darkness. He looked around for a light switch, found it and clicked it on. Neon strips on the ceiling flashed into life. He closed the door behind him, took off his mask and hung it from the door handle, and descended the stairs. There was a stuffy, musty smell, along with a faint undertone of cleaning fluid. The walls and stairs were white-tiled and looked like they were regularly

277

cleaned. He counted 64 steps before he reached the bottom, where there was another steel door. He used the same key to unlock this one. He opened it into darkness, felt along the wall until he found a switch and clicked it.

This time, only an overhead light fitting came on, illuminating only the immediate area. He was in a wide, high-ceilinged cavern. The floor and walls were roughly cemented and there was a black iron handrail on both sides. The cavern, which had a slight downward slope, vanished into the darkness. Down there, about a mile and a half ahead, according to what MacAnamy had told him, there would be a door leading directly into the Channel Tunnel. He didn't have to go down that far; the transmitter was designed to work from where he stood.

Carter carefully placed the case on the floor. From his pocket, he took a small cellophane envelope and emptied its contents on the floor: two cigarette stubs, some tobacco ash and an empty Swan Vesta matchbox, which he had surreptitiously collected in the bar of the Savoy a few hours earlier. He crushed the matchbox with his foot and kicked it into a corner. He figured that these false clues would confuse the later investigation considerably.

The air in the cavern was stifling and he was already beginning to perspire. Quickly, he opened the case. It was exactly as he had been told. It consisted of a plastic panel with a series of coloured buttons and several small lights. On the top half of the case, a sheet of neatly typed instructions were affixed. All he had to do was follow them. He hoped his press visit had done the job.

First, he pressed the green button and immediately there was a low humming noise and the lights lit up. Good. Next he twisted the blue light, marked Number 1, to the right. He counted to thirty and nothing happened. He waited a few more seconds, and the little blue light started to flash, which meant that it had connected with the device he had placed nearest the cave entrance in the Tunnel. He waited. After a few more seconds, the Number 2 blue light flashed on and off. Then the Number 3 light did the same. Apparently, the damn thing worked. Until that moment, he had wondered whether the IRA's technological expertise was as good as they claimed.

All that remained was to press the red button and Carter did so. Again, there was a few seconds' delay, then a red light directly under the red button started flashing on and off and the case emitted a low, urgent beeping. In five minutes, all going well, the signal would be sent in a microsecond via the three transmitters in the cave to the detonator in the Centre, exploding the Semtex. Simultaneously, a powerful miniature explosive would blow the case itself to smithereens.

Time to go. He mentally calculated that it had taken him no more than ten minutes from the time he had left Tara. He looked at his watch. Nine minutes, forty-seven seconds. Close enough.

When he got back to the customs office, he slammed the steel door closed, took out his gun and waited quietly. After a pause, Tara called out to him, "Martin, we've got visitors. I'm with Jonathan Jones and Margaret Blake but everything is OK for the moment."

Her voice was relaxed, without tension. There was no hint that she was speaking under duress. He doubted, anyway, that she would set him up.

Then came a man's voice. "Mr Carter, I'm Jonathan Jones, Assistant Director of MI5, British Intelligence. Miss Blake is with me. We need to talk to you, we want to make you a fair and reasonable proposition."

Carter waited, saying nothing.

Jones spoke again. "The three of us here are all armed, and I'm sure you are, too. But we've established a détente of sorts. We've got guns in our hands but we're not aiming them. Could I please ask you to join us and do the same. Believe me, you'll want to consider what I have to say to you."

"He's speaking the truth," affirmed Tara. "We've agreed a temporary truce."

Carter thought about it, then, with his gun hand at his side, he walked towards the room. He heard Jones say, "Margaret, don't take your eyes off our friend here. I'll watch our good friend Carter."

Something in his tone the way he had said 'Margaret' suggested to Carter that there was more than a professional relationship between them. Jones, you've just made a real dumb mistake, he thought as he came into the room. Jones and Blake were standing on the left, a few feet apart, their guns by their side, pointing down. Tara was on the right, half sitting on a desk and resting her hand with the gun on the desktop. Tara and Blake watched each other, almost casually, and neither looked at him.

Tara said, "Jones tells me that MI5 has us surrounded. They followed us both down from London in the taxi."

Carter understood. Whatever Jones was going to say, there would be an element of bluff in it. Jones frowned slightly, aware that the girl had given Carter some sort of message but couldn't work out what it was. He said to Carter, "I want you to consider carefully"

But Carter interrupted, saying to Blake, "You know what they're going to do to you for fucking up an Agency operation."

"Crap," answered Margaret, keeping her eyes on Tara. "I've checked you out, Knight. You're not working for the CIA, so don't try that line."

"Did you check with the Director?" he asked softly. "Did you check with Tony Lake? That's where my orders came from. Who gave you yours?"

She still didn't look at him. He saw an almost imperceptible doubt appear on her face. Then it was gone, and her tone was scornful "Drop it. No one gave you orders to join the IRA and kill British cops."

"Ignore him," said Jonathan, too loudly. He had assumed that he would talk with Carter, the threat of their two guns keeping the truce between them, while Margaret neutralised the threat of the girl. But it didn't work if Margaret switched her attention to Carter. He said quickly, "Carter, we don't have a lot of time"

Carter said to Blake, "This has nothing to do with the IRA. Margaret, they should have told you. We're tracking the men who killed your father."

Startled, she looked over at him. Then everything happened very fast. There was a dull boom, distinctly audible, seeming from a great distance. The room started to shake. Tara lifted her gun and shot Blake. Acting instinctively, Jones swung round and fired at Tara. He was already swivelling back when Carter's bullet took him in the head.

Carter did a quick check of the three bodies on the floor. Jones was dead, his head oozing blood and brain. Tara, too, was dead. She had taken a bullet in the nose and her once beautiful face was a mess. Margaret Blake was alive. She lay on the ground, her legs shaking violently, a growing red stain on her chest. She tried to sit up, but couldn't.

Breathing heavily, she looked up at Carter and said with a rueful smile, "Bringing up my dad, that was really playing dirty." A trickle of blood began to run down her nose.

"Didn't they teach you at Quantico that there's only playing dirty?"

She grimaced in pain. "You're finished, Knight. The posse will be here any second."

Ha, the trap hasn't closed yet, he realised.

"I hurt bad, man. How is it?" she asked.

He looked. Tara had shot hastily, taking her under her right breast. Her ribs had almost certainly deflected the bullet. There was a lot of blood, a lot of pain but basically it was a survivable wound.

"You're not going to make it," he said flatly.

She sighed. "Something I want to ask you. This morning, you had me in your sights and you didn't take me out. Why?"

He said, "Then, I didn't have to." Before she could work it out, he brought up his gun and shot her twice in the head.

280

He wiped his gun carefully, placed it in Tara's inert hand and wrapped her fingers around it. Another small thing for the investigators to puzzle out. He took up Margaret's gun, the only one that hadn't been fired and went out front.

Maybe Flynn had heard the shots or felt the vibrations of the blast, because the black taxi was outside the door, facing the road, its engine running. When Carter opened the car door, Flynn asked, "Where's Tara?"

"She's dead. I'm sorry, Paddy."

Flynn stared at him, blinking hard, not wanting to believe. "Are you sure about it? How can you be sure?"

"Tara is dead," he said flatly. He sat in the front seat. "You're going to have to believe it. There was shooting and Tara got hit."

"I watched those two go in," he muttered, talking to himself. "I knew they were Brits. I should have gone in after them." He looked into space for a few seconds, then gruffly asked Carter, "Did she take care of them?"

"Yeah. She killed them both." He guessed it was what he wanted to hear.

At that moment, they saw the convoy of cars coming down the road from the right, heading towards them at high speed. In the lead was a large black saloon car with four men inside, followed by two dark green Landrovers packed with additional manpower.

"Out of the car, out, now," snarled Flynn. He was quickly pressing buttons on the radio. Without hesitating, Carter flung the door open and dived out. He landed on the grass verge and, ignoring the jolts of pain, he began rolling his body away from the taxi as fast as he could.

With a screech of tyres and a spray of gravel, Flynn gunned the car across the short driveway and onto the road, accelerating as he made straight for the oncoming cars. Carter flattened himself on the ground, tucked his head down and clamped his hands over his ears.

He heard a crunch of metal on metal. It was immediately followed by an enormous explosion. The blast hit him in a great hot wave, lifting him off the ground and flinging him a few feet in the air. He thumped into the ground and again tried to flatten himself as much as possible. He was struck by several small objects as a rain of debris fell around him. Then there was complete silence.

He got unsteadily to his feet and looked at the road. All he could see in what was now a deep hole in the road was a great mass of twisted, blazing metal, like something out of a scrapyard. Flynn's cab and the black saloon that had been leading the convoy had simply vanished. The Landrovers were no longer recognisable as motor vehicles. There were no bodies to be seen. It looked like they had all been blown to bits. Thick, oily smoke was rising high into the air. He realised that he had very little time to get away from the scene.

He turned round and swore softly when he saw that the two cars that had been parked outside the building were both lying on their sides, petrol seeping out onto the ground. What looked like an engine block had smashed through the rear window of the Citroen. The building itself was a shambles, windows and doors smashed and most of the front caved in.

* * *

The Chief of Staff of the IRA smiled with satisfaction switching off the radio in a small apartment in Mayfair, owned by a Dublin property developer who liked to keep a few rooms for his frequent visits to London, where he always combined business with pleasure or vice versa.

"So they think they've got me under lock and key. Let them dream on. This has not been a good day for British Intelligence. Dies IRA has become *dies irae*, so to speak. Poor old Sinn Fein Councillor Sean Anthony Mosse, Sam to his few friends. Talking about being in the wrong place at the wrong time but having these initials as well. How would he get out of that one? Wallace of MI6 would be delighted for awhile. Barry McGrath of the IRA had better disappear quickly for he would have both of them after him if "Sam" Mosse survived MI6!"

Feargal Colgan didn't know what the Chief was talking about, but, assuming it was some witticism, said, "Good one, Sam."

Sam was still smiling. "They've no idea just how bad this day is going to turn out for them. It's time for us to be off and laying out the honey for Trousers."

Trevor Wallace parked his car in Albany Street, a few yards down from the Regent's Park entrance and contemplated his day with the greatest satisfaction. An hour earlier, the Director had invited him to his office and poured two generous glasses of single malt whisky, while congratulating him on securing the information that had enabled MI6 to unmask and capture the Chief of Staff of the IRA in London. The intelligence coup was all the sweeter for taking place on the very day that MI5 had suffered an unmitigated catastrophe in St Christopher's Place, with four dead policemen, two of them senior officers of Scotland Yard, and a nest of IRA terrorists permitted to escape. Neither the Director nor Wallace indulged in gloating. They both solemnly agreed that the tragedy that had befallen their sister organisation had been most unfortunate, and they expressed the greatest relief that, in apprehending the infamous Sam, they had been able in large part to turn around what would otherwise have been disastrously negative media comments on the capabilities of British Intelligence.

It was especially gratifying that what might have turned out badly had, in the end, gone very well indeed. MI6 had broken the rules in doing a solo run on Sam. As soon as Wallace made his initial verbal report, the proper course of action would have been for the Director to immediately inform Stella Rimington, who was officially responsible for co-ordinating the war with the IRA. Instead, the Director had suggested that perhaps Wallace's intelligence required further checking before it could be formally confirmed and, in the meantime MI6 would take the precaution of placing Sean Mosse, the man who was supposedly Sam, under close observation. Wallace had immediately concurred that an intelligence sub-committee should review his information and conclusions before it was passed to Rimington.

When MI6 learned that Rimington had unexpectedly flown to Scotland, they decided to seize the opportunity. An Eyes Only memorandum was sent by courier to Rimington. Within the hour, Wallace ordered his operatives to seize Sam. It went without a hitch. When armed MI6 agents burst into the hotel suite of Sean Mosse, he was meeting with three men. They were all too shocked to offer much resistance, and vehemently protested that they were respected businessmen, and it was all some terrible mistake.

They were handed over to Scotland Yard's anti-terrorist division, who would get joint credit for the arrests. The three businessmen were identified straight off by Scotland Yard as Eddie and Billy Seary and Morris "Crowbar" Pfanz, who ran a notorious south London criminal outfit. The initial reaction of both MI6 and Scotland Yard was one of consternation that the unthinkable had happened and that the IRA had formed some sort of unholy terrorist alliance with English professional criminals. But then a briefcase with £150,000 was found in the room, together with several packages of high-grade heroin. It was just business. It was also enough to ensure that Mosse's trial would result in enormous embarrassment for the IRA leadership.

"On the other hand," the Director had said with a chuckle, "by the time Sam appears in the Old Bailey, I don't expect that there will be any IRA leadership or even any IRA at all to speak of, hm?"

Wallace smiled at the recollection. From the glove compartment, he took out a dark blue tie decorated with playing card symbols in gold hearts, clubs, diamonds and spades. He removed his red satin bow tie and replaced it with the tie. He disliked wearing a tie but wearing one was a rule of his Club. He locked his car and made his way down Albany Street to enjoy a relaxing evening at the Red & Black Club.

One of the most basic maxims that applied to anyone in the espionage business was to avoid routines and regular patterns of behaviour. It made one vulnerable to enemy action. Wallace was well aware of this. In the past, he had mentioned it when he gave talks to new entrants to MI6. Of late, he had often shaken his head at the folly of prominent IRA leaders in slipping into well-trodden paths always visiting the same pub or club, leaving home and returning at more or less the same time, frequenting the same restaurants, turning up at the same sports grounds every Sunday afternoon. It made surveillance that much easier. And an assassin knew precisely when and where to strike.

But it had never occurred to him that the maxim applied to himself. He had an illusory belief that he was a largely unknown and anonymous Intelligence functionary and was highly unlikely to be anyone's target. Consequently, he paid no attention to the blue Toyota Hi-Ace van that was parked directly across the road from the Club, nor did he notice the couple in the red Volkswagen Golf that was parked further up the street.

The young boy in the Cumberland Hotel had to be alerted if the MI6 man reacted as he normally did when under extreme pressure, making his way to a certain pub to get relief in more ways than one. They did not know that an even more important guest was staying there also.

MI5 Headquarters, London

Sunday 29th

The next day's newspaper carried the expected headlines:
"Big Explosion at French Customs Post in Folkestone".
"Number of Casualties not certain."
"Official Secrecy on Folkestone Explosion."
It was left to a local paper to mention reports of a bigger explosion coming from the direction of the Channel Tunnel minutes earlier and that was only in the first edition. The black car from the Ministry of Defence and the four people in it who met the editor before he had time to go home to lunch, made certain of that. The poor man nearly had a heart attack and decided on early retirement.

Over at MI5 Headquarters in Millbank, the situation was also confused. The senior officers sitting around the big conference table were all wondering what the hell was happening when the Deputy Head, this time a man, entered the room. Unlike Stella Rimington, the lady who headed the organisation, he went by the name of "The Boss", a title he had held for so many years that none of those present remembered his real name, if they had ever known it or if it ever was his real name.

"Do you want the bad news or the worse news first?" was his opening as he glared around the table at each of them in turn, before continuing:

"You all know my views on our people going off on hunches of their own, without official authorisation and without keeping in regular contact. Now two of our best agents, Jones and Manning, the Director General's own body-guards to make it worse, have disappeared and are presumed dead. Manning was involved in some sort of a Wild West shoot out in Christopher's Place off Oxford Street which left four dead, including a chief inspector from Scotland Yard and two others whom we can only suppose were IRA terrorists. But Jones and the bloody nuisance of a CIA woman who insisted in sticking her nose in, Blake her name is or was, have disappeared."

While he paused for breath and a drink of tepid water which had been on the table since morning, they wondered was this all the bad news or could it get

285

worse. They were not kept in suspense long.

"Now we have word of a big explosion at Folkestone where Customs Officials say at least a dozen people were blown to bits. Two couples were seen going into a Frenchman's hut in the compound there at different times. Then armed police went in. Then some maniac with a London black cab of all things drove straight into the whole bloody lot of our men and cars. There was this terrible explosion and they are still picking up the pieces. What a bloody awful shambles. Our lady has been called to Downing Street and you all know what that means. So if I were you, I'd go and have a good lunch before she gets back because I have a feeling it's going to be a long night. See you all here at 15.00 hours," and he marched out of the room, without waiting for any comments.

"Was that all the news?" one or two of them wondered as they headed for the canteen while others went to the nearest pub. Those who knew Jonathan Jones and Andrew Manning well just remained seated at the table, stunned at the news and mourning two good friends. They sat in silence, not feeling like eating or drinking, just thinking of other days: of dangerous love affairs, families, all the things they had shared together. Finally, one of them, without speaking, went out of the room and returned later with welcome doughnuts and cans of coke which they took without a word. They barely had time to finish the drink and hide the cans before she entered the room. One look at her face was enough.

She sat at the head of the table as usual and the others, the most senior officers of MI5, filed in to take their places after her. When all twelve were in the room, she suddenly got up from her chair, crossed to the door and locked it, an action which made the hearts of even some of the toughest agents beat a little faster and those who had drunk the coke wish they had gone to the toilet.

"Gentlemen, you have heard the bad news. Two of our best agents, two of my best friends, are dead. What more can I say. They tell us it comes with the territory but that does not make it any better for those left behind. We will all pray for them in our own way and grieve for them in our hearts."

Nobody dared break the long silence that followed and there was not a sound in the room until she spoke again:

"To some, and I will not mention any names, that is not the worst news we have today," a statement which startled her audience, people hardened to tragedy and sorrow.

"Yes, something even worse happened that you do not know about and I cannot tell you much about either. All you need to know is that a secret chamber hidden beneath the sea, a spur from the Channel Tunnel, was completely wrecked by a mysterious explosion, shortly before the one which killed our friends overground. This supposedly atomic-bomb-proof room, packed full of the latest British, American and Japanese technology, costing much more than a billion pounds, is gone. The Tunnel entrance is, as you know, well guarded. Nobody who should not be there went past. The doors to this chamber can only be opened by three secret codes, one of which I hold myself. Another is in Six, the third at the Yard, yet the bloody thing is gone, disappeared, no more."

It was quite a while before anyone said anything, not sure that she was finished and afraid to draw her obvious pent-up anger on themselves. In fact, she herself continued before any of them could pluck up enough courage to comment.

"So, gentlemen, it is all-out war now. It is them or us. Some of you may have heard rumours that we were preparing a special surprise for these murdering terrorists and it is true. But, if you heard those rumours, forget them, just as you will not repeat a single word you have heard in this room today. If you do ..." she let the silence hang in the air until she was sure everyone had got the message, then continued:

"I am asking all of you to be on your guard. Four of you are to be around me at all times in the usual eight-hour shifts as there is no knowing what those mad bastards will do next. The only bright spot, a small one, is that we may, I don't know how yet, have managed to wipe out their entire active service unit as they call it, which will set them back a bit. I promise you, they have seen nothing yet. If they think the past twenty-five years have been bad over there, wait until they see, or rather feel, what will hit them in the next few days, I can promise you that. I suppose we can count this as a draw if we leave the personal element of Andrew and Jonathan out of it and that old fool Scott of the Yard. But the MOD and the Treasury do not see it that way, neither does Downing Street. They spent all this money on the most top secret project which does not exist anymore. The less said about the Prime Minister and the government, the better."

As she looked around the table, she could detect the beginnings of a smile on more than one face and thought:

"There is still no love lost between the lot of us. Sometimes one would wonder whether we are all on the same side." She had dismissed them with a wave of her hand and a simple "Good-bye and Godspeed" before returning to her own attack-proof office. At least she hoped it was, after the mysterious explosion in the guarded tunnel, she thought, as she entered the room which was almost her home these days.

Immediately, she picked up the secure red phone and dialled Belfast:

"Is that you, Chief Superintendent Taylor? Stella Rimington here." She cut short his greetings and usual small talk with the words:

"We are putting our project into operation immediately. Have your twenty-five people on standby within forty-eight hours. The situation was never more critical so this is our D-Day. I will be back to you within that time and rely on you to have all the selected people ready to go. Remember only the best and, as that other lot says, 'who dares, wins' so it is our turn now to wipe them all out. 'Bye."

IRA Headquarters

Falls Road, Belfast

If the situation was confused at Millbank, it was even worse among the seven people who formed the all-powerful Army Council of the Irish Republican Army, who had been fighting to get the British out of Ireland since 1916. The new and youngest-ever Chief of Staff had recently taken over and what was to have been a major blow against the British in England appeared to have been a complete disaster. The facts were hard to get. There seemed to be increased Army, Royal Ulster Constabulary, British Intelligence, activity in Belfast, Derry, Lurgan, Armagh, and the other big cities in the entire six-counties of Northern Ireland, and even out into the countryside.

Meanwhile, the Chief of Staff was nearly frantic, trying to find out what had happened to the entire elite Active Service Unit based in Central London. Even in those far off days when Sean McBride was Chief of Staff before going on to become a Government minister, then winner of the Nobel and Lenin Peace Prizes, or when Sean MacStiofain and Daithi O'Connell had been in command, there had seldom if ever been a disaster of this magnitude. Here was a special unit cultivated over some twenty-five years for major jobs in London only, a Unit which was to be used very seldom and only on targets of the greatest importance, which had just disappeared. The secret messages on the Internet were unanswered; there was no reply to the coded e-mail; even a few very secret and dangerous phone calls were getting them nowhere.

The chief made a decision and then decided not to tell the others, playing for time instead by promising to let them know shortly. There was so much enemy activity in the entire area that none of them were too keen to hang around and wanted to get back to their homes or mostly safe houses, before darkness made it more likely that one of them might be picked up for questioning, if only by accident. They were all told to be sure to log on at the appointed times, to observe strict security, encrypting every message, a brief 'Slan Abhaile' with a firm handshake to each of them and the chief was left alone.

Musing about what might have been, what should have been, only made it worse. The chief had hoped to announce the complete destruction of Britain's most valuable and irreplaceable secret technological project, the chamber under the sea off the Channel Tunnel. Instead of that good news, there was nothing and the ASU itself had gone missing, all five of them! It's enough to drive you to drink, which was a good idea thought the chief, pouring a stiff vodka and not too much coke into a Tyrone or was it Cavan Crystal tumbler, who cared? The drink still tasted great. The chief sat by the fire, alone, sipping the drink, thinking of the decision they could not be told about. They would prevent it. Another drink and it did not seem so dangerous. It was the only thing the chief could do now.

But there had been glimmers of hope as brief and vague reports of an explosion or something unusual happening near the Channel Tunnel had been carried on some foreign radio stations and then... nothing. Perhaps it was time for another Stoli before bed.

Urbanisation Playa Serena; Roquetas De Mar, Almeria, Spain

The bell ringing on the beach told him that the German had the baked potatoes ready and he was looking forward to having them with the half bottle of wine left over from last night's party. He knew he should have got rid of her earlier but time flies when you are having a good time. He had just crossed the pavement from the Banco de Andalucia where the monthly transfer had arrived in his account as usual and it was always good to feel the big wad of notes in his wallet.

As he walked along the hot sandy beach in his shorts and sandals, he thought to himself as he did on that one day every month that it certainly had been a good decision to live in Spain. He liked to relive in his mind the main events of his life and his work before settling down to yet another major challenge. The expertise he and others had gained over the years would now be essential for the success of this, his most difficult project to date. He remembered how he had become tired of America and had made enough money in California's Silicon Valley in the '70s and '80s to do him for a long time. Working for IBM when computer genius Gene Amdahl was pushing out the frontiers before he left to establish his own Amdahl Corporation, had been a great experience together with his short spell at Microsoft in its earliest days. It was just what he wanted after NASA and the National Security Agency. For once, at college, he had been in the right place at the right time although he did not know it then. What started out as a safe method of communication for the Defence Department in the event of nuclear war had gradually been extended to the universities. His college, Berkeley, was the first to design the early system for the military in the '60s before it became commercially available in 1990. Soon there would be at least 30 million users world-wide as the numbers were growing every day.

The start-up of the Internet, he thought to himself, had been the lucky break he deserved and his lifelong knowledge of computers for war and peace had made him one of the few experts who could name their own price.

Then he had met her. Sitting now in his comfortable apartment looking out over the blue Mar Mediterranean, as she always called it, he still marvelled that the Internet, with his own specially developed methods of encryption which was different and confidential for each client, had made him a small fortune and it was only the beginning. Many companies, including banks, had been scrambling information for a long time so that nobody could hack into confidential data on the so-called new information superhighway.

Security concerns in many companies centred on external threats from "hackers" with transactions from financial institutions being intercepted and unwanted users gaining access to corporate networks. These concerns were usually eased by the use of firewalls, a more basic system of encryption than he had perfected and state-of-the-art authentication mechanisms. A firewall was a computer placed between the Internet and the internal corporate system. Simple encryption used a key to scramble and, of course, unscramble data. Authentication was often provided by the use of digital signatures which could help prove that the right person actually signed the documents. The strength of any encryption algorithm was determined by the size of its key, with 56 bits being regarded as secure, although he could now break that code within two hours of the software being ready. He was using 128-bit encryption, with special variations and nobody had managed to even get near breaking it yet.

But there was no such thing as an unbreakable code. It just took time, expertise, equipment and, often, in spite of all the technology, a bit of old-fashioned luck. Sipping a glass of the local red wine before his short siesta he still found it difficult to get used to the early afternoon heat he always liked to remember how he got involved in hacking before words like World Wide Web and Cyberspace became commonplace.

It was the challenge of BSkyB satellite television in 1990 which said its system could not be decoded that started him off. Within four years, Sky had issued ten generations of new Smart-cards as expert hackers like himself found ways to unscramble its encrypted signals for paying, or rather non-paying, customers.

Then there was the GSM mobile phone system used almost everywhere except America and which was initially also supposed to be secure. The British Royal family, the Ministry of Defence, the Home Office and other Government departments were later dismayed to find that even an amateur electronics or computer enthusiast could track and steal their numbers with equipment legally purchased in any specialist telecommunications store on the Tottenham Court Road. British Telecom and Mercury had estimated that, in one year, over £3 million in revenue could be lost through people with scanners picking up radio signals of mobile phones, transferring the numbers to another phone with connecting leads and then using these phones to make calls world-wide. In Hong Kong, an electronics expert was going one better by developing a mobile phone which could store 100 different phone numbers with electronic serial numbers which allowed the user to switch numbers anytime to avoid detection. Codes and code-breaking operations went far back into history, the most famous location probably for this work being Bletchley Park during World War Two. There, thousands of Englishmen and women worked day and night to decrypt ever-changing German codes which guided the U-boats towards the British fleet. Even at that time, one of the German codes had over 100 million permutations so now, fifty years later, the advances of new technology were mind-blowing. Phone conversations, fax messages, e-mail, were all easy to intercept. The Internet, with expert-encrypted messages, now offered the best security, providing the person you were sending the messages or information to had the right software to decode it, of course. While in June 1993 there were only 130 World Wide Web pages, now they were multiplying faster than rabbits. He estimated there would be over 20 million in a few years.

"Was any system 100 per cent secure?" he mused as he helped himself to more wine and visualised two celebrated cases of computer hacking. Robert T Morris's worm had infected thousands of computers, replicating itself endlessly until the systems crashed. This could no longer happen, at least not so easily, as many big companies had already inserted security "firewalls" to isolate the Internet gateway from the rest of the system. But more of interest to him, and the subject of further study, was the alleged planned attack by hacker Kevin Mitnick which was set to shock the computer experts before the end of the year if it happened.

A computer used by Tsotomu Shimomura, a computer scientist, could perhaps be subverted, using an attack known as "IP address spoofing". The Internet Protocol (IP) address spoofing attack would rely on the fact that, although IP "sequence numbers" are supposed to be random, many Unix and TCP/IP software vendors use a simple algorithm which is far from unguessable.

Kevin Mitnick, another famous or notorious hacker, could determine that the target machine trusted another machine to run commands with "super-user" privileges, without passwords. He could then overload the trusted machine with packets so it would not notice the forged packets and force them to be ignored by the target. Once this was done, he could test the sequence-number generator on the target which would allow him to work out the generation algorithm used.

He could then send a barrage of packets, containing the appropriate sequence numbers, which would convince the target computer that a legitimate connection was in progress. Since the trusted computer was overloaded, it could not warn the target that these were forgeries. Once the connection was established, he could run a command as the "super-user" on the target computer and its defences were subverted. The man in Spain, one of the very few to hear of the secret plans, was very excited about this project, if it ever happened.

He knew it would be commented afterwards by most experts that if the target computer had been protected by a good router, this attack would have failed, in fact that it would be impossible. Impossible was a word the man in Spain never even considered-it was just a bigger challenge. He decided then not to do any more thinking or work that day-it had been a hard night in more ways than one but he wanted to look into what he called his "secret room" before lying down.

She had certainly brought him luck. He would never forget the night he had met her in Chaplin's Fluffy Duck bar up the road. It was her eyes that got him-at first. The Internet was now bringing him money, plenty of it for an inexpensive country like Spain. Few, if anyone, knew where he was, yet he could reach almost anywhere in the world in seconds.

He had been lucky with the apartment in Spain. He had just completed its purchase when he heard the time-share company next door was going into liquidation, so with a bit of negotiation-and a few cash payments-he was able to get a studio apartment added to his own two-bedroomed mini-villa. This was now his base for world communications and when alone he liked to take a look at his "toys" as she always called them.

The latest mainframe IBM and Amdahl stood side by side for practical as well as sentimental reasons but that had nearly been the end of his Spanish adventure. Nobody had told him that the electric current was, to say the least, unreliable in that area at certain times. Even light bulbs did not last long. But he had got there just in time when extra power was needed for the three luxury hotels in the area, like the Trinidad, so a little cash here and there solved that problem too.

From the beginning, he had decided to go with CompuServe as the on-line network to the world. He would not be surprised to know that it would soon have three million subscribers in 150 countries with almost half a million of those in Europe. He kept in contact with American on-line Delphi Prodigy and

Microsoft for future needs as well as the newcomers. Looking at his PCs and software, he was proud of his collection Dell Compaq, Sun, Motorola, Hewlett-Packard, Sharp, Windows he met Bill Gates once many others including the Viglen Genie PCI and the one he always carried with him, Psion, which was about the size of his wallet.

He was keeping an eye on the new boys on the block as well remembering that most new computer products are out of date before they get to the customer 25-year-old guys like Marc Andreessen and his Netscape Navigator for the World Wide Web multimedia section of the Internet. Multinational giants like Philips would soon even make it possible to surf the Net from a home TV set. This latest development was now of particular interest to him.

Time for his siesta. Then back to work on a project for a new client who wished to remain anonymous but wanted a further check on a top-security Internet communication system, his own creation, which could only be decoded by seven people in the world. That would be tomorrow's challenge for his mind tonight's challenge for his body would be when she returned home, so better have that siesta now.

* * *

The young university graduate they had sent him had nearly killed him or, rather, worn him out more than the girl. He was an electronic genius when you could get him to work but with the cheap drink, the discos, the senoritas, he was often coming into bed when the older man was ready for breakfast. Nevertheless, they had become very friendly and, every afternoon, when most of the inhabitants of the area were taking a siesta, they would be deep in concentration on the computers and how they could solve the problem. The assignment had come over the Net in one of his most difficult codes and, at the beginning, did not seem of special importance. It was from his most valued client.

Cloning the phones had been relatively easy and they soon had a press full of them, all with different numbers. Then they struck a brick wall. How to get them all, with their different numbers, to ring exactly at the same second. They had linked them up to the computers in different ways but there were always difficulties. After two weeks, they still could not solve it to the degree of certainty and accuracy always demanded by his best customer, who would be thousands of miles away when he would be expected to make it all happen.

Communication with this VIP customer was not easy as every word had to be encrypted and that message then encoded again before transmission at the agreed time to the designated screen, wherever that was, which was only to be used in an emergency. However, he had to use it many times over the past weeks.

A possible solution had come to him during the night and he had jumped out of bed to jot it down before sleep, or the girl, put it out of his mind. Would it serve their purpose if all the phones had the same number? Then, from Spain, with his bank of computers, it would be no problem to make them all ring at the same time. The reply had come quickly in one word Yes. It was easy to show his young friend how to implant the same number on many different phones over and over again, so that he could bring the expert knowledge away with him. What they did with him or it did not concern the man in Spain as he knew the lodgement would be in the Banco de Andalucia nearby within a few days. In a way, he was sorry to lose the company of the young man. In another, he had his computers, the girl, and the good life in the sun. Now for his siesta and much-needed sleep. He slept better not knowing that all his hard work on this project would be in vain as the telephone plan had been put on the back burner for use sometime in the future or maybe never. His sleep would also not have been so peaceful if he had known that the most difficult and dangerous challenge of his sheltered life was now on its way to him, one vital to his future safety.

In his dreams, he again seemed to be reliving his whole life as he did every time he walked from the Banco de Andalucia. Although asleep, he knew he had done it again today in spite of what his doctor had told him. "Forget your past, your computers, this girl, when you are out in the beautiful sunshine beside the sea and enjoy the great life you have here every day." The old Spanish physician had said in his broken English as he made out the usual prescription for Valium and muttered, as he produced his bill with its usual complement of noughts added to the pesetas; "Why do you not, maybe this is how they say it in English, just smell the flowers?" For some reason the mention of 'English' even in his dreams made him wake up suddenly. He hoped it was not an omen.

Cumberland Hotel

Marble Arch, London

The chief knew it was taking a big chance, probably the biggest chance of a career that had seen action, promotion, capture, escape, and election to the top job in the IRA. If the others in the Army Council knew, it would be all over and back to the ranks. There was no record of course, there wouldn't be in any event of the Chief of Staff ever staying in a central London hotel, although under an assumed name and with forged identity papers. Just as bad, if not worse, was baiting a trap with a boy-child (they would call him) for one of the top people in British Intelligence.

The first task had not been as difficult as expected. With the right code developed by the man in Spain, it did not take long to contact No 2 Active Service Unit based in outer London, around Hampstead and White City, ordering them to be ready to replace the elite "Mayfair" unit as the others jokingly called it, which the chief had now discovered could be all dead. The chief sat in silence in the comfortable old-fashioned hotel room, looking out the window, at the crowds rushing to Oxford Street, Edgware Road, Bayswater Road and down into the Underground to a hundred other destinations, wondering:

"Do they ever think of Ireland at all? They have their own worries like everyone else. Yet how would they like it if one-fifth of their country was occupied by the Germans, the Russians or the Chinese just because they had marked out a geographical area in which they would always have a majority in favour of the presence of a foreign army there?" Then the phone rang and the only good news of the week: In fact, the best news of the year!

"The goods were delivered as ordered. The building completely demolished." As the chief sat digesting this bit of exciting news, knowing for the first time that the elite ASU had hit the target of the secret chamber in the Channel Tunnel, although depressed that they had all probably died in the action, the phone rang again;

"The situation is deteriorating rapidly. A major move is being planned against us. You can arrange contact with potential client at 9 p.m.."

That was the news the chief had come over to hear but dreaded it when it came so abruptly. There were a few hours to kill and, resisting the vodka and orange in the mini-bar, the chief decided to try to relax with a movie. Tom Hanks in *The Man With One Red Shoe* was so funny and stupid that the evening's meeting was forgotten for some ninety minutes at least. Then it was time to shower and dress properly for a meeting which had to take place but which sent waves of revulsion through the entire body. Contact had to be made with the boy, more like a child, Charles, but nevertheless on the game for two years. He needed the money, air ticket, and the visa, for, hopefully, a new life in Australia. The chief felt the bulky envelope, which would be his reward if all went well.

Coming out of the main door of the Cumberland, Charles turned left as instructed and was soon swallowed up in the crowd. Another left turn, then across a quiet side street, and there was the bar. Entering it, he noticed a sudden lowering of the noise from the conversation and knew the regulars there, maybe twenty or thirty men, were sizing up a newcomer, a novelty of fresh white flesh for the establishment. Going up to the counter, aware that most of the eyes in the room seemed to be watching, the usual order of coca-cola and ice was delivered and paid for, without any unnecessary pleasantries.

A seat almost facing the door gave a good view of the occupants and any newcomers. The target did not seem to have arrived and he hoped it would work out, as another night there might be difficult. Just when the coke was on the way, he entered to be greeted by a group of friends. Charles knew him from the photo slipped under the hotel room door and now destroyed.

It was like a club there and the newcomer was not a member. It was better being ignored than being the object of attention but contact had to be made. Commander Trevor Wallace, whom the intelligence data supplied by the Irish person he met in the hotel had said could never resist a fresh face, but who preferred young boys to older men, made it easy.

"You are new here. May I buy you a drink?" he asked as he wandered across the room, ignoring the jealous looks of some of the others and sat down beside the newcomer, who thought that back home in Scotland such relationships were more private. Conversation was easier than expected and the cover of being down from Edinburgh was not too difficult. The Commander liked asking questions, that's what he did a lot of in MI6. Charles had been warned:

"Be careful of him. He is one of the inner circle in the British Intelligence services but, with this one peculiar habit." Charles, of course, did not know the chief. He had been contacted by a man over a week ago in a similar pub and made an offer he could not refuse. Just one night's work, off to the other side of the world the next day with £1,000 in his pocket. He had agreed quickly, perhaps too quickly, he thought now. Maybe he should have asked for more. They were chatting comfortably now and soon the landlord, at the far end of the bar, was shouting "Time, gentlemen, please" as glasses and bottles began disappearing from the tables. "The English are certainly a disciplined lot" thought Charles, "back home, that would be a signal for everyone to order doubles or an armful of pints," but Commander Wallace "please call me Trevor" was talking again:

"It looks like we have to go. How long will you be here for? Maybe we could get together earlier tomorrow?" was met by the disappointing reply:

"I'm afraid I have to go back in the morning. Only down for the day and to-night really" which gave Trevor Wallace his opening:

"Where are you staying then?" his hand already straying, more like brushing, against the boy's leg.

He brightened up when he heard "The Cumberland" saying,

"That's almost next door. What about a nightcap there?" Charles could only nod before they left the gay bar to the stares of Trevor's friends.

'Lie back and think of England' used to be the old music hall joke and it came to mind as the boy realised Commander Trevor Wallace of MI6 did not believe in wasting time. After helping himself to the only Martell brandy in the mini-bar, Wallace was already taking off his clothes. As Charles followed his example, thinking he looked ridiculous in his shoes and socks with those multicoloured boxer shorts, Trevor Wallace made his move or rather the first of many moves. He liked to be rough and dominant and Charles, face pressed into the pillow, nearly cried out as the big man thrust his full weight, panting like a dog enjoying a new bit of fresh meat. The boy was suffering in silence but Wallace wanted more and Charles could not disappoint the hidden camera which was picking up every action from its ideal vantage point over the bed. "Remember to turn your face towards the picture on the wall," the only thought that came to his mind.

Soon, but not soon enough for the boy, Wallace was spent and fast asleep on the bed. The tiny Japanese camera in the picture was now getting some excel-lent shots of him nude, his organ like a limp frankfurter, still dripping.

"Just as well I do not have a knife," thought the chief later when the nega-tives were developed, "or I'd be tempted to cut it off and post it to that Stella Rimington, who has wiped out the ASU and made this ordeal necessary. It need not have been like that. The man was a beast, a bully, used to getting his own way. Well, MI6, or at least commander Trevor Wallace, would be getting a bit of a shock in a couple of days, when tonight's pictures joined those they already had of him with some very young boys from that bar. These thoughts passed through the chief's mind when looking at the negatives later:

"Why had there been so many homosexuals in British Intelligence, Philby, Burgess, McClean, Blount, when it was so rare in the IRA?" No quick answer came. But the chief knew what the rest of the Army Council would think of anyone gay.

"You have to get dressed and get home before hotel security notices you leaving" had been enough to hurry Wallace up and he left without a word to the boy just another one-night stand for him. One of the Irish maids would take down the hidden camera, remove the film, remember to dump the camera before giving it to the courier and... The chief could think no more, no further than a hot bath and plenty of sweet-smelling hotel soap to try to wash away the filth of that night. It would take much more than that to bring forgetfulness. "The things we do for Ireland." It was as if there had been a personal involvement. "Just looking at the pictures was enough to make one vomit," was the chief's last thought before sinking into a troubled sleep later.

The room for Charles had been paid in advance as he was only fourteen, the chief had just discovered. He would now be on a British Airways flight to Australia.

* * *

Early the next morning, after destroying all records of the stay in the Cumberland, except the strips of valuable film, the chief paid in cash and, just a short cab ride, checked into the Hilton, which was the same as every other Hilton except for the rooftop view. Before leaving the Cumberland, the chief had made a few calls from the pay phones in the lobby, which could not be traced back to any room. The courier arrived at the Hilton soon afterwards for the evidence which the chief needed returned in photographic print form within two hours. The chief was using a different name and identity now, just someone on business in London who would not be even noticed among the other business people in the lobby with the never-ending comings and goings of an international hotel chain that spanned the continents. The other photos, collected over three years, were in a locked briefcase in the hotel's strongroom. Time to get them now.

The courier was back sooner than expected and waited quietly while the chief looked at the photographs, happy in the knowledge that the original film was now stored in a safe house in Wimbledon, while making a mental note to destroy it personally when all this was over. The young messenger, a relatively new recruit to the IRA who had never been to Ireland yet, did not know the chief's identity nor did anyone else in London, so he waited patiently for instructions:

"Please deliver this envelope to Commander Trevor Wallace at the address on the envelope. You will see it is marked 'Personal; Confidential; Urgent' so all you have to do is give it to the receptionist and get out of there as fast as possible. Then, to be doubly sure, do not go outside your home for the next two days. Do this right and we will arrange a nice holiday in Ireland for you very soon." The young boy was delighted at getting his first important mission for the IRA and the prospect of a free holiday so was gone in a flash.

The chief was not so happy. Maybe the photographs and the requested typed note should have been sent from the Cumberland. If the courier was caught before he could get out of the building, would he talk? Unlikely but better be prepared. It was a nice day so the chief took the elevator to the lobby, bought the *Times* and the *Guardian* before strolling down Park Lane and across to Hyde Park, joining the hundreds sitting on benches in the summer sunshine. Only the chief had a special interest in the big hotel. Nothing happened. Soon it would be Heathrow, Paris, Dublin, then back to Belfast again. It was best to be careful. The chief was imagining Trevor Wallace of MI6 opening the envelope, perhaps during his weekly meeting at MI5 as this was the day for it. It brought the first smile since arrival in London. The message would do wonders for his blood pressure:

You will be contacted in Belfast, Europa Hotel, tomorrow night and you had better be there. Otherwise, these photos and many others will be sent to your mother, your family, the heads of MI5; MI6; Scotland Yard and, of course, to the Sun *and other tabloid media.*

Central London

Monday 30th

Commander Wallace was just entering the meeting of Intelligence chiefs when the porter handed him the envelope. Fortunately for him, he took it into the gents' toilet, then promptly got sick when he saw the pictures and read the message, three times. Wiping his mouth with the paper towels, particles of which stuck to his beard, he looked at his white cheeks in the mirror, splashed some water on his face, and made a brave gesture in getting himself together to go into the room for what he knew would be a difficult meeting.

Stella Rimington was sitting at the head of the table and there were only four of them there, including himself. A bad sign, he thought as he tried to pull himself together and act normal. When he looked around the room, he felt a bit better as the chief superintendent of Belfast's RUC and Clive Reid of Military Intelligence did not look too happy either. She was speaking:

"You will be pleased that I can confirm we have liquidated the entire IRA unit which has given us so much trouble in the past," but she hardly paused for the "Hear, here" and "Jolly good show", drowning them out as she continued:

"But we have lost four people who were here on the day of our last major planning meeting, Jonathan Jones, Andrew Manning, two of my best and most trusted men; chief inspector Geoffrey Scott of the Yard's Special Branch, and that CIA woman Margaret Blake. I have decided, as time is short, that they will not be replaced at this top command level so it is now all down to us around this table." When she paused for a drink of water, the others knew it was very unusual to hear Clive Reid speak first:

"You know, madam, that I am not in favour of this operation at all?"

"What would you suggest instead?" was the icy reply.

"We had a way of dealing with terrorists like these in Aden, Cyprus, Israel, India, Palestine, Nigeria and several African countries."

"And what way was that?" she asked, baiting the trap.

"Leave them in cells to rot or put them all up against the wall and shoot the buggers." How Trevor Wallace hated that last word, but he kept silent as the

Director General of MI5 was speaking:

"Yes, Clive, and we lost all those countries. We even tried it in Ireland in 1916 and again when we sent in the Black and Tans and now they are going to make a big Hollywood movie about the man who beat them, Michael Collins. We can't ignore the fact that we had to give them back twenty-six of our counties to get that lot sorted out when Lloyd George was prime minister and now they are at it again. Trying to get us out of the remaining six where our own British people have settled. That's why we are here, gentlemen, whether we like it or not."

As there was silence after that interchange, she asked:

"What do you think, Ian?" and the big Belfast man took his time in replying:

"What we discussed at the last meeting should work. Anyway it is our best option now. Take out the fifty leaders for good which should please Clive and, at the same time, pour troops into the Province to round up everyone connected with that terrorist organisation. Lock them up and throw away the key. We can leave it to the Government, the Ulster Office, the media who are on our side, to take the flak from all the do-gooders not only in Ireland but here and in America as well. We can expect reprisals to this internment but give us the manpower and throw away the rule book as Para One did on Bloody Sunday, '72, in Londonderry, then we'll soon settle them." She was looking at Trevor now so he knew he must say something, always aware of the note with the photographs in his briefcase:

"Yes, I agree and I think the sooner we put it into operation the better."

He was not expecting the next question from Stella Rimington:

"Would you be prepared to go to Belfast this evening with Ian in Jonathan's place as he may need help in co-ordinating this important, this vital, operation?" He was going to plead urgent MI6 business, in any event it was her and MI5's show, then he remembered the note and quickly agreed.

"Very good," was her equally prompt reply, "so just to recap-within a week, perhaps within the next forty-eight hours, our twenty-five key senior officers from all the intelligence and security services will be brought together at a secret secure location for one meeting only. There, they will be fully briefed and given all the resources they need to carry out the job. Each of them, including you Ian, I understand, has a complete dossier, and I mean really complete, on two of the IRA's leaders, commanders, killers, fucking terrorists, call them what you like, as long as we get them off the face of this earth for ever. Everything will be explained at that meeting and the plan, some of you call it the 'FS' project, will then be put into full operation immediately you

303

will be given all the intelligence, military and especially SAS support you request. There will be no delay and those murdering bastards will never know what hit them. They have blown up our pubs, our offices, killed too many of our people, and now they think they can even attack Downing Street and the City which, of course, we cannot allow. We are going to end it all and all of them, for good this time. Fifty of their leaders dead and all the others in prison here on the mainland, not Belfast, will finish them." She pressed one of the three buttons on her desk and there was a knock on the door, followed by two porters with tea and biscuits on one tray and a bottle of Gordon's gin, tonic and glasses on the other.

They began to relax but conversation was difficult, especially when the gruff Ulsterman asked:

"Any confirmation yet on what happened to Jonathan and Andrew?"

Stella Rimington hesitated a long time before replying:

"Andrew's body was recovered from that shoot-out off Oxford Street but not much of Jonathan was left I'm afraid after the explosion in Folkestone. We never did discover the identity of that maniac in the London cab who seemed to be trying to rescue the IRA prisoners. The whole place just went up with such an explosion and a burst of flame that he must have had a bomb in it. It's still a bit of a mystery but I am trying to forget it as we turn our thoughts to the operation in hand which, when it is successful, should make certain that nothing like that ever happens again."

Trevor Wallace, as he was now committed to the Belfast end of the operation and expected he would have his own personal problem to deal with there, decided he'd better show some interest and asked:

"What about over here? They seem to have some of their so-called Active Service Units here on the mainland so what's being done about them?"

"Scotland Yard, under Geoffrey Scott, with our help, had been working on this for quite a while before he was killed. There will be a few important arrests, a few mysterious gas explosions in what they call safe-houses around London. But they are difficult to spot in a city of more than ten million. There are only five million in the whole island over there. The Yard will be sending a man to Belfast on the same flight as yourselves, to replace poor Geoffrey who was a likeable old sod. In the interests of security and the fact that they all come from that part of the world in the first place, we decided long ago to concentrate this entire operation within the high-security Army compound in Lisburn. We have the whole place guarded day and night with a crack SAS regiment flown there in secret to reinforce the already excellent security put in place by Ian's RUC chaps and Clive's army colleagues. So a good job so far all round."

It was difficult to keep the small talk going any longer but while she was drinking the tea, the three men had poured themselves three stiff gin and tonics with Trevor needing it most.

"One final word," she cautioned just as they were beginning to relax, "this is the most important mission any of you, of us, has ever been involved in and nothing can go wrong. That is why we will be taking our twenty-five elite officers out of Northern Ireland for a final briefing in a place even more secure, which you probably find difficult to imagine, but, while you cannot tell them that, do have them all on permanent stand-by, ready to go when the order arrives. Then, there will be no time to waste. Good luck, gentlemen."

* * *

Chief Superintendent Ian Taylor wanted to do some shopping, the kids had a list of things they wanted from Hamleys in Regent Street. Trevor Wallace agreed to meet him at the InterContinental Hotel in three hours so that they could go to Heathrow and Belfast together. Another call was made by one of Stella Rimington's new bodyguards before they left the Millbank HQ and it was arranged that a Jeremy Morley from the Special Branch anti-terrorist section of Scotland Yard would also meet them there.

Trevor wanted time to think. In the toilet of the Tower Hotel he steeled himself to take another look at the photos. By now, the gin and tonic had settled his stomach but the thoughts of them going to his mother, brothers and sisters, the neighbours, his boss, the media, almost made him sick again. Getting his lighter, he burned each of them in turn and flushed the ashes down the toilet. He read the note once more, noted the Europa Hotel which was already well known to him and then it too was flushed away into the Thames or wherever. A couple more double gins at the bar made him feel better, calming him down as he phoned the office, his mother now in her seventies, and a few close friends, including two from the pub near the Cumberland, telling them he would be out of town for a few days, which was nothing unusual in his job.

He tried to relax, cursing that night which was now obviously a set-up. But they had many other homosexual pictures as well so must have been watching him for a long time. In line for promotion at MI6 or even one of the other Intelligence Services, following the new official policy of changing officers around now and then, he must get those negatives back and make certain there were no copies. He considered going back to the office to draw out arms and ammunition but decided that might cause hassle at the airport. Then he remembered he would be with Ian Taylor and knew he would look after him. If there was one thing the RUC was not short of, it was guns. He wondered what this new fellow from Scotland Yard would be like. You never know, he might be in luck, was a fleeting thought until he remembered the previous night and vowed, yet again, never to pick up strangers no matter how young and attractive, but to stick to his own circle of gay friends. A promise he had made and broken often but these pictures and what they would want for them made even him begin to feel fear. He had the commissionaire hail him a cab, slipped him a pound coin, and was in the bar of the InterContinental before the others.

There was a nice young man in the corner who looked at him now and then over his newspaper but whom Trevor very pointedly ignored. He had had enough excitement, and trouble, already this week.

When Ian Taylor arrived, it was amusing to see this big gruff man laden with the distinctive Hamleys bags. Trevor began to feel better, until he noticed the young man who had been watching him approaching their table.

"Commander Wallace? Chief Superintendent Taylor? I'm Jeremy Morley, Geoffrey Scott's replacement from the Yard." They shook hands, and were soon engaged in conversation, the cricket, football, tennis, everything except politics and that which was on all their minds.

"Ever been in Belfast before?" asked Ian Taylor and was not surprised by the reply:

"No, it will be my first time and I am looking forward to it."

"Will they ever learn", thought Taylor, 'another ambitious young lad not long out of nappies coming over to make his name among the natives' but he only said:

"I hope you will enjoy it," thinking you will not get much of a tourist's view from the slit of an armoured car. Jeremy Morley was also making up his mind about the two older men. 'Taylor' he thought "is a bit rough and ready but a genuine sort of bloke who could be a good friend, while Wallace is another kettle of fish. Unless I'm very wrong, I would not like to be in a dark room alone with him," he concluded, smiling a little to himself as he looked forward to his first assignment out of the country and the stories he would have to tell Nancy and the children when he got back. He had come up through the ranks fast, studying hard at night after university while Nancy held down a job in the local bank. He was now the youngest senior officer at Scotland Yard, in his mid-thirties, but looking much younger, thanks to her good cooking, Nancy always said. The children, Tommy only five and Jeanie almost seven, would miss him but he had promised them both a day at the zoo and another in Brighton when he returned to his small but cheerful detached bungalow in Hampstead, which they loved to call home. He had promised to ring them every night but you never knew when you got mixed up with these army bods and the spooks, he had also warned them. The promise of presents had made the parting easier.

Now, Trevor Wallace was speaking:

"Well, I've been in Belfast a few times. Not my favourite place I must say. No offence, Ian," while the big Belfast man only nodded, more interested in how they made that terrible mild-and-bitter piss they called beer in London. Personally he could not wait to get back home for a real drink and some real people. He'd had enough of those ponces in London, although young Morley seemed a nice lad, if too young for a man's job. He would have been surprised to know that Morley was not his real name and that he was the head of Scotland Yard's anti-terrorist section now that Geoffrey Scott was dead. A protégé of Geoffrey's, he knew all about the mission but had often found it useful to use his youthful innocent looks to plead ignorance, you got more information that way especially from colleagues who were drinking much more than you.

The arrival of a porter signalled that the car Jeremy had requisitioned from the Yard's pool to impress them on the way to the airport had arrived. They said nothing but obviously enjoyed the comfort of the latest '94 Toyota, which was now built in Britain by the Japanese, and the police driver made Heathrow faster than they had ever done before. While both the older men went to the duty-free to have a look around, the new arrival made a few calls on his Panasonic mobile, one of which was to Belfast, another to his children, which was almost a mistake as he had to rush to the plane by the time they would let him go. Seated together, none of them felt much like talking during the hour's journey although they did manage to knock back a couple of double brandies each, which helped their humour "For medicinal purposes only," Ian Taylor had told them.

Arriving in Belfast, even Ian noticed more troops than usual around the airport and could feel that tension that had kept him alive all these years coming back into his body. His car and escort were waiting and he had forgotten to tell the others of the arrangements.

"We have quite good quarters in the barracks and I think you will find the mess well stocked, Trevor," he remarked as they came down the steps and was more than a little surprised at the reply:

"That's kind of you, Ian, but I had my people book me into the Europa where I always stay when I visit here. As a businessman, of course," he added when he saw Taylor's face.

"Are you sure that is wise, especially in these very special circumstances?" the RUC man persisted.

"Don't worry about me. I'm always careful and they look after me well there," he replied, already wondering if that young Italian waiter still available.

"Well, all right but I'll have a couple of my men in plain clothes keep a special eye on the place tonight," then continuing before Trevor could tell him that was the last thing he wanted:

"You know, there is not much that happens in this city that we do not know about. Trouble is, the other side usually knows about it as well. I'll be glad when this operation is over and all you crowd can go back safely to London," he could not resist remarking.

It was Jeremy Morley who broke the obvious tension between the two older men:

"I'll come along with you, Ian, and look forward to meeting your colleagues in the officers' mess for dinner."

Europa Hotel

Belfast

Trevor was relieved when they dropped him at the security entrance to the Europa Hotel where a look into the car, and a flash of his card, rushed him quickly through the checkpoint.

Inside was the same as he remembered it and soon he was in his room which was no different to a hundred, maybe a thousand, other hotel rooms he had stayed in during his long career in MI6, except for the thicker glass, perhaps bullet-proof he wondered, in the windows of what locals glorified with the title of "the most bombed hotel in Europe". They have a strange sense of humour in Belfast, he thought, but then the Irish were a strange lot. Not like the civilised British, no Eton or Cambridge, only some jumped up technical college they pretended was a university. A humourless crowd in Belfast, he told himself, not like Dublin which was an exciting city, full of culture. Then he remembered the one time he had been there, to show those stupid so-called Loyalist fellows who had gone down with him in the car how to make and prime the bombs and how he had been lucky to get back to England alive. Enough of these thoughts, he told himself, as he showered, shaved, changed to casual blazer and slacks before making his way to the bar and booking a table for dinner.

It would be a nice evening but for that blasted note. He began to wonder again, when they would contact him, who would do it, what they wanted from him, but decided to put these troubling things from his mind as he ordered a Famous Grouse, he liked a good Scotch whisky for a change, and studied the menu. The restaurant was pleasant if not spectacular, the service was excellent although he did not see the Italian waiter, and the food he knew would be as good as anything you could get in London. He was flicking through the wine list to find a good Burgundy to go with his chef's special fillet steak flamed in Bushmills whiskey, when a voice said:

"May I join you, Mr Wallace?" and the shock was almost too much for him, in fact he spilled some of the second Famous Grouse he had brought in with him from the bar. They had sent a woman, and a pretty one at that, if you liked that kind of thing. Before he could reply she continued:

"I understand you got the holiday photos and the note from our friend in London?" which confirmed that they had wasted no time.

"What do you want?" he asked abruptly and she smiled in reply:

"Some pâté to start, followed by the roast chicken with all the trimmings would be nice and, of course, you can choose the wine."

By this time a waiter had arrived and was taking down her order so he had little choice but to play along with this dangerous game. As it turned out, dinner was as enjoyable as it could be in the circumstances, the conversation trivial but polite. She made the point that she was only a courier carrying out orders from London, which he felt was about the only thing they had in common.

She had not told him her name, not that she would give her real one in any case, but he felt it was the proper thing to do to ask.

"You can call me anything you like, providing you don't call me too early in the morning," she replied laughing at him now while adding:

"Of course, I suppose this does not apply in your case."

When he looked around to see if anyone had overheard, she continued:

"You have nothing to worry about, Trevor. May I call you Trevor? And you may call me Marian. You need not worry about the Italian waiter. He was one of ours, that's how we got some of the pictures the last time and he is now safely back home in New York. So it will not damage your reputation too much, being seen with a woman," she added with a grin. He let this insult pass, thinking of what he had done with Giorgio last year and wondering how long they had been setting him up, watching his every move, especially those in bedrooms.

She cut in on his reverie with:

"We always keep our word. I wish the same could be said for your side but, nevertheless, we will keep our word to you. Film negatives, prints, destroyed. No copies made. Your past adventures of no concern to us anymore. All for this last job which will be very simple for you."

When she stopped, he found himself believing her and thinking it would be wonderful to be free of this sword, this guillotine, hanging over him and promising himself that he would get a live-in boyfriend when he got safely back to London, no more casual pick-ups, no more one-night stands. Then it struck him:

"What do you want me to do?"

"All in good time, Trevor. I'm staying in this hotel also. There is no use telling your RUC friends as I only know what they tell me and that's very little, while you have everything to lose back in London, your family, your friends, your colleagues, your job, your ..."

"Don't!" he almost shouted, "I get the message. Now what is it your lot wants?"

"Simple, every single detail of this top-secret operation you are planning against us. The when? The where? The how? The why now? The time? Everything. Don't look surprised. Before they disappeared, probably murdered by your SAS killers like our three unarmed volunteers in Gibraltar, the Central London ASU told us there was a big operation begin planned against us but did not have time to find out any further details. We have seen the increased traffic at Aldergrove and other places. More of your chaps coming and going to and from London. Increased surveillance on some of our top people who have to move around more than usual. People like Cahill, Adams, McGuinness, were around too long not to notice things like that. They are not involved now but trained us well. More security patrols in the Falls, Creggan, the Bogside, even Crossmaglen if only by choppers with night scopes and cameras. So we wonder. Is it internment again? But as that did not work the last time, is it something worse? So here we are, Trevor, having a lovely dinner for which I thank you. You can solve the puzzle for us."

It was a good dinner, he had to admit that to himself as he took the lift to his room. More like the last supper, he thought. They had parted as she said she was going to a downtown disco but gave him the number of her room which he was to call if there was any sudden development.

When he got inside his room, his hands were shaking and he had difficulty fastening the security bolts. He considered phoning Ian Taylor of the RUC who could have her picked up easily, as he had heard rumours of what they could do to prisoners at Castlereagh, but decided against it. She probably knew nothing and her friends in London could and would ruin him if she did not contact them regularly, she had told him before they parted.

He felt trapped. He was trapped. Could only do as they asked and hope he could get away with it. Although he had had plenty to drink, probably too much, he decided to raid the mini-bar and have a miniature Hennessy before falling asleep on the covers without undressing.

* * *

Meanwhile, the girl, Marian, as she was calling herself tonight in the hotel, had taken the waiting black taxi to the house in the Malone Road, one of the last places they would expect the commander of the Belfast Brigade of the IRA to live, among all the doctors, the lawyers, the businessmen, with his children going to the same schools and his wife on the same committees. She often thought of her own little flat on the Falls as she entered the big hallway. They even had a maid to open the door. But she had always liked and admired him. Making her comfortable in a plush armchair beside the fire, with a nice glass of smooth red wine in her hand, it was easy for her to tell him everything that had happened in the Europa, especially her impressions of how Trevor Wallace would react. She was confident he would do what they wanted and give them the reliable information which was now essential. Taking a sip from her glass, she remarked:

"Well, look at it this way. If I'm wrong they will be waiting for me at the hotel and this is the last time you'll see me," adding with a smile:

"Look at all the good wine you'll save."

She handed him the tape of the entire evening from her bag as they both knew she should be getting back before the next patrols were on the streets. She was confident that everything would go as planned and his last words cheered her up a little:

"You'll soon be an officer. Don't worry. I'll have someone looking after you, near you all the time, if there is any trouble. You are doing a great job. Slan Abhaile, Marie," and the taxi was waiting to take her back to the hotel.

Trevor Wallace would tell them everything they needed to know. A good 'nights' work, she told herself, as she slipped into the unfamiliar bed, falling asleep instantly.

FRANCE

Sunday 29th

After the gun battle in London and the Channel Tunnel explosion, Carter could not believe he was still alive. The last thing he remembered was holding Tara's dying body in his arms and seeing Pat in the black cab drive directly at the oncoming cavalry. His thirty years' training with the American Special Forces in far-flung corners of the world had stood him in good stead. He had automatically thrown his body out of the way and, after that, all he remembered was the biggest bang he had ever heard. Now, in the distance, a voice seemed to be calling:

"Over here, Irish; over here, Yank."

Very slowly at first, he tried to move his arms and his legs, surprised to find that they were working and that, apart from a bad wound in his shoulder and a torn suit, he seemed to be all right.

"Vite, vite, monsieur," it was that voice again and suddenly Carter remembered the Frenchman whom he had forgotten during the fight and who was now limping towards him.

"Quick. Your only chance. The ferry with some of my family working on it. It is there now. I have some old, what you say, boiler suit here. Quick. Now."

Martin Carter struggled to his feet, looking around at the destruction and the confusion as rescuers and sightseers rushed all over the place. The bodies, including Tara's he suspected, were buried in the debris and before he could feel any regrets, his arm was grabbed by the Frenchman, whose name he had forgotten, who then helped him into an evil-smelling, oil stained work suit while whispering:

"We are crew. I see my brother coming this way. He will hide you to France and then you are on your own." Carter was grateful he had not been rough with the Frenchman when they had first arrived and had let him finish his wine before tying him up.

Being helped on board, looking and feeling like a member of the crew who had had too much wine, as two big Frenchmen were on each side of him, Carter relaxed in their strong arms and soon was hidden in the depths of the vessel. It sailed almost immediately and, with great difficulty, he raised himself to peer through a porthole at the hundreds of police and army arriving at the scene.

"My last view of England" he thought before becoming unconscious again. It was only a short journey across the English Channel and soon the Frenchman was trying to wake him again.

"You must disembark with the rest of the crew, monsieur, and my brother and I will get you on the train to Paris. Here is five hundred francs. It is all we can spare. You Yanks helped our family during the war so now we repay."

Struggling to his feet again, Carter thanked him and was almost embarrassed when the big Frenchman kissed him on both cheeks before leading him down the special gangway with the rest of the crew who had finished their shifts for the week. Soon the Frenchman handed him a single ticket for Paris and the change, and said:

"Au Revoir" at least five times as he put him on the Paris train and, again, Carter fell asleep. He had the ticket sticking out of the top pocket in the boiler suit so he was not awakened again until the train pulled into the Gare Du Nord.

Paris

"What to do now?" thought Carter as he sat on a wooden bench in a corner of the very busy station. It was only a matter of time before the Gendarmerie started checking the area, but where could he go? He did not know anyone in Paris and then he remembered:

"Nicole! Nicole! Those enjoyable hours they had spent together in the city and in bed! His clothes under the boiler suit were almost destroyed, his wallet, passport and Foreign Press card gone, and he did not know, or could not remember, where she lived. Again it was his lifetime of living dangerously which came to his aid. Once, when she had left to go to the bathroom, he had memorised the number of the mobile phone she had left on the table. Could he remember it now, he kept asking himself. The more he tried, the more other numbers came into his head. Then he decided to try the old Dale Carnegie method of association of ideas, numbers with things or events. An hour later, he was sure he had it. There had been a lot of telephone numbers, codes, passport, car, military numbers in his life.

He got a shock when the voice answered in English "British Embassy. May I help you? Who is calling, please?" and dropped the phone quickly, wondering how on earth he had got that number. Going over the method in his head once more, he realised he may have dialled one digit incorrectly so tried again and and he was through.

"This is Nicole," the tape on the answering machine was starting when he kept shouting:

"Nicole, it's Martin. For God's sake, answer the phone," and suddenly she did:

"Martin? Martin who?" was the careful reply, to which he replied loudly:

"Martin Carter of Les Bains, the bateau mouche, your lover. That Martin." There was a minute's silence and Carter could see his last francs running out before his eyes just as she replied:

"Martin. I had to be certain. Where are you? Why are you back in Paris?"

"Nicole, I need your help now, this minute, more than anything in the world. I'm in the main concourse in the Gare Du Nord, opposite platform seven. Please collect me. I can't last much longer. I am ...." but was cut short by her reply:

"Hold on, Martin, I'll be there in less than fifteen minutes", and the phone went dead, the way Carter almost felt. It was the longest fifteen minutes of his life and then he saw her. He tried to get up to rush to meet her and fell flat on his face, into complete darkness.

* * *

He seemed to be drifting on a cloud, from a rainbow of colours into a bright light and tried to close his eyes, not realising they were already tightly shut. He felt something gentle touch his hand, the light was getting brighter, he could hear music, then panic as someone was calling his name in the distance.

"I'm dead," his brain seemed to register, "but at least I'm in Heaven." He lay there for what seemed an age, listening to these pleasant sounds in the now bright surroundings but unable to move. He began to think a little more:

"Heaven is not so great if you cannot move," then back to blackness slowly, his mind telling him:

"I should not have thought that, now I'm going to the other place." Several times the same thing happened, happiness and darkness until even the moments of happiness began to lose out to despair:

"Is this all there is?" He began to remember things from his childhood, his mother and father, but every time they seemed to be almost within reach, he slipped back again into nothingness. Then his teacher made a fleeting appearance followed by the old priest who had convinced him there was a God. He started to cry out:

"Father Murphy, please help me," and was startled to feel a cool hand on his forehead and a voice, louder this time, calling:

"Martin, Martin. Wake up."

This time he struggled hard and finally managed to open his eyes, closing them immediately in the brightness, then opening them again to see this beautiful face bending over him.

"An angel," he thought before she said:

"It's Nicole. You have been asleep for two days. A friendly doctor fixed your shoulder and gave you a strong injection. You are safe here."

A smile as she touched his lips with hers and then he was gone again for another twelve hours before he startled her still sitting beside his bed:

"Where am I? How did I get here? Where are the others? Who are you?"

Suddenly he started to cry as the memories flooded back to Folkestone, to

Tara. She let him cry, cradling his head in her arms like a child until there were no more tears left.

Soon he was able to sit up, drinking chicken soup with a dash of cognac which made his recovery even faster. She told him how a helpful taxi driver had brought him to her apartment, about his wound, the doctor, while he kept thinking, "how like Tara she really is" but put it down to his imagination trying to compensate for his loss. He was surprised when she told him that he had been there two days and that he would have to leave tomorrow evening. When he questioned her, her reply was vague as she remarked:

"Now that your strength is back, we will have a good night together like the last time and we'll discuss the future tomorrow," which suited him fine. He remembered the last time and now felt her slide into the big bed beside him.

"I'm in heaven all right," he thought again as they kissed.

When he woke up the next morning, she was cooking breakfast. She had bought him an off-the-peg suit at La Printemps, which fitted him perfectly, new shoes, shirt, tie, but had forgotten underpants.

"You can wear one of mine" she laughed when he told her, "but be careful when you go into les hommes toilet at the airport."

"The airport?" he asked and he could see she had not meant to let that slip, at least not yet.

"Yes, Martin, I am sure you want to get home to your children in New York but perhaps you would like to make a small detour to get revenge on those who killed Tara?"

"How do you know about that?" was met with a prompt reply:

"You have talked about nothing else in your sleep for the past twenty-four hours and also I received a message telling me what happened. It was dreadful. I am so sad just like you are."

He saw her on the verge of tears and moved to put his arm around her on the couch. She looked into his face and said words he would never forget:

"Very few people, only our family, know what I am going to tell you, Martin, as I feel you deserve it. Tara was my sister."

She saw his look of astonishment, then embarrassment, perhaps shame and was eager to reassure him:

"I know you loved both of us, Martin, and both of us loved you."

He was speechless. It was almost like being shot all over again. He knew he was blushing, feeling such a heel, when she continued:

"Did you not notice the likeness? At home, before the Troubles, people used to think we were twins. There was only a year between us, we did everything

317

together, joined up together, went for two weeks' holiday in far-away places once a year, always together."

Martin was deep in thought as she finished with a kiss and whispered:

"So it was only natural that we would both fall in love with the same man."

"What can I say?" pleaded Martin.

"You can say you loved Tara and now you love me."

"That's easy as it's God's truth," was his reply as he took her in his arms again to make more passionate love, the breakfast forgotten.

He must have fallen asleep again. When he awoke, he lay still as he could hear her at the computer in the little nook of the apartment she called her office. Messages were going back and forth and he knew they were encrypted by her actions, so he moved quietly off the bed to stand behind her. She sensed his presence and told him:

"It is better you do not see this. Please get the breakfast, Martin, I'm starving for food this time," she laughed, so he left her for the kitchen.

He decided to boil four eggs, make some coffee, which, with the fresh French bread she had obviously got when he was asleep, would bring some life back into both of them. He arranged it all nicely on the floral tray, added a rose from the windowbox and could see her happy smile as he entered the lounge. Then he rushed back for the salt and pepper and the knives and spoons and the butter, which made her laugh out loud before kissing him and thanking him for breakfast.

He had decided he had to know what was going down but waited until she had eaten one egg, a big chunk of bread and finished her first cup of coffee, before asking;

"What is happening? Where am I going? Will you come with me?" Again, the sad look in her eyes, yet a smile on her lips.

"Was this how a woman looked at you when she really loved you," he thought to himself before she replied slowly and very quietly as if choosing every word carefully:

"The good news is that you are going home, back to New York via Dublin and Shannon so you will not have to go near England. I suppose another bit of good news is that I am due to take my annual holidays in two weeks' time and can join you there if you wish."

"That's wonderful. Fantastic. A dream come true," jumping up to kiss her, but this time her eyes did not close as their lips met, so he stopped to let her continue:

"The not so good news is that you will have to make a slight detour for us to deliver a small package." He was quick to interrupt:

"I don't like bombs. Guns are my style. I've had enough of bombs and what they did in Vietnam to last two lifetimes."

"It will not be a bomb, Martin, just a package that none of us can get through within the next twenty-four hours, when it is needed, due to the heavy security everywhere since the Tunnel chamber explosion. The British are grabbing everyone Irish and they are trying to get the European Union police forces to do the same so we have to lie low for a few weeks. Anyway, it will help you get revenge on all those who were responsible for the death of Tara and I would want that just like you. She was my sister you know. I promise you, on our love, no innocent people, no civilians will be killed, even hurt, as a result of your mission."

He answered her quietly with one question:

"Where do I have to go?" and when she replied:

"Belfast" he knew it was a dangerous job, no matter what she said; but she was still talking:

"You will fly Aer Lingus direct to Dublin, take the express train to Belfast Central, be met there, deliver the small package, then back to Dublin on the train. Depending on timing, a direct flight to New York, maybe with a short Shannon stopover. Your new papers, everything you need and, of course, the package. Another pack of cigarettes, actually, are on their way here now. After Belfast and Dublin, I'll meet you soon in New York. I love you Martin and you love me, we are so lucky." They kissed again.

Spain

Monday, 30th May 1994

The man in Spain had not been happy. He did not like being ordered to leave immediately the security of the little world he had created for himself over the years when the final instructions came in early April. He had left soon afterwards: although a month ago, he remembered it as if it was yesterday. In fact, it would be a pleasant drive along the coast with short detours on the way there or back, to take in Estepona, Marbella, Funengirola, Benalmadena, Torremolinos, Malaga, Torre Del Mar, Nerja, and other playgrounds of the rich. Probably half of them crooks, he guessed, as he made his plans. Although always in dispute between Spain and Britain, Gibraltar was still British territory and he remembered what had happened when the SAS had ambushed the three unarmed IRA volunteers on holiday there, shooting them several times and then coming within less than three feet to finish each of them off, including the girl, as they lay bleeding on the street. He made a mental note to avoid the spot where it happened.

But he would not be able to avoid British security as the whole point of the mission was to pass openly through all the police and army checkpoints before joining the RAF crew based there. He hoped the papers they had given him were in order and that his contact would be there as arranged. He had agreed to go on condition that, if and when he was able to invent what they wanted, he would only return as far as the Spanish border town of Rosas in the other direction. They could come over from France to pick it up. If he could do it.

He had set out early as he wanted to get the long drive over before the dead heat of the Spanish sun, which even after all these years still sapped his energy, sometimes a problem with his girlfriend who liked to make love in the afternoon. He parked his Spanish-registered Peugeot before crossing to the entrance security check, knowing that he, like all the other tourists, would be under observation by the hidden cameras and the plain-clothes British detectives who also found it difficult to maintain interest in this burning climate. There were no problems with the two security checks as his Spanish passport and driving licence were genuine. After all, he had lived there for years and

320

day-trip visitors who looked like they would spend a lot of money were welcome in this outpost. Now would come the difficult part, he thought, as he approached the army garrison barracks to ask for another American, Samual Brown, who was a former colleague at NASA.

All went as planned and soon they were deep in conversation, over a giant seafood platter, bread and red wine, while they exchanged news and gossip spanning the twenty years since they had last met. There had been cards and sometimes phone calls at Christmas but being together again after all these years was something special.

The afternoon was passing too quickly, especially after the second bottle of wine, and looking at his watch, Brown remarked:

"It was a wonderful coincidence you phoning me to test out the latest digital mobile phones which are supposed to be completely secure and I was able to tell you I was coming here so we could get together. By the way, I suppose you know you can now program your computer to instantly intercept digital calls just like the old reliable analogue? A handy little gadget based on, say, the Sanyo laptop can lock on to a digital signal sent by any phone between the nearest antenna mast and the operations communication centre. Your movements can also be tracked even if you are not using your mobile as long as you have it switched on to receive a call. But there I go again, rabbiting on about our old hobby when I suppose you are too busy with the senoritas, the wine and that book you are always writing. How is it going?"

The man in Spain knew he had to be careful as it was obvious Samual Brown knew nothing of his secret work or the real reason for today's meeting.

"Yes, it's hard to concentrate, especially with the heat. Like you, I get a regular royalty cheque on those little security gadgets we invented in our young days. It would not be enough to live on in the States but here it is possible as everything is so cheap. Then I write travel-type articles, "An American In Spain" kind of stuff, do a few brochures for travel companies and sometimes, for a bit of fun and a good deal of money, show rich Americans around mini-Hollywood as they call it, where Clint Eastwood made those spaghetti westerns we both loved."

"Yes, I remember *A Fistful of Dollars* or was it *For a Few Dollars More*. Then there was *The Good, The Bad, and The Ugly*."

The man knew that, once started on films, Brown could go on forever and time was flying, so he said:

"I suppose I should see a bit of the place while I'm here as it's a long drive back to where I live," hoping for the right reply:

"Why don't you stay the night? Like the old days, all expenses paid by the company."

"That would be great but I don't want to cause you any problems. After all, you have work to do here, you told me earlier."

"Why don't you come with me?" was the question he had come all this way to hear but he did not want to appear too eager:

"Are you sure it will be all right? What about security?"

"No problem," was Brown's reply, "as a matter of fact, there was a colleague supposed to meet me at Kennedy when I flew in from Seattle but he never showed up, so I have his security pass which will be OK for you. We were always good at fixing passes," he laughed, and his companion joined in.

The man from Spain had a fair idea why the colleague never made the airport. Probably still in Eamon Doran's pub or another of the many Irish bars in New York, enjoying what they called "the craic", and would be kept happy there until Samual Brown returned, so nobody would know.

By this time, Samual had ordered a third bottle of wine, taken out his mobile and his American Express Corporate card to book another single room on the company account and decided they would make a night of it, leaving work until tomorrow.

"Already you have learned an old Spanish custom" he laughed, determined to try to keep a clear head for the important task ahead.

Morning came quickly, followed by four Alka-Seltzers, three cups of black coffee and he was ready but where was his friend, Brown? He had left him at his room the night before, or rather early that morning, but a quick check by the maid showed his bed had not been slept in. For a few minutes, the man from Spain considered getting out of Gibraltar quickly, away in his car to Almeria and safety.

There was a loud noise in the street and he looked from the window to see Samual Brown, a married man with six children in the Big Apple, saying a very romantic "goodbye" to a somewhat tired-looking but attractive big-busted Spanish girl, while dripping a handful of pesetas down her now buttonless blouse. Then he saw his friend upstairs at the window and shouted:

"Just like old times, eh? I wanted to prove I could still do it! Remember the nights on the town in Manhattan we had together? Make sure they have a good breakfast ready while I shower, shave, change, and we will be on our way to work."

Within half an hour, they were being checked through RAF security and there it was the famous Boeing Chinook twin-rotor helicopter which had served the US and other countries in so many wars over the past thirty years, during which more than one thousand of them had been built by Boeing. Samual Brown, now a senior inspector, was there for a final surprise check on this giant which could fly more than fifty fully armed fighting men almost over the roof tops at speeds of one hundred and fifty miles an hour.

While the man from Spain could hardly believe his luck, Brown was still going on about:

"This 'old motherfucker' is the best of them all. I'll show you the new equipment as it will soon be almost automatic pilot, while the crew have an easy time just watching the instruments and deciding which girl to fuck."

While Brown was trying to make it even safer, the man from Spain wanted ideas on how to make it crash, without anyone ever knowing why.

* * *

They had given him six weeks' notice. A lot of the time had been spent, maybe wasted, on the mobile phone technique. It was feasible but there would have to be an exchange of phones with his pre-programmed numbers and there had been a problem at their end. They never told him much nor did he want to know but he gathered that one of their inside men had been captured. However, they had not ruled it out and told him to see if he could come up with some refinements which would make it more practical. Then the new urgent instructions.

He still remembered those two days in Gibraltar with Samual Brown and his amazing luck when Brown had not very surprisingly fallen asleep in the cockpit, allowing the man from Spain all the time he needed to check everything on board for a potential weak spot. This would be useful to him when he got home to design a very special undetectable secret weapon, for that is what they had ordered and wanted urgently.

The message in April had been brief and to the point as usual but the fact that the special double encryption code had been used probably meant it came from the person they called the "managing director", which was unusual. After decoding, it read:

Top priority. Now very urgent. The product must be small enough to fit several of them in a cigarette packet. It must be able to operate long range, your base to anywhere. Must be undetectable to all known security devices, including the new Millivision handheld device working on the heat, or lack of it, principle now under final development by US forces. We expect delivery end of May latest. Your biggest challenge. Your biggest fee.

That last bit had cheered him up and he began making contact with several of his former colleagues in NASA, the computer industry and firms like Motorola. He still favoured the electo-magnetic device he had developed with the young man but had no idea of what had being happening in this area until he made his overseas connections.

Electromagnetic interference (EMI) had already caused more than fifty proven cases of near air accidents. When passengers turn on their mobile phones or personal stereos, microprocessors emit radio waves on 1-10MHz within a 30ft range which are picked up by the vast amount of cables behind the luggage racks and transmitted to the autopilot, which can cause it to give the wrong information. In addition to mobile phones, a walkman, laptop or camcorder in use by a passenger could also cause complete distortion to the computers in the pilot's cabin.

This was worthy of further research and days of almost non-stop work revealed that: Unexplained computer failures were unofficially blamed for an air crash in Thailand; a Boeing 747 which, when the pilot had selected the flight plan, the autopilot would not follow it, sending the plane off track (a hand camcorder was the cause); a jumbo jet losing all communication with ground control (a phone, walkman and laptop being used by passengers at the same time); even false signals being sent to an autopilot which caused it to alter course (several passengers using personal electronic devices simultaneously) and there were many more.

A very significant fact of this research, from his point of view, was that all aircraft seemed most vulnerable while taking off or just before landing. Among all the data he had on file in his own personal computer was another interesting fact the flight computers of a Boeing jumbo jet had told pilots it was descending while in fact the plane had increased speed significantly and a crash was narrowly averted, all due to a passenger's digital tape recorder. This meant it was technically possible to influence the on-board computers used by the pilots themselves, not just the autopilot; but the problem was not that simple. He wondered if a strong electromagnetic radio signal could be transmitted to an aircraft for a certain brief period and then discontinued almost at the moment of impact. If it could be done it might allow all the instruments to revert to their true readings,. leaving no evidence. There had even been unconfirmed rumours about problems with the multi-million-pound Concorde.

Questions crowded into his brain. Did you have to be on board to do it?

What was the range of any device he could make? How could he perfect a device that would make the pilots' computers, all the instruments, show that the aircraft was at least '500 to 1000 ft'higher than its actual altitude? How could he make something that could be controlled by himself in Spain for a distance of more than a thousand miles? Above all, how could he make a device which was undetectable by the strictest security and so small that several of them could be hidden in a cigarette package?

He had a headache which even his girlfriend could not cure, but he knew he could not let them down. To clear the decks for work in his secret computer room, he sent the girl with her sister for a week's holiday in Rosas, that nice little border town where he would deliver the goods if he could make them. He finished all his other projects, made up his mind to set his alarm clock for 6 a.m. each day, eat in, not drink, work and sleep. His last thoughts, before going to sleep early on the first night without his senorita, drifted to the times when he had made regular contact with the astronauts speeding through space from his desk at NASA and once when he even had a long conversation using a VHF radio. So, sending very powerful electromagnetic signals from Spain was just another challenge he told himself as he closed his eyes and remembered no more.

* * *

It took twenty-seven full days, sixteen hours a day, with many trials and errors until he was satisfied. He sat back, alone, looking out at the deep blue sea, examining the packet of cigarettes. As always, he had added a little touch of his own which is why they paid him so well. There were twenty real cigarettes in the pack, which was slightly longer than normal, while the cigarettes were slightly shorter, but neither enough for anyone to notice. He had chosen Marlboro, heavily advertised, popular in America, identified with sport sponsorship, but not the favourite in the part of Europe which was the package's final destination.

He was tired, weary even for the first time since he had come to Spain, and promised himself a good holiday in nearby France as soon as the money arrived in his account. But first he had to send the message to Paris that the gift package was ready. Then the relatively short journey to Rosas to hand it over to the courier, probably another girl on summer holidays from university, before meeting his own lover and her sister. Perhaps they would try "a three-some" they were always going on about in the thrillers he read for relaxation on the sand.

With this happy thought in his mind, although wondering would he be able for one of them, not to mind both, he remembered his short time in the Philippines with Samual Brown many years ago. He owed him a dinner, next time they met, if ever. Yes, the Philippines. The girls there knew how to treat a man. Just lie back, spread your legs naked on the bed and they would rub you all over with sweet-smelling oils. His favourite was Jasmine, the name of the girl and the perfume, always stopping and relaxing you again, just when you were sure you had to come. They could keep you that way, not sure whether you were asleep or awake, as the petite beautifully formed figures would kneel over you, their small pear-shaped firm breasts touching your lips while their hands, light like a butterfly, went between your legs again and again. As Brown had said afterwards:

"They could wake the dead."

He was beginning to feel the need for his senorita now and decided to concentrate on his driving. But he hoped the device worked. He was as sure as anyone could be that he had met all the specifications and that, given that they did as instructed in his last encrypted message, all the instruments in the aircraft would confirm to the pilots that the aircraft was flying at an altitude at least 500 to 1000 ft higher than it actually was. It was also essential that, even if the pilots tried to avert a crash at the last minute, the controls would not respond no matter what they did. That was vital, they had said. That's what they had asked for. He had to be back home on stand-by from June 1st to press the keys to activate all the devices at the exact time they would tell him. That was the last vital part of the project and he had to be alert for the signal. He had met the deadline and the goods were delivered. Then the money. The holiday. The girl. Everything he wanted. No more work for a long time. Until they called again!

He was happy when he got home. He had done it all well before the end of May deadline and, already, after the final action in early June, he was looking forward to the big, very big, cheque and the rest, especialy the girl

JUNE 1994

Dublin

Wednesday, 1st June

Martin Carter had wished he could have stayed in Paris longer but the small parcel had arrived quickly by courier from Spain. There had been a long painful farewell with Nicole. "Why am I always leaving the people I love?" he wondered, cheered slightly with the firm promise to get together in New York soon. But he could not help thinking of the same promise he and Tara had made so he was feeling depressed until he looked out the window and saw the lights of Dublin, a city he had never visited although most of his friends would dig up an Irish grandmother after a few drinks in any bar in New York. With a couple of hours to kill before the evening express to Belfast, he took the airport bus into the capital.

O'Connell Street was very busy, full of shoppers and litter which annoyed him. A beautiful street, one of the widest in Europe, ruined by fast food joints, amusements, and people trying to sell you things. Then he turned the corner, after crossing the river Liffey, and was impressed by the illuminated Bank of Ireland and the famous Trinity College opposite it. But it was Grafton Street which took his fancy. Here, the people were well dressed, as good if not better than in London or Paris, seemed very happy, plenty of street musicians, little streets with sidewalk cafés, big expensive department stores like Brown Thomas, and the smell of coffee from Bewley's Oriental Café which he could not resist. Inside the building, which looked as if it had not changed in two hundred years, the friendly waitresses still wore frilly white aprons over black skirts and stockings. You could serve yourself as well so he helped himself to what they called the big Irish breakfast although it was late afternoon. Then a visit to a few of the pubs made famous by such Irish writers as Joyce, Wilde, Synge, O'Casey, Dean Swift, Bram Stoker, Brendan Behan at least that's what the friendly customers told him as he went to Neary's, McDaid's, the Bailey, Davy Byrnes, then a new very fashionable place called Café En Seine which the Irish promptly christened Café Insane. He was sorry to have to leave Dublin, the people were so friendly and he could hear the Irish music and ballad singers start the evening which he was sure, if New York was anything to go by, would last until the next morning. But his final duty called and soon he was at Connolly Station waiting for the train to Belfast. A friendly porter told him the station was named after one of the leaders of the 1916 rebellion against the British in Dublin. James Connolly had been wounded in action when the rebels surrendered and the British had brought him to Dublin Castle for overnight medical attention before taking him out the next morning in a chair to face the firing squad. He was sorry when the Belfast Enterprise Express arrived and he had to leave the bar.

* * *

The man with the peaked cap and the "Taxi" sign was waiting for him when the train pulled into the centre of Belfast, just as the message from Nicole in Paris had arranged. For about the tenth time that day, Carter felt the precious cigarette packet in his inside pocket to make certain it was safe. He would be happy to get rid of it. After the man had identified himself as "Sean" and made certain he was Martin Carter, they were soon off into the traffic. It was then that he noticed the soldiers on the streets, the police with machine guns, the armoured cars, all the things he had not seen in Dublin.

"Is it always like this here, Sean?" he asked the driver, getting the usual short sharp Belfast reply:

"Sometimes it's worse."

After another silence, during which Carter imagined he saw the station again although they had been travelling for almost ten minutes, he asked:

"Have we far to go?"

"It depends?"

"On what?" persisted Carter.

"On how long it takes us to shake off that blue car behind."

Then Carter saw Sean was on the taxi radiophone and a few minutes later the driver accelerated dangerously at a roundabout, while three other identical black taxis immediately followed them.

"Very clever," remarked Carter.

"Plenty of practice here," replied Sean, making certain the street behind was now clear before turning yet once again, until they reached a road of fashionable expensive houses, manicured lawns and trees. Suddenly stopping, Carter almost hit his head off the roof.

"You get out here quickly, please," he was told and he could see the light from the doorway up the short path. Then the taxi was gone. Although the door was open, he could not see anyone until he stepped into the hallway and it closed abruptly behind him, which made him jump.

"Welcome to Belfast, Mr Carter," said a pleasant-faced, smiling woman, probably in her fifties, her hair turning grey, neatly dressed in a cream jumper and a black skirt, adding:

"You have come to see himself. You must be hungry after your long journey. There's plenty of food on the table in the study for you, and himself will always have something stronger hidden away."

She gently steered him down the long hallway which was almost in darkness, into a pleasant room with deep leather armchairs, paintings on the walls, a big blazing coal fire in the grate and, as she had said, a table laden with food, cold ham, turkey, salads, bread, even wine.

"Help yourself to anything you want. He's on the phone but will be with you in a few minutes," she said before departing. Carter looked at the paintings and pictures. Wolfe Tone 1798; Padraig Pearse 1916; and many others he had never heard about even from his Irish American friends. He helped himself to a good plate of food, a full glass of Budweiser, and placed it all on a small tray while settling himself down beside the fire. He was finishing his food and just about to get another glass of Bud, when a voice behind him said:

"Sorry to keep you waiting so long, Mr Carter, but these are exciting times we live in, at least here."

The man was tall, late forties or early fifties, clean shaven, fair haired, fresh faced, someone who liked the open air and spoke with a soft Irish accent. He was dressed in casual clothes, slacks, open-necked plain green shirt, and was again apologising for the delay while refilling Martin's glass. He did not offer his name as he gave a firm handshake and Carter thought it was better not to ask. The man was speaking again:

"Thanks for coming such a long journey. I hear you have had plenty of adventures since you met up with some of my colleagues. I'm sure you will be glad to get home in a couple of days."

"A couple of days?" repeated Carter. "I had expected tomorrow."

"No problem. We can talk about that later. Meanwhile may I trouble you for the wee package as a courier will soon be here and I have to divide up the contents. Sometimes I think we make things too complicated. In any event, your packet of twenty cigarettes will soon become two packets of ten, one of which will leave here soon. I'll be back in a few minutes. Meanwhile, help yourself to some more beer and we will have a chat with a real drink when I come back."

Martin did as he was told and was soon dozing at the roaring fire. He did not know how long the man had been away as he was enjoying the comforts of his home and needed the rest. He had been slightly troubled when "a couple of days" was mentioned but the food, beer, heat and exhaustion had numbed his fears as he sat alone in this stranger's room in a city which seemed full of police and soldiers, like some of those in South America he never wanted to see again. Telling himself he had completed his last mission by delivering the package safely, he relaxed so much that he did not hear the door opening behind him and almost jumped from his chair when the voice said:

"Now would you like Bushmills whiskey?: This is the only real whiskey in the world," the man added with a smile. "You can't beat a Black Bush!"

* * *

The man later told Carter that his name was "Michael" adding:

"Probably after Michael Collins rather than the one in heaven, knowing my father."

Seeing Martin they were on first name terms now looking around the large well-furnished room, he seemed to read his mind:

"You are probably wondering how and why I live here?" and when there was no reply, continued:

"I have great neighbours although we almost never see one another, which is just as well. This section of the road is one of the safest in the city with doctors, accountants, dentists and, of course, the judge further up who is under twenty-four-hour armed guard to make sure no IRA riffraff get near him," he concluded with another smile.

While Martin Carter took another long sip of the drink the man had told him the Irish called "the water of life", he was still talking:

"As you are going back to the States soon, there is no harm in telling you that I am in the legal profession myself. This is a perfect cover for meeting all kinds of people like suspected terrorists. Although it is often a waste of time defending them here after the RUC Special Branch have had them for a while and they are in front of a one-judge, no-jury, Diplock Court. Sometimes I have to take cases for the other side, otherwise they would get suspicious."

"It must be difficult leading this double life," remarked Martin, remembering the times he had gone undercover in the US Special Forces, hating every minute of it.

"You get used to it. There are only the two of us here at home now and ...," the man called Michael took a long drink of whiskey, to cover what Martin thought was a break in his voice, maybe a tear in his eye, or was it just the light, before continuing:

"Anyway, enough of that and of me. The first thing I would like you to do, Mr Carter, I mean Martin, is to make a phone call," and seeing the surprised expression, continued quickly:

"Back home to your bank which, due to the five-hour time difference, will soon be closing. I want you to be satisfied that the money we agreed is actually in your account."

"Please follow me."

Martin found himself in a dark corridor heading for what they used to call "the smallest room in the house" when they were kids.

"Yes," said Michael as if reading his thoughts again, "this is where we keep our most secure telephone. A cleaning lady comes here for a couple of hours each day which is nothing unusual in this area where they all employ nannies, housekeepers and what have you. But ours does a different kind of sweeping, a top electronics graduate from the university who has specialised in counter-espionage, anti-bugging, or whatever they call it, of all things," again that hint of a laugh.

"Wait until I show you this little gadget she has hidden, almost impossible to find even in this tiny room."

He pressed the embossed wall studding in a certain order, opening a secret panel to reveal a telephone and went on:

"See this little device which plugs into the telephone already connected in the ordinary way but going through another part of the same invention. Through something she calls a scanning circulatory exercise this puts any bugging device out of action and even tells you when it is safe to make, and, of course, receive calls. I'm not a technical person as you can see but I know that it works. Otherwise, I would not be here now."

Martin was impressed at the efficiency of the organisation and Michael having left him alone with the phone, proceeded to call the Chase Manhattan Bank, quoting his account number and other details requested. He was relieved to hear the reply:

"Yes, Mr Carter, the amount arrived a few days ago from Geneva and has been distributed equally to the four accounts as you instructed. In the unlikely event of anything happening to you in the future, your share will be divided equally between your two daughters, while your wife will retain her present entitlement. Hope to see you soon and that you are having a relaxing holiday in Europe. You must tell me all about it. In fact, I'll take you out to lunch as there are some good investment opportunities I would like to discuss with you now that your family accounts are very substantial. Will you ring me when you get back?" concluded the chief clerk, obviously keen to earn some extra commission. "What family?" he said to himself before replying; "Sure will, as it's not often the bank takes me to lunch. And I'll tell you all about my relaxing uneventful holiday in Europe as well," Martin added with a smile, before saying "Goodbye!" While he was there he decided to use the toilet and sat for some time reading the *Belfast Newsletter* before returning to the big room, where Michael was pouring two more glasses of whiskey.

"Everything all right Martin, the money there safely?" and when Martin said he was very grateful, Michael got a little more serious as they sat down in the comfortable armchairs beside the fire.

"How would you like another one hundred thousand pounds in your own hand before you go home?", the suddenness of the question startled Martin out of memories of his two lovely girls, but Michael was continuing before he could reply:

"Please hear me out before you say anything. We have this operation planned for months and it is as follows. We know the British intelligence services, military chiefs, RUC Special Branch, do not want our cease-fire and peace negotiations to be successful. They are at a very delicate stage now with our people not only in meetings with senior officials of the British Government but also the Government in Dublin and your own US Administration as well. But the Intelligence Services, MI5, MI6, Military, together with the Special Branches of both Scotland Yard and the RUC here in Belfast, do not want peace. Ever since the end of the Cold War and the fall of the Berlin Wall, the Russians have become friends not enemies. Add to that, the British have to hand Hong Kong back to the Chinese in 1998 and you can see that the once great empire, which even at the end of the last war controlled the lives of 250 million people, will then only have about 250,000 on a few mickey-mouse islands nobody cares about. The lot I mentioned, MI5, who are now in charge, and the rest, will all be out of jobs, so they want to hold on to our six counties in the north of Ireland at all costs."

He stopped to pour another drink remarking:

"All this talk makes one thirsty. Sorry for getting on my favourite subject, but you will appreciate that I do not meet many people I can talk freely to especially about these topics."

"No," protested Martin, "I find it all very interesting but where do I come

334

in? You mentioned another operation?"

"Yes, Martin, we know your record. Awards for bravery. The lot. But of equal if not more importance to us at this moment are those covert flights low over the jungle and the cities to avoid radar and at such a high speed that nobody on the ground would have time to take a shot at you. Yes, Martin, you did great work in those troop-carrying Chinooks."

Although Martin had thought he could no longer be surprised about how much they knew, this was still a shock as the Chinook flights were top secret on direct orders from the Pentagon itself. They obviously had people everywhere. Of course, there were over forty million Irish Americans over there so some of them must be on their side. Still it was a big surprise to hear it mentioned in this room so far from home.

Michael observed him carefully before continuing:

"Two RAF Special Forces officers filed the flight plan yesterday for the Chinook they will pilot tomorrow with more than twenty of Britain's top intelligence chiefs, the real top senior men from London as well as here, to a secret conference in a fortified compound that we have no chance of getting near. All along we understood it was to draw up a list for sudden widespread internment without trial again. But then Tara, God rest her, got a message to us the day before she was killed, that it is more serious than that. They are drawing up what you would call a hit-list for assassination of all our leaders, including the Chief of Staff, the Army Council and, of course, myself."

Both men were silent for awhile after that. Carter with memories brought back at the mention of Tara's name and what they had shared together. But the other man was so long-winded that he had to ask the same question again:

"Where do I come into all this, Michael?"

"We have these two pilots under close observation and later tonight we will kidnap them so that you, with your Chinook experience and another young man who has only flown conventional jets, will take their place."

"To do what?"

"To hijack the aircraft with all their VIPs on board and fly them to the real north of our country, Donegal, or Tory island to be more exact, where some of our men disguised as fishermen in well-armed boats are already waiting."

There was a sudden silence. Something that had been troubling him since he first became involved with the Provisional IRA in New York clicked into place in the back of his mind. So that is why they were paying him so much money! This had been the real objective all along! Not many people could fly the big Chinook as well as himself. He had proven that in Vietnam and

Columbia. They all knew that, even if it meant battle conditions, he was the best man for the job and had the decorations to prove it!

Martin was speechless. Could only look at him in amazement before asking:

"What will you do with them? What will happen to me on this island, wherever it is?"

"Martin, we have not let you down yet. You have served us well. There will be a small plane there to get you direct to Shannon in time for the New York flight so you will be well gone before the excitement starts. As to what we will do with them? Interrogate them, of course, make them tell us their plans. We will have all their secret documents. Remember the island is off Donegal which is the most northerly county in our country and it is in the Republic, so we will create an international incident. We will have people overseas ready to contact the world media who will invade the place. Imagine what will happen when Major, Reynolds, Clinton, get the news. More than twenty, the high command, of British intelligence captured and being held hostage by the IRA. We will try to bargain to get all our prisoners released in the three countries. But, at the very least, we will have information on the entire British intelligence network, including identity of spies, informers, and God knows what else. We will at least be able to get safe passage for all our people on condition we release the hostages unharmed and, after all that world-wide publicity, there is no way they can kill us."

"It's certainly a daring plan. It reminds me of Bruce Willis in *Die Hard* but I suppose it could work. I've probably done worse in my time. How much extra did you say? Was it one hundred thousand dollars?"

Michael simply nodded and raised his glass to clink with Martin's when a small buzzer rang quietly near the fireplace.

"That's just the phone call I was expecting with full details, time, etc. for tomorrow's operation. Help yourself. Will be back soon." And he went out of the room, leaving Martin with plenty to think about.

It was a long time before he returned, his face seemed to have lost its ruddy glow, and he said nothing as he poured himself an even larger glass of whiskey which, so far, did not seem to have had any effect on him. He sat in silence and Martin also sipped his drink, feeling it was better to let Michael speak first, which he did about five, maybe ten, minutes later:

"All this dangerous work and all for nothing," he muttered almost to himself.

"What's happened?" asked Martin, stealing a quick glance at the door and straining his ears for the sound of any sirens, before thinking:

"If they were coming for us, there would not be any sound." The room was still, almost peaceful, which Martin found ironic with all this talk of war, almost unaware that his question had not been answered. Even the room seemed to have changed. There was a sombre atmosphere of gloom there now where a few minutes ago there had been excitement amid the comfort.

"Sorry, Martin, about all this but I have just got a bit of a shock although you would think I would be used to them in this business," finally came the quiet reply: "They must have got on to us. It might have been a coincidence but you live longer here by not believing in them." He stopped again so Martin prompted:

"Michael, what has happened? Please tell me."

"The two RAF officers who plotted and filed the Chinook course have suddenly been told that they will not be flying it tomorrow. They are to be replaced by two others, also two of the very best they have, but we don't know who they are and have no time to do anything about it now. It is very unusual. There could not have been a leak from our side. Maybe they are just being extra careful."

Again, the gloomy silence with only the stirring of the fire, the sound of their breathing and the purring of the old black cat which now sat at Michael's feet, to be heard in the room.

Then Martin remembered why he was there and asked:

"What about the package I brought? What was in it? What was that all about?"

"Oh, yes, Martin. I almost forgot about that with the great disappointment of that phone call. I suppose I was looking forward too much to the excitement of being on the world stage. You're right, of course, all is not lost yet."

By now, Martin had learned it was better to let Michael continue at his own pace and soon he was explaining the package further:

"Our new and youngest ever Chief of Staff had another idea. That was always 'Plan B' which we now definitely need and, here again, Martin, we want your help, for the same fee. Do you still have those Boeing documents and pass our friend Samual sent from Gibraltar to Nicole in Paris?"

"Yes, Nicole said I should keep them safely so I did," producing them from his wallet and stretching them towards Michael who did not hold out his hand.

"No, please keep them, Martin. Tomorrow morning, I'll confirm the time later. There will have to be another few phone calls, including an urgent one to Tory island!" and he left the room abruptly.

Martin considered leaving now but thought better of it as he felt he would probably be shot dead by one side or the other before he reached the city centre, wherever that was, so he stayed in his chair for a half-hour until Michael returned again in better humour this time.

"It's all settled. Your pass will get you into the RAF base at the airport. If they get suspicious, you can give them Samual Brown's number at Boeing to confirm that you are carrying out a final check but naturally pointing out that he will not like to be disturbed at home due to the time difference. Your reason for a final check will be the same as that of the RAF who had one of their top men, John Coles, even take a trip in it today. The Mark II Chinook is the first of this type to be used here and has all the very latest technical equipment. It only arrived on the 31st and, as there is no love lost between any of the British services here, especially between MI5 and the rest, there will be plenty of confusion when all these spooks are coming tomorrow. The RAF there will be glad to see the back of them."

"But I can't simply walk in, overpower the security, and hi-jack the chopper on my own," burst out Martin. "I'm not Superman."

"Nothing as drastic is needed now, Martin, you just have to take, say, half an hour to check it out, while planting these tiny listening devices in the pack you brought at strategic places on board. We need all of them, completely hidden of course, in the cockpit if possible as it will confirm the location, which is important. We want to hear all they are saying about us and their plans. They seem to have this top-level secret conference in the same place annually so to cheer ourselves up, Martin, in a war that has been going on in one form or another for eight hundred years, we could sing, if we knew the words, our northern winner of the Eurovision contest, "What's Another Year?""

The whiskey and the shock of the big operation blown is getting to him now, thought Martin, but I had better play along. He had not much choice, he felt for the first time. "OK. I'll do it, provided your people get me to Dublin or Shannon in time for the New York plane," replied Martin quickly.

"A done deal," said Michael, shaking hands, "now we'll go over the new plan, as our lives depend on it."

Hotel Europa, Belfast

While Martin was enjoying his Black Bush Irish whiskey with the man on the Malone Road, Marian was sitting down to her second dinner with a very reluctant Commander Trevor Wallace of MI6, once again in the dining room of the Hotel Europa where they were both staying. A big change from her own little apartment off the Antrim Road, she thought to herself before asking:

"Afraid people will talk about us?" she teased him, thinking of the graphic homosexual pictures she had of him in her bag. He must be on a good expense account as she knew the Pommard they were drinking with the duck in orange sauce was not cheap.

The more she could get him to drink the better and when he went to the gents, she beckoned the waiter to bring another bottle when this one was finished.

Trevor had obviously decided to make the best of his situation, although very worried about what they wanted him to do in return for the photographs, which still almost made him sick even remembering them. Marian was very chatty, cheerful, which led him to suspect there were other IRA people in the large restaurant, maybe a waiter like last year's Italian. Then his whole life was built on suspecting people, on deceit, and sometimes he wished for early retirement or, better still, for promotion where he could sit behind a desk, have long luncheons, tell others what to do. He liked giving orders, now he would have to take them like a man.

Even he almost smiled when she suggested, as they finished their third Martell:

"Your place or mine, Trevor?"

For what seemed an age he did not answer as he had seen the jealous glances of other men when he dined in the room with her. It was not as if he had never had a woman that way but, somehow, since university, it didn't give him the same enjoyment, any thrill at all. But he pictured himself on top of her back, hurting her, hearing her screaming for him to stop, degrading her, making her... Then he stopped that line of thought. It reminded him too much of London and the young boys in the pub there. They would probably come in and shoot him or worse so he replied:

"It really does not make any difference to me. It's your show."

So she had picked his room. He thought he knew the reason and they were now facing one another in two small armchairs, an attractive glass-topped table with two miniature Hennessy brandies between them, and she was speaking.

"We are letting you off easily, Trevor, you have been such a sport and taken it all so well. First, here are half the pictures and half the film as evidence of our good faith. You will get the rest after you do one small job for us tomorrow."

He said nothing, just sipped the brandy, realising he had taken too much alcohol, but at least this time he had a good reason.

"Don't look so worried, Trevor, it will be all over soon and you'll get the rest of the original film on your desk by the time you get back to London. Some of our people do not trust you as much as I do, so they are keeping it there in case anything happens to me."

"Put me out of my agony. Don't drag it out. What is it your lot wants?"

"Just what your lot have been doing to us for years. We just want you to plant a few tiny listening devices so that we will be able to hear them talking about us. Simple, as I told you."

He was silent. He supposed it could be worse. They might have wanted him to kill someone or fake an accident, a speciality of MI6. Planting a few bugs which would probably be discovered by the next security sweep. He would make sure of that, after he got his pictures back of course. Or he might use it to set a trap for some of those IRA leaders and pull a fast one on those jumped-up rotters in MI5 who had told him this morning that he would not be needed on tomorrow's trip to Scotland. Hold the fort in Belfast, they had told him and no doubt thought that was funny, considering where they were going for a weekend of golf, food, vintage wine, with this latest wild scheme of "Five's" under discussion, another final solution, she had called it. Maybe there was a nice young chap in Belfast he could ...

She was speaking again:

"Trevor, this looks like a normal small packet of cigarettes and they are cigarettes, but hidden underneath each one is a tiny magnetic listening device, a bug if you prefer, which we want you to plant tomorrow. That's all."

"Plant where?" and the answer made his hands shake and his face turned white:

"On board the Mk2 Chinook that is due to leave Aldergrove for a secret destination around 5.30 p.m. in the evening."

He sat in silence while she watched him closely, fingering the "panic button'"as she called it, in her pocket. Everything depended on his reaction now.

"But I won't even be on it. I'm not going," he said weakly, to which she replied sternly:

"As the senior MI6 officer here, you are entitled to carry out a security check on an aircraft which only arrived in Belfast for the first time yesterday and which is to carry such important passengers."

He said nothing more, simple holding out his hand for the cigarette pack, looking at her, his eyes close to tears.

"I'm sorry, Trevor, I really am. But it's war, you know that. I'll phone you early in the morning with the time you should do the inspection. Just plant these tiny bugs where they won't be seen, put several of them near each of the pilots as they might say something interesting and, of course, the others near where your friends in MI5 usually sit, the best seats naturally."

During the night he had told her everything they wanted to know and would do what he had been told. He had little choice. She was beginning to feel a little sorry for him and wondered if she was going soft in her old age of twenty-five.

This last brought a faint smile to his lips for the first time that evening and she held out her hand, gently guiding him to the bed. She took off his shoes, his jacket and his tie, without a sound, covering him up with the warm duvet before she slipped silently from the room. Tomorrow would be a busy day.

Belfast

Thursday, 2nd June

It was not surprising that Martin Carter slept late at the house on Malone Road the next morning and it was almost 11 a.m. when he, finally, with the help of several black coffees, got his mind working after all the Irish whiskey of the previous night. He had intended to do the job early, get it over with, and head for home. On his way out, he noticed a large envelope with his name on it in the now empty house and read:

After you have carried out the wee job, enjoy yourself in Belfast. Slan Abhaile (safe home!). You did great work for us and "Our Day Will Come". Slainte.

In the envelope were crisp new £500 notes, two hundred of them, which he put in his pocket as he phoned the number, also on the envelope, for a taxi which must have been waiting around the corner, it arrived so soon.

He had no trouble, after showing the Boeing pass and promising he would be less than half an hour, getting into the RAF base at the airport at 12 noon. He sensed some confusion and a certain amount of nervousness about the imminent visit of unknown VIPs, with one crew member telling him it was probably British prime minister John Major. After the expected security at the two entrance gates, he was surprised there did not seem to be any arrangements for a check-in of some light luggage, including golf clubs, already arriving, nor of the orange survival suits they told him the people travelling in the giant Chinook would be wearing. He was only happy that this seemed to be at least one thing the IRA did not know, otherwise they would have him in there with Semtex instead of just listening devices, he told himself.

Although he found the tiny bugs at the bottom of the cigarette pack difficult to handle with his big fingers, there was no problem fixing four near the area where both pilots would sit. They stuck like glue. The NCO escort had slipped into the toilet for a quick smoke "The only one I will get today, so I hope you don't mind, sir?" had brought quick permission from Martin. He placed the other devices under the two rows of seats down each side of the aircraft. He was driven back to the gates well within the half-hour, to the relief of the only

342

officer he met, who was obviously happy to see the last of him. One less of the blighters to worry about on a busy day when they should be getting on with real work, instead of waiting hand and foot on a crowd of desk jockeys who, from the look of their luggage and golf clubs, were only off to enjoy themselves.

As he walked out to the waiting taxi, a voice called from the back seat.

"Hello, Mr Carter," said an attractive redhead, "my name is Mollie and we have some time for a little tour of Belfast before your train to Dublin and home to New York. Would you like that?"

He could only nod, assuming that the taxi man had collected her while he was inside and replied:

"I'm Martin but I'm sure you already know and I would like to visit some of the places we see on TV back in the States," he replied.

They went through what she called "our strongholds" with a running commentary which was very entertaining, full of Irish humour, on the way. He remembered Ballymurphy and New Barnsley Estate which she told him was not far from where some of the loyalist gunmen hid in Highfield on the Springfield Road. Then went on to point out what she called one of our favourites, the heavily fortified British army RUC barracks. A fast drive down Lower Ormeau Road and across to Andersonstown which she told him was less than ten minutes from the Malone Road, although they looked worlds apart. He commented on the Irish tricolours of green, white and orange flying in many of these areas and wondered why the army or RUC did not take them down.

"They would not dare," she was quick to reply, "anyhow, they have their Union Jacks," adding "but not for too much longer, we hope."

His next remark seemed to take her by surprise and brought a slight blush to her cheeks:

"There seems to be a lot of very pretty girls in your organisation."

"Oh, yes, we are certainly an equal opportunity organisation. Do you have a problem with that?" to which he was quick to reply:

"Certainly not. I enjoy it and if I was staying here much longer, might even join myself if they were all like you."

She changed the subject, with a big smile:

"Would you like to see the City Hall and perhaps do some shopping before you leave for home?"

"Yes, this time tomorrow I'll be in New York. I have to wear formal clothes in the Waldorf Astoria so could do with something more casual for a change."

He went into Austin Reed, a branch of the store he had liked in Regent Street, and Burtons, the one new to them. She preferring Marks and Spencers. When they met again in half an hour, he with his purple bag, she with green plastic, there was no way Mollie could restrain a laugh:

"They certainly knew you were American. Nobody here would be seen dead in that," as the multicoloured plaid sports jacket certainly did make an impression. He had shirts and ties in the bag.

"Maybe you're right. Now I know why he gave me 25 per cent off and suggested I wear it now."

"I'm sure they will like it in the Big Apple with its genuine McGee Irish tweed," she smiled adding: "you are still lucky that nobody knows you here."

But she was wrong.

* * *

Commander Trevor Wallace of MI6 had decided that he had no alternative but to do as he had been ordered by Marian and wanted to get it over with before lunch. He had pulled rank to get an official car with an armed RUC Special Branch driver, who brought him the Browning automatic he had also requested as he always felt Belfast was a dangerous city. She had said 2pm.

That gave him his first problem of the day. There was no way that snotty-nosed young upstart at the security gate would let him bring that pistol in with him. As he was carrying the cigarette pack in his inside pocket, he decided that discretion was the better part of valour and, under protest, left it with his driver outside the airfield. It cheered him up to see that another armed SB man was now in the car as well.

"At least they know who I am now," he thought to himself as he marched the long distance towards the giant Chinook, sorry he had refused the offer of a lift but happy to be accompanied by a recently commissioned young lieutenant, who had possibilities. But first things first, he always said to himself.

When he told, then ordered, his young escort to remain at the entrance to the aircraft, the lieutenant got as far as:

"But, sir ...", before Trevor bellowed:

"Don't you know who I am? This is the army, or the airforce if you like, but you still do what you are told by a superior officer. Or perhaps you would prefer six months shagging sheep in the Falklands which is even worse than this bloody place, if that is possible."

"No, sir. I mean, Yes sir. As you say, sir," stammered the young man and

Trevor was pleased to see he was blushing like a girl although there was no doubt he was an athletic young man. Maybe it might be his lucky day after all, so he decided to appear pleased:

"That's the spirit. I'll only be a few minutes as I am sure it has been well secured by now."

"Oh, yes sir. An RAF expert has already had a test run in it with the pilots, one of whom had even taken it to its destination, wherever that is, before coming here. And I think Boeing have already sent a man earlier, so they are taking no chances, sir."

But Trevor was already alone on board the unguarded aircraft, taking his time to place the magnetic listening devices where they would not be found, including under the pilots' seats. That was a big part of his normal job after all, planting bugging devices, he thought, as he went through the task almost routinely, wondering would the young lieutenant be off duty tonight. Until he reached in to place the last bug along the metal bars which led to the cockpit and found one already there. These last few days have been very stressful, I need a holiday, he told himself as he did not remember placing it. This one must go somewhere else and he went back to the cabin where there was an almost inaccessible nook near the automatic pilot, muttering:

"Now they can hear all they want but with the noise of this big flying machine, they'll probably only hear the engine. Anyway, I have done the job and that's their problem. It will not matter in a week as the top fifty IRA leaders will all be dead, and the rest locked-up, when plans are finalised at this conference," he told himself again.

"Now, young man," he said to the officer still standing to attention outside, "at ease. Job's done. As safe as a house."

"Yes, sir."

"By the way, are you free tonight to show me some of the nightlife in the city?"

"I might be, sir, I am," replied the slightly confused and rather frightened young man, who was not accustomed to conversation with such senior officers, especially not this kind of one.

"Shall we say 8 o'clock at the Europa Hotel then?" brought a quick reply:

"Yes, sir. Certainly, sir. A pleasure, sir."

"I hope it will be," Trevor muttered silently to himself and he was gone.

The two Special Branch men were not too pleased when he asked them to take a roundabout route back into the city centre as he wanted to see what he called "the trouble spots". As far as they were concerned, the whole place was now a trouble spot and half the time they did not know which side was going to shoot at them first. They were even less pleased when he went back to the hotel for lunch leaving them outside in the car but at least he did not stay too long.

"Now, I would like to stretch my legs and get a bit of fresh air," he told them, so they had to accompany him on a stroll along Donegall Place, looking at the shops. They consoled themselves with the thought of overtime and, if they were lucky, with a bit of extra money for VIP protection duty.

* * *

The three-man Active Service Unit of the IRA on the roof of the high flats had a good view of the city streets, while the girl was standing guard at the entrance downstairs.

Their new special US sniper rifle with an accuracy range of almost a mile and already a record of killing three British soldiers with only three shots fired, had to be protected even more than themselves. They had been told:

"Don't come back without it or you will face a court martial." They knew that, due to a combined British Intelligence FBI sting operation in New York, the IRA only had four of these lethal weapons and were still waiting on the latest heat-seeking surface-to-air missiles which were not only ordered but paid for in advance. They were taking it in turns to look through the magnificent telescopic sight and would do the same that night when they had been assured it was even better. This was purely an exercise to make them familiar with handling the weapon and picking out make-believe targets on the streets. Next week they would be off to a secret training camp in Glencolumcille for the real target practice.

The three had been together since schooldays, had gone to their first dance together, where they all had their first dates and like their fathers before them had joined the IRA together when they were sixteen. But they had been told not to take "the big one" out today as something special was going on in the city, to lie low, keep well out of sight, not attract any attention. Yet they could not resist it since it arrived early that morning and told themselves:

"Sure, what was the harm in taking it up on the roof of the flats where we live and, anyway, we could see the soldiers coming a mile away now?"

The girl had jeered at them that they were like little children with a new toy at Christmas when they asked her to act as look-out, but their commanding officer, himself only twenty-five, who had just arrived, had not been very amused. Still he remembered what he had been like at their age, eighteen, and thought it better to give in to their youthful enthusiasm as they had a tough week's training ahead of them in the hills of Donegal.

His hands trembled a little as he took the rifle from his comrade. This was the big one they had been waiting for since the British decided that it was no longer safe to travel by road in South Armagh. In the early 1980s, the IRA had killed eighteen paratroopers with a landmine at Warrenpoint so now all troop movements were by air except in special circumstances when making quick ground patrols and sudden checkpoints. By the mid-80s the IRA were negotiating in the United States to purchase the most powerful and effective sniper rifle ever built, the Barrett M82AI 12.7mm semi-automatic. It had been used by American soldiers in the Gulf War against almost everything. It had a range of almost five miles and a good sniper could be sure of hitting even a small target a mile away. There was no body armour protection against it and at least nine British soldiers and RUC men had been killed with them since the first consignments arrived from New York and Chicago. "God help me if anything happens to it," he said in a whisper to nobody in particular as he looked through the sight again at the events on the street.

So there they were, taking turns picking out make-believe targets on the streets and each imagining in his own mind what it would really feel like to actually pull the trigger. Down on the streets, not much was happening.

* * *

Trevor was becoming a bit of a nuisance as far as the Branch men were concerned and they both looked at their watches more frequently in the hope he would take the hint to call it a day. It would be nice to get home early just for once. Walking openly through Belfast streets, especially some of the smaller ones he insisted on seeing, was not their idea of a good time or even a safe one. Still, it was overtime now and they did their best to keep up their end of the boring conversion with yet another Englishman who could never understand the Irish, even those like themselves who were supposed to be on his side. By now they were both walking and talking almost automatically and when he stopped suddenly they had gone on a few yards before noticing it.

But they did notice that his face had gone white and he was moving his hand towards his heart, so they hurried back thinking:

"That's all we need. The bloody idiot is getting a heart attack." When they reached him, he gave a loud whisper:

"He looks exactly like Carter- but he's dead," and they wondered how they would get him back to the hotel without too much fuss, as he was obviously cracking under the strain. When they saw he had been reaching for his gun, not his heart, one of them took it from him, pocketing it quickly before anyone could see it. Wallace remembered a CIA photo of Carter.

He was speaking to them again, more calmly now:

"See that man in the bright coloured jacket with the red-haired girl? One of you go over across the street, as near as you can without being seen. Come back and tell me if he is speaking with an American accent."

* * *

Martin and Mollie were enjoying each other's company, helped by the fact that they had stopped at a couple of pubs along the way. She had even got him drinking Guinness and now they could both laugh at his new jacket. He was thinking, "This is the last place in the world the British will be looking for me in the unlikely event they suspect I am even alive."

"I would love to take you to my favourite pub or bar, as you might call it, the Crown, almost opposite the Europa, which still has gaslight but it's not safe today. There's time for a walk up the Falls before your train. We'll be safe along there. See, there are two of our lads outside that bookies shop beside the pub," she told him.

"Why don't we put on a bet?" he asked her. "I feel very lucky today."

The two young men smiled at Mollie and nodded to him as they entered the shop, he picking three horses by sticking a biro in their names on the racing page of the *Belfast Telegraph* and giving her the ticket, saying:

"You can collect the winnings tomorrow when I'm gone. I'll be thinking of you in New York." But, inwardly, he was thinking of Nicole in the bed there the next week.

Across the street, the RUC bodyguard had confirmed to Trevor that not only had the man an American accent but that the girl, although she had no terrorist record, was an active member of Sinn Fein, the political wing of the IRA.

"I'm right," Trevor almost shouted, "the bastard was not killed at Folkestone at all after costing us five billion pounds."

The RUC men did not know what he was talking about but were taking him seriously now.

"Call for back-up. You have your mobile but don't let him see you. Tell them to seal off both ends of that street and any other exits where they might run.

But tell them to leave him to me." Trevor was taking command now and they did as ordered, both RUC men freeing their automatics from under their coats but still keeping them hidden.

"Remember, and tell them, we want this bastard alive. Repeat alive. He knows a lot. We will wring the last drop out of him before he dies."

* * *

The four men on the roof did not know what to make of all the sudden activity on the streets below them. They recognised one of the Special Branch men who was talking into the mobile phone in a shop doorway and then saw him rejoin two other men who were crossing over. They appeared to be following the man in the bright jacket they had joked about earlier:

"The first of the American tourists. You'd think he would go to Miami or Disneyland in this weather instead of here," one of them had remarked, while the youngest one laughed:

"Sometimes I think this is Disneyland." They were intent on watching the RUC men now, there seemed to be three of them, when suddenly the youngest member of the ASU who was having his turn with the scope, almost shouted:

"Jesus, that's Mollie down there."

"Give me that quick," ordered the man in charge, who peered through the sight on top of the gun before saying:

"You're right, Padraic. Not only is it Mollie but she is with that American," continuing almost immediately with:

"Christ, I know we had an American over here to do a very important job for us early this morning. He was at the commander's home last night and Mollie must be bringing him to the station. I don't know any more."

"Well, he's in trouble now," said Sean, who had taken the rifle for a look. He hated to let it out of his hands and the others had joked he would take it to bed with him tonight instead of his wife.

"There are unmarked RUC cars at each end of that street now, these three are following him and, if you look over there, you can see an army patrol is on its way. The poor devil."

* * *

Martin was enjoying himself, even laughing at her Irish humour when Mollie suddenly said:

"I think we are being followed."

She did not have to add "Don't look around" as Martin, with years of training, knew what to do. They stopped, as they had many times previously, to look into shop windows but, this time, they did a little more, and what they both saw confirmed her fears.

"It's probably me they are after," she said softly, "as they have seen me at parades and meetings. You are just a tourist and I'm showing you to the station, which is that direction by the way. Now, I'll double back to that bookies shop where the lads will get me out through another door and you can continue your walk. Don't worry. I'll be OK and they could not know you."

Not giving him much time to think, she shook his hand, saying:

"Now you can kiss me 'Goodbye' to make it look well," which he did before she was off back down the street whispering "God Bless". Martin continued his leisurely stroll, wishing he had his Browning or Smith and Wesson automatic just in case but the street looked very quiet so perhaps she was wrong, or perhaps, it was too quiet.

* * *

The hidden watchers on the roof were getting agitated now.

"Maybe, with all this sudden activity, we should disappear," said Kevin, "we can't afford to lose our baby here," fondling the rifle.

But the commanding officer took it from him and, once again, looked intently down on the trap the American was innocently walking right into. It would only be a matter of a few minutes now.

"They want to surprise him and take him alive," he remarked to nobody in particular while the other three younger men turned to face him.

"Otherwise, they would have moved in earlier. They must think he knows a lot and want to break him in Castlereagh."

"I could take out two maybe three of those following him. They are well within range, almost too near, for this one," whispered Kevin, eager to get his first shot from the new gun.

"But what about the two car loads at each end of the street and the army patrol which is much nearer now?" asked Padraic.

Sean, the young IRA officer who had not spoken for a while, realised the others were looking at him, relying on him. He had been honoured to have been put in charge of a Belfast Brigade ASU but now the responsibility was his and his alone. They were waiting on him for an order and time was short.

Kevin, the best shot with the Armalite and the Heckler & Koch, had the supergun now and was eager to become the sharpshooter.

He nodded to Kevin who immediately sighted the gun at the targets, zooming in on the one in the middle of the RUC group first.

"Take him out!" came the order, to be met with:

"What? ..... Who?" from the others almost simultaneously.

"The American," said the officer sadly, "he knows too much. He was in the safe house last night. He knows too much and one of our biggest jobs is going down today. We can't save him. So do it!"

Kevin, the sharpshooter, got Martin Carter in his sights, zoomed in again, this time to see a happy if tense face, moved his armrest and elbows slightly, hesitated, looked again at his young commanding officer who had now gone white in the face, but who nodded immediately.

* * *

Martin was thinking. They could not know me. It must be Mollie they are after and she seemed certain she could escape, so all was well. He could hear a train in the distance and knew the station was not too far away. He had enjoyed his time in Europe but it would be good to get home to his daughters. Poor Tara, then Nicole, and now Mollie, what wonderful girls, any of whom would have made a good new mother for the girls. But Nicole had promised to come to the Big Apple so who knows? Mollie's "Goodbye" kiss was very nice, was his last thought as the high-velocity bullet hit him straight between the eyes and he was dead before his body hit the ground.

The sharpshooter, Kevin, who fired the shot, blessed himself saying:

"I hope we did the right thing," and the young commander was thinking the same. They were all deep in thought, until he said:

"Maybe we should say a little prayer for him, lads," and all was quiet again, as they knelt on the roof with heads bent. "Hail Mary, full of grace, the Lord is..."

Then they heard it but it was too late. They were caught off guard. An army helicopter was suddenly overhead and they could see the concentration on the face of the machine-gunner as he finally braced himself before riddling all their bodies with bullets.

"Another IRA Active Service Unit has been wiped out, sir," reported the pilot on the radio to HQ.

"The area might be booby-trapped so we will collect the dead bodies and what looks like that American sharpshooter rifle we have been after, in the morning. Meanwhile, I suggest we cordon off the whole place as things have a way of disappearing around here at night. Over and out. Roger."

Meanwhile, below on the street, Trevor and the Special Branch men did not know what was happening. They dived for cover, thinking they had been led into an ambush. They had heard a sharp powerful shot, seen the American fall to the ground, then more firing on a roof out of their line of vision, which seemed to involve an army surveillance helicopter.

"What a day for helicopters," thought Trevor, shouting to the RUC man to give him back his gun. Edging along from doorway to doorway, Trevor got near enough to the American to see he was not moving but, with promotion suddenly flashing before his eyes, he fired another shot into the already lifeless body just to be sure. As the man who killed the IRA's most valuable agent, the one who destroyed the Tunnel Chamber, they could not deny him in Whitehall now. As he stood over Carter's body, automatic in hand, he knew the helicopter would be taking pictures and made a mental note to get a copy of the film before he went back to London tomorrow. The American's would not be the first body that disappeared without a post-mortem in Belfast. Commander Trevor Wallace of MI6 would make certain nobody would ever know he was first shot by a high-powered rifle and not a revolver. All in all, not a bad day's work. If the IRA kept their word and gave him back the other film and, if the young RAF lieutenant was at the hotel tonight, it would be even better.

Still Thursday

2nd June, 1994

The first message reached the man in Spain at 8 a.m.. Very early by local standards, he did not know that Marian had been up all night, first to get the essential timetable information from Trevor after persuading him to do the job, but then to avoid the increased Army-RUC patrols to get the message to the Chief of Staff. There was no way she could keep even a phone much less a computer in her flat on the Antrim Road which was raided regularly.

After the double encryption was decoded by the software and when the day's password was keyed in, the message was simple as usual:

Our visitors leave today (2nd June) ETD 17.30 hrs (5.30 p.m.) our time. Send them Interflora surprise ten (repeat, ten) minutes later exactly. But take no action until actual departure confirmed. Stand by. Good luck.

He smiled to himself. Nobody, only the "managing director" who had sent the message, knew that he had added his usual little "extras" to the devices, so that two of them, distinguished by a slightly different coloured top, were actually transmitters. He had suggested to the "MD" that one be included in each pack. He was already logged on, the big screen was ready and it reminded him of NASA except that instead of months and years, this time he would have only fifteen minutes maximum, to take action. He checked all the electronic equipment again, particularly the special computers enhanced to emit the maximum signal technically possible to the receivers aboard the aircraft. He hoped it would work but had no way of knowing. It would be a long day and he promised himself, when it was over, he would take a holiday. He felt he deserved it.

* * *

The giant Chinook stood well away from the Wessex helicopters usually used in Northern Ireland, which now looked like midgets in comparison to this, the ultimate in fighting flying machines. With over a thousand seeing action under battle conditions in jungles, mountains, anywhere in the world where the Americans, or even the British, wanted high-speed, low-level flying, they knew there was nothing like the Chinook.

Boeing, the manufacturers, were particularly proud of HC2 ZD 576, the one that now waited like a giant American eagle on the runway near the RAF base at Aldergrove airport, a few miles north of Belfast. It had recently been completely serviced by the best aircraft technicians in the world and put through the most rigorous testing that any helicopter had ever experienced. It had been fitted with three independent positioning systems which made the pilots joke among themselves that they would soon be redundant as this chopper could almost fly by itself.

The Racal RNS 252 Super TANS, positioned in a console between the two pilots, would process information from the Global Positioning Systems (GPS) based on twenty-four satellites which circle the globe and the Doppler Velocity Sensor would provide velocities of the aircraft with respect to the earth's surface by transmitting signals from the aircraft and then measuring the returns reflected from the surface. The helicopter was as invincible and safe as state-of-the-art technology could make it. Everything was ready for action.

* * *

5 p.m. The crew were driven to the aircraft. Flight lieutenants Jonathan Tapper and Richard Cook were two of the most experienced RAF Special Forces pilots with more than two thousand helicopter flying hours between them, mostly in battle conditions that made today's journey look like a Sunday drive in the country. Flight Lieutenant Tapper had recently landed the Chinook on the pad beside the Mull of Kintyre lighthouse so that he would be completely at ease with the aircraft, and familiar with the route, before arrival in Belfast.

The two pilots were accompanied by equally experienced loadmaster crewmen, Graham Forbes and Kevin Hardie. Soon they were busy carrying out the usual pre-flight checks and procedures while awaiting arrival of their twenty-five top secret VIP passengers.

* * *

5.10 p.m. Most of the passengers had arrived at the hangar, some in their own cars, some driven by wives or friends. In the small reception hut, they were putting on orange survival suits while waiting for the bus to drive them to the aircraft. Within another five minutes, they were all there and ready for Chinook Mk2 Zulu Delta 576.

* * *

5.15 p.m. The twenty-five passengers in their orange survival suits boarded the bus, some of them talking to one another, joking to those with golf clubs that it was work not a holiday in the sun.

* * *

5.20 p.m. The bus left the hangar for the short journey to the helicopter and the passengers were aboard the Chinook a couple of minutes later. They sat facing each other along both sides of the aircraft, with their baggage placed along the centre of the cabin.

Officially on board were, in addition to the four crew:

Head of the RUC's Special Branch, Assistant Chief Constable Brian Fitzsimons and nine other senior Special Branch officers: Detective Chief Superintendent Maurice McLaughlin Neilly; Detective Inspectors Dennis Bunting and Andrew Stephen Davidson; Detective Superintendents Philip Davidson, Robert Foster and Ian Phoenix, Detective Chief Superintendent Desmond Conroy; Detective Inspector Kevin Magee; Detective William G. William; the six MI5 officers on board were: J. R. Deverell, M. G. Dalton, J. S. Haynes, Ann James, N. B. Maltby, S. L. Rickard, although it is not certain that these were all their real names; nine top British Army Intelligence officers were also on the passenger list: Major R. Allen, Colonel C. Biles, Major C. J. Dockery, Lieutenant Colonel R. Gregory-Smith, Major A. Hornby, Roy Pugh, Major G. Sparks, Lieutenant Colonels J. Tobias and G. Williams.

It was suspected that there were at least two high-ranking SAS officers included in this list as were two equally senior members of MI6, neither organisation wanting to be seen to be still actively involved in Northern Ireland, so worked undercover and used other military titles on official duties. The passenger list was shredded as the helicopter took off.

* * *

5.43 p.m. The giant Chinook, originally scheduled to leave at 5.30, rose into the sky, its twin rotor blades covering those on the ground with dust and the noise of its powerful engines drowning out any conversation.

* * *

5.45 p.m. The couple with their arms around each other near the seaside village of Carnlough punched in the four PIN numbers on their new Motorola mobile phone, before throwing it into the sea when nobody was watching them.

At the same time, another boy and girl, this time on bicycles with binoculars, bird watching books and sandwiches in their saddle bags, a little nearer the airport, were doing the same. None of them knew that their message was being received in Spain.

* * *

But MI5 knew better.

At 5.45p.m. that evening, about two minutes after the Chinook had lifted off, an enigmatic message had been transmitted to Stella Rimington's confidential e-mail address. It read: *"An Indian, not from India. A rocky wind blows east and west. It leaps from pacific waters. It crashes down to earth. Recommend you drop Fortress Salvo. Regards. Sam."*

Its arrival caused some consternation, especially the reference to the imminent Fortress Salvo Operation, coupled with the name of the IRA Chief of Staff. There was also serious concern that MI5's e-mail security had been breached. Technical experts tracked the origination of the e-mail to a supposedly locked room in Queen's University, Belfast, where the trail dried up.

The message was sent to the cryptologists for analysis, but it was not given the highest level of priority and they did not receive it for over an hour after it had been sent. It took them less than ten minutes to solve the basic riddle and by that time its significance was understood. A Native American Indian tribe, a Rocky Mountain wind and a salmon indigenous to the North Pacific Ocean all had a common name, Chinook.

The following day, the message was given the highest level of classification and locked away.

* * *

5.47 p.m. Aldergrove's control tower said "Goodbye" to the Chinook's pilots as it was now leaving the airport's zone, heading into the Scottish Military Aircraft Control area at Prestwick.

* * *

By this time, the man in Spain was already tracking the aircraft by the two devices hidden on it in Belfast earlier that day. The confirmation from the two visual sightings at 5.45 were only a back-up procedure insisted upon by the "managing director" whom he sometimes thought was being too careful but, in the end, he supposed it was better that way.

The message was also already on his screen and he hardly needed to decode the even more obscure encryption but, following orders, he did:

Our visitors left just before 5.45 p.m. as expected. Send them our Interflora greetings in ten, repeat ten, minutes exactly. It will be a surprise. It's not Christmas but the bird must die today! No further contact necessary. Have a good holiday.

He moved over to the battery of mobile phones which he had linked up to his computers to give the most powerful electromagnetic signal outside of NASA to the moon, he mused to himself. He watched the hands of the two big clocks on the wall, thinking of his high-powered tiny bugs on the aircraft just waiting for his signal. For a moment, he felt himself all-powerful, like God he thought, before forcing it from his mind to concentrate on his work. Just another job, but the timing had to be right. Had to be perfect.

As he watched the clock and the tracker screen with his hand poised over the keyboard and the master switch, he could feel trickles of perspiration on his forehead.

* * *

5.55 p.m. He pressed the master switch which set off the all-powerful electromagnetic interference which would immediately be picked up by the enhanced hidden receivers on the aircraft. Even the Super TANS would not be able to correctly process the information from the GPS and DVS, with the result that the instruments on board the helicopter would give a false reading. The pilots would be confident they were flying at least 500 ft higher than the aircraft actually was, with the result it should crash into the mountain if his calculations, his timing, his devices, were all correct. The best pilots in the world could not override this system even if they realised something was wrong. He hoped. He was sweating now.

* * *

It was a routine flight for Lieutenants Tapper and Cook. Not like the many times they had flown in battle conditions low over the jungle at full throttle with hostile fire all around them or on search and rescue missions against the raging sea. Some of these had been really tricky. Their destination, Fort George, located on an isolated peninsula eight miles from Inverness, was surrounded on three sides by water, and with only one access road, was probably one of the easiest places in Europe to guard against attack. Crews had never been made very welcome there on previous visits and were always happy to get back home to the mess with their colleagues.

The special unit of the SAS, which always surrounded the place when a VIP conference was being held, made it clear they did not like any intruders whether they were from the RAF or the 600 officers and men of the Royal Scots regiment for whom the base was their headquarters.

While the flight was almost routine, the twenty-five passengers were certainly unusual. With weekend cases, mobile phones and golf clubs, there was little to indicate that they were Britain's most senior intelligence officers in the war against the IRA. One of the crew recognised Special Branch Head Brian Fitzsimons, often described as the finest intelligence officer in Europe, who always had a cheerful word for them. Others recognised senior MI5 officer Matthew Maltby, Major Gary Sparks of Army Intelligence and the woman Ann James, head of Irish GCHQ operations, who had a fearsome reputation only equalled by Stella Rimington herself. Mostly they kept to themselves, guarding their eyes, their briefcase and hand luggage in the middle of the cabin.

Before the flight, one of the crew had been told in a whisper:

"Your passengers are the high command in the fight against the IRA. The top people in MI5, MI6, Special Branch, SAS, Military Intelligence, the lot. They are on a very sensitive mission which will change the entire situation in Britain and Ireland. They are irreplaceable. So get them there safely as usual and we will have a big drink waiting for you in the mess."

He had not told his companions, especially as his source had added with a laugh:

"They probably have files on all of us," which he did not think that funny.

Another few minutes and they would be there. The two pilots and their crew checked all the instruments to make certain yet again that everything was in order and one of them looked down at a sailing boat as they passed the Mull of Kintyre lighthouse. The words of Beatle Paul McCartney's late '70s hit record often came to mind as they flew over that beautiful rugged countryside.

They sometimes hummed it together. Everything was normal. They had alerted Control. The Chinook was thundering across the final piece of Scottish coast when suddenly they saw it, right in front of them, too late to do anything about it. The 1,405 ft high Beinn na Lice hillside which should be well below them.

"It could not be! How had it moved? Why was it there? It should not be there at all!" must have been one of the crew's last thoughts.

* * *

The crash was heard and seen over a wide area as the big Chinook hit the mountain some 800 ft up, broke into two pieces as it ploughed along the mountainside, then seemed to disintegrate into a ball of fire, with wreckage and debris covering a wide area. Within minutes, three Navy Sea King helicopters from HMS *Gannet* were on their way to the scene, together with all the emergency services, including mountain rescue teams from RAF Boulmer in Northumberland and RAF Lossiemouth in Morayshire. Nine fire-fighting appliances and heavy lifting equipment, coast guard rescue services, Strathclyde ambulance service and a host of volunteers joined in the rescue bid.

Within three hours, all the would-be rescuers were cleared from the area which was suddenly cordoned off by the SAS and troops from nearby Fort George. The media were asked to leave. Crash experts from Boeing, the manufacturers, were not immediately allowed to examine the wreckage. Newspaper editors in London were warned to be careful about what they published under threat of a "D Notice". Questions were being asked-was there something to hide? But there were no answers, and...

There were no survivors.

SOON AFTER

Immediately after the mysterious crash of Chinook HC2 ZD576 at the Mull of Kintyre on 2nd June, 1994, British Government officials intensified peace negotiations with the IRA. Neither side mentioned the crash but began to meet more frequently. The IRA's two main current objectives were discussed the release, or at least the return to prisons in Ireland, of all IRA people held in British jails and, of equal importance, the quick entry of Sinn Fein, the IRA's political wing, into meaningful talks on a permanent peace settlement. These conditions were suddenly agreed by the British officials. On 31st August 1994, just three months after the crash, the IRA declared a cease-fire to end a war which had gone on for twenty-five years. In November 1994, the Ministry of Defence in London cancelled a £300 million contract with an Armagh firm to fortify British Army bases in Northern Ireland against IRA attacks.

* * *

Within months, Stella Rimington, Director General of MI5, told the then Prime Minister, John Major, that she wished to retire after less than three years in the £100,000 p.a. top job which she had wanted all her life. He accepted her resignation with regret, perhaps wondering whether it had been a wise decision to allow the Home Secretary, Kenneth Clarke, to announce publicly in the House of Commons on 8th May, 1992, that MI5 would take over from Scotland Yard's Special Branch the fight against the IRA in Britain.

* * *

The day after the crash, an official Board of Inquiry was established at RAF Benson and they visited the scene for the first of three such occasions. Air accident investigators, RAF technicians, technical experts, eye witnesses, all gave evidence but, after six months, could find no definite evidence of either human failing or mechanical malfunction which would account for the crash, which was still a mystery.

A year later, the inquest opened at the Sheriff's Court in Paisley with Sir

Stephen Young presiding. Again all possible avenues were explored, all witnesses and technical people examined, but with the same result. No official explanation as to the exact cause of the crash could be reached. When on the last day of the three-week hearing, the coroner asked an expert witness, an RAF wing commander, if he could offer any explanation, however far-fetched, as to why the Chinook was where it was, when it was, the reply was of little help:

"I cannot, my Lord, I wish that I could, but I cannot."

They had come to the end of the final investigation and the coroner remarked:

"It could be something beyond our imagination ... I've been in this job long enough to feel that truth is often stranger than fiction."

EPILOGUE

Commander Trevor Wallace had good reason to be happy and was relaxing with a vintage Armagnac, a cigar, listening to the Three Tenors on his prized stereo, less than forty-eight hours after the biggest disaster ever in British Intelligence. He had come out of that Belfast caper smelling of roses, he told himself, as he took another sip. With the twenty-five top people killed in the Chinook crash and rumours that the old battle-axe from MI5 would soon retire, he was next in line for one of the top jobs in British Intelligence perhaps the big one, TCG, directing all the intelligence agencies, MI5, MI6, Military Intelligence, Scotland Yard's Special Branch and even the RUC's Special Branch based in Belfast for, after all, he was one of the few senior officers to have come out of there alive. Yes, he would pour himself another brandy.

It had been quick thinking, that day on a Belfast street. Shooting that already dead American IRA man and standing with the revolver in his hand, while the army helicopter filmed him, had certainly impressed the top brass when he got back to London. Maybe he would look at his copy of the film again. Suddenly, his thoughts on film moved in natural progression to the girl in Belfast called Marian and that film which he was expecting any minute. He had told security downstairs to grab any courier or messenger with a letter marked "Personal" for him, just in case he might get a lead.

Then, the porter brought in the afternoon's post and there it was. He recognised the block capitals and they had even put two stamps with the Queen's head in the corner when one would have done, so they, or at least she, was back in London. Investigations later proved that the letter had been posted round the corner from his office. But he was more interested in the note:

Enclosed as promised the film you wanted. You will notice we have retained a few of the more exotic erotic shots, especially you with famous people, as our insurance. Remember Philby, Burgess, McClean, Blunt. You can have a job like theirs now but working for us. You are the only reason we cannot claim international publicity in the media, and full responsibility for our greatest single victory in the 25-year war. We have to protect you for the future. But we promise not to contact you very often. Only in an emergency like the last time. Congratulations on your impending promotion. M sends her love.

Trevor was white and shaking as he smashed the glass into the fireplace which brought the guard from outside the door into his room with gun drawn.

"It's all right, Christopher, just a little accident," he managed to say and, when the man left, got another glass, filled it to the top and kept drinking it until the potent liquid seemed to set his insides on fire. Slumped in his chair now, he cursed the IRA, his boyfriends, that girl Marian and the whole dirty business. Then, he thought, those she mentioned got away with it for almost a lifetime and, maybe, now that there is a cease-fire, they will not want his services at all.

The thought cheered him up and his mind wandered back to the idea of promotion, to being the head of one of the senior intelligence services or maybe of all of them. He felt better now, looking forward to another five or ten years behind a big desk telling others what to do, taking no risks himself. Maybe he would try a few advertisements in the gay magazines, using a Box Number like the one they used to have when they were in Curzon Street, he smiled to himself. Yes, a few good years in the job, then retirement to that country cottage in Brittany, after he got the knighthood of course. He fell asleep thinking of the Palace, the Queen, the title. His life had taken a turn for the better.

* * *

She had been busy all day. All week in fact. Underestimating the amount of work involved in moving into a newly built apartment had almost worn her out. Visiting the big stores, ordering the furniture which never came at the agreed time; looking in shop windows, always seeing something she was sure would look nice until she put it where she had imagined it and then did not like it. Still, it was beginning to take shape. The pictures on the wall, reproductions mostly but a few originals by unknown artists; the little ornaments from the antique shops; the flowers in the window

box and others in full bloom on the nest of tables. The latest slim-line TV and stereo system, her music centre as she called it, which the man at Dixons had assured her was the first one of its kind in the country. Habitat had taken more of her money than she expected, there were so many nice things for a first-time homemaker there. Then there was her casualwear and underwear from Marks and Spencers before she went to the Body Shop for cosmetics, sweet-smelling soaps and lotions. A couple of party dresses at Next, then to Boots for the more practical household things, not forgetting Disprin for the hangover she expected to have after the party. She was reluctant to open the bag with the new shoes. Gucci, Versace, Rocca, were names she associated with the big fashion shows and magazines, not the shoes in her bag and the American Express receipt which she did not want to spoil her evening.

Suddenly, she remembered it was Friday. How the week had flown and the girls would soon be arriving. She expected the three of them had not changed much since the school prom even if they were a doctor, a lawyer and an accountant now. That meant, if her memory was correct, that they would each arrive with the best bottle of wine they could afford none of them were near the top of their professions yet and would insist on drinking the lot at a reunion party of their own, before going on to the other party, whatever and wherever that was.

It was eight o'clock as she stepped out of her new clothes which she had tried on for the third time and looked at herself in the mirror. Her body, while not that of the skinny models in the fashion magazines, was still in great shape and she felt better now than at any time in her thirty-five years. A natural brunette with long hair that was always noticed, her youthful face with its unblemished complexion, blue eyes and sensual mouth, would someday attract the right man, she hoped. Her breasts were firm, now jutting out as if to demand attention, her stomach flat, her legs long and slender, her ... yes, she was looking forward to the night, she told herself, softly soaping her entire body in the shower.

She dressed herself slowly and carefully, not just to impress the girls she had not seen since her college graduation day or any eligible man she might meet, but just to make herself feel good. As she pulled up each of the Dior stockings and fastened them to the suspender belt above her silk French panties, she decided she would wear the simple but not cheap Paul Costello black dress and the single row of expensive pearls she had picked up on holiday abroad. Examining herself in the mirror again and then looking around the now fully furnished apartment, she decided to start the party herself with a glass of nicely chilled Chablis. She almost forgot her favourite Opium perfume. She had been tempted to try Poison for a change.

She opened the window and, in the distance, could hear the sound of music and singing from the pub on the next corner. The city lights were like a rainbow reflecting in the river nearby and, when she leaned out, she could see couples strolling along the narrow streets, arm in arm, sometimes kissing, sometimes laughing, sometimes in silence. Everywhere there were signs of gaiety, of fun, of entertainment, of enjoyment. She took another small sip of wine and sat down in the big comfortable armchair, with a small sigh of satisfaction.

The Chief of Staff of the Provisional IRA, Irish Republican Army, was feeling very happy to be home among her friends in the town she loved so well, which had now become a city. Already it felt good to be able to use her full name again after all these years. She had another sip of the Chablis as she whispered "Samantha"... "Samantha" almost to herself.

What the critics said about Michael O'Reilly's last book *"The Bravest of the Brave."*

"Men of action are the subject of Michael O'Reilly's book, 'The Bravest of the Brave' published by Anna Livia Press and is a racy account of the lives of eight national heroes. Whether you agree with him or not, he won't fail to engage you",
- Review by Maurice Devlin on the RTE 1 national network TV programme, Book Lines;

"The True-Life Adventure thriller of the Year", editor of the international magazine, People and Places.

"A most entertaining book, difficult to put down" Tony Knowles, Horizon Radio.

"Michael O'Reilly's book is a timely reminder of many of the men who made the ultimate sacrifice for Ireland. Worthy of a place on your bookself", - The Sunday Press, national newspaper.

"A celebration of Irish patriots" - Phoenix magazine, Dublin.

"The author brings life to one-dimensional heroes who inhabit history books and the ballads of old", Suzanne Crosbie, Cork Examiner.

"The Bravest of the Brave by Michael O'Reilly is history of a more popular nature. It is a most worthy illustrated 166-page paperback", The Irish Post, London

"The Book is a tribute to Bravery! Bart Cronin, IN Dublin magazine.

"O'Reilly's admirable book looks at Irish history through the lives of eight Irish heroes", Hot Press magazine, Dublin.

"I bet Michael O'Reilly will have the last laugh as the tome slowly but surely climbs to the top of the best sellers lists". The Daily Star.

"Michael O'Reilly, that well-known gentleman of the PR world has, for the first time in his 25 years in journalism and public relations, been sending out invitations to a personal event - the launch of his first book". The Sunday World, national newspaper.

"Michael O'Reilly, a journalist, has taken the bright lights of Irish history and dramatised them in a style that has not been done much in this country but is popular elsewhere - it is what he describes as a 'true-adventure' style, more about people than dates and details". Sunday Tribune, national newspaper.

The launch of the book, mostly with photographs of the author and the well-known people attending, was covered by the Irish Times; The Irish Independent, The Irish Press, The Evening Press, The Evening Herald.

The most quoted passages were the two introductions: "In this book Michael O'Reilly has very sensitively dealt with the lives of some of the giants of Irish history", Sile de Valera, T.D.;

"A powerful book which I strongly recommend" US Congressman Joe Kennedy.

Michael O'Reilly was a national newspaper columnist, then a senior official with the Irish Government's Industrial Development Authority, before becoming over the past twenty-five years, managing director of five successful PR consultanices including Michael O'Reilly Associates, Wilson Hartnell O'Reilly and US giant Edelman Worldwide in Ireland. He is now a full time author. He is a member of the NUJ; the PR Institute; the Foreign Press Association in London; and the Arts Club in Dublin, where he lives. His book *The Bravest of the Brave* sold out following enthusiastic media reviews and *The Chinook Must Die* looks set to become the international thriller of the year.